Girls
of the
Great War

OTHER TITLES BY FREDA LIGHTFOOT

FREDA LIGHTFOOT

Girls
of the
Great War

To Pat
with love and best wishes

Freda Lightfoot

Take care

LAKE UNION
PUBLISHING

Text copyright © 2018 by Freda Lightfoot
All rights reserved.

Published by Lake Union Publishing, Seattle

www.apub.com

Amazon, the Amazon logo, and Lake Union Publishing are trademarks of Amazon.com, Inc., or its affiliates.

ISBN-13: 9781612187198
ISBN-10: 1612187196

Cover design by Lisa Horton

Printed in the United States of America

PROLOGUE

1894

She was running as fast as her legs could carry her, rocks constantly tripping her up, and a blanket of trees towering around so that she could barely see where she was going. The sound of heavy feet pounded behind, filling her with panic. Was he chasing her again? Would she be captured? Breathless with fear, she ran all the faster, knowing what would happen if she did not escape. She could feel her heart hammering, tension freezing every limb. Then pain rattled through her back with merciless precision. She felt utterly powerless and vulnerable, petrified of what might happen.

A hand tapped her cheek and she jerked awake in panic.

'Wake up, Martha, it's time for breakfast.'

Staring into her mother's eyes, the young girl gave a small sigh of relief. So this had been yet another nightmare, a trauma she suffered from constantly. The emotion attached to it always cloaked her in absolute terror. At least she had managed to sleep a little last night, which was never easy. Tension would mount within her whenever she went to bed, no longer a relaxing time. Now pain and fear escalated through her once more and she cried out in agony.

It seemed that having spent nearly five months virtually locked away in her room, she was now about to give birth, although she had only just turned seventeen.

A part of her longed to vanish into oblivion, to disappear back into the world she'd once enjoyed, not least her happy and privileged childhood. Why had that all gone wrong after her beloved father died? Would she now die? Many women did when suffering this traumatic event. Would the good Lord take her to heaven? Her soul having no real attachment to Him, it was doubtful He would trust in her innocence and accept her. Nor did her mother, who'd made it clear she didn't believe a word her daughter said. She no longer viewed her as respectable and had offered no sympathy or support, declaring that no one must ever learn of her condition.

Martha gazed up at the window, her blue eyes glittering with desolation. How she ached to catch a glimpse of the sun, the cliffs and the sea. Oh, and how she missed her life. Her mind flicked back to the young man she'd once grown fond of. He was most handsome, dressed in baggy trousers, and lived in one of the fisherman's huts. Whenever he wasn't away at sea working in smacks and yawls to catch fish, he'd be in a local pub eating, drinking or gambling. He also spent much of his time sitting by the harbour mending nets. They'd sometimes listen to the band down on the bay along with crowds of spectators, or watch a concert and dancing. Claiming he adored her, he'd give her sweet kisses and had her name tattooed on to his arm. Then one day, when she'd excitedly hurried to meet him, as usual, he'd told her he was off to America in search of a new life, having become bored with fishing. She'd felt utterly devastated. He was so charming and helpful over her family problems that she was almost falling in love with him. How she missed him, but if he were still around why would he ever agree to marry her?

Now water suddenly flushed out of her and the sound of her screaming echoed around the room, bouncing against the shutters that blocked the window. Over the next several hours, she sank into more agony with no doctor or midwife around to help, only Enid her maid and of course Mama. Whenever another bolt of merciless pain struck, she struggled to sit up in a bid to resist it, only to be pushed back down by her scolding mother.

Finally, something solid slid out of her, leaving her breathless and exhausted. She felt hands pressing upon her belly and more stuff flopped out, including blood that soaked the bed sheets. Then she found herself being briskly washed, wiped, stripped and dressed by the maid, making her feel like a piece of dirt. Not a single word had been spoken to her, save for orders to push hard and stop screaming. And no comfort offered.

Whatever child had been delivered was now swept up into her mother's arms and she marched away, slamming the door behind her. Martha gave a small sob of distress, aware she'd been informed the baby would instantly be given away for adoption. She certainly would not be allowed to keep it. If only her life could return to normal, but the harsh, uncaring attitude of her mother proved that would never happen.

It came to her then that with the agony of her imprisonment and this birth finally over, she had no desire to stay here any longer. In order to maintain her safety, she needed to go as far away from here as possible, and change her name. The time had come for her to leave home and build a new life for herself. Then she'd find herself a husband and become respectable again.

PART ONE —
THE GREAT WAR

ONE
CHRISTMAS 1916

LIGHTS DIMMED as a man dressed as Pierrot in a bright blue costume and pantaloons, peaked hat and a huge yellow bow beneath his chin, skipped merrily on to the stage singing 'All the Nice Girls Love a Sailor'. He was quickly joined by a troop of dancing girls. They too were dressed like Pierrots, all of them looking ravishing in a pink costume with a wide frilled collar, long swirling skirt decorated with fluffy bobbles, and a tight-fitting black hat. They were complete visions of beauty who brought forth roars of excited approval from the audience. Pierrot waved his gloved hands at them, the theatre being packed with British and Belgian soldiers who responded with cheers and whistles.

Cecily smilingly watched from the wings as she loved to do most evenings. A part of her ached to join the singers, something her mother would never agree to. Viewing herself as the star performer, she expected her daughters to wait upon her hand, foot and fingers. Not that Cecily believed herself to be a good assistant, being too involved with working as a conductor on the electric trams now that most men were caught up in the war. Her mother disapproved of that. Cecily, however, firmly believed in making her own choices in life.

Feeling a gentle tap on her shoulder, she found her sister at her side. 'Her royal highness Queenie requires your assistance,' Merryn whispered, her pretty freckled face wrapped in a jokey grin. 'I've been dismissed, as she's engaged in her usual bossy mood.'

'Oh, not again!' Stifling a sigh, Cecily accompanied Merryn back to the dressing room. Gazing in the mirror, she recognised the familiar lack of focus in her mother's blue eyes, proving she'd again been drinking. Despite seeing herself as a star, Queenie too often felt the need to overcome a sense of stage fright before she performed.

'Merryn has made a total mess of my hair,' she stuttered in a slurry voice.

'I'm sure she didn't mean to, Mama,' Cecily calmly remarked, and reaching for a brush began to divide her mother's curly blonde hair across the back of her head.

'*Never* call me by that name. You know how I hate it.'

She'd chosen to name herself Queenie years ago as she considered it more appropriate for her career than Martha, the name she was born with. And that was what she required her daughters to call her, having no wish to be reminded of her age. Merryn seemed to accept this. Cecily always felt the need to remind her of their true relationship, which irritatingly was not an easy one. She carefully twisted up a small strand of her mother's hair and clipped it, then tucked the other portions neatly around before pinning them together with a glittering silver hair slide on the top of her head.

Grabbing a curl, Queenie pulled it down to loop it over her left ear. 'I've no wish for my hair to be all pinned up. Flick some over my ears.'

'I thought you liked to look as neat and tidy as possible, Mama,' Cecily said.

'No, fluff it out, silly girl. How useless you are.'

Cecily felt quite inadequate at this job and checked her success or lack of it by viewing her mother in the mirror. She was a slender, attractive woman with a pale complexion, pointed chin and ruby lips frequently curled into a pout, as they were doing now. But she was also vain, conceited, overly dramatic, emotionally unstable, selfish, overbearing and utterly neglectful. Queenie was never an easy woman to please, even when she was stone-cold sober. She was an exhibitionist and a star who demanded a great deal of nurturing and support, a task Merryn was extremely skilled at and happy to do, save for when Queenie was completely blotto, as she was now. And having been scolded and dismissed countless times when her mother was drunk, her sister would sit in the corner reading *Woman's Weekly*, taking not the slightest interest. Once Queenie sobered up she would happily treat her younger daughter as her favourite child in order to make Cecily feel unwanted, even though she'd done her best to help. Not that she ever felt jealous about this, always eager to act as a surrogate mother towards her beloved sister as Queenie could be equally neglectful of them both, wrapped up in herself and her tours.

There came a rap on the door. 'Three minutes on stage, please,' called a voice.

'You should have a drink of water,' Cecily quietly suggested. 'It might help to mobilise your voice and cool you down.'

'How dare you say such a thing! My voice is fine,' Queenie snapped.

Reaching for a jug, Cecily poured a glass and placed it on the table. 'Do take a sip to improve it, Mama.'

Filled with her usual tantrum, she snatched the jug and tossed the water over her daughter's head. Then she swept the glass of water, a box of make-up, brushes, jars of cream and all other items off the dressing table onto the floor, swirled around and marched away.

Grabbing a towel, Merryn rushed over to pat Cecily's damp hair and face.

'Don't worry, it'll soon dry off,' Cecily said, rolling her eyes in droll humour. 'Come on, we need to make sure Mama calms down and performs well.'

Giving a wry smile, Merryn nodded, and they both scurried after her.

∽

When Cecily reached the stage, she heard the audience yelling at Pierrot who was running around cracking jokes, the dance being over. They were obviously bored with him, growing increasingly impatient and eager to see the star performer. Finally, the curtain opened at the back of the stage and Cecily watched with relief as Queenie stepped forward, her head held high and arms outstretched. Clutching her sister's hand, she felt a sense of pride as silence fell. Their mother looked truly gorgeous, elegantly dressed in a sleeveless frock, the décolletage as low as on an evening gown and her back also daringly exposed. And for once, she was not tightly bound in a corset.

Queenie began to sing 'Who Were You With Last Night?'. It was one of her favourite songs from her music hall days, a period in which she'd made a small fortune until it began to fall out of fashion. How Cecily envied her ability, always having longed to sing herself. Kissing the tips of her fingers, Queenie waved to her audience with a smile.

'She so loves to proudly display that gloriously large diamond ring she wears on the third finger of her left hand, all she has left of her late husband,' Cecily murmured.

'I hope to have one of those some day,' Merryn said. 'And you definitely will before too long.'

'Maybe,' Cecily said.

She smiled at the memory of becoming secretly engaged to Ewan. How her heart yearned to see her beloved who was somewhere on the high seas, battling in this dreadful war. It was when Queenie had purchased a large house on Grand Parade close to the Sound in Plymouth, the city where she was born, that Cecily had first met Ewan at the fish market near to the Barbican. They'd become true friends and would spend hours walking barefoot along the beach, happily holding hands beside the comforting sound of the sea. They'd go fishing, swimming or sailing in one of his father's boats. He'd admitted his love for her the moment she turned sixteen, when he held her in his arms to give her a happy birthday kiss and Cecily had confessed she loved him too. Two years later, war broke out and it had been utterly heartbreaking when he'd joined up for the King's shilling.

'You will be here waiting for me when I return, won't you, my darling?' he'd asked, on the day he admitted to having visited the recruiting station. She told him how much she loved him and would look forward to his homecoming. His spirit was high, excitement buzzing through him as he held her close for a tender kiss. Like thousands of other men, he was a loyal patriot determined to protect his family and country from foreign invasion.

His parents received this news in distressed silence, particularly his mother who quietly expressed her gratitude to Cecily for her support. They'd agreed she could see him off at Millbay railway station, an inability to say goodbye to their son in public very strong in them. Cecily would never forget the sight of dozens of young men gathering on the platform to depart, with sobbing mothers, wives and sweethearts all around.

'Don't cry,' Ewan had told her, giving her a loving smile. 'This war will be over by Christmas, so there's something I want to ask you.'

It was then that he went down on his knee and asked if she would marry him. 'I love you so much, I wish you to be with me forever as my wife.'

She'd squealed with delight. How she loved the memory of that moment. Oh, and had ached to say yes. Knowing it wouldn't be easy to acquire the necessary permission from her mother, she promised to speak to Queenie and persuade her to agree. They'd kissed and hugged each other and as the train chugged away, the tears she'd been holding back ran down her cheeks at last.

'You will write to me, my love?' he'd asked.

'I most certainly will,' she'd promised, adoring his choice of words. She lived in hope the war would end soon and they'd be together forever. Right now, her joyous memory of him was interrupted by the sound of fidgeting and groaning coming from the audience.

'Oh dear, Queenie's performance is not being well received,' Merryn whispered. 'She looks slightly warped and there's a hoarseness in her tone of voice.'

'Very likely the fact she drinks too much gin before each performance,' Cecily sharply remarked.

They met each other's gaze in bleak despair, feeling a deep concern for their mother. Queenie was not at all as popular as she'd been in her younger days. There were rarely any fans by the stage door here at the Palace Theatre waiting for her at the end of a show, and few men around, save for the odd occasion like this evening. And these young soldiers here on leave would prefer a song that was much more lively and up to date.

'Fly away, bird, if that's what you are,' yelled one soldier.

Queenie had gone on to sing 'A Bird in a Gilded Cage', almost as though that was how she saw herself. Her blue eyes flashed with temper, looking as stormy as a rippling tide. Then forgetting the next verse, she went back to singing the chorus slightly out of tune.

Cecily cringed. 'Oh Lord, will she calm down and win them round, do you think?'

'We can but hope so,' Merryn muttered, sounding entirely unconvinced.

A soldier in the audience began to boo and others joined in. Looking livid, Queenie lurched forward to wave her clenched fists, apparently ordering these grumpy young men to shut up. It was then that she lost her balance, tripped and fell flat, letting out a loud scream. Cecily froze with shock.

The audience jeered and booed all the more as the curtain was brought quickly down. Coming to her senses, Cecily rushed to help, Merryn already having dashed to their mother lying sprawled on the stage, her legs spread wide and her eyes completely blank. As they attempted to lift Queenie to her feet she screamed again, the pressure on her ankle proving that she'd injured it and was in great pain. The backstage men ran to help them and carried her back to the dressing room. Seconds later the dancing girls came on stage again, quickly lightening the mood of the disgruntled audience.

༄

Before they'd had time to do more than settle her on the couch, the door burst open and the director stormed in. 'Why on earth did she fall? She certainly has no time to sit here feeling sorry for herself. She should be back on stage *now*!'

'I'm afraid that's out of the question, she's in considerable pain,' Cecily said, making no mention of the fact that Queenie was drunk.

Hovering over Queenie, he growled with fury when he sniffed the reek of gin on her breath. 'Ah, I understand why she fell, the stupid woman. So that's it, she's finished. I will not allow her on this stage ever again.' Looking from one to the other of her daughters, he pointed at Cecily and said, 'The audience is still waiting, so you'll have to take her place.'

'Don't be ridiculous. My daughter is not a star,' Queenie retorted. 'This lass can sing.'

'Absolute rubbish! She has no talent at all.'

'I've heard her quietly singing to herself and been quite impressed. She has a most pleasant, well-modulated voice with a London accent and she's a lovely girl,' he firmly retorted.

Cecily listened in stunned disbelief to the argument that ensued between them. She did not see herself as lovely. Her mousy-brown hair was a tangled mess, not sensibly bobbed. It was also soaking wet right now, thanks to the deluge of water her mother had tossed upon her, drooping over her pale oval face and violet-blue eyes. Yet a part of her felt the urge to do as he requested. 'I do enjoy singing, although I'm not convinced I can sing well enough to please this audience.' As neither the director nor her mother responded to this comment she felt a tension rise within her, destroying her determined sense of quiet reserve.

Merryn gave her hand a squeeze. 'You sing with a wonderful tone of voice, so why not have faith in yourself?'

Cecily met the glow in Merryn's hazel eyes with deep appreciation, recalling how the two of them would sometimes entertain themselves with her singing and Merryn playing her piano accordion. She could hear the audience yelling for someone to sing, surely not a request that could be ignored.

'It's Christmas Eve so we can't let the audience down. Smarten yourself up, girl. You are needed on stage *now*. You have three minutes to get ready,' the director sternly announced before marching off.

'Don't you dare do as he demands!' Queenie strictly informed her. 'I need you to stay here and care for me, not take over my role in life.'

Should she obey the director or her mother? Over the years she'd developed a strong sense of independence, regardless of giving way to most of Queenie's orders in a bid to create more affection between them. Deep in the core of her, Cecily was all too aware that she deeply enjoyed singing. Was this the moment she'd always longed for? Much as she felt the urge to obey the director's instructions, could she truly perform well? Panic welled within her. 'Will you join me, Merryn? You could play your instrument.'

Merryn shook her head. 'The band is in charge.'

'Then sing with me.'

'You'll do fine on your own,' her sister assured her, and quickly tugging off Cecily's damp dress, she pulled a pretty blue silk gown over her head. Within seconds, she'd tucked up Cecily's hair and pinned it with a matching blue slide. 'There you are, you look lovely. Now go out there and please those poor men and do have faith in your ability to sing well, lovey.'

Ignoring her mother's furious protests, Cecily nodded, straightened her shoulders and hurried off, her heart thumping.

Walking on stage, she gazed out at this audience of men who had gone strangely silent. Below, in the pit, the leader of the band stood holding up his baton, his expression clearly asking what she wished to sing. Cecily felt paralysed with nerves. Never in her life had she performed on stage or in public. Yet as she gazed into the faces of these brave young soldiers, the need to please them banished the panic within her. She might not be the star her mother was but this could prove to be the experience she'd so longed for – how she loved to sing!

She began with 'Keep the Home Fires Burning', a song written by Ivor Novello at the start of the war. Giving a big grin and a wink of the eye, the leader waved his baton and the band instantly started to play for her. A glow of happiness brought forth the instinctive pleasure Cecily experienced whenever she sang for herself, and to her amazement and delight this audience appeared spellbound by her performance. When the song came to an end, the soldiers roared with pleasure and loudly applauded. From the corner of her eye, Cecily could see Merryn in the wings, grinning and clapping her hands with jubilant appreciation. Growing in confidence she went on to sing 'It's a Long Way to Tipperary', 'Pack Up Your Troubles in Your Old Kit Bag' and many other favourites. The men joined in whenever she urged them to do so, clearly loving every minute of her performance, as did she. When she finished singing and gave a little bow before leaving the stage, feeling dizzy with excitement over the success she'd experienced, she heard them call out for an encore.

'Give them one more song,' the director eagerly instructed her when Cecily reached him in the wings, his usually arrogant face a picture of satisfaction.

'He's right, you were wonderful, so do as he says,' Merryn urged, giving her a hug.

'How is Mama?' The prospect of facing Queenie's anger at her star performance being taken over by her least favourite daughter was too dreadful to contemplate.

Merryn wrinkled her plump little nose. 'Johnny the drummer has taken her home in his Ford car, so Nan will take care of her.'

'Thank goodness for that.'

As the director pushed her back on stage, Cecily grinned and happily went on to sing 'Roses of Picardy', fulfilment echoing in her heart.

TWO

SEATED BESIDE her mother who lay fast asleep in bed, Cecily gazed wearily out over the Sound. She watched a couple of fishing boats plough through the white horse waves, tossed about like mere toys by the vicious wind on this cold winter day. The grey clouds unexpectedly split open to reveal a shaft of sunlight that encircled the boats. Would that Queenie's behaviour could light up as brightly. She'd barely slept a wink last night, sobbing and crying as she suffered yet another nightmare. Cecily, along with her sister, had rushed to offer comfort, never certain what caused this, assuming it to be a consequence of her addiction to alcohol.

This time the nightmare could have been in consequence of her fall on stage or else she felt racked with guilt over the failure of her voice, having worked hard at singing her entire life. Queenie could also have been irritated at seeing her star role pass to her daughter. Guilt echoed in Cecily at the thought.

It was difficult to decide how to resolve her mother's problems, knowing surprisingly little about her past, something she refused to speak of, save for being considered quite a talented singer as a child. Her parents had encouraged her to sing at local churches and shows. They apparently treated her very like a star and had lovingly spoiled her, buying her many gifts. These comprised pretty frocks, teddy bears, a pretty doll's house and a family of dolls that still sat upon her bedroom window ledge. Later, she'd moved on to success in the theatre, viewing herself as a celebrity of great talent. This now seemed to be on the wane, which naturally made her increasingly ill-tempered.

Queenie woke when the door opened and Nanny Aldcroft, or Nan as she preferred to be called, walked in. She'd looked after her mistress and themselves as children for years. Born in the East End of London, she and Merryn had spent their entire lives constantly moving around the country: Bristol, Liverpool, Preston, Newcastle, Brighton and here in Plymouth. Queenie had always insisted that she needed to tour in order to perform. Forever on the move, they hadn't felt they belonged anywhere and rarely found time to develop any friendships. It had, however, created a closeness and dependence between them as well as a deep affection for Nan, who felt much more like a mother to them than Queenie ever had. Loyal, efficient, disciplined and utterly reliable, she was a woman with a strict routine, giving out instructions on life as if she knew best. Not easy to defy, but filled with love for the two of them. Giving Cecily a cheerful wink, she placed the breakfast tray across her mistress's knee in her usual brisk, unfussy manner.

Glowering at the plate of food, Queenie looked as though she felt the urge to toss the sausage and toast on to the floor. 'This is not at all what I wish to eat. You are well aware that I prefer scrambled eggs.'

'We've none left,' Nan retorted, her wrinkled face exceedingly stern, her wide mouth tightening over the obstinate jut of her square chin. 'Food ain't easy to come by with this war on.'

'Then try hard to find some for tomorrow,' Queenie haughtily ordered.

Folding her hands across her plump belly, Nan gave a chuckle and the kind of scalding look she used to give them as children whenever they were naughty. 'If I succeed in finding some eggs, you can't have them every day or there'd be none left for these girls. They too deserve the odd treat. I'll go out to do some shopping later on today. It's a pity you aren't well enough to come with me, as you so like to do. Is there anything else you'd like me to buy for you?'

'I need a new gown since I tore my favourite one in this accident,' Queenie said with a scowl.

'Now I wonder why that happened,' Nan drily commented, busily tucking in the sheets and pretending she didn't know Queenie had been drunk. 'Would you like me to find you one?'

'No, you are no good at shopping, fussy woman.'

Cecily put her hand over her mouth to stifle a giggle as she listened to their familiar dispute. Her mother always wished to be dressed in a most stylish fashion, swamp herself in jewellery and spend money as if there was no tomorrow, so loved exploring all the marvellous shops here. Cecily had little interest in such things.

Now Queenie gave Nan a dismissive nod. 'I've no wish to eat this breakfast, so you can take it away.'

Nan stubbornly placed the tray on the side table and poured Queenie a cup of tea. On her way out, she paused to speak to Cecily. 'When that young drummer Johnny fetched your mother home, I sent him in search of the doctor who has promised to call round this morning to examine her injured ankle.'

'So glad to hear that. Thank you, Nan.' Giving her a grateful smile as she marched off, Cecily returned to her mother's side to plump up her pillows and gently suggested she should eat her breakfast in order to aid her recovery.

'I am still in pain and in desperate need of relief, not food.'

'I'm sure the doctor will supply you with a little opium, once he arrives. Meanwhile, drink your tea, dearest, and take a slice of toast if nothing else.' As Queenie at last began to eat, Cecily risked changing the subject. 'You may be interested to hear that my performance went well. Not as good as yours is, Mama, but so thrilling,' she said, her violet-blue eyes glimmering with a stir of excitement.

Queenie gave a twisted little smile, envy marring her expression. 'Do not imagine for one moment you will always perform well. Being an actress or singer can be fun if also highly stressful. Performances can easily go wrong.'

'I can't say yours ever did, Mama, not until you started to over-indulge yourself on alcohol – a little foolish. The doctor could make that point too.'

Her face flushing, Queenie sharply retorted, 'Gin is produced here in Plymouth at the distillery in the Barbican, so why would I not take advantage of it? You should appreciate that having endured a consider-able amount of anguish throughout my life, I feel the need for a glass or two before a performance to help deal with my nerves or possible stage fright. Now that I've been dismissed from the Palace Theatre, will nothing ever go right for me?'

'I know it was opened as a music hall back in 1898 but it is still hugely popular, so I'm sure we can persuade the director to change his mind, as you are also popular,' Cecily assured her.

'I am indeed. They may have featured many famous stars such as Lillie Langtry, Gertie Gitana singing 'Nellie Dean', and the illusionist Harry Houdini performing his escape tricks, but I too am a true star.'

Cecily gave her a smile. 'You are, Mama. So if I stand in for you again, it will only be until you are fully recovered. Oh, and I really enjoyed singing.'

'You should be aware that it's far more important for you to find your-self a husband, not to spend your life trapped on stage, as I have been,' Queenie snarled. 'That would not be wise as most men tend to treat actresses, dancers and singers as prostitutes. It could destroy any hope of a decent offer of marriage and children for you. Raising a family is what we women are expected to do with our lives, a tradition you'd be wise to follow.'

Giving a little sigh of frustration over her mother's obsession with marriage, Cecily perched herself on the edge of the bed. 'Do stop boss-ing me, Mama. I'm in no rush to marry.'

'You are almost twenty-one years old and growing older, Cecily.'

'With luck I won't be much older when this dratted war ends.' She paused, wondering if this was the moment to reveal the truth. Taking a breath, she said, 'Actually, Ewan having been my sweetheart since I was sixteen, we became secretly engaged before he left for the war and fully intend to marry once it is finally over.'

Queenie's eyes opened wide in astonishment. 'Goodness gracious, the notion of you marrying that fellow is too dreadful to contemplate. Ewan Godolphin is a scraggy mess, only employed as a fisherman by his father. Not at all the kind of man I wish for either of you girls to cavort with. He is obviously keen to take advantage of your money and status.'

'That's a dreadful thing to accuse him of. He loves me as much as I love him.' A frown puckered Cecily's brow as she recalled how her mother had always been entirely disapproving of their friendship and did her utmost to destroy it. She was a complete snob, uncaring of Cecily's chance of happiness, being more concerned that her own reputation could be ruined if her daughter married a working-class lad from low society.

Oh, and how she missed him. The last she'd seen of him was over a year ago when he'd come home on leave. Cecily remembered that day well. Hearing the train come puffing into the station she'd run along the platform, anxious to find him. The instant he saw her she'd fallen eagerly into his arms, delighted to see his face beaming with delight. 'Oh, I've missed you so much, darling,' he'd told her, pulling her close.

'I've missed you too,' she'd cried.

He was instantly kissing her, coaxing her lips open to devour her in a way that brought a thrill of excitement into her heart. Cecily had pulled off his cap to stroke her hands through the short locks of his brown hair, loving the fact he was pressing her tight against his chest.

Ewan Godolphin was tall and athletic with powerful shoulders and long lean legs, dark brown eyes and gloriously good looking. His face had appeared a little more rugged and tired than usual, as a consequence of all he was suffering in this war. His expression was still filled with warmth, compassion and love. Once he'd returned to his battalion, Cecily continued to write to him most days and received regular letters in response. There were periods when she heard nothing at all from him in ages, as had been the case recently. A quiver of fear would rustle through her until his next letter arrived.

'That boy has little hope of ever earning a decent living,' Queenie sternly announced. 'And do not assume for one moment that I will supply you with the necessary funds if you do marry him. I have quite enough expenses, not least dealing with the upkeep of this fine mansion house. You need a man with money and status who can provide you with a wonderful life.'

The irritating thing was that she seemed perfectly content for Merryn to remain at home as her carer, while constantly urging Cecily to marry a rich man with whom she could live her life elsewhere. She'd no intention of obeying such ridiculous instructions, while Merryn was most keen to marry.

'Happiness in marriage is not about money,' she remarked dismissively, giving a little chuckle in the hope of lightening her mother's temper. 'I really have no wish to be a domesticated, stay-at-home wife with a man I don't love. I fully intend to live the kind of life that suits me. Ewan is not against my working for a living and proud of the job I do for the electric trams. It's not quite what I would have chosen to do, but with this war on, I feel it's right to do my bit. I accept it won't be easy to find more interesting employment once it is over, or earn sufficient money, particularly as women do not get equal pay let alone the right to vote. That could change with time, and I'll find something that appeals to me.'

'Why would you? A young woman's job should end once she marries.'

Cecily groaned. 'You sound so Victorian, Mama.'

'Nonsense! Once a woman is married, she must devote herself to being a good wife and mother. I mistakenly did not do that.'

'How brave of you to admit that, Mama. What was it you did wrong?' Cecily asked, surprised to hear her confess this fault.

'There were times when I felt as if life was treating me like a piece of rubbish. I encountered endless problems, not least the lack of love from my husband. I have no wish to remember his dismissive attitude towards me. You should do what is right and proper in order to find happiness and prosperity.'

Cecily had constantly asked questions about what sort of a man her father was and why he had left them and tragically drowned, receiving no response. Both girls felt bereft at losing a father of whom they had very little memory. There was no point in harassing her further on this subject. 'Please don't assume that because your marriage failed, mine will too. Ewan and I are happy together and will make a success of it. If you made the wrong choice of husband, do tell me why?'

Frowning, Queenie again turned away, avoiding meeting her enquiring gaze. 'Your father was not an easy man and I was most thankful to see the back of him.'

'If that is the case, why do I still find you crying for him sometimes, even in your nightmares?'

'I'm not weeping *for* him or longing for his return. I'm merely furious at the mess he made of my life, which is why I advise you to ensure *yours* is better. When I was young, I was entirely naïve and dreamed of a perfect marriage. Nothing worked out quite as I'd hoped. Dean ruined my life and I was left feeling in desperate need of love and care. As a consequence, I am extremely thankful for my success on stage and have no desire to discuss this issue further, with you or anyone.'

Cecily stifled a sigh. Was that because her mother had little patience with other people's points of view, being obsessed with her own opinions and insisting upon complete control of her life? She suspected Queenie might have acquired the art of adjusting her life story by making up false tales in order to avoid revealing certain heart-rending facts. Cecily found it so frustrating that she refused to confide in them about what went wrong with her marriage, and whether their father had suffered an accident or killed himself.

THREE
JANUARY 1917

CHRISTMAS PASSED in a blur, then as the New Year dawned, Johnny the drummer called round to ask if Queenie was feeling any better. 'I thought you'd like to know that I've now spoken to the director and persuaded him to allow Queenie to carry on working for him,' he told Cecily.

'Oh, how very kind of you,' she said, giving his hand a little shake to thank him. He was a lively young man and a smartly dressed dandy. 'Mama will be delighted. I'm so grateful you brought her home in your Ford car, as the theatre's chauffeur was not around at the time. And you thankfully called the doctor. He has assured Mama that it is a sprained ankle, not broken.'

'Thank goodness for that,' he said, beaming at her.

'She's resting in the parlour. Would you like to see her, so you can tell her this wonderful news?'

'I would indeed. She's a lovely talented lady, as are you, so why wouldn't I be glad to help? I have to say that I was greatly impressed with your performance, managing to see some of it before taking your mother home. I do hope to hear you sing again. You're not only beautiful but could be the next star.'

Aware that his gaze was sliding over her, his eyebrows twitching as he gave her an admiring wink, she recalled how Johnny Wilcox did have something of a reputation for attracting women. Not that she had any interest in him, her heart enraptured with another young man. Carefully avoiding any response to the compliments he was paying her, Cecily merely chuckled and led him across the hall in a most practical fashion. 'If Queenie is to be allowed to continue working at the Palace Theatre, I doubt the director would ever make me another offer.'

'Then put yourself forward for auditions in other theatres or at the Pavilion on the Pier. I'm sure they'd be delighted to welcome you.'

'I'm not convinced they would, but I will give it some thought. Now do come and see Mama. I'm sure she'll want to thank you too.'

Her mother's face had been most gloomy lately, but lit with interest as he entered. 'Ah, you've brought this lovely young man to see me. What a treat.' When he cheerfully explained how he'd managed to recover her role at the theatre, she clapped her hands with joy, smiling at him in delight. 'What a wonderful treasure you are, dear boy. I am most grateful for your assistance.'

He grinned. 'Should I also attempt to gain a role for your lovely and talented daughter? She's a brilliant performer.'

'Nonsense, she's never had a singing lesson in her entire life,' Queenie retorted.

'I was provided with lessons at school, Mama, and joined the choir. You are unaware of that as you were commonly away on tour.'

'There you are then,' Johnny said. 'This girl does have talent and experience you can be proud of. I've suggested to her that she should perform again.'

'Indeed not! She already has an important job to do while this war is on, one she's much better at than singing.'

'Really, how could that be?' he asked, looking puzzled.

'Mama could be making a valid point. I work as a tram conductress and it is an important job with so many men no longer around.'

20

Recalling her mother's furious attitude over that unexpected performance, Cecily was unsurprised to see her lips tighten and her smile vanish in another surly fit of jealousy. It destroyed any sign in her of kindness or compassion, qualities Cecily firmly believed in. She made a vow to steadfastly avoid such envy herself, viewing it like a plague. Nevertheless, as she only worked part-time, she would love to take part in the occasional evening concert, possibly in some place other than the Palace Theatre.

Merryn entered at that moment, carrying a tray of tea and biscuits. Turning to smile at her sister, Cecily said, 'Johnny has suggested I apply for an audition at the Pavilion on the Pier. Would you join me, lovey, if I were ever granted a performance?'

Merryn blinked with excitement. 'Ooh, do you think that might happen?'

Queenie's face lit with fury. 'It most certainly will not, Merryn. Not for a moment would I ever allow Cecily to perform in a rival theatre.'

'Why ever not?' Merryn asked, looking surprised. 'She surely has a right to a good career.'

'She has no right to compete with me. I shall contact the director and make it clear that he must never invite my daughter to take part in a concert, otherwise I will not agree to appear on stage for him ever again.'

Cecily's hopes instantly died. How controlling her mother was, still viewing herself as a star even though her talent was beginning to fade, and obstinately refusing to allow Cecily the right to fulfil her own dreams. Queenie had taken part in several concerts at the Pavilion in the past. Not much recently as she was busily engaged at the Palace Theatre. Feeling a stir of resentment flicker within her, Cecily warned herself that this was not the moment to enter into a dispute when her mother was still unwell. Dampening this sensation, she gave her a conciliatory smile. 'Don't fret, Mama. I doubt it would ever happen. Thank you, Johnny, for this suggestion. I won't pursue it right now. Maybe one day.'

And giving him and her sister a warning glance, she caringly smiled at Queenie and poured out the tea.

※

In the weeks following, Cecily received no further invitations to appear on stage. She felt a swell of disappointment that singing for the soldiers at the Palace Theatre had achieved nothing. This was exactly what she'd expected to happen. Oh, but how she longed to perform again. Could it be that she hadn't performed well enough to impress the director? Although, Queenie could have talked to every stage manager in Plymouth, ensuring they never allowed her daughter to perform, dismissing her as a foolish amateur. Thankfully, Queenie had fully recovered within days and as a consequence of Johnny's support was soon back to her normal routine at the theatre. Cecily and Merryn must now try harder to keep her off the gin.

Urging herself not to fret about the loss of her own dream, Cecily concentrated upon her job. It was not an easy one. Each morning or evening she was required to scrub and clean the tram in her charge, and make sure that her smart jacket, long skirt and peaked hat were also respectable and clean. She spent hours studying the routes, timetable and stops she'd have to deal with each day. Then when the tram set off, she concentrated on collecting fares and giving out the right tickets, carefully noting who'd paid and who hadn't. Some passengers might try to sneak off without paying their fare, and Cecily would find herself caught up in conflict with them. She was happy to help old ladies, children and injured soldiers get safely on and off the tram – not easy on cold winter days when everywhere was wet and slippy. And she enjoyed many of the places they visited, in particular the Theatre Royal in George Street, trips to Saltash and Devonport, Plymouth Argyle football ground, and most of all Little Ash Tea Gardens, where a brass band would sometimes play once spring came.

Today, being a much-needed day off, she walked along the limestone cliffs of the seafront, then up the slopes on the Hoe to where Francis Drake had played bowls before sailing out to defeat the Spanish Armada. From here she could see a marvellous view of Drake's Island and Plymouth Sound. Gazing down at the Pier, a part of her recalled Johnny's suggestion that she should apply to take part in an audition here at the Pavilion. Would it be worth the risk?

Unable to decide, she couldn't resist walking along to the Pavilion to hear music playing and somebody singing. She quietly slipped in to listen and, looking around, saw the man in charge with a queue of people waiting to audition. She watched folk come and go, noticing the director sitting mainly with his eyes closed, only occasionally glancing up to view the person on stage in order to wave his hand and dismiss them. He looked extremely bored and Cecily doubted he'd be interested in her either. Fearful of offending her mother, which could drive Queenie into another jealous tantrum and more drinking, Cecily quietly slipped out, promising herself to concentrate upon more important issues in her life.

❧

Spring was now upon them, the March weather quite warm and sunny, with fluffy white clouds filling the skies that sometimes delivered the usual showers. At weekends, in order to give themselves some exercise, Cecily and Merryn would walk along to Smeaton's Tower, past the Citadel and go to the Barbican to enjoy the fish market and stroll along the harbour to Mayflower Steps, from where the Pilgrim Fathers sailed to America. On warmer days, they would take longer walks along the sandy beaches and over the cliffs. They would hear the singing of buzzards and kestrels and enjoy the glow of violets and primroses. On rare occasions, the sight of dolphins playing out at sea would captivate them.

Cecily felt reasonably content with her work on the trams, banishing all disappointment over her inability to sing from her mind. Merryn too was happily doing her bit for the war, being employed part-time at Dingles drapery store on Bedford Street. Neither of them was well paid, yet revelled in this new sense of independence, so much more interesting than sitting endlessly at home for no real purpose. In this respect, the war had proved to be an advantage to women.

This afternoon, being a Saturday, they were attending a suffragist meeting, which offered much satisfaction. Cecily had worked alongside this organisation from before the war, taking part in parades and demonstrations. She'd always felt a sore need to help, as she strongly believed in the rights of women. She'd spent every evening the previous week happily delivering notices to encourage people to come to this meeting.

'The place is packed,' Merryn softly remarked, seated beside her on the front row and glancing around. 'You did an excellent job encouraging so many to come.'

'Thank goodness there are plenty of women here.' This had been helped by the fact that Annie Kenney, a most special lady, was attending the meeting. As a working-class factory girl who started to follow the Pankhursts, she was now almost as famous as them and she certainly gave excellent talks, being very down-to-earth. 'Unfortunately, some working women are unable to attend these suffrage meetings because they have families to feed after they finish work, or else they fear to offend their bosses or family. Irritatingly, the occasional sour-faced father or husband would toss away the notice I delivered!'

'Men can be very commanding,' Merryn agreed.

'I would never allow one to control me,' Cecily sternly remarked.

'I can understand that your sense of independence is partly the reason you enjoy working with the suffragist movement to help them seek the vote. Me too, although I am in favour of marriage and willing to be a fairly obedient wife to make my husband happy.'

Cecily chuckled. 'Hang on to your rights, darling. I have no doubt that we will both achieve the vote one day and find the love of our life.'

'Exactly.'

Stifling their giggles, they listened to Annie Kenney explain how Lloyd George, who had always been supportive, was now helping ladies achieve their goal, having finally replaced Asquith as Prime Minister last December. 'We have every reason to believe that a vote will soon be granted, if only to women of a certain class who own property and are over thirty,' she announced.

'Why is that?' Cecily quietly asked her sister, only to find herself hushed.

She firmly disagreed with her mother's attitude against the working classes, particularly regarding her beloved Ewan. It seemed politicians were equally disapproving. How would she, Merryn, and most other women, ever achieve the right to vote unless they succeeded in improving their status and raised enough money to buy themselves a house? Deep in some secret part of her soul, there lurked the hope that by stimulating the new talent she'd discovered in herself during that one performance on stage, it might happen again one day and earn her an independent income. Shutting down these dreams, she realised Annie Kenney was explaining the reason for this puzzle.

'The government is wary of the fact that women are in the majority. Men have been in short supply for some years. Many went to work in the colonies before the war in order to find employment, a situation that could grow worse once this war is over, as so many young men have already been killed. Therefore, the number of surplus women will increase.'

'Is this lack of a vote for all women, whatever their age or income, because the government has no wish to be taken over by us?' Cecily asked with a wry smile. Others in the audience laughed and cheered at this remark.

'I'd say that is the reason, yes,' Annie replied with a cheerful nod. 'As a young Yorkshire lass wishing to help women get the vote, I packed my little wicker basket, put two pounds safely in my purse – the only money I possessed – and started my journey to London to join the Pankhursts. Fortunately, Lloyd George and Asquith both now agree that the heroism of hard-working women doing men's jobs during the war has made them reconsider our situation. This bill will make a start on improving our rights. Given time and more effort, we will hopefully succeed in widening its scope.'

As the meeting came to an end, Cecily joined the group of stewards to help collect donations from those women able to contribute. Some carefully ignored this appeal, not being well enough off, but she did manage to gather a fairly large sum.

'That was a most inspiring meeting,' she said to Merryn as the two sisters walked home, arm in arm. They went on to talk about how one day they too might be granted the vote, even if they weren't as fortunate as their mother and able to buy a property. Putting her key in the slot, Cecily was startled when the front door burst open and they found Nan waiting for them in the hall. Leaping forward, she wrapped her arms around Cecily, pulling her close to give her a hug.

'Goodness, don't tell me there's another problem with Mama?'

With an expression of pity she shook her head, then, wiping tears from her eyes, handed her a telegram. 'Sorry, dear, this has just been delivered to you.'

Cecily stared at the telegram in complete shock, her hands starting to shake as she opened it. Then her knees buckled and she fell to the ground, sobbing in anguish as she read that Ewan had drowned.

FOUR

CECILY FELT numb with grief and horror, so utterly devastated that her mind became completely blocked, leaving her quite unable to think or speak, as if she'd fallen into a dark pit. Merryn held her sister tight in her arms as she sobbed, tears running down her cheeks, sharing her grief. Nan rushed to fetch Queenie, who came within seconds.

'Oh, my dear girl, I'm so sorry.'

Taking her to bed, Queenie hugged her as if she were a small child. 'I know how it feels to lose a loved one,' she said, as her hesitant smile rippled with compassion. 'My heart goes out to you, my dear. I do hope you will manage to build yourself a new and better life, and find yourself a new man.'

Cecily felt utterly speechless at this tactless remark, unable to imagine planning a future without her darling Ewan. Yet she was deeply moved by her mother's sympathy and lay in her arms for the entire night, the closest they'd been in years. When Cecily had learned of the death of her father, she'd felt an aching void within, loneliness in her heart and a need to know more. Now she felt far worse, but was pathetically grateful for her mother's support.

Finding the right words of condolence for Ewan's family when she went to see them the next morning was heartbreaking. His mother held her tight in her arms as they both wept, then bravely attempted to recall the activities he'd taken pleasure in throughout his life, his ability to swim, fish and sail, even in a stormy sea. Cecily then learned from his father that the ship, upon which Ewan was a part of the crew, had sunk after being hit by a German submarine. The Kaiser continued to flex his military might, determined to challenge Britain's dominating presence on the seas and destroy their brave young sailors and soldiers.

No funeral was possible as his body was lost, but determined to celebrate their son's life, Ewan's family held a memorial service at the St Andrew's church close to their home. It was packed to the doors with friends, old fishermen he used to work with, siblings, cousins, aunts and whatever uncles were still around. Queenie claimed she was unable to attend, as she was busily involved in rehearsals for her next concert, again revealing her lack of care. Accompanied by Merryn, Cecily listened to the memories and stories they all told about him with a strange combination of pride and despair in her heart. It was a day that would live forever in her soul, as would Ewan.

Over the coming days, Cecily sat huddled in her room, rocking herself in misery, going nowhere and doing nothing, feeling as if she'd been ripped to pieces, her heart broken. All too aware she would soon be required to return to work on the trams, she could hardly persuade her brain to think of how she could go on living without him. How many other men too had lost their lives? Thousands had died at the Battle of the Somme last summer, some of them merely young boys, having joined out of a sense of patriotism. What an appalling war this was. Would it get better or worse? She could hardly bear to think.

Having barely slept a wink and filled with depression, one morning she rose early and walked down to the seafront along the terraces to the beach changing rooms. Moments later she was swimming fast and strong in the sea close to the Pier. Several swimming clubs met here and would swim early each morning. Cecily had often joined them and Ewan would be with her. Now she was alone and wrapped in grief.

Swimming mainly beneath the water, she lifted her head only occasionally above the gently lapping waves to draw breath. The sun winked and shimmered on the surface of the water, blotting out all sight of land and Smeaton's Tower. There was nothing sparkling about her mood, which was at complete odds with this sunny April day. Locked in pain, her mind felt as if she was swamped in dark, heavy, wet clouds.

Turning her back on the shoreline and the unwelcome sight of dozens of boats, she dived deeper, heading further out to sea, her eyes glaring at the pebbles slowly vanishing beneath her. She had no wish to relish any sight of the sun, nor children playing on the various beaches. How she'd longed to bear Ewan's child. Now, with no hope of marriage, she would have none. How could she face life without him? Filled with the desire to join Ewan, wherever he was, she considered letting herself drown in the murky world at the bottom of the sea.

Is this what her father did when his marriage had apparently failed and he'd presumably found himself facing an empty life? Whether his death had been suicide or a freak accident was a question her mother had never answered.

It came to her then that she'd not lost Ewan because of his lack of love for her. He'd joined the Navy to fight in the war at just nineteen because he loved the sea and was a brave young man, keen to do his bit for the country. Filled with pride for him, how could she blame him for taking such a dangerous risk? Hadn't many valiant young men joined up for the King's shilling? She recalled how he'd proposed to her before being sent off to France, so keen to marry her. In spite of her deep love for him and being only eighteen at the time, she'd claimed to be too young to contemplate marriage with no hope of the necessary permission from her mother. Now, three years later, not having seen him for over a year and turned twenty-one last month, the war was still going on and Ewan was lost forever. How she deeply regretted putting off their marriage. If only they had eloped in defiance of her mother, instead of always giving in to her demands. They could then have spent some time together before he departed this world.

Holding firmly to the image of his handsome face, the way he used to smile at her, the touch of his lips and the warmth of his arms whenever he held her close with love in his eyes, Cecily told herself that drowning was not the answer to her troubles. She needed to keep Ewan forever in her heart. Nor must she abandon her beloved sister.

With enormous effort, Cecily forced her tired limbs to swim back up to the surface. Taking a breath, she allowed herself to be encased in a bubble of brilliant, magical light from the sun. Approaching the shore, she saw Merryn waving to her from Tinside Beach, then she stepped into the water, doing battle with the waves and looking desperate to reach her. Panic echoed through Cecily, knowing her sister was no great swimmer, particularly dressed in her long skirt. Quickly lifting her hand, she shouted, 'Stay there, Merryn, I'm on my way back.'

Gathering her strength, she swam as fast as she could, feeling almost thankful when her feet touched the sandy beach. Merryn was waiting for her anxiously and handing her a towel, slipped her arms around Cecily to give her a tight hug, clearly aware she was still suffering from the pain of her loss. 'I came looking for you, to make sure you were all right.'

'I'm in better health now, thank you,' Cecily said with a weak smile as she began to rub herself dry.

Merryn pulled a face. 'Queenie was displeased to see you go off alone for a swim. She wishes to discuss plans for your future.'

In mournful silence, Cecily tickled a sea anemone in a nearby rock pool with her toe, coaxing it into opening its delicate fronds. Finding a mussel close by, the waving tentacles gobbled it up and closed again. How precious and short life was! Glancing around, she reminded herself that she adored this place. Ewan too had loved living here. They used to hunt for crabs in rock pools, swim in the sea and walk for miles along the coast or fish in the Sound. Not that she was as good at fishing as he had been. They'd spent such a happy time together, climbing over rocks, dipping in rock pools and laughingly stalking each other. She would secretly allow him to catch her so that he could steal a kiss any time he fancied. He'd been the love of her life, and always would be.

Now she gave a rueful shake of her head, feeling quite unequal to breaching the rigid stance her mother took. 'I suspect these plans will be whatever suits her, not me.'

'I agree she can be a bit of a problem. Don't let her bully you. You're a clever and talented girl. I'm quite certain you'll find something useful to do with your life.'

'I'll try my best to think of something. Goodness knows what that will be.'

'I'll help you to decide,' Merryn said with a smile. 'You can sing so wonderfully, but as we know, Queenie does not wish you to perform ever again. I do, however. Goodness, she's here!'

Cecily looked up in dismay to find her mother striding towards them, looking angrier than ever, her feet getting blocked in the sand with each furious step as she wore pretty heeled shoes, more suitable for a stage than a beach.

'What the hell do you think you're doing? Have you gone mad?'

Her mother's sympathy had now clearly vanished, and Cecily felt a shaft of pain again clench her heart, as it did a hundred times a day. Worried about how many lifetimes it would take to pull herself out of this grief, she'd spoken to the vicar. He'd kindly explained that you never did get over losing a loved one; you just had to learn to live with the reality and be thankful he was at peace. The truth of this would not resurface her mother's compassion or her lack of interest in a young man of whom she'd highly disapproved.

'I woke this morning feeling the need for some fresh air and exercise after the agony I've suffered. What is wrong with my taking a swim?'

'Swimming with barely any clothes on is no way for a young woman to behave. Get dressed this minute.'

Glancing down at her striped swimming costume, which covered her arms and shoulders and almost reached her knees, Cecily felt the urge to laugh out loud at such a ridiculous comment, even though her wide, generous mouth felt far too stiff to manage a smile. The tension etched within her made her banish this desire with a burst of anger over her mother's constant disapproval. 'I surely look perfectly respectable and what I do with my time is no concern of yours, Mama.'

'Oh, you heartless girl, how can you say such a thing?' As Queenie burst into tears, she wrapped her arms around her daughter, hugging her tight. 'I feared you were hell-bent on taking your own life.'

Cecily was filled with shame at hearing this comment. Realising she'd said or done entirely the wrong thing she gave a soft apology. 'I'm so sorry, Mama. I assure you I'd never do that.' She made no mention of the depressive, crazed thoughts that had driven her to swim ever deeper, perhaps seeking that hidden kingdom beneath the sea that the Cornish so like to believe exists.

'Oh, thank goodness. Pray do not deny me the right to be concerned about your future,' Queenie said in a surprisingly soft tone of voice. 'I believe it's time for you to return to work.'

Cecily appreciated that she would forever grieve for Ewan and dreaded the prospect of facing a lonely and solitary future. Since his death a few weeks ago, she'd felt filled with pain, as thousands of other women experienced because of their losses in this dreadful war. The United States had now entered the conflict, declaring war on Germany, so there was little sign of it ending soon. Once it was over, would she ever become close to another man? She felt no desire for that to happen. Her life had changed forever. Now it was time for her to move forward.

'You are right, Mama. Going back to work will give me a reason to go on.'

Over the next days, Cecily was still unable to relax and sleep. She would spend hours struggling to think through what she should do with her life, struggling not to remember the foolishness of swimming out to sea, which had so upset her poor sister as well as her mother. Then one night, remembering how Merryn had reminded her of that wonderful performance she gave before Christmas, an idea sparked within her. It felt like a flash of light across the bay, creating a glint of unexpected excitement. Pulling on her dressing gown, she crept to her sister's bedroom. Slipping quietly in without bothering to tap on the door, she was pleased to find Merryn reading a book by candlelight, as was often the case.

'Can I join you for a moment?' she whispered.

Pulling back the blanket to let her in, Merryn gave a little chuckle. 'You've constantly done that since I was small, so why not? Are you still feeling in need of help?'

Cecily happily snuggled in beside her. 'I've been speaking firmly to myself and have resolved to find happiness some way other than the marriage I'd looked forward to with Ewan. I feel the need to build a new life. Also, I want to thank you for your opinion of my so-called talent, lovey. It's given me a wonderful idea. You are right, I *can* sing quite well, if not how Mama used to,' she modestly stated. 'So why don't I do that for the soldiers in France?'

Merryn gazed at her sister, astounded. 'Are you serious?'

'I most certainly am.'

'I can't believe what you're saying,' she said, tossing her book aside. 'Tell me more.'

'I've no idea what it might entail. I desperately feel the need to support Ewan's efforts in the war, as well as do my bit to help other brave young men trapped in the trenches. It would give me a new purpose in life, one that might also help me deal with my loss. Would you be willing to play your piano accordion for me?' Cecily asked, her expression changing to a broad grin.

'Oh, my goodness, you want me to join you?'

'I do. We're a very close team and you're a better musician than me. I'm just a singer.'

'Not for a moment would I claim to be more talented than either you or Queenie.' Merryn's hazel eyes narrowed as she gave the matter more careful thought. 'You realise we'd have to give up our jobs. It would also involve travelling to an unknown foreign place close to the battlefront and danger. Are you sure you want to do that?'

'A part of me would like to stay in Cornwall or Devon forever, but life is presenting new challenges so I'm prepared to take the risk. And why stay here with our disapproving and neglectful mother? She's so hard to live with. We can come back to our jobs once the war is over, and find peace and happiness.' She met her sister's confused gaze with deep pleading in her own. 'I'm keen to do my bit in memory of Ewan and for the men in the war. Please say you're willing to help too.'

Merryn's face lit with a grin. 'I am indeed. Let's do it. You and I are indeed a team. Off we'll go to entertain the troops.'

FIVE

THEY SPENT much of the night talking through what they needed to do to make the necessary arrangements. It felt like a turning point in Cecily's life, a commitment that set the reality of war above such trivialities as personal happiness. Performing in concert parties in France had not at first been considered an appropriate role for women. She was aware that because of the shortage of men, the authorities finally did give permission, accepting that touring parties needed to be mainly female. It could certainly prove to be dangerous, but Cecily prayed they would survive unharmed.

'Do you plan to persuade anyone else to come with us?' Merryn asked.

'I'm not sure who we could ask,' Cecily admitted.

'What about Johnny the drummer? He isn't a conscientious objector. The Army rejected him because he wears spectacles, having an eyesight problem, and he's not terribly tall or fit. I think he's been hounded by the white-feather campaign on more than one occasion but I don't believe he's a coward. He's just not exactly big and strong.'

'You sound as if you know him well. Is he your new sweetheart?' Cecily teased her.

'No, of course not.'

'But you'd like him to be?' Cecily smiled as her sister's cheeks flushed bright pink. She'd had only a few over the last year or two and more often than not, Queenie would dismiss them after only a few weeks, just as she'd attempted to do with Ewan. Merryn never once protested, being three years younger than Cecily. Could she be much more captivated by this young man? Unlike her dear sister, Cecily no longer nursed any desire for marriage, caring little for her own well-being. Bearing in mind the traumas they might face, she vowed to do her best to protect her.

'He's just a good friend,' Merryn said. 'Johnny is quite talented so I believe he'd be a useful addition to our team.'

'Good idea. I'll let you know when it's safe to ask him, once I've acquired the necessary passports and permits. And say nothing about this plan to Mama either. I've no wish to risk any further disagreement between us.'

'Oh, I do so agree.'

'I'll write to the local authorities first thing in the morning. We should be aware it could take a while before I get a response.'

It was barely a week later that Cecily arrived home from work to find she'd received a letter inviting her to take part in an interview. Bursting with excitement, she showed it to Merryn as they sat having supper together.

'How wonderful to get a response so quickly!' her sister said in surprise.

'Would you believe they wish me to attend the Army Headquarters first thing tomorrow?'

'Will I have to attend too? I do have a day off from work.'

Cecily grinned. 'As I'm the one who planned this project, it's up to me to get the necessary permission, then you can go and speak to Johnny.'

Cecily sat in the waiting room, her nerves jangling slightly. She'd worked out what to say with regard to their various skills and overall plan. More importantly, she'd rehearsed her speech on her strong desire to do her bit for the men in the war. Hadn't she been involved with the battle for the women's vote for a long time, so this surely couldn't be any more difficult?

A young woman approached her with a smile, and leading her into the office directed her to a seat before a large desk. Cecily struggled to calm her pounding heart by taking deep breaths. The stern-faced man seated behind it did not look up, being engrossed in reading a pile of papers stacked before him. Finally, he lifted his head to stare at her over his reading glasses.

'Lieutenant Trevain, at your service. You are this . . . er . . .' he glanced again at the paper, 'Miss Hanson?'

'I am, sir, yes.'

He glowered at her, scepticism clear in his face. 'So you are claiming to be a singer capable of entertaining the troops?'

Determinedly ignoring the patronising tone of his voice, Cecily instantly began to relate her skills and her sister's musical ability, carefully making no mention of their famous mother. If she revealed Queenie's name, he might opt for her instead, which was not at all what she wanted to happen. Before she managed to explain what she could offer, as well as the possibility of persuading others to join them, he briskly interrupted her.

'You're just a skinny little miss and far too young. I think you'd best leave.' Banging the bell on his desk, the door quickly opened and the young woman again appeared. 'See this girl out, please.'

Cecily felt utterly devastated at being dismissed before she'd been allowed to properly speak of her plans and the reason for this project. He hadn't asked her a single question. 'I may be young but I *can* perform well,' she retorted smartly, and leaping to her feet in a blaze of passion instantly began to sing 'Take Me Back to Dear Old Blighty'. She saw how his eyes widened in surprise, his secretary coming closer to listen, with a smile of appreciation on her face. Cecily dipped her knees, saluted, and stamped her feet up and down as if she was a soldier in uniform on the march, then hugged her chest by the end of the chorus.

Take me back to dear old Blighty
Put me on a train to London Town
Take me over there, drop me anywhere
Birmingham, Leeds, or Manchester, well, I don't care
I should love to see my best girl
Cuddling up again we soon would be,
Whoa
Tidley-iddley-ighty,
hurry me home to Blighty
Blighty is the place for me.

When she'd finished, there was no applause, only a strange, eerie silence. 'This song is very popular,' she quietly informed the Lieutenant. 'Tommies who feel homesick do love it.'

Glancing across at his secretary, he said, 'Bring us a pot of tea, please, Mrs Marsden. Now do take a seat, Miss Hanson. You should be aware that there are rules for any concert party going abroad to entertain the troops, many required by the French as well as the British Government.'

Cecily felt a flurry of excitement that he hadn't thrown her out, and beamed at him with pleasure. 'That makes sense. I'd be interested to know what these are.'

Firmly clasping his hands, he proceeded with instructions. 'No artist who has a husband in France is allowed to take part in this project. Are you married or do you have a lover there?'

Cecily drew in a breath and gave her head a little shake. 'No, my fiancé has just been killed, drowned when his ship was attacked by a submarine.'

'Ah, I'm so sorry to hear that.' Flicking quickly through his sheets of paper, he regarded her with a stern expression. 'You need to appreciate that King George has disposed of all German names and titles in the Royal family, realising it could create issues for them. Do you, by any chance, have any German relations?'

'Not at all.'

'Or a German ancestor?'

'No.'

'If this answer proves to be false then you could find yourself suspected of being a German spy.'

'I assure you it is the absolute truth,' she firmly declared. 'We have a small family, not connected in any way with Germany or France.'

'Hmm, that's good to know. You should also be aware that if German officers spot you, they might also demand to be entertained. Could you deal with that?'

Cecily paused, struggling a little as she searched for a sensible answer, this being a possibility that had never occurred to her. 'I am aware there may be danger, but having lost my fiancé I'm prepared to support his efforts. I'm a strong, patriotic woman willing to do my bit for other brave men.'

'Excellent!' Sitting back in his chair, Lieutenant Trevain smiled at her. 'As you seem perfectly capable of presenting a good concert for our troops, I assure you the War Office regards that as of great importance for their morale. We're willing to deliver permits that would last for four to six weeks, or several months if you prefer.'

'Oh, thank you so much.' Cecily could hardly believe what she was hearing. 'A few months would suit us best, I think, making our work much more worthwhile. Where do you recommend we go, and how do we get there?'

'You'll be transported by the Navy across the sea to a particular place in north-east France. Thereafter, the Army will move you to different locations on land whenever they deem it to be appropriate. You will be fed and granted free accommodation in billets. Costs will be nil since you are volunteers with no wages paid. On occasion, you may receive a small payment to cover other expenses, should you feel the need for that.'

'That all sounds wonderful!' she agreed, giving him another beaming smile. 'And so very well organised.'

'It is indeed, thanks to Her Royal Highness, Princess Helena Victoria, our late Queen's granddaughter, who is in charge of various committees and organises much that is involved in these projects. She is a lady of great patience, good humour and generosity, and offers to help with any issues suffered by voluntary workers.'

'We'll do our best to cope with whatever difficulties we may have to face.'

'Let us hope you succeed. You need to be aware, Miss Hanson, that the conditions and accommodation in France will not be easy or comfortable. You could find yourself surrounded by injured men, as bases get struck with bombs on occasions. Are you still of the belief that you can cope?'

A small quiver of fear flickered in Cecily's heart. 'As I said, my sister and I are both eager to do our bit.'

His smile now was warm as he thrust out his hand to shake hers. 'Then I look forward to hearing how you get on.'

Cecily thanked him, then rushed home to give her sister the good news and tell how she'd done a small performance in an attempt to prove her worth.

Merryn hugged her with excitement, popping a kiss on each of her cheeks. 'How could that fellow resist making an offer when you're such an achiever, good at everything you do?'

'I'm not at all.'

'Oh yes you are, darling. I've worshipped you since the day I was born. I know Nan looked after us wonderfully, making sure we were properly dressed, bathed and well fed. She also taught us the three R's whenever we couldn't manage to get to a new school. But I preferred to think of you as the one in charge. You were so protective of me and made sure I was taught how to play the piano, write poetry, ride a bike, play games, jump and skip. With a mother I rarely saw, how would I have found any happiness without you to love and care for me?'

Cecily too gave her a warm hug. 'Why would I not adore my little sister? I loved looking after you and did manage to find people to teach you the things you wanted to learn. I also made an effort to personally teach you how to swim and drive, having been taught the latter by the tram company, but failed that completely. Is it worth my trying again?'

'Nope, I'm hopeless at such tasks,' Merryn said, and they both burst into a fit of giggles. 'I can cook and sew, which you can't.'

'There you are then. We're a perfect team.'

⁓

Later that afternoon, Merryn eagerly hurried over to the Palace Theatre just a short distance away. The young drummer was fully engaged in rehearsal, the bandleader constantly hammering his baton to stop the musicians playing while he issued more instructions to them. She knew she would have to wait a while before he was free, so taking a seat, she watched him. He was a cheerful young man with reddish hair, soft grey eyes that were constantly alight behind his spectacles, a slightly gap-toothed smile and a chiselled chin. Being a bit of a joker, Johnny Wilcox was great fun. When finally he was allowed a break, Merryn offered to buy him afternoon tea at a nearby café.

'There's something I'd like to discuss with you over a little tiffin,' she said with a smile.

'That sounds good,' he grinned, his expression filled with curiosity.

As they sat enjoying tea and biscuits, Merryn told him of her sister's plan to create a small concert party and entertain the troops in France.

He looked a little taken aback. 'Blimey, that'll be a challenge. I wouldn't want anything dreadful to happen to either of you two girls.'

'I don't think we'll be anywhere near the front line where the fighting is going on. We just plan to entertain the soldiers at their bases. I know you appreciated how Cecily discovered her talent for singing. Oh, and by the way, I can play the accordion.'

He gave another wide grin. 'What a brick you are, a real sport. As you know, I play drums and cymbals, so can I come too?'

Merryn blinked in surprise, amazed by this instant offer, having fully expected she'd need to persuade him. 'You most certainly can. I was about to ask if you'd be interested, as we'd welcome your support. I doubt there'll be any wages paid since we'll be volunteers fed and accommodated by the army.'

He creased his lips into a pout then gave a little smirk. 'I'll do my best to accept that fact. You're a girl with great talent, as is Cecily. I'd love to work with you both.'

The weather being sunny, he walked with her to the beach, talking about the music they loved to play and how long it had taken each of them to learn these skills. 'I've been playing drums all my life, ever since Dad bought me one for Christmas when I was ten. It kept me sane when I was suffering his loss.'

'Oh, how dreadful. How did that happen? I know very little about your past.'

'I was born in Barnsley in Yorkshire, part of a working-class family who became even poorer after Dad was tragically killed in a mining accident. Such bloody bad luck. Following his death, my mam worked as a cleaner, earning barely enough money to feed her six children, all of them younger than me. I eventually was able to help by getting myself a job playing my drum kit at a local pub. I was so thrilled with Dad's present that I was determined to improve and learn how to play well. Thankfully I succeeded.'

'Good for you, Johnny, I'm glad to hear that. My father sadly drowned in the Thames when we were quite young, although how that happened has never been explained to us and we have little memory of him. Queenie refuses to say anything on the subject, not even explain why her marriage went wrong.'

'My mam didn't talk much about her early life either. Far too distressing for her.'

Merryn decided that they had a great deal in common and could be well suited to working together, both being musicians. 'I'm delighted to hear that you wish to join our team.'

'Why would I not, when you're so attractive?'

Merryn rolled her eyes in amusement, having no belief in her own looks. She saw herself as quite plain, a little too round and simply practical, interested mainly in fashion, sewing, make-up and hairstyles. Cecily had always been the pretty one with talent and plenty of young men falling for her, whereas she'd never found a boy who really took a shine to her. Merryn adored her sister and felt quite proud of her famous mother too, readily willing to deal with Queenie's problems. His next words startled her out of those thoughts.

'Can I give you a little kiss of thanks?' Johnny murmured.

'I'm not sure that would be a good idea,' she stuttered. He was a most pleasant young man, if a little flirtatious.

'I must confess that I've always felt the need for more closeness between us.' Taking hold of her hand, he kissed it gently.

The golden sun slipped closer to the horizon, bathing the landscape and their entwined figures with a glorious glow, his warm breath igniting a stir of excitement within her. Aware of his gaze sliding over her, his eyebrows flickering in admiration as he studied her feminine curves, Merryn felt a trembling beset her. So badly did she want him that his nearness almost unnerved her. She stepped away from him. 'It must be time for you to prepare for tonight's performance.'

Glancing at his watch, he sighed. 'You're quite right, I should go. We could continue with this "discussion" some other time,' he said with a twinkle in his eyes.

Merryn felt herself blushing at such a prospect. Thanking him and promising to inform Cecily of his offer, she hastily rushed home.

SIX

CECILY AND Merryn were seated on the sofa in the parlour, happily discussing their plans when Queenie arrived home following her matinee performance, her eyes flooded in fury. They glanced at each other in dismay. 'Oh dear, what do you think her problem is now?' Cecily whispered.

Stifling a sigh, Merryn spoke with a grimace. 'Looks like she's come a cropper again.'

Watching her storm back and forth in the drawing room, Cecily's heart plummeted. 'Is there a problem, Mama?'

'Yes indeed. Thanks to the director, my career at the Palace Theatre is over. It seems that this time there will be no change of heart from him. That dreadful man has dismissed me.'

'Oh, no! I'm so sorry.' Catching the warning glance in her sister's eyes, Cecily carefully avoided asking why this had happened. It seemed fairly obvious, knowing her mother's issues and recognising her slurring tone of voice, so what was the point?

'I believe it was because neither of you were with me this afternoon. Why neglect me when you know how much I require your assistance?' she said, staggering a little as she paced back and forth.

'We cannot always be with you, Queenie, as we're both busy working,' Merryn quietly reminded her, making no mention of the fact that she'd had a day off.

'Should we try to persuade the director to change his mind?' Cecily asked, not sure it would work and feeling a degree of sympathy over that man's decision in view of her mother's inebriated state.

Flopping into a chair, her anger finally dissipated in a sorrowful cloud of tears, Queenie shook her head. 'That upper-class bully never listens to a word I say. I'd only enjoyed a couple of small glasses of fizz before the performance. What's the harm in that? He's very pop-wallah, never touches a drop of alcohol himself so shows no tolerance.'

Merryn and Cecily exchanged a weary glance, each finding it difficult to give the right response. Clearing her throat, Merryn calmly asked, 'So what do you plan to do now, Mama?'

Leaping again to her feet, Queenie went to ring the bell. 'I shall get Nan to help us all start packing. The only answer is to go back on tour.'

Merryn gasped. 'We can't do that. We both have jobs here.'

'We certainly couldn't accompany you.'

'Rubbish! Your main responsibility is to be dutiful daughters. I accept that the music hall is not as popular as it once was, particularly with this war on. There's little chance of my finding employment in London so you could send out letters or ring some theatres, Cecily, and acquire new offers for me elsewhere.'

Going to put her arm around her, Merryn led Queenie back to her chair. 'Don't bully my dear sister, she has enough to deal with. Besides, such a request would only work if you finally agreed to turn teetotal,' she calmly pointed out, which brought a flush of crimson to her mother's cheeks in addition to a tense scowl.

Cecily reached over to give her hand a gentle squeeze. 'You need to accept that too much drinking does you no good at all, Mama. I'll be happy to write to the many theatres you've appeared in across the country, so long as you do as Merryn suggests. However, as we explained, we won't be available to accompany you.'

'Why on earth not? You can give up those stupid jobs and work for me.'

'No, Mama, we cannot come because we have a tour to do of our own,' Cecily said, fully aware there was a far more important reason she should mention.

'What nonsense!'

Merryn grinned. 'Do tell her, Cecily, how you've managed to get the necessary permits for this special tour. How long will we be staying in France?'

'Oh, for some months.'

'France! What on earth are you talking about?' Queenie yelled.

Turning back to her mother, her face lit with excitement, Cecily briefly outlined their plan to entertain soldiers in the war with music concerts.

Queenie blinked in amazement. 'Good heavens, is this a joke? I thought I'd made it clear what you girls should do with your lives: be good wives and mothers, not engross yourselves in unsuitable jobs. Although I'd have my darling younger daughter stay with me forever.'

Cecily froze, feeling the usual stir of annoyance at her mother's dictatorial attitude. Hadn't she made it very clear that she had no desire to sacrifice herself to a Prince Charming, or a knight on a white charger? Nothing of the sort would ever happen. And hadn't she helped to campaign for votes for women as well as better rights for them? 'This is a decision I've made because of losing Ewan. I need a new purpose in life.'

'You certainly can't sing,' her mother scornfully remarked.

Cecily gave a weary sigh. 'You are fully aware, Mama, that is not strictly true. The Army Lieutenant was sufficiently impressed by the little performance I gave him at my interview and has happily provided the necessary permits and instructions. I think my talent must be developing quite well.' Then turning to her sister, she asked, 'Oh, did you speak to Johnny, our drummer friend?'

Flushing a little, Merryn nodded. 'I did, and he's very keen to join us. He feels he was rejected by the Army for no good reason and has readily agreed to do his duty for the soldiers.'

'That's good to know,' Cecily said with a grin. 'He seems to be a lively and helpful fellow.'

'Oh, he is, very much so,' Merryn said, not quite meeting her sister's enquiring gaze.

'I didn't realise you were friends with that working-class lad,' Queenie said.

Here we go again with her snobby disapproval, Cecily thought, but before she could defend her sister, Queenie's next words left her speechless.

'Well, if this Johnny boy has offered to go with you, dear Merryn, then I will too. You'll certainly be in need of parental protection with all those fit young men around. In addition, as your talent is limited, Cecily, having me as a star performer would make this project much more likely to be a success.'

Cecily blinked, appalled by the threat Queenie was making to stamp over her plans to build herself a new life. She'd paid little attention to her needs when she was young, being far too engrossed in her own destiny and success. Cecily remembered being constantly bullied by a girl at whatever school she'd been attending at the time. Her mother didn't listen to a word she'd said about that, dismissing her pleas as fussy. The bully would tug her hair, trip her up, pinch her shoes, and once tied her to a tree close by a river when the tide was coming in. Thankfully, Merryn had found and freed her. Thanks to her brave young sister, who punched the girl in question on her belly and kicked her bottom, the problem was resolved. She and Merryn had always been strong on protection of each other, with little support ever offered by their mother. So why on earth was Queenie declaring they needed her protection now? The more likely reason was that, in a fit of jealousy, she strongly disapproved of not taking the top role. Cecily felt a knot of fury grow within her. Such an attitude and proposition could destroy all hope of building a career for herself.

'I believe you're being too dismissive of me, Mama. You should appreciate this foreign tour will not provide the comforts you are accustomed to. Neither will it be entirely safe. There is a war on in France, remember.'

'I'm sure we will be perfectly safe and well, dear, otherwise no permission would have been granted,' Queenie firmly remarked. 'And if I can no longer work here, why would I not wish to join you and perform for the troops? Otherwise, what else can I possibly do with my life? And how would I cope if I were left all alone?'

Cecily caught a glimpse of warning in Merryn's hazel eyes, recognising a message that she should take into account the fact that if left in such a situation, Queenie would become more inebriated on gin.

Slamming down her despair, Cecily gave a little nod of agreement. 'Very well, Mama, you could come for the first few weeks, if you wish. However, I cannot allow you to sing. You don't perform as well as you used to because of this foolish indulgence of yours. Your obsession with drinking must stop, then I'll give you due consideration. We are required to give the best possible performance, so you could instead help to train us. If you'd be willing to do that, then you may join us.'

Silence fell as Queenie gave no reply to this demand.

Merryn gave her a kind smile. 'Do listen to Cecily, as that would be an excellent idea. And bear in mind that there'll be no gin or alcohol available, so you'll thankfully escape this problem. One of the soldiers in the audience told me that the most popular teetotal drink for Tommies is a sweet fruity citron and tart grenadine. That's the best you'll get.'

Queenie took out a hanky to wipe the tears from her eyes, a flush of embarrassment still evident on her lovely face. 'Very well, for the sake of my health and to restore my voice, I will accept what you suggest.

And yes, I can offer you training and tips on how to sing well. I doubt you have the first idea what needs to be done.'

'Thank you,' Cecily coolly remarked. 'It would be good to have you help us with the start of this project. Once you are well, I'm sure you'll have new offers coming in and can then return to your own career.'

'I'm not convinced that will ever happen,' she mournfully remarked. 'I agree there are moments when I fail to sing as well as I used to, probably due to pressure. I can act though, so we could look into the possibility of putting on small plays too if you wish.'

'An excellent idea,' Cecily said, and within seconds the three of them were discussing possible one-act plays to perform, which helped to lift her hopes. 'We'll also need to buy some equipment including lamps, candles, suitable costumes, sheet music and I'm not sure what else. We need to think this through, then start packing.'

'I'll ring Johnny and invite him to join us tomorrow,' Queenie remarked. 'Then he can help us arrange such details.'

'Don't worry, I'll do that,' Merryn said. 'Right now, I'll put the kettle on and find some paper to start making a list.'

∽

'You need to have a strong voice, which I'm not convinced you have,' Queenie said when Cecily's training began. 'Stand before me and sing. I need to check that you present yourself properly balanced.'

Straightening her back, Cecily did as she was told and sang 'It's a Long Way to Tipperary', the one she'd performed for the soldiers.

Clapping her hands, Queenie merely snorted with disdain and ordered her to stop. 'Do not allow your jaw to close or narrow; pull it down to hold it in place while you learn to sing correctly. And keep the angle of your head held in the right position.'

As she continued working hard under her mother's coaching, Cecily would often shake with apprehension and exhaustion, not finding it at all easy. Nevertheless, she was learning a great deal. Whenever she went wrong, she listened carefully to obey every instruction Queenie made, and could but hope that with plenty of practice she might improve her voice.

'First take in a long breath, then exhale. It's important to keep the right balance in your breathing. Breathe in and out. Breathe again. Now sing the scale, *Do, Re, Mi, Fa, So, La, Ti, Do*. Hold on to each note for as long as possible with your chest raised to acquire the necessary power and muscle strength. Do not lift your chin too high. It's also vital to make sure your jaw opens to the right position on your vowels or you'll lose the control to sing well.'

As she slowly improved, Cecily became increasingly appreciative of Queenie's support, even though Merryn was the one who received a kiss on her cheek from her mother when she played well, while Cecily would receive no more than a grim nod of approval.

'Press on your chest to maintain control and ease the pressure. Don't let your head bob up. Now relax, keep your jaw open and sing again. As you reach the end of a phrase, give it a little tremor, changing the pitch with some vibrato.'

Johnny had come to join them and, as instructed by Queenie, was required to help by ordering equipment as well as playing his drums. 'It's bloomin' hard work. Came as something of a surprise to find that in addition to the performances in which I'm involved every evening, plus twice weekly matinees, I'm also engaged in countless rehearsals each and every day.'

'Do say if we're overworking you,' Cecily said, noting a sign of alarm and exhaustion etched in his pale face. 'If this is too much for you, then you're free to leave and not come with us to France.'

'I do have to keep a careful watch over my state of health, so I shouldn't do too much work.'

'You do look rather tired. Maybe you could find other musicians or actors to join our team? I've so far failed to find any. Most young male artists and actors joined up in the war, apart from the odd one too old to fight. Do you know of any?'

He frowned as if he resented her making more demands upon him. 'I'll ask around, just in case. I'm delighted to be a part of your team. I'd move heaven and earth for you lovely ladies. Anything that is within my grasp I'll happily do for you,' he remarked softly, his gaze holding hers for a long moment.

'He's not greatly helpful in spite of the compliments he offers us,' Cecily later told her sister.

'He's doing fine,' Merryn hastily assured her.

Cecily curbed herself into silence, not wishing to upset her sister who appeared to be highly captivated by this young man. Later, whenever she asked him what progress he was making, he'd simply blink and say he was still searching. He didn't seem to be an easy person.

The day before they left for France, after Cecily had sung 'Roses of Picardy', Queenie this time clapped her hands in cheerful applause, giving a nod of approval and a loving smile. 'Congratulations. You are singing so much better, dear girl.'

'Oh, thank you, Mama. I greatly appreciate your help.'

Then to her astonishment, her mother put her arms around her in a warm hug. 'You could well become a star too, given time and more practice.' Her blue eyes were clouded with a flush of tears and Cecily felt filled with gratitude, a surge of emotion eminent within her over this sudden show of closeness.

SEVEN

EMBARKING IN the early morning upon a naval vessel, it took nearly twenty hours to cross the channel to France from Southampton. Nan had remained in Plymouth to care for their house. She also agreed to protect Queenie's diamond ring from the danger of war by locking it in the family safe. The sea clogged with submarines greatly troubled Cecily as it reminded her of how she'd lost Ewan, the love of her life. She battled valiantly against the grief that had once again thrown her into a dark pit, striving to move on. At least this decision to sing to the troops would honour his memory. When first she'd declared her intention to go to France and do her bit for the war effort, not for a moment had she imagined that her mother would wish to accompany them. It was most certainly the last thing she'd wanted and a part of her shivered with despair at this prospect, mixed with a sense of shame. Queenie had been most sympathetic over her loss, a fact Cecily felt she should appreciate.

These thoughts were interrupted by Johnny coming over to join her on deck. He drew a cigarette from a silver case and lit it. 'It's a pity I wasn't allowed to bring my precious Ford car. That would have made it a much quicker and easier journey with me in charge,' he said.

'Except that as we don't know the way, we might have got lost,' Cecily drily pointed out.

'That would be a typically female problem. Being a man and an excellent driver, you could have trusted in my ability, as I can easily follow a map.'

'Oh, for goodness sake, Johnny, many women can drive and follow maps. I certainly can, having been involved with tram transport, both driving and conducting. A foreign land is not easy for either men or women. In any case, I think your motor car would have had problems crossing the Channel. I'm enjoying this sailing and quite happy with the transport arranged for us,' Cecily brightly explained.

'Absolutely, and happy to chat with you,' he hastily remarked. 'By the way, I did ask around to find other men to join the troupe we've created but it proved impossible. I asked one chap who'd been invalided out of the Army, but he made it clear that he had no wish to return to France or risk losing his current job in Blighty. So I'm afraid I got nowhere.'

She sighed, not entirely convinced that he'd made a good effort, but then she'd failed to find any either, so could hardly object. 'Not to worry, we're a small, smart troupe, as you implied.'

'We are indeed. You are a most talented and attractive young woman. I'm an equally gifted chap and greatly appreciate that you approve of my drumming and allowed me to join you.'

'We're grateful to have you with us,' Cecily blithely commented.

'I must admit I do hope you'll be the one in charge. Not Queenie, who seems to be growing more irascible and neurotic, perhaps for some health reason.'

Cecily turned away, keeping her gaze fixed upon the sea, not wishing to reveal her sense of irritation by the fact her mother was attempting to turn herself into the director. She was still a woman of talent and surprisingly willing to train them. But if she attempted to take over this project entirely, Cecily would again be in battle with her, having no wish for Queenie to control her. Coping with her obsessions was not going to be easy either.

'I admit Mama is not easy to deal with because of her addiction, but my sister and I are working on resolving that. You may have noticed how we never allow her to sneak off in search of gin, and constantly check her cabin here on the ship to make sure she hasn't hidden a bottle there.'

Johnny grinned. 'Blimey, you girls are both so clever and intriguing. Do be aware that I greatly appreciate that and would happily offer to support and protect you.'

'I assure you we are not in need of your protection, thanks all the same.'

'Really? I think you will be, considering there's a war on. Women cannot look after themselves. They obviously require a man's advice and support.'

This comment, as well as his tone of voice, seemed to indicate that he was an arrogant male who believed women should do as men instructed, not an attitude she was ever willing to accept. Cecily smiled. 'I'm sure we'll all be looked after by the Army and will enjoy putting on our concerts. It could prove to be jolly hard work and maybe quite dangerous, so yes, we will have to be strong and brave, but can manage that perfectly well for ourselves.'

'I do reckon we'll have great fun together, although your sense of independence is a puzzle to me.'

Cecily gave a little chuckle. 'Ah, we can't have you understanding us women too well. That would never do.'

He then fell into a fit of coughing. 'Sorry, I don't often smoke but it does help to drive the tension out of me.'

Removing the cigarette from his hand, she tossed it into the sea. 'You really shouldn't smoke at all till that cough is better. And as I say, listen to my advice and take a rest before our main work begins. I certainly feel in need of one myself while it's still possible,' Cecily tact-fully pointed out.

'A chap is allowed to have a little comfort, a sensation we could share,' he said, and with a grin slipped his hand around her waist to pull her close.

She was about to slap his hand away, turn on her heel and briskly return to her cabin when her mother appeared.

'May I have a word with you, dear?' Queenie sharply remarked, her expression irate.

'Of course, Mama.' To her relief, Johnny quickly departed. What an odd man he was. Hadn't her mother told her about the dismissive attitude of men towards actresses, dancers and singers? Was he like that too?

'What on earth possessed you to flirt with that young man? You should behave with more propriety,' Queenie said.

Cecily's mouth dropped open in surprise. 'What are you implying? He was the one engaging himself in flirtation, not *me*! I was about to escape when you appeared, Mama, since I view him as something of a philanderer. Aren't all men like that?'

Queenie frowned. 'Nonsense! You were clearly encouraging him to take a fancy to you.'

'I certainly was not! Please do not accuse me of such a thing. I have no wish to seek new love right now, if ever. I was simply disagreeing with his poor opinion of women. I also find his flamboyant and atten-tion-seeking attitude most irritating, constantly attempting to prove how useful and gifted he is.'

'Johnny is a resilient man, quite respectable and caring. He means no harm, merely feeling the need to improve his status, coming from a poor family. Do not assume that you are more talented and clever than him, or me either, girl.'

There was something about what Queenie was saying that made Cecily wonder if she could be making a valid point. Her dispute with

Johnny had possibly been a little shameful. Caring about one's class and abilities was surely the right of everyone? He could simply have been trying to be friendly and his flirtation just a joke. Maybe she'd viewed him wrongly because of her loss. If that was the case, she'd done herself no favours by treating him with such contempt. 'You're possibly right, Mama. I'm not a patient soul who tolerates people as well as I used to. I'm afraid I have little trust in anyone because of my grief.'

A mixture of sympathy and disapproval flickered in her mother's face. 'If only you'd made an effort to find yourself a good husband, we would not be here putting ourselves in danger.' And turning on her heel, she marched away.

Cecily felt herself sink into that familiar dark pit of despair. Why would her mother blame her for everything and never believe a word she said, or agree with what she wanted out of life?

However rare it might be to find an attractive and respectable young man in this dreadful world, let alone one who showed a genuine interest in her, a relationship was not what she longed for any more. And she must keep a careful watch on this Johnny Wilcox. There was something about his attitude that she didn't at all approve of or comprehend. He did seem to be a self-opinionated idiot. Admittedly he was a talented drummer and Merryn was quite fond of him. Not a fact she should share with their mother as Queenie would be sure to disapprove of a possible relationship between them since he was not at all rich. Firmly setting this issue to one side with a sigh, Cecily returned to her cabin, pulled out her song sheets and began learning the words of the next one.

❧

When they finally reached Le Havre, Cecily looked excitedly out over the flat wide estuary, seeing how it stretched for miles. It was engulfed in mists, the wind whipping the waves, with pools of seawater filling hollows in the sand. There was a great beauty to it, and it appeared so peaceful. If only that were true of the rest of France.

On arrival, they were checked for passports and *cartes de séjour*, obliged to go through an endless interrogation by French sentries. They were required to answer a number of questions about themselves, their journey, and the reason they'd come to France. It took some time before they were finally allowed in, then taken by boat along the River Seine to Rouen. It was not an easy journey, as the craft was constantly tossed about by the strong tide and currents. It took even more hours, gradually becoming calmer as they sailed further inland. Cecily enjoyed viewing the green woodland that surrounded the river, pretty villages tucked amongst them here and there, and felt most relaxed.

In Rouen they were transported in a scrubby old wagon through the town, passing rows of beautiful black and white houses. To their surprise, they spotted a theatre that looked very like the Theatre Royal near Covent Garden, generally known as Drury Lane, where their mother had performed in the past. 'We could ask to perform there,' Merryn said with a grin.

'The soldiers prefer to visit *Folies Bergères*,' the driver told them.

'To watch the women dance?'

'Indeed,' he smirked. 'And there's the memorial of Joan of Arc behind those iron railings.'

'So that's where she was held?' Cecily asked.

'Aye, and faced trial and execution here in 1431.'

She shivered, hoping and praying nothing of the sort would happen to them, and their singing would appeal to these soldiers. Possible danger and their ability to perform were both of concern to her.

Once they reached the camp on top of a hill, they saw a wonderful view of the town below, more hills in the distance and forests all around. The camp itself was a mess of mud with only a few duckboards to walk on, hundreds of bell tents all around and a few Nissen huts. The stench was appalling, mainly of smoke and injured men with putrid limbs, and other smells she preferred not to contemplate.

Stars were lighting the dusky skies as the ladies were shown into their tent. It was not particularly clean and they saw a number of beetles scuttling across the ground. Merryn screamed then started to stamp on them. Cecily did too. Having largely swept them all away, at least for now, they settled in their beds. She closed her ears, not wishing to hear her mother ranting on about the dreadful state of their accommodation, too exhausted after this long journey to deal with Queenie's moans and groans or to start unpacking and tidying. 'We'll give this tent a good clean up when we unpack tomorrow,' she said with a weary yawn.

Merryn agreed, and making up her own bed quickly lay down, anxious too for a proper rest. It was then that the bugler sounded 'Lights Out'.

'Goodness, I'm not ready for bed,' Queenie declared, peering in her small mirror by candlelight as she smoothed cream upon her face.

There came a pounding on the sides of the tent. 'Put that light out!'

'I reckon that's the sergeant checking we're doing as we're told, Mama,' Cecily whispered as she quickly blew the candle out.

Merryn and Cecily stifled their giggles beneath the brown blankets in their cold uncomfortable camp beds, listening to the sergeant stamping around outside, banging his cane on other tents while Queenie continued with her grumbles.

'Well, really . . . What a fusspot that fellow is. We haven't even had dinner.'

'We arrived too late for that. Tomorrow morning we'll be supplied with a decent breakfast.'

It was then that they heard a terrifying barrage erupt, the roar and shriek of shells and guns firing, sounding very like a thunderstorm. The reality of war pummelled into Cecily's head. Would they indeed be given the necessary protection?

EIGHT

GIVEN ASSURANCE that this battle was taking place close to enemy lines, not in the camp, they spent the night tucked in their beds, barely sleeping until the sound faded. They were so thankful when dawn and silence came at last. It was then that Merryn went in search of breakfast for Queenie, since she always liked to have it in bed. She discovered there were field kitchens and a bakery at the camp. 'The bread is packed deep in a tunnel glowing with heat, and left to cook overnight,' the chef told her, handing over a tray of bread and jam. 'The Tommies' diet is a bit boring but must be substantial enough to keep them fighting.'

Merryn smiled. 'I'm told soldiers declare that an army marches on its stomach?'

He laughed. 'Aye, while wags on the front line claim the appalling rations they are given can create more dangers to their health than German bullets.'

Feeling peckish and not wishing to complain about the dark, solid-looking bread, she quickly returned to their tent with the tray and mugs of tea, learning later that the chaps in his tent had provided Johnny with a bacon sandwich.

Merryn and Cecily spent the next hour or two cleaning and tidying the tent and camp beds, finding some duckboards to walk on in order to avoid the mud and stacked all essential equipment in a corner. They chose to leave all costumes and other stage equipment carefully packed away. After that, they set about washing a few grubby clothes and mending stockings.

Queenie merely reclined upon her camp bed, taking what she declared to be a much-needed rest. 'It was so dreadful, I barely slept a wink last night. We should not be here.'

Neither of her daughters made any comment upon this, merely exchanging a roll of their eyes, each irritated that she'd chosen to join them. 'Let's leave her in peace while we go and find out where we'll be able to present our concert this evening,' Cecily murmured.

'Good idea,' Merryn agreed, and they scurried off, paying no further attention to Queenie's moans and groans.

The camp looked even more smoky and dusty than they'd noticed when they first arrived, the lines of sandbags all around. Thankfully, they found a young man waiting for them. He gave them a beaming welcome and shook their hands. 'I'm Corporal Lewis. Good to meet you and glad to help.'

He was most friendly, small with a bone-thin body, looking as if he hadn't enjoyed a decent meal in a long while, his face pale with dingy-looking skin. Nor had he much hair visible on his virtually bald head, clearly having shaved it all off in an effort to protect himself from nits and lice. Cecily introduced herself, then asked where they would be allowed to perform. He showed them a range of boxes that had been set up to form a small stage. 'Not perfect, just the best we can do,' he said, giving an apologetic smile.

'This will be fine,' Cecily assured him as she stepped carefully over it. The boxes rocked slightly, but as they wouldn't be doing any dancing, she decided it should work well enough. Already she could see groups of men hovering around in eager anticipation of the event. Stretched along the pathway by a hut was a row of camp beds upon which injured soldiers lay wrapped in blankets, many of them swathed in stinking wads of blood-stained bandages. Gazing upon them, Merryn's heart pumped with sympathy. Those poor men were clearly suffering from physical or mental problems, having endured desperate dangers. They looked in deep distress, some with empty blank eyes as if these pains had blocked out their minds.

Recognising the compassion in her expression, the corporal said, 'These lads are badly in need of a bit of fun and are filled with excitement at the prospect of this concert you're going to give them. They've insisted on having their beds brought out so they can watch.'

Cecily felt emotion block her throat. 'We'll do our best to brighten their lives and cheer them up,' she promised.

∽

There was no proper stage, no curtains, dressing rooms or footlights, but they did have acetylene gas lamps glimmering brightly around the boxes. They worked for hours rehearsing, and enduring more instructions from Queenie on what and how they should perform. Cecily suffered a flutter of panic as she became aware of hundreds more men gathering in the audience. A few were seated on boxes or benches, the rest of the area packed with a solid mass standing shoulder to shoulder. Many had been patiently waiting hours for the concert to start. Looking at the state of them, it was evident that many had come direct from the trenches, where they'd probably been trapped in horrific conditions for months. Those unable to move from their tent pulled the flaps open so that they too could hear the concert.

Heart pounding and nerves jangling, Cecily felt the urge to turn and run as the moment for the concert to start came closer. Was her mother right and she couldn't sing well after all? Would they roar and boo at her as they had that time at Queenie?

She steadied her breathing, smoothed down her skirt with sweaty fingers and when she walked on stage, the men gave a loud cheer of welcome. The excitement in their faces filled her with hope and as she stepped forward to the front of the boxed stage, the audience instantly fell silent, looking enthralled and spellbound. She exchanged a swift glance with Merryn, counted one, two, three, four . . . and her sister and Johnny both began to play, sounding most professional. Cecily started to sing:

> There's a Long, Long Trail A-winding.
> Into the land of my dreams,
> Where the nightingales are singing
> And a white moon beams.

As she sang, her fears, depression and worries vanished in a surge of elation, soaring into a new life, and bringing these soldiers pleasure and relief from the war. When the song was over, she received a tumultuous applause, cheers, whistles and roars of appreciation from them. Smiling broadly, she went on to sing 'Roses of Picardy', followed by 'Pack Up Your Troubles in Your Old Kit Bag' and many other popular favourites. Most of the Tommies would readily join in with singing the chorus whenever Cecily invited them to do so. Others would weep, as if fraught with emotion because they were homesick and felt greatly moved by this reminder of England. Then they would again cheer and roar with happiness at the end, urging her to sing an encore.

'You're doing quite well,' her mother casually remarked during the short interval, a comment Cecily greatly appreciated. 'Now sing some of those jolly music hall songs that I recommended.'

'Right you are.'

Cecily went on to sing 'Burlington Bertie From Bow' and 'Fall In And Follow Me'. These brought bright smiles and laughter to all the Tommies' faces. She finished with 'Your King and Country Want You', bringing forth loud cheers of agreement. How she loved singing to these soldiers. If she hadn't been a star before, she certainly felt like one now.

∽

Over the coming weeks, they finally settled in, again often hearing the sound of shellfire in the distance, but fully concentrating upon rehearsals and entertaining these troops. They went on to perform at many other bases, driven there by Corporal Lewis in the scrubby wagon. And whenever she passed by soldiers in a camp, they would click their heels and salute, treating Cecily with great respect. She found it most rewarding to perform for these brave young men, notwithstanding the exhaustion of putting on two or three concerts a day. They would often feel badly in need of a break having done so many performances and naturally made sure that Queenie did not spend her time drinking, which did affect her temper.

Today, rain was heavily pounding on the roof of the large tent where they were about to give their latest performance, again packed with men eagerly waiting with considerable excitement. A tarpaulin had been hooked up around it to protect some of the audience, plenty standing around outside to listen with the rain sheeting down upon them.

Johnny looked at Cecily with concern. 'You've no coat on. We can't have you getting cold and wet.'

'Unlike those poor Tommies I'm safely inside the tent, not stuck out in this dreadful rain. I'm warmly dressed in a sort of uniform: a decent long skirt, jacket, shirt and tie and most suitably attired,' she said with a smile, carefully placing a broad-brimmed hat upon her head.

He flickered his gaze over her with a slightly quizzical expression in his grey eyes. 'True, except you look a bit – how should I put it – plain. That outfit is neither appropriate nor sweet. I think it's time the Tommies saw you dressed in something far more glamorous.'

Cecily laughed out loud. Johnny frequently came over to suggest what she should sing before the start of the concert. She was carefully acquiring the ability to tolerate his eccentricities and odd sense of humour, his recent fondness for smoking and growing accustomed to his foolish flirting. She'd willingly listen to his suggestions, as he was a good musician. This comment about how she looked highly amused her. On the subject of costume, they were completely at odds. 'Are you suggesting that I should wear an evening gown? Sorry, I wasn't expecting to go dancing so didn't bring one with me. I think wearing a version of uniform is entirely the right thing to do. It makes me look like I'm part of their squad.'

He gave a firm shake of his head. 'You're a woman, so would never look like a Tommy Atkins, not in a million years. I confess that prettily dressed females do make me hot around the collar, but it's *art, dahling*,' he teased.

'Nonsense!'

'I could make you one,' Merryn offered casually, interrupting their disagreement. 'We brought some net curtains with us, so I could use some of those to make you a more attractive gown.'

'Really? Well, if you're sure you wouldn't mind doing that, Merryn, that'd be wonderful.'

'You know I love sewing as much as music. I'll look into it.'

Queenie came strolling over to join them, having been chatting with the young men, as she so loved to do. 'It's good being here to do our bit for the Tommies, and so exciting. You must sing a little louder, Cecily, as there's no way to extinguish the sound of this hammering rain.'

Fortunately, the performance went well, and the rain did ease off a little during the course of the day. Merryn gave a short solo performance playing some French tangos and 'Mademoiselle from Armentières' on her piano accordion – catchy tunes that brought a good response from the audience. Johnny did a solo performance on his drum that brought forth more cheers and the hammering of hands. Then Cecily recited three poems, *Break of Day in the Trenches* by Isaac Rosenberg, *My Boy Jack* by Rudyard Kipling, finishing with her favourite, *The Soldier* by Rupert Brooke, which the soldiers loved.

It had felt most disturbing to see these men in their scruffy clothes, knee-high socks and thick muddy boots, many with arms wrapped in slings, bandages around their heads, or blank expressions of shell shock on their ashen faces. Some were unshaven, while others had shaved their heads to avoid nits, lice and other scourges. But they roared, laughed, cheered and happily joined in the singing, clearly loving every moment of the show.

∾

At the end of the concert, Cecily could still hear the men singing in parts of the camp. The wind was gusting all around as she struggled to walk almost ankle-deep in the mud. She was barely halfway across the field when Johnny caught up with her. 'I hope you didn't object to those comments I made about your uniform. You are a real beauty and I just want you to display it more diligently.'

Cecily gave a cynical little smile, feeling no urge to agree with him on this or discuss the matter further. She simply felt the need to escape the rain that was soaking through her. 'I do appreciate the advice you offer, Johnny, so we'll see if this idea works.'

'I'm sure it will.' Putting up his hand he gave her cheek a gentle rub. 'You look tired and feel quite cold. What a nincompoop you are to be out walking with no coat or scarf and this wind bringing more rain.' Taking off his own coat, he wrapped it around her.

'Don't nag me, and I don't need this coat as I've nearly reached my tent,' she said, attempting to hand it back.

'Yes, you do, and I'll give you a warm hug.' Wrapping his arm around her, he pulled her close, gazing at her with interest. 'You're smart and clever, Cecily. I recognise that in you, being pretty smart and clever myself.'

Pulling herself free from his hold, she gave him a scathing look. 'If that is the case, why were you rejected by the Army? I often see you coping without those spectacles. Why is that?'

He laughed at this as if making a joke. 'I forget to put my specs on sometimes. It was not just my eyesight that was the problem, they thought me too small and unfit.'

'Nor do you limp much any more. And why do you behave like a licentious fool?'

'I beg your pardon if that's the case. You should be aware, I might blunder a bit because of how much I care for you.'

Cecily's feet slipped in the mud as she hastily tried to escape, and when she almost fell, he grabbed her again. Flicking his head sideways, he grinned, making no move to release her for some long seconds. His expression was now so filled with desire that a sense of disquiet stirred within her. Then, as he lowered his pouting mouth to mere inches close to hers, it disturbingly occurred to her that he was about to give her a kiss and she shoved him firmly away. 'Don't you dare do that. Let go of me this instant!'

With languid courtesy, he slowly bowed his head. 'My apologies. It's just that I find you absolutely irresistible, so why wouldn't I offer you more attention and a little fun?'

'I don't need your attention. Nor do I view your flirtatious attitude as "fun". Refusing to treat me with proper respect when you are perfectly aware of the grief I am suffering, puts you perilously close to being rejected and sent back to Blighty,' she sternly informed him. 'If you wish us to remain friends and continue to work together, do not touch me ever again, Johnny Wilcox.'

'Not unless you want me to,' he said with a grin, as she marched away.

❧

Within twenty-four hours, Merryn had successfully created a most beautiful cream lacy gown with a long, frilled skirt and a daringly low neckline. Cecily felt utterly thrilled when she tried it on and her sister beamed at her, saying she looked wonderful.

'Blimey, ain't she cute?' Johnny said, giving a whistle.

Queenie too appeared stunned, a touch of jealousy evident in her piercing gaze. 'Not at all the small, plain girl you usually are. So where is *my* gown?' she demanded of Merryn.

'Why would you want one? You brought a whole trunk of clothes with you, far more than we did,' Merryn reminded her.

'Nothing as beautiful as this one. I too will soon be performing, so why would I not have the right to look equally lovely? Eventually, my fussy daughter here will allow me to sing, which is what I'm best at. I'm certainly more of a star than she'll ever be.'

Silence followed this remark, Cecily's sense of humour dissolving in frustration. They'd strenuously attempted to keep Queenie well away from alcohol. Her voice not at all improving, it was hard to be assured they were succeeding. 'You'll be welcome to perform, Mama, once you are getting better,' Cecily tactfully informed her. 'And I'm sure Merryn will do what she can for you, won't you, lovey?'

Merryn sighed. 'If I can find any more material, I'll give it a go.'

'You will happily oblige me since you're my darling daughter. If you don't have what we require, then go shopping in the town,' Queenie sweetly instructed her, giving her a warm hug.

This time when Cecily walked on in her beautiful new gown, silence fell, the men's jaws fell open, their faces rapt with such wonder and emotion it brought tears of delight into her eyes. Their reaction was completely overwhelming. Perhaps Johnny did have some good ideas after all, even if he was an irritating playboy. She would wear the uniform on occasions, but it felt good to cheer these men up by looking more glamorous.

~

'What a clever girl you are,' Johnny told Merryn as he walked her back to her tent. 'You look gorgeous too, sweetie. Can I give you a kiss by way of thanks?'

'Goodness, no.'

'It's all right. I'll do nothing too naughty,' he said, and kissed her with such passion that Merryn gasped, her limbs feeling like liquid fire.

'Johnny, you must behave with absolute propriety.' She tried to speak with suitable hauteur but couldn't quite find the strength to give proper emphasis to her words. She was struggling to breathe as his tongue circled the hollow beneath her ear and a pain started up somewhere it shouldn't.

'I will in a moment, I promise. It's just that you're such a lovely girl, I'm becoming utterly enchanted by you. Can I just unfasten this pearl button on your blouse and caress you?'

'No! You shouldn't be doing this. Please stop!' Desperately striving to recover her composure, Merryn firmly refastened the neck of her blouse. 'I'm becoming quite fond of you too, but please be aware that you must behave.'

Drawing her close in his arms, he nodded as he kissed each of her flushed cheeks. 'What a treasure you are.'

'Oh, so are you,' she said, feeling a stir of excitement. 'Don't ever mention our growing friendship to Queenie. She is most dictatorial about who I spend time with.'

'Rightio, I promise I won't say a word and look forward to us growing ever closer.' As he began to kiss and caress her even more, her breathing quickened, leaving her unable to resist. Merryn found herself astonished and thrilled by the attention he was paying her. This time she made no protest as he unfastened the top button of her blouse to kiss her neck and gently stroke her breast, making her gasp as desire escalated through her. Was Johnny falling in love with her? That would be wonderful, but she should take great care to protect herself. Waving, she quickly fled to her tent.

It took her a long time to fall asleep, her entire body buffeted with emotion. As she tossed and turned, she felt a whirl of happiness in her heart. Oh, and she did need to confide in Cecily about how she was emotionally captivated by Johnny, let alone deeply moved by his kisses. She decided to reveal this secret to her sister some time when they were alone, making sure their mother was nowhere around. All too aware that her gaze would instinctively follow his every move, Merryn resolved never to allow her eyes to meet his whenever they were working together, fearful of Queenie noticing how a relationship was developing between them. The last thing she needed was to have her mother dictating whom she could love or marry. And men were so hard to find.

NINE
AUTUMN 1917

T HEY MOVED on with the battalion, transported in the old wagon or else in an armoured vehicle driven by Corporal Lewis. Today they were travelling in an old London bus, painted grey, heading to a camp close to Saint-Omer. It was a large town situated less than fifty kilometres southeast of Calais and a hospital centre. It had suffered many battles, the enemy anxious to reach Ostend or Calais and then move on to attack Britain. The camp was situated at the edge of town in a large field, holding dozens of lines of tents and a few Nissen huts, many of them used as wards for patients, a small rough platform set up at one end for the concerts. Surrounded by beautiful meadows and woodlands here at Longuenesse, Cecily ached to walk out and explore them. They were not allowed to do that because of the dangers involved. At times she could hear the sound of birds instead of guns firing, which helped to take her mind off the horror of war. Shrapnel shells would frequently burst from the sky, bringing black smoke everywhere, or the sound of heavy fire would zip around, the entire area constantly under attack. Very scary.

This morning, as she sat scribbling on a script, she heard the rumbling sound of a plane overhead. Glancing up, she watched in awe as it flew closer. The speed of its approach indicating it was an enemy plane caused her to leap to her feet, realising she should run for cover in case it fired at them. Fear began to pound in her as she turned to go, making her entire body shake at such a prospect. It was then that she found herself grabbed and flung upon the ground a few yards away, hearing the plane roar back up into the sky and disappear. Gasping for breath, she glared up into Johnny's grey eyes.

'Thank God you're safe,' he said, smoothing his hand over her face.

'What the hell did you do that for?' she cried, slapping it away. She felt a quiver of panic within her as she strove to recover.

'That plane was only fifty yards or so above us, no doubt about to take photographs not just of you, beautiful though you are, but also the entire camp, guns, rifles plus other equipment and details. Not even the soldiers fired at it, probably equally shaken and overwhelmed by such an audacious pilot.'

'I was alarmed by its closeness, although about to run for cover in case he fired at us. I was perfectly capable of doing that so not in need of your assistance,' she smartly responded, brushing the mud from her arms and legs.

Heaving a sigh, he said, 'How is a poor confused male able to decode such signals of independence in a classy lady?'

'You should appreciate that women can look after themselves. I know that for a fact, being involved with the suffragists. Although I suppose I should thank you for attempting to save me, Johnny. Quite brave of you to take that risk,' she grudgingly admitted, not at all appreciating what he'd done but wishing to sound polite.

'My pleasure,' he remarked softly, his gaze sliding over her. 'I believe there could be something special growing between us. Surely I'm not wrong about that?'

Cecily almost stopped breathing. Was he attempting to awaken a desire in her, as he clearly had with Merryn? She almost gave a mad little laugh at such a prospect. He was a most pretentious young man, and wolfish. Still feeling his arms holding her tightly around the waist she pushed him away and stood up, releasing herself from his grip. 'You're talking absolute tosh, Johnny, sounding far too coquettish.'

A sparkle lit his eyes as he blinked provocatively. 'I do relish the opportunity to have fun in my life, some of that with a lovely woman. You look so glorious I find you utterly dazzling. Let me know if you ever feel the same.'

Cecily met the teasing flicker of his gaze with a glimmer of dismay in her own violet-blue eyes. He surely wasn't declaring love for her, merely giving her a snippet of his aspiration for pleasure. Foolish man. 'I assure you that however much I might still ache for Ewan and the loss of love in my life, nothing of the sort will ever happen again, certainly not between you and me.'

After a lingering moment of silence, he jumped to his feet, a frown once again marking his face. 'My sympathies for your loss, although I'm sure you'll change your attitude towards me, given time. I did make a valid point that all women are in need of protection from a man.'

The urge to argue over this comment faded in her, feeling the necessity to remain polite in consequence of this terrifying incident. 'Possibly there are occasions when that may be appropriate. So long as you learn to calm your emotions and stop trying to flirt or control me. Keep your hair on, as the Tommies would say.' Walking away, Cecily vowed that in spite of his eagerness to protect and flirt with her, he would never win her round. It was her sister who cared for him, not her. But was Merryn right to trust him?

❧

The next day, they attended a local hospital packed with more pain-wracked boys. Seeing them was quite traumatic. How they must have suffered from the torment of fighting, leaving them badly injured and in such need of care and comfort. Often stuck in the trenches, death seemed imminent whenever a raid or attack was launched. The nursing staff welcomed Cecily's offer of entertainment with equal delight to the Tommies, many feeling lonely in this remote part of town, clearly drained of energy and they too constantly having to dodge shells. The misery, distress and torment the patients were subjected to were instantly relieved by smiles and laughter. As well as lively songs, Cecily sang 'Take Me Back to Dear Old Blighty'. Their response was a moment of silence, ripe with emotion, followed by a whoop of applause.

Her heart went out to these Tommies, who were finding this performance a good way to shut out the awfulness of war from their troubled minds. As the concert proceeded, Cecily noticed a line of German prisoners approaching, led by a group of sentries. Some looked very young; others wore an Iron Cross tied to a buttonhole with a black-and-white ribbon, obviously attempting to prove their pride and bravery. They all seemed entirely immune to the scream of shellfire. Could that be because they were already in a serious state of shell shock? Stretchers too were being brought in, carrying the wounded. Some patients would lift their heads to try and see what was happening, striving to ignore their pain. They might even offer a weary smile.

The performance lasted only an hour, the medical staff insisting that patients could not stay out of their beds too long. When it was over, Cecily, Merryn and Johnny went round the wards to entertain those unable to attend the performance, being trapped in their bed because of a fractured limb fastened to a system of slings, ropes and pulleys, or other serious injuries. Johnny couldn't carry his drum around, but chatted with the patients. Queenie was nowhere to be seen, not interested in caring for men who stank or were covered in blood. Cecily asked Merryn where she was.

'She declared herself far too exhausted and went off to the orderly room in search of a cup of tea,' Merryn said. 'I feel pretty exhausted myself after all the sewing and other jobs I've done in recent weeks, running back and forth to clean her clothes or do her hair. Whatever I find for her to eat rarely pleases her. At least she's stopped demanding

I buy her gin, which is a bit of a puzzle. That could be the reason she frequently visits the orderly room. There is the possibility that the bottle of water she constantly carries around with her is not water at all but something much more alcoholic. I vow to find the opportunity to investigate that.'

Cecily gave a weary nod of her head. 'You could be right, love. We'll look into that later.'

Shutting out that problem for now, she found it most exhilarating to spend time chatting with the wounded and singing to them. One young man, who looked about eighteen, was propped up against several pillows in bed, listening to her, his face etched in pain. The lower half of his left leg had gone, a cloth soaked in blood wrapped around the remaining stump. She went over to him, held his hand and began to sing 'Every Cloud has a Silver Lining'. He joined in the first line or two then lay back, looking quite relaxed and smiling happily at her.

'Did you enjoy that?' she asked him when she'd finished singing. It was then that a nurse came over and quietly told her he'd passed away peacefully.

'Thank you for singing to him. It gave him a little pleasure before departing this life.'

Quivering with emotion, Cecily kissed the boy on his brow then walked away to find Merryn who was happily playing her accordion to other patients.

⌒⌇

They continued to work hard over the following weeks in various camps and bases, and it was one day in early October as she prepared for their morning rehearsal that Cecily told Merryn she had an idea for a one-act play. 'It might take a while to rehearse and perfect our performance, but it would provide a lively event for Christmas.' Looking around, she again asked where their mother was. 'I do hope she hasn't gone off in search of more gin.'

Merryn pulled a face. 'Nope, I provided her with breakfast in bed as usual, and she then went back to sleep.'

'We need Johnny too, so when you've helped Corporal Lewis set things up, can you go and find him?'

'Rightio, happy to do that. You go and drag Queenie out of bed.'

Cecily chuckled and hurried back to their Nissen hut to do that. As she approached, she heard the sound of a man's voice. Peeping through a slit in the door, she saw her mother still lying in bed, her hands patting Johnny's cheek as he knelt beside her. Then pulling him close, she kissed him.

Alarm reverberated through Cecily. Good grief, was Queenie attempting to seduce him, as she had done many times in the past with other men? She remembered when they were on board the ship how her mother had ordered her not to attract him. That could be the reason if this difficult woman was jealous. Queenie was always sweetly and cleverly demanding of Johnny, constantly flashing a smile or gazing adoringly at him. Did she dream of inspiring him to fancy her? Cecily felt she really should attempt to protect him from her mother's demands. More importantly, she surmised there could be a growing attraction between her dear sister and Johnny, so must protect her too.

Quickly backing away, she felt a waft of shame for having such a sex-mad mother. Gathering the necessary courage to approach again, this time she called out to her before reaching the hut. 'Are you ready, Mama? It's time for our next rehearsal.'

When she entered, Cecily found her entirely alone, her face a picture of blithe innocence and her rosy lips twisted up into a charming smile. Had Johnny slipped out through the back door, eager to escape? 'Ah, there you are. It's time for our rehearsal. Please go and join Merryn while I find Johnny.'

'Very well, dear. I feel more than ready to help. Sorry I'm late. I'll go this very minute,' Queenie said, and taking a sip of water from the bottle the cook had provided for her, she quickly dressed.

Going in search of Johnny, Cecily found him a short distance away from the Nissen hut. Gently touching his arm, she gave a sorrowful smile. 'I feel the need to apologise for my mother's behaviour. I should have warned you that she has always had an obsession with young men. Do take care not to allow yourself to be – how can I put it – captured by her ardency. She is most promiscuous.'

He looked startled by this remark. 'Are you saying that you saw us together just now?'

'I'm afraid I did, quite by chance.'

'I assure you I was just delivering her letters from her maid and checking that she was feeling well. If you assume I was attempting to seduce her, you are absolutely wrong.'

Why would he assume she was blaming him, even though she'd apologised for her mother's behaviour? An alarming thought. 'I simply wished to warn you that Mama has had more sweethearts than I care to count. She adores men and . . .' Cecily clamped her mouth shut, blushing with embarrassment as she had no wish to use the word 'sex'.

'Why would she not? Queenie is a beautiful woman and single. So are you accusing her of being a tart just because she thanked me with a kiss?'

A sense of anxiety seeped through her, worrying how Merryn would react if she learned that her mother had kissed this man of whom she was becoming fond. There was evidence of her sister's true feelings glinting in her eyes whenever she glanced at him, then she'd tactfully look away. Cecily now studied him most cautiously, wondering what Johnny's feelings were towards her sister. He was a very self-obsessed man. Infuriatingly, he'd attempted to flirt with her too, a fact she'd still avoided mentioning to Merryn, not wishing to offend her. 'I – I just have no wish for you to get the wrong idea and assume yourself to be of special importance. Mama's problem is that she's obsessed with . . .' To her dismay, the words again stuck in her throat.

He laughed. 'Ah, so you're jealous, is that it? Do not for a moment imagine I would prefer her to you,' he said, pulling her into his arms and placing a sweet kiss on her cheek. 'You're a beautiful young woman.'

This response was not at all what she'd expected or hoped for. Cecily pushed him away. 'Don't start your silly joking or flirting with me again. I'm sorry if I've offended you. I appreciate that Mama might only have been thanking you for bringing that letter. It was wrong of me to suggest otherwise.'

'It was indeed.'

Seeing Merryn approach, Cecily firmly closed her lips, hoping her apology had been entirely appropriate.

'Ah, there you are, Johnny. I've been looking everywhere for you,' Merryn said, then meeting the glimmer of consternation in her sister's eyes with a puzzled query in her own, she frowned. 'Is something wrong?'

It came to Cecily that, possibly having misjudged what she'd seen her mother doing, she had no desire to reveal this embarrassing mistake to her sister. Saying nothing about what she'd seen seemed a sensible option. But if Johnny was the one at fault, then maybe she should warn Merryn to take better care of herself. Now was not the moment to discuss this.

Quickly moving on, she said jokingly, 'No, lovey, dragging Mama out of bed was not easy, and it took me a while to find Johnny. Good to see they're both here now as I have a suggestion to make.' She turned to Queenie and spoke more openly to her. 'I know that our music, songs and poetry are popular and the audience loves to join in. I thought it was time we offered a little play as well, as you recommended, Mama. One that we could perform without props or scenery would, I'm sure, be welcomed with open arms. I thought we could perform a short extract from *The School for Scandal*. Mama, would you play Lady Sneerwell, as you did say you could act?'

'I can indeed, so I would be delighted to play that part,' Queenie said.

'Oh, what a good idea, and Johnny could be Sir Peter Teazle. I'm sure he'd be brilliant in that role,' Merryn suggested.

'Blimey, I've never acted in a play in my entire life, but I'm prepared to give it a go if you all believe me capable.'

'We do,' Queenie said, giving him a bewitching smile.

Cecily struggled not to reveal her censorious frown. Was this another attempt to win him round? Nevertheless, his role in the play must be accepted. 'Whether you can act or not, Johnny, we don't have any choice but to give you a part in this play, being short of men,' she said, before glancing again at the cast list. 'Merryn, would you play Lady Teazle?'

Merryn looked thrilled and gave a little smile. 'I suppose so, only I've never acted before either.'

Cecily rolled her eyes in amusement. 'You'll be fine, lovey, and we're only going to do an extract. We'll do the scene where Lady Teazle speaks to Lady Sneerwell, or the one where Sir Peter believes his wife is having an affair with Joseph. Which of us should play him, that is the question?'

Johnny grinned. 'Hey, I could play Joseph and you could be Sir Peter, Cecily.'

She laughed out loud. 'Why not? As I said, we are definitely short of men.'

'That would not be appropriate,' Queenie said with a sniff of disapproval. 'You can dress up as a man, by all means, Cecily, as you've done men's jobs these last few years. You should play Joseph and be the one to flirt with your sister.'

Merryn frowned. 'I don't think they do have an affair. Joseph just suggests that Lady Teazle should make her husband jealous,' she tactfully reminded her mother, catching an echo of that emotion in her eyes. 'I'm happy with whatever you prefer, Cecily.'

'I will play Sir Peter so that I can have a moustache and beard to make clear I'm a man, not a woman,' Cecily said with a grin. 'Right, here's the script. Now we must read it and start to learn our lines.'

TEN
WINTER 1917

SMOKE HUNG heavy over a nearby village, where trees and the once beautiful brick houses now lay wrecked. Merryn stared in apprehension as they drove past. The fields and orchards were full of shell holes. There were no people left living there, with many killed and the rest having fled to safety. The old trenches had been so badly damaged by shellfire, new ones had been dug from where the Tommies furiously fought. They felt extremely exposed to the enemy, being so close to German lines, standing for hours at a time in case of further attacks.

Merryn was filled with admiration for their courage and the increase in their confidence. Corporal Lewis explained how things had improved since the battle of the Somme, the Tommies' skills being now much more efficient. Communication too was apparently better with new technology in the form of wireless, field telephones, as well as runners, signallers and pigeons that carried details for battalions and brigades. Whenever another terrifying barrage began, everyone would run to their dug-outs.

Most nights, Merryn and her sister remained in their hut or tent, listening to German machine guns and bullets bouncing off walls and trees, valiantly attempting to curb the fear sparked by this sound. This evening, Cecily was fast asleep, but Queenie was again absent. She often came quite late, putting off going to bed as she did still suffer the odd nightmare. Or else she could be trying to bribe the chef to give her a spot of rum. In view of the fresh danger that had erupted recently, Merryn was concerned and went in search of her.

Walking across the camp, she suddenly heard a grunting sound and saw Queenie on the edge of the woodland, tightly holding a young man in her arms. They were safely hidden in the dark beneath a tree, and whomever this soldier was he laid atop her, pounding into her as she squealed with pleasure. Her mother had always liked to indulge in sex, revelling in affairs with various men throughout her life. This was not something Merryn had any wish to investigate and turning, she quickly ran away and slipped back into bed, making no comment when her mother returned some time later.

Determined to keep her mind off Queenie's foolish obsessions and these increasing dangers, Merryn happily spent days rehearsing. The opportunity to act as Johnny's wife filled her with excitement if also a slight nervous tremor. Not that she was against spending time alone with him rehearsing. She simply had no wish for Queenie to guess her attraction to him.

'How perfect Johnny is for this part,' her mother declared, her chirrupy laughter lightening all their hearts.

'He certainly is,' Merryn agreed and received a hug, as her mother once more treated her as her favourite child whenever she was in a good mood. Had Queenie truly recovered from her lack of gin, her temper at last in decline or was she still acquiring alcohol? Watching her take a sip from her water bottle, Merryn again felt a pang of concern. She really should look into that, but carefully pay no attention to her obsession with sex.

Queenie interrupted these thoughts by making a smart retort about her lack of costume. 'I should be wearing a crinoline and a stole: do we have any of those? My curls need ribbons to turn them up into ringlets. Oh, and do we have a fan, Merryn?'

'Sorry, the answer is no to all of those questions. I certainly can't make you a crinoline,' she firmly stated. 'It would require a great deal of fabric, which I no longer have. Nor do I have the time for all the stitching involved.' Let alone the energy, Merryn thought, feeling far too overworked in this muddy and dangerous situation, her heart constantly bursting with fear at the sight and sound of guns, shells and injured men. 'We could borrow a uniform for Johnny. I'll speak to Corporal Lewis about that,' she offered.

'So long as we give it a good wash first. Most of them are filthy and stink like hell,' he grumbled.

'I'll see to that too,' Merryn said, and he thanked her with a smile that set her heart racing. His closeness was at least putting some happiness into her life.

'Sewing is an important part of your job, not simply playing that stupid accordion.'

Seeing the glower on Queenie's face, Merryn held up a hand to silence her. 'Stop fussing over such things, Mama. I've already made us some lovely gowns and I'm sure you'll find one you wish to wear.'

'You're quite right. What a darling you are,' Cecily said. 'We must next go through a dress rehearsal and find some chaps to watch it.'

It began well, attended by a small audience of sick men who cheered and clapped to welcome them. When Queenie came trotting on stage, elegantly dressed in her favourite blue evening gown, Merryn noticed at once how glazed and bloodshot her eyes were. She looked utterly inebriated. Stumbling forward, she constantly tripped from side to side, completely unbalanced. Her curly blonde hair, twisted up into a knot on top of her head, had fallen loose from the glittering hair comb Merryn had used to pin it in place. It looked entirely dishevelled as she kept flicking her hand through it. And the slur of her words when she began to speak was atrocious.

'I abso-lu-tely adore these men,' she stuttered, skittering over to the front of the boards to beam at the audience. Forgetting she was supposed to be acting as Lady Sneerwell, she then began to sing 'The Boy I Love Is Up In The Gallery', her tone of voice completely outrageous.

Merryn turned to Cecily with a weary sigh. 'She's drunk yet again. What on earth do we do?'

'I've no idea,' Cecily groaned.

The pair of them watched in dismay as Queenie pulled down the strap of her gown and leaned closer to these Tommies. Shaking her shoulders, she gave them a glimmer of her breasts and a sexually flirtatious smile. They roared with laughter, taking this as a fun and exciting part of the scene. Tottering among them, she smoothed their cheeks, slipping her arm around their shoulders erotically as she grinned and offered them little kisses. She then started whispering in their ears, possibly offering something sexually suggestive or making inappropriate comments. Some men shoved her away, while others captured her in their arms to give her a more passionate kiss.

Alarmed at what Queenie was doing, her performance going from bad to worse, the two sisters met each other's gaze in equal panic then rushed over to capture her, as they had done that time she fell on stage at the Palace Theatre. She shouted at them in fury as they dragged her away, the audience still roaring with laughter. They applauded and cheered, obviously having enjoyed Queenie's drunken behaviour. What a nightmare their mother was. The sisters took her to her tent and Merryn struggled to settle her in bed.

Cecily said, 'I'll rush back to inform the audience we'll give a far more appropriate dress rehearsal another day, once Queenie has sobered up.'

'That went well,' Merryn commented cynically, glaring at Queenie as she lay on her camp bed with a damp towel over her forehead. 'You made a complete fool of yourself, Mama, absolutely forgetting how you were supposed to act *and* remain sober.'

Clearly drained of energy, Queenie responded by denying she was drunk. 'Oh, darling child, don't say such a thing. I've on-y had a couple of drinksy,' she stammered.

That evening, while brushing and cleaning costumes, Merryn searched through Queenie's possessions and unsurprisingly found a bottle of rum tucked away in a drawer beneath her nightgown. Pouring out the alcohol, she replaced it with clear water, then put the bottle back where she found it. She could but hope that her mother would not surmise she was the one responsible for this loss. Determined to resolve her mother's problem, she went at once to speak to the chief cook to explain what had happened.

'May I beg you not to provide Queenie with any alcohol in future? It badly affects her.'

He quickly apologised, saying he'd believed he was doing her a favour in this dreadful war. 'Soldiers too are given a glass of rum each day to ease their suspense and distress.'

'I appreciate that, but she is an addict and no doubt managed to receive more.'

'Sorry if I filled her water bottle with too much.' Just as Merryn was listening to his assurance he would not do that again, a fusillade of machine gun fire suddenly erupted. Part of the hut roof collapsed, and she screamed as something hit her in the back. Her knees buckled and Merryn found herself smacked down on to the ground, then was blocked into silence as she lost consciousness.

When she came round some moments later, Merryn found herself locked in a world of smoke, could hear the sound of moaning and cries for help, some of it perhaps coming from herself. Barely able to breathe, she struggled to pull herself up, anxious to escape, terrifyingly aware that the army canteen had been attacked and was now on fire. Could she manage to get to her feet or had her spine been snapped into pieces? Convinced she was about to die, she was lit with relief when she became aware that someone was dragging her along the ground past men who'd been wounded or killed. Pain enveloped her, but then Merryn found she was being lifted up and seconds later, gasping for breath, she was laid out on a duckboard. A voice close by spoke of someone dying. Were they referring to her? Closing her eyes, she assumed she was and sank back into oblivion.

૭

'How are you feeling, lovey? Oh, what a relief that you're now awake.'

Blinking open her eyes, Merryn was astonished to find herself tucked in her camp bed and her beloved sister holding her hand. 'Oh, thank God I'm still alive,' she said, fear still thumping in her chest.

'You are, and praise be to those who saved you! I'll send word to Mama who is desperately upset by what you've suffered.'

'What happened to the chef I was talking to? Is he all right?' she gasped, struggling to speak clearly.

Cecily smiled. 'He was the one who saved your life by carrying you out, dear man. He is slightly injured but yes, alive and reasonably well. Many Tommies who acted as cooks and kitchen workers for the battalion did manage to escape. Others were caught up in the fire and tragically could not. They died. It was a terrifying attack.'

'Oh, it was,' Merryn murmured, the memory of it resonating through her and making her choke, but she was so thankful she had no serious damage to her spine.

Cecily gave her a drink of water and a warm hug. 'The loss of a large amount of food from the canteen will prove to be a problem and some of the Tommies have already been sent off in search of replacements. Not an easy task. We'll be on tight rations until more can be delivered. Are you hungry now?'

Merryn gave her head a little shake, then saw her mother come rushing in to wrap her in her arms, sobbing as she hugged her close. 'What on earth were you doing in the canteen?' she cried.

Making no mention of how she'd been investigating her mother's addiction to alcohol, Merryn remained silent. Then, ordered to rest, all thought of resolving this problem, let alone other issues and the sewing and rehearsals she should be involved in, vanished from her head and she slipped back to sleep.

∾

Days later, Cecily was delighted to find her sister fully recovered if still suffering from a sense of trepidation that flickered through her whenever they heard the roar of a gun or shellfire some distance away. Queenie was now stone-cold sober and as a result, the next dress rehearsal went much better. Cecily thanked their small appreciative audience when they gave their applause, which was a relief and most encouraging.

'Normally we say break a leg when we really mean good luck for our main performance, which will take place to celebrate Christmas. Right now, that sounds the wrong thing to say,' she said with a smile. 'And I'm sure we'll perform it brilliantly.'

The play did indeed work wonderfully, cheering everyone up and giving them a great sense of satisfaction after all the terrors they'd suffered. It was followed by Cecily singing a few melodies and Merryn playing her instrument. At the end, standing tall and straight, Corporal Lewis presented each of the ladies with a bouquet of winter holly. He gave a smart salute, then with a click of his heels turned and marched off the platform.

'How kind of him,' Cecily said, welcoming his gift of red berries with delight. 'What a charming and helpful man he is, and this play extract has been a real success.'

Lewis returned a few moments later to say, 'You've all been invited to take lunch with the officers who were present at this concert.'

'Thank you, that would be lovely.' When he left, Cecily turned to her sister, looking highly irritated. 'Oh, for goodness sake, is Mama missing again?'

'She's gone for a little walk around the camp, presumably to see the Tommies.'

'By herself? Goodness, will she be safe? There are quite a lot of prisoners of war here and Mama is not very sensible.'

'I'll go and find her and make sure she's all right,' Johnny offered, 'then bring her to the lunch.'

Once he too had left, Merryn gave a weary sigh. 'I recently saw Queenie involved in a passionate embrace with a soldier. She could well be with another right now. Not something I wish to consider.'

'Ah,' Cecily said, giving a small shiver. 'Not a surprise! As we know, Mama is a bit of a nightmare. In spite of her always being a very determined, self-obsessed lady, albeit with vulnerable addictions, she also has an insatiable sexual appetite. Being a star, she's a woman who has always loved frolicking with various men friends, viewing herself as an adored Queen. Whatever she's up to now, with a man or alcohol, is her choice. I can think of no reason why you and I should not attend this lunch, Merryn, since we are desperately hungry. Let's quickly change and savour some good food, as well as receive the support of those officers.'

ELEVEN

WAITING FOR them outside the Nissen hut, when they came out looking quite smart, Corporal Lewis greeted them with an approving smile and led Cecily and Merryn to the Mess for the lunch. There were often many officers in the audience who would offer their praises, applause and thanks, as they had done for this latest show. The moment they sat down, the Major General turned to them with a scathing expression in his eyes.

'I'm surprised that you bothered to come and entertain us. In my opinion, women should remain at home, not involve themselves in the war, particularly here in France,' he said, looking extremely sour-faced and disapproving.

Cecily was staggered by this remark. Merryn was too, judging by the way she blinked. They'd each made sure they were wearing a respectable skirt and jacket, not a fussy costume, and a hat, aware they needed to look smart for this lunch with the officers. Now her nerves jangled with a spurt of anger. How could this man say such a thing after all the applause and roars of delight they'd received from the audience? His dismissive attitude caused Cecily to feel the need to stand up for women's rights all the more, as she had done while working with the suffragists and even when talking to Johnny. She would continue to do so whenever necessary. Men could be so obstinate and dictatorial.

'Are you saying women should only be wives and mothers and keep to the kitchen or bedroom?' she asked, giving a little smile in an attempt to appear courteous.

'Indeed. That is their duty in life.' His view of women seemed to be entirely disrespectful and old-fashioned.

'With this war still going on and rarely anyone at home to cook or care for, women having lost their husband, father, brother or some other loved one, why would they not find suitable duties?'

The Major General made no response to this, merely making puffing noises with his tight-lipped mouth, his flabby nostrils flaring. Turning his face away, he began to sip his soup.

'Most women have a strong sense of duty,' Cecily continued, 'and have taken on jobs normally done by men. Women are working in factories, making ammunitions, and as bus conductors, cooks, clerks, waitresses, mechanics, nurses and ambulance drivers, or sewing shirts for soldiers. All are viewed as pioneer women. My sister Merryn and I too did our bit back home and now are perfectly happy to serve the troops here in France as entertainers. Why would we not?'

'Utter rubbish! We may well be in need of nurses to work for the doctors, definitely *not* women singers and actresses.'

'The Tommies would not agree with you there, sir,' Merryn gently pointed out. 'They always welcome us with delight, saying we've lifted their morale.'

'Indeed they do,' Cecily agreed. 'We are greatly enjoying this trip and would be prepared to move closer to the firing line, as near as we are allowed by the military.'

'They would never agree to that,' he said with a snort of disapproval. 'It's against the rules, and there's also a limit to how long you'll be allowed to stay here.'

Cecily gave him a polite smile. 'We have been granted several months' permit, as no one knows how long this war will last. We're happy to stay as long as necessary and visit more camps and base hospitals.'

'You would require new passes in order to do so,' he stated firmly.

'We're perfectly aware of that and have had no difficulty in being granted one for each base and hospital we've visited already, including this one, thanks to Corporal Lewis who organises these for us. He's first-rate at helping and keeping us informed of such rules. Getting the necessary petrol and vehicle to transport us does take him some time, with quite a few formalities to go through.'

'You will never be granted a pass again, not if I have any say on the matter,' he growled. 'I'll make damn sure of that.' And with a sardonic smile, he turned his back on her and spoke not another word.

'Goodness, he was such a difficult man,' Cecily said, as she and Merryn later packed their equipment and costumes ready for departure. 'What a dreadful attitude he has, stating that women should only be wives and mothers. Mama has constantly attempted to push us into a domestic lifestyle, which she herself has no interest in. Even though because of the war, there are few men around and none that we love. She hates the fact that we both abhor the idea of marriage.'

'You certainly do,' Merryn said with a smile. 'I'm much more in favour of it.'

'Then do take care whom you choose for a husband, assuming you can find one. Marriage is a form of tyranny that can chain women into slavery. This Major General's attitude illustrates that entirely. He looks upon dancers and singers as prostitutes, as Mama claims many men do.'

'Sometimes actresses are accepted by men of distinction and become pretty grand ladies. Mama once told me that Papa was a high-class gentleman from a well-to-do-family, so that could be how she sees herself.'

'Really? I didn't know that. I assumed he too was involved in the theatre.'

'Not that I'm aware of.'

'That's something of a puzzle. And as we know that his name was Dean Stanford, then why is she called Hanson?'

'I assume, having lost him, she returned to her maiden name.'

'Ah, yes. Apparently, he was not an easy man to live with, so must have made bad mistakes too. I wonder if that is the reason for her inappropriate behaviour, and why she never speaks of her past? Do we have any notion why their marriage failed?'

Merryn gave a shrug as she carefully folded the costumes away. 'No idea. Like you, there's very little I've been told about him or what went wrong between them. One day, Queenie might explain the reason but it's not something we should ask her about right now. We have enough anguish to deal with, not least the problem this Major General has created. He sounds as if he's wanting to send us back to Blighty for good.'

'As he stoutly declared, he'll make damn sure of that,' Cecily said, adopting his resolute tone of voice. Then she firmly remarked, 'And I'll make damn sure that he doesn't succeed.'

❦

Due to the dreadful weather with snow blocking all the roads and frost freezing everything, a decision was finally made to call an end to this latest battle, at least until spring came, which was a great relief to everyone. Many of the troops were transported away by bus or train back to Rouen, some to Ypres and other places. As she felt eager to carry on entertaining the Tommies still present here in Saint-Omer, singing, reciting poems and performing their play extract, Cecily found herself again engaged in battle with the Major General. She asked for her small troupe to be granted the necessary pass by the military to remain with this battalion. Corporal Lewis was standing by her side, ready to offer his support.

'It's time for you to leave for England,' the Major General informed her decisively. 'We've heard enough of your performances.'

'I appreciate that you are clearly no longer prepared to accommodate us, however, we fully intend to visit more bases and local hospitals,' she said. 'At least for a while longer.'

'Why would I allow you to do that? You should consider going home to your family.'

'They are all here, including my mother, who is a star performer and happy to assist me. Also my sister Merryn and Johnny, our friend and drummer. We're busy rehearsing new songs, music, play extracts and poems, happily doing our bit and have no wish to return home until this war comes to an end, which could be soon.'

Clearing his throat, Corporal Lewis stepped forward, clicking his heels together to stand stiffly erect. 'Sir, I assure you neither the patients nor the Tommies are bored with these performances. I accept it is essential for this concert party to entertain at other bases. But can we welcome them back in a few weeks, sir?'

'Never!' the Major General roared. 'I'll make damned sure no further passes are provided.'

⁓

To her dismay, before the end of January, Cecily received notice that their permit had been cancelled and they were ordered to quit and return home. Still determined to contest this decision, she again hurried to speak to Corporal Lewis.

'Can you arrange for me to be escorted back to Blighty?' she begged him, showing the details of the letter. 'Lieutenant Trevain initially granted us permission so I need to return to Cornwall to speak to him and gain a new permit. It was my idea in the first place, so I feel the responsibility to resolve this problem and restore the Major General's faith in us. I'll make sure it's a short trip.'

'Of course, ma'am. We'd feel lost without your team of entertainers and you should have the right to visit more camps and bases. Men always feel enraptured by you, and your performances boost their morale. I'll see that you get home safely.'

Cecily wrote to Nan to tell her she was coming, explaining that Merryn, Mama and Johnny had agreed to stay and continue working. Nan wrote regularly to them all, and it was always good to hear how things were back home in Plymouth. Queenie, in particular, loved receiving many letters and postcards from her.

'I've certainly no wish to travel anywhere in this freezing temperature, let alone cross the sea,' Queenie stated with a shiver, despite being dressed in several layers of clothes.

'We will miss you, love, and live in hope you get the necessary permission,' Merryn said, giving her sister a hug.

'It's most brave of you to risk taking this journey on your own,' Johnny said. 'Would you like me to accompany you?'

Cecily shook her head. 'No need for that. Corporal Lewis is finding me an escort. You stay here and care for Mama and Merryn.'

Merryn gave him a shy smile. 'We'd be lost without you too, and would feel in more danger.'

'We would indeed,' Queenie said. 'And we need you to keep on drumming for us.'

It had proved to be a cold, hard winter and their booted feet were crunching through snow as the two sisters took a walk together that evening around the camp, Cecily feeling the need for a private chat. 'The Tommies have clearly been through a difficult time, with this latest battle destroying more lives. Because of their heroism, I firmly believe we should continue to support and entertain them. Keeping their spirits high is vital.'

'Oh, I do agree. They love to sing with us instead of thinking how they could be blown to bits any day. And these brave men sometimes keep singing our tunes in the trenches. You're so clever, Cecily. I'm sure you'll succeed with this problem the Major General has created for us.'

'I'll certainly do my best. And do take good care of yourself while I'm gone.'

'Don't worry, I will, and I'm sure Johnny will help.'

Cecily gave her a wry smile. 'I suspect you're becoming very fond of him. Has he declared his fondness or love for you too?'

Merryn blushed. 'Oh, don't ask. We are becoming good friends and, yes, he has kissed me on a few occasions. It turns my heart over with excitement. Whether we'll get any closer, I really don't know.'

Cecily wrapped her arms around her sister to hold her close. 'I hope you are happy with him. But as I say, do take care and protect yourself from too much of his constant flirting.'

By the end of the week, Cecily was on board ship, and a young man who was due a leave was happy to escort her. She thanked him most gratefully and promised herself that she would do whatever was necessary to achieve her goal.

TWELVE
FEBRUARY 1918

NAN WAS waiting for Cecily at Millbay railway station in Plymouth. 'Oh, I'm so pleased to see you, darling,' she said, welcoming her with a warm hug. 'I've missed you so much. I do hope Merryn and Queenie are safe and well.'

'They are indeed,' Cecily said with a smile. How she loved this woman who still felt like a mother to her.

To her delight, they took a tram home. It felt like she was stepping back into her past and she instinctively helped an elderly woman climb on board with them. As she contentedly sat as a passenger instead of a conductor, Cecily spoke of how popular they were, having achieved relief and happiness for the troops, making no mention of the dangers they'd had to face. She went on to briefly explain the problem the Major General had created.

'Good for you. We'll celebrate your triumph this evening with a delicious dinner.'

Back on Grand Parade, Cecily could hardly believe that she was home in this charming Victorian white house with its elegant bay windows, rosewood furniture, oak-panelled walls and her personal bedroom. She'd always relished its braided chintz curtains, mahogany bed, bureau and wardrobe, not least her own private bathroom.

She eagerly took a bath, something that had not been possible at the base camps in France, then dressed herself in a lilac chiffon gown that reached in a straight line down to her ankles with a crossover draped bodice and ruffled waistband. It was one of her favourites, which she hadn't worn since before the war. She also adored being able to wear her pretty heeled shoes. Glancing in the mirror, Cecily modestly admired her elegant appearance, so different from the plain uniform she'd normally worn for years, either on the tram or in camp and sometimes on stage. She looked much thinner though, and more tired. A few days off might do her good.

Thinking of this visit as a little treat that couldn't last long, she went down the curved staircase to take dinner with Nan in the dining room. Expecting there to be just the two of them, Cecily was surprised to find a young man seated beside her.

'Ah, hello, darling. I hope you don't mind that my nephew has come to join us, being keen to hear all about your achievements.'

'Pleased to meet you,' she said, reaching out a hand to shake his.

He introduced himself as Boyd Radcliff: a young man who was quite good-looking, if somewhat reed-thin. His left eye looked a little narrow and blank while the other was a lively and bright velvet brown, the same colour as his hair. Hobbling over to her, using a crutch, he gently shook her hand. Cecily quietly asked if he'd suffered injuries in the war.

'Yes, a bash to my head when I was hit with a shell and lost part of my left leg.'

'Oh, you have my deepest sympathy. I've met many other young men and boys in hospitals where we perform who have similar problems. You must have suffered considerable pain.'

He nodded and went on to tell how prosthetic technology was improving and that he had not succumbed to gangrene or any infection. His leg had been amputated just above the knee, then fitted with an artificial wooden limb. 'I call it a peg-leg, something I'm slowly growing accustomed to,' he said with a smile. 'I spent some time in a military hospital with an excellent doctor, where we were given exercise and assistance to get walking again. Not easy, but if one wishes to return to reality it's worth the effort.'

'I greatly admire you for that and wish you every success,' Cecily said, smiling with admiration at his courage.

Nan came bustling in carrying a tray stacked with dishes of chicken, vegetables and gravy. Boyd quickly hobbled over to lift it from her and place it on the table.

'Look at this boy, always so keen to help despite him having no chance of getting that knee back.'

Boyd laughed. 'Aye, I do tend to walk a bit stiffly and one day my peg-leg should become much more comfortable. I'm enjoying this much-needed rest here in Plymouth. It was kind of you to invite me, Aunty, and I'm delighted to meet you, Cecily.'

She found herself blushing as she met his appreciative gaze. 'I'm pleased to meet you too. I love Plymouth. I used to constantly explore the Sound, Drake's Island and Wembury Bay. It was a delight to come and live in this house in the city where my mother was born.'

Nan gave her a startled look. 'Queenie was born in Whitstable in Kent, not Plymouth.'

Cecily blinked at her in astonishment. 'Goodness, that's news to me. I thought Mama said that was the reason she bought this house, as well as the fact she'd always loved views of the sea. Did I misunderstand?'

Frowning slightly, Nan looked a little embarrassed. 'Possibly Queenie doesn't always explain things very well. After her mother died, she had no wish to return to the house where she was born, so she bought this one instead.'

'I see. She has, in fact, told us little about her past. Is there more you could tell me about her and my father?' Cecily asked quietly, hope flickering through her.

'Not without her permission, dear. I probably shouldn't have said what I've just told you. Now do help yourself to some chicken.'

Frustration brought a small frown to Cecily's face, thinking how difficult it was to find simple answers to her mother's past. She noticed how Nan avoided her gaze, as if nervous of having said the wrong thing. This was a subject she should not have asked about, she decided, as they settled to eat the delicious meal Nan had provided.

'I wondered if you were at all interested in the suffrage movement,' Boyd asked, skilfully changing the subject.

Now she tactfully smoothed her disappointment away. 'I am indeed interested in the suffragists, having been involved with them for some years. Nothing too violent, but I've willingly offered my support by raising funds and gathering new members for them. When this war began, the suffrage movement ceased their political activities, cancelled their hunger strikes and focused their attention on the war effort. We women eagerly volunteered to take on jobs normally carried out by men, which has surely proved how capable we are. As a result, I think the view of women by the government has improved. They agreed to release all the active suffragettes who'd been imprisoned.'

'And now they have successfully reached their goal, at least to a degree.'

Cecily gave a sardonic little smile, fully aware, as was he, that only women over thirty who also owned property were the ones to gain the right to vote. Whereas all men over the age of twenty-one were now allowed to vote, while those in the armed forces could vote from the age of nineteen. 'The suffrage movement is pleased that votes have finally been granted to some women, but there is still evidence of inequality between us and men.'

'I agree that's entirely wrong,' Boyd said, with a firm nod. 'At least it's a start and will improve.'

'It certainly should, as this war has proved women's ability,' she stated, meeting his bright gaze. How she appreciated his support. He seemed to be a most friendly man. 'I'm so glad we agree on this subject.'

'Indeed we do, and you may be interested to know that on 6th February there is to be a suffrage parade to celebrate this granting of votes for women, not only in London but in many other places too in the days following, including here in Plymouth. I've definitely been in favour of it so will be attending. Would you care to come too?'

'Oh yes, I'd love to.' There was something about this young man that caused a warm glow to spread through her, rather a surprise considering how she'd felt little interest in men recently. Smothering a yawn, she leaned back in her chair and patted her tummy. 'That was a delicious meal, Nan. Such a treat. Can't say we're ever well fed in camp, particularly lately when we ran out of food, the canteen having been attacked by a bomb.' She briefly told what Merryn had suffered from, but that fortunately she was not seriously injured.

'Oh my goodness, thank heaven for that. What dangers you must have faced. Do you intend to stay in France and continue with your concerts?'

'We do indeed. We feel it's our task to keep these men's spirits and morale high.'

'That is very brave and noble of you,' Boyd remarked softly.

'Now you'd best go off to bed for some much-needed rest,' Nan instructed her, as she had done so often when Cecily was a young girl.

'You're quite right, I do feel pretty whacked. And tomorrow I need to make an appointment to see Lieutenant Trevain. Let's hope I don't have to wait too long for that.'

∽

A few days later, Cecily received word that he was looking forward to seeing her again, whenever it suited her. At ten o'clock the next day, she sat before him relating what their troupe had achieved and went on to explain why she had come to see him.

'Oh dear, that sounds odd,' he said. 'I've received good reports of your performances so why would you not continue? I'll be happy to provide you with a new permit, one that should see you through to the end of the war. I'll write and explain to that fellow why I trust you to perform for them, as you are a most talented and brave young woman.'

Her heart swelled with relief at his generosity. 'Thank you so much, Sir. I really appreciate your help. We've worked hard and do find great fulfilment in what we do.'

Leaning closer, the Lieutenant quietly remarked, 'In return for this new pass, may I respectfully request that you contact me with any information you might come across, should you be willing to speak with prisoners of war?'

Cecily stared at him in blank astonishment, falling silent for some seconds. 'Are you suggesting that you wish me to act as a spy?'

'We call them agents, not spies. It is considered to be an element of your duty, one that women are particularly good at, being able to persuade men into handing over information by offering them a sweet smile and a bat of their beautiful eyelashes. Would you be prepared to do that?' His eyes widened as he patiently awaited her answer.

Swallowing the panic that blocked her throat, Cecily worried whether she could cope with such a challenge. It surely wouldn't be easy. She'd seen PoWs tucked in tents watching their performance, but had never approached them or attempted to converse with them. How on earth would she find the courage, let alone be aware of the right questions to ask? It then came to her that this might prove to be a form of revenge for the loss of Ewan, so why shouldn't she give it a try, assuming she was told exactly what to do? Clearing her throat with a little cough, she met his questioning gaze with one of her own. 'Would I receive training on how to go about this?'

'I will teach you how to achieve anything that could be useful for us.'

'If this is what you wish in return for the permit, then yes, I'll do the best I can for you, Sir. No promises, however, that I'll succeed.'

'Excellent! I know you're leaving soon so I'll be in touch with you in the next day or two to arrange an element of training for you.'

It turned out not to be easy. Lieutenant Trevain assured Cecily that her success as a spy would be largely dependent upon practice and experience. He began by lecturing her on the growing threat of conflict in Europe and how the Germans were determined to invade Britain. He then informed her that she should look into the possibility of interrogating prisoners-of-war to gain essential information. First, she should attempt to identify their name, rank and number and possibly their chief officer; where they were planning to go before being captured; as well as more important details of the enemy's military capacity and their future plans. Becoming part of an undercover spy operation, he explained, would also be useful.

Achieving that seemed highly unlikely, let alone questioning PoWs. Were members of the local population involved in such activity, even though so many villages had been under attack? Her team had performed quite close to the enemy front line, where German armies occupied a section of northern France as well as nearby Belgium. The Netherlands were neutral, but would she ever find herself in a situation where she could acquire information on when the Germans planned to invade her home country? Cecily suspected that being a spy, or agent as Trevain preferred to call them, would be a lonely and dangerous occupation, with no certainty she'd find the necessary support.

Asking how any information she managed to find could be sent to him, she was instructed on who to contact at a local station of the Royal Navy in France; how they would pass on whatever she'd discovered through their Marconi wireless telegraphy system and what code she should use: something she was not allowed to write down but must firmly fix into her head. She listened to these instructions with increasing concern. Learning how to carry out such tasks was a terrifying prospect.

When the training session was finally over, Cecily hurried back home, filled with a sense of panic, all faith in herself having vanished. Her instinct was to try and help, whatever the risks involved. She flew upstairs to her room to write a letter to Merryn, telling how she'd successfully gained a new permit, carefully making no mention of the deal she'd agreed as a consequence, let alone the training she'd been through. She simply promised to return to France soon. After she'd posted it, she joined Nan in the parlour to tell her the same.

'I congratulate you on your success, dear. You always were a smart, clever girl. I thought so from the moment I first met you.'

She laughed. 'I was only a baby at the time so how could I be?'

'Actually, you were a toddler of about two.'

Cecily's eyes widened in surprise. She'd learned that her mother had not been born here in Plymouth, now here was another puzzle. 'Are you seriously suggesting that Mama took the trouble to care for me without your assistance when I was first born? Or presumably she employed some other nanny whom I don't remember, only being a baby at the time. Was she then sacked?'

'I expect that was the case. I'm not sure who your first nanny was before I was appointed to care for you and your mother. Being quite old now, I forget such details.' Nan turned away to fuss over a mistake she'd made on the cushion cover she was embroidering. 'Now, what would you like for lunch? You look in need of good food to renew your energy.'

'Very true. I'll delightedly accept whatever you have to offer.' In her heart, Cecily didn't feel at all smart or clever, simply willing to do her bit for the war, as did the rest of her troupe. For now, she concentrated firmly on looking forward to the suffrage parade, due to take place the next day, which could help to restore her courage.

◦◦

Cecily and Boyd caught a tram and she expressed her delight that due to the reason she'd been obliged to return to Blighty, she was at least able to take part in this parade. 'I'm so excited I can hardly wait. Thank you for telling me about it. I'd lost touch with them and I'm sure it'll be a great day.'

As they got off the tram, things started to go wrong. A woman approached and stuck a white feather in Boyd's hat, accusing him of being a coward, then gave him a shove. He lost his balance, dropped his crutch and fell to the ground. Cecily rushed to rescue him, then seeing the woman who'd assaulted him start to scamper away, she grabbed hold of her and shouted, 'How dare you do that to this brave man? He damn well isn't a coward. He's suffered enormous damage as a consequence of this war, not least the loss of a leg. Apologise to him this instant!'

Several suffragettes had hurried over to help lift him back to his feet, and brushing the dust from his jacket, he shook his head. 'It really doesn't matter. I've had this happen to me many times before. There is a stupid obsession with these white feathers, handed out for entirely the wrong reason and I've no wish to make a fuss. I shall simply return it.' Handing it back to the woman, he met her sour-faced grimace with a polite smile.

Blushing, she picked up her skirts to turn and run away. Cecily yanked her back. 'I said you should apologise.'

'I'm sorry,' she whispered, and stuffing the feather in her pocket dashed off down the street, many people shouting and jeering at her.

Anxiety creasing her face, Cecily asked Boyd if he was all right. 'Can you still walk? Or do you wish to go home?'

'No, I'm fine and can walk,' he said, giving a plucky grin.

Slipping her arm through his, she gently led him to Old Town Street. It was crowded with people, all smiling and cheering as the suffragettes set off marching, waving banners or flags. Dressed in her white suffrage gown, brimmed hat and a purple sash that declared the words *Votes for Women*, Cecily felt privileged to be allowed to join in this parade. They were led by a fine-looking lady riding along in a horse and carriage at the head of the procession. Constantly checking that Boyd remained well as he walked close by, she handed him a flag to wave and they frequently shared a grin. What a thrilling day it was proving to be, setting aside that annoying insult he'd suffered.

Later, as the suffrage movement gathered in the square around Derry's clock, they began to sing: 'I'll not be a slave for life'. Cecily happily joined in. She'd attended so many meetings in the past and loved to do battle for the rights of women. Then the lady who'd led the procession finished off the meeting by giving a little speech, introducing herself as Lady Stanford. Cecily jerked with shock. Wasn't this the name of their father, apparently a high-class man? Could this woman be related to him?

Highly intrigued, Cecily began to edge herself forward through the crowd, listening closely as Lady Stanford went on to speak of how she'd helped to organise the parade in London so had readily agreed to come and share this one with them. By the time her speech came to an end, wishing them a good future, Cecily had finally reached her.

Edging closer, she said, 'Excuse me, Lady Stanford. Thank you for your interesting talk, but I'm intrigued by your name. May I enquire if you are by any chance related to my father who was called Dean Stanford?'

Glancing at her in startled disbelief, the lady dismissively remarked, 'Of course not. There is no one of that name in my family. Are you claiming Stanford to be your name too?'

'My name is Cecilia Hanson, usually known as Cecily, and my mother was . . .'

'Ah, my apologies, dear girl, I must now leave.'

Cecily felt a flush of disappointment as the woman waved to a friend and hurried away, not having shown the slightest interest.

❦

She spent the next few days shopping and packing, buying a few essentials she'd promised to take back for Queenie and Merryn, including some food provided by Nan. On her last evening when Nan had gone to bed, having enjoyed another good supper she'd cooked for them,

Cecily and Boyd sat in the courtyard at the back of the house, enjoying a small glass of port. She quietly told him of the dismissive attitude Lady Stanford had shown towards her, giving little response to what she'd deemed to be a perfectly reasonable question. Cecily went on to explain how she was all too aware that some high-class people could be rather snobby, which often caused them to be entirely indifferent to ordinary folk. 'Very like that woman who flicked that white feather at you and gave you a shove.'

'I did appreciate your assistance, and am willing to forgive that silly woman.'

'At least you're alive and well, thank God.'

'Indeed, so no complaints,' he said, sharing a warm smile with her.

'There's so much I feel the need to know about my father, as does my sister Merryn, our mother not having told us anything. I got nowhere by speaking to that Lady Stanford, despite her having the same name.'

Looking quite sympathetic, Boyd said, 'Nor should you accuse yourself of doing anything wrong by asking her that question. I too feel the urge to find out more about my own family. I could look into him if you like, and happily write to let you know, were I to find out anything.'

Meeting his gaze, Cecily again felt a warm glow spark within her, almost one of excitement. An interesting friendship did seem to be growing between them. 'Thank you, that could be most helpful. We love receiving letters from family and friends, as you know, sent to us by The British Army Postal Service. Feel free to contact Lieutenant Trevain, who'll happily pass it on to them for you,' she said, with a smile of gratitude.

Reminding herself that she'd vowed not to engage with any man, she quickly changed the subject and they moved on to share tales of their youth. Cecily told how she'd become involved in singing in a choir at school and he said how his passion had been playing football and cricket, sports he could now only watch.

'I admit to being very stubborn, so have no wish to lose face by going down the wrong path now my life has changed,' he said, with a shrug and a grin. 'I have complete confidence in my ability to build myself a new life and eventually find a job.'

'Good for you.' Cecily felt a stir of emotion, greatly admiring this belief he had in himself and was interested to hear how he happily lived in the East End of London with his doting parents, where she'd been born. Unless she was wrong about that too, her mother being a most uncommunicative woman.

Then, speaking of the war, he laughingly told how he'd left his rifle lying on the ground when he'd gone to the latrine, then had seen a German crawl over the parapet to steal it. 'I was scared out of my wits, but it was a daft thing for me to do,' he said. 'Thankfully he didn't fire at me, just ran away.'

'Thank heaven for that,' Cecily said, not wishing to discuss the horrors they'd endured. Finishing the last sip of her port, she rose to her feet. 'Now I must say goodnight and retire. I leave on a naval ship early tomorrow morning to head back to France.'

'Goodnight and good luck,' he said, standing beside her with an expression of deep concern on his face. 'I wish you well and do hope you remain safe.' Then lifting her hand, he gently kissed it. 'I've been so pleased to meet you and look forward to seeing you again.'

'Let's hope that will be quite soon,' she told him softly, and walked away with a sense of happiness and a reluctance to leave him sparking in her heart.

THIRTEEN
SPRING 1918

ARRIVING BACK in Saint-Omer, Cecily was welcomed with cheers, waves and salutes from the soldiers still here in the battalion, a response she found quite touching. The snows were melting from the mountains, running in cascading rivers down to the lake, gushing with all the new force of melted ice released from bondage. Merryn came running, giving a squeal of delight at seeing her sister wave the permit she'd obtained. She quickly enveloped her in a tight hug.

'Thank goodness for your success, love. We've been promising everyone that we will not be leaving any time soon. Do tell us what you had to go through in order to achieve this.'

'Lieutenant Trevain was most impressed with our efforts,' Cecily confidently told her, not wishing her sister to know about what she'd been obliged to agree to as a consequence. That evening, when Queenie went off for her usual walk within the camp, Cecily sat beside Merryn on her camp bed to tell her how Nan's nephew had been accused of cowardice when they'd taken part in the suffrage parade. 'It was so interesting, but an odd thing occurred there for me too.'

Merryn appeared full of curiosity to hear of her sister meeting a Lady Stanford. 'Goodness, her lack of interest must have been so distressing.' She sat in silence for some moments before adding, 'We could ask Queenie if she knows this woman.'

'We're clearly thinking along the same lines because I've been trying to decide if we should do that. Dare we take the risk, knowing how Mama hates to speak of the past?'

'We'll give it some thought,' Merryn said. 'No rush, and we are a bit busy right now.'

∽

Over the coming weeks, they continued to travel to various bases, still transported by Corporal Lewis in the old wagon. He too was delighted they'd been granted the required pass, despite the threat from the Major General. Sometimes they performed in a large tent or out in an open muddy field, often obliged to use only candles to light the area of their performance, and always took with them a couple of chairs for Merryn and Johnny to sit on when playing their musical instruments, in case none were available.

Their accommodation varied greatly, and once they were put up in a convent. It was cold, but they were at least offered comfortable beds and a bath. Queenie had greatly welcomed this, if not the prospect of some nun offering to unpack their battered, strapped suitcases, their garments looking most shabby and not at all as clean as they should be. With soap and hot water at last available, she insisted Merryn wash all their clothes. Being next lodged in a Nissen hut where they were allotted bunk beds, lice kept falling upon them, which was a real problem. Held responsible for tidying it, Merryn would again often find a bottle of alleged water that turned out to be rum, which she would remove or substitute with water, receiving sour expressions from Queenie as a result.

One morning, Merryn was stripping the sheets off the beds, planning to get them washed, when Johnny appeared by her side. 'Do you need help with this? If so, I'm the man for the job.'

She laughed. 'Why would you be? In fact, you shouldn't be in this section of the hut. It's for us women only.'

'It obviously needs tidying, so I'm happy to carry these sheets and blankets to the laundry for you. You work far too hard and should be granted some time off. After that, why not let me take you for a relaxing walk. Or we could go and take a rest out in the sun?'

'In this wind?' she said, tossing the soiled sheets to the floor. Breathing deeply in an effort to control her emotion, she calmly said, 'No thank you, just leave me in peace, Johnny. That wouldn't be at all appropriate and could risk us being spotted by my mother. Nor do I need your help, as I'm quite happy working at this job.'

'Blimey, it's long past time you accepted that you should relax, and why not with me? You must realise how much I adore you. I'd love to introduce you to the fruits of pleasure. We could have so much fun and I'll make sure Queenie doesn't see us.' His arms came around her and he pushed her down upon the bunk bed, plundering her mouth with his tongue.

Merryn felt her pulse start to beat wildly. Filled with anxiety that her mother might walk in, she pushed him away. 'Get off me, and do behave.'

'Why would I? I know you desperately want me.'

'Don't flatter yourself. I'm far too busy and it wouldn't be right.'

Releasing her, he leapt to his feet, holding up his hands in a show of apology. 'So you're dismissing me? All right, I'll leave you alone and never touch you again.'

Merryn watched in dismay as he marched off, feeling she'd lost him forever.

∽

On their next trip to a far-away base, they were billeted in a cottage, Cecily and Merryn sharing a double bed with a straw mattress. Queenie was provided with a single bedroom of her own, a situation she loved. Each morning they would be called down by the elderly woman who owned it to be given bread and a boiled egg, so delicious and greatly appreciated, except by Queenie.

'Don't you dare complain, Queenie,' Merryn firmly instructed her, seeing the resentful expression on her face, all too aware she objected to not being allowed to take breakfast in bed, as she so liked to do. 'This is a wonderful meal and there's always a hot cup of black chicory coffee to go with it.'

Lunch was usually soup as the old woman had a tiny garden with a small vegetable patch, surrounded by a shallow ditch of water. Merryn would often help her to dig up the necessary vegetables and trim and chop them for her. Her mother's reaction to this food continued to be derisory. 'I shall go and speak to the camp cook in the hope he can provide some meat for us.'

'I confess I enjoyed some marvellous meals back home in Plymouth, cooked by Nan,' Cecily admitted. 'It was such a treat.'

Johnny gave a groan. 'Blimey, we should have come with you, Cecily. I feel so jealous.'

'How fortunate for you,' Merryn said, clicking her tongue and glaring at Queenie, suspecting that what she really longed to ask the chef for was yet again a tot of rum. And as this was a different man, he'd probably agree to indulge her. 'Anyway, Queenie, the camp cook is desperately overworked, dishing out plates of scraggy bully beef, sometimes brawn and kidneys. Not much else, so why bother?'

'Besides, you need to appreciate our hostess's generosity, Mama, despite living the life of a poor peasant,' Cecily said.

'And you should appreciate your daughter Merryn too, as she helps this woman do the cooking and other tasks,' Johnny reminded her.

Looking suitably scolded, Queenie clipped her lips together and at least savoured the coffee.

Merryn felt delighted at Johnny's support and how he shared a secret smile with her. So they were still close, after all.

∾

April came, and they arrived at Ypres over the border into a French part of Belgium, even closer to enemy lines. The land was quite flat with canals and rivers linking it to the coast. Parts of this territory had been controlled by the Germans since the start of the war. They'd been driven back, but now that the weather had improved they were once more attempting to take it over and capture the town. In June 1917 many mines had been detonated and as the war continued, the Allies had suffered terrible losses. In and around Ypres, including Passchendaele, Broodseinde and many other parts of Flanders Fields, thousands of soldiers and civilians of all nationalities had been killed or wounded.

The country roads leading to the town were flat and muddy, cluttered with smashed vehicles, tanks, maimed horses, broken guns. There were wounded men lying on stretchers waiting for an ambulance, including Germans. Revulsion pummelled through her as Cecily noticed there were skeletons, unmarked graves and rats all over the place. Rotting corpses lay all around, some having fallen into the muddy trenches, pools or shell holes where they'd drowned, and fat maggots were crawling over them.

'Why has no one removed them?' she asked Corporal Lewis.

'Squads are not allowed to help casualties when on their way to the front line, that task has to be left to stretcher-bearers whose job it is to rescue the wounded. Burying corpses is another matter. A group of men were destroyed in their tent by a single shell, leaving just a crater. They were blown to pieces, no bodies found.'

A sickness came over Cecily. 'Did their families receive a telegram saying "Missing, presumed dead" sent from the War Office?'

He gave her a sorrowful smile. 'Ah yes, they did. Fortunately, others escaped as walking wounded.'

'All of this horrific mess makes travelling extremely difficult, the effect upon soldiers far worse. I can see the fear and tension, strain and anxiety in their faces as they fall into a grim silence the nearer we come to the battle zone.'

'Their thoughts do turn inward. Younger, single men and hardened veterans manage to deal with such problems more easily. While many are marching here, some Tommies are coming by train, all prepared to try and block the German attempt to take over this area.' At that moment, an aeroplane came flying over, more shrapnel shells bursting forth. 'These planes have entered the war to drop bombs and attack the British or to check on what's happening,' Lewis muttered grimly and slowed down the wagon to avoid them being hit.

Flying to and fro, the aircraft quickly came under attack from the Tommies and Cecily saw one of the plane's wings blown off. Within minutes, it plunged down to earth where the enemy pilot must have been instantly killed. Thankfully, they remained safe. She could see men running around, then they would drop down into a trench before emerging to move on in a different direction. It couldn't be easy for them in such muddy ground, which made movement extremely difficult. This must be an experience they'd endured many times before and Cecily worried over whether she could cope with such dangers as she might be about to face.

෴

Their next concert greatly cheered her up. As always, it was packed with soldiers who happily applauded whenever she sang to them. The entire area stank of smoke as so many of the men were puffing on their Woodbines, including Johnny while playing his drum. Cecily began with 'Keep the Home Fires Burning', then went on to sing many more songs, encouraging the Tommies to join in with the chorus, which they so loved to do. How she enjoyed these performances, brightening her mind and dismissing all fear and worries over the drastic reality of war. It had that effect on these men too. Once it was over, some would hover around, begging Cecily for her autograph or, more daringly, inviting her to take supper with them. She discreetly declined, not wishing to succumb to their flattery. Queenie, however, cheerfully flirted with them, batting her eyelashes and kissing their cheeks, her fascination with men still very evident. Unlike her mother, Cecily felt not at all interested in courting any man, although her grief for Ewan had now reduced to sweet memories of his life. She did remember the slight attraction she'd felt for Boyd, Nan's nephew, then blocked him from her mind too.

As well as being attended by hundreds of able-bodied soldiers, the wounded, stuck in tents often overpacked with as many as twenty injured German prisoners instead of the usual eight Tommies, were also keen to watch their performance. Sentries bearing rifles stoutly guarded them. Once recovered from their injury, these prisoners would be moved on to an internment camp some distance away. Cecily was always surprised when some of the German PoWs joined in the singing, presumably those capable of understanding some English.

She saw a young nurse calming a sick patient as she gently washed his swollen grey feet, which looked freezing cold, inflamed with blisters, ulcers and peeling skin. Cecily couldn't resist going over to help. 'You must be in a sorry state,' she remarked softly, and holding his hand, began to sing to him.

His expression, which had been locked in pain, now twisted into a small smile of appreciation.

'We do our best for these boys and greatly enjoyed your performance.' With a smile, the nurse washed his face with a sponge and combed his hair, then told him he must stay put until they were certain he wasn't suffering from gangrene.

When she moved outside, Cecily stayed with her as she introduced herself as Lena Finchley. She appeared most caring, smartly attired in a blue uniform dress, a bright red cross on the centre of her white apron and a firm white collar around her neck. Her dark brown hair with its centre parting was capped with a neat white hat. 'These men suffer a great deal, not least from rats, lice, fleas, slugs and beetles, as well as scabies, trench-fever and trench foot – what this young man is plagued with. Boils too are very prevalent because of their poor diet,' she said, her golden-brown eyes filled with warmth and compassion.

'Goodness, how dreadful, and very brave of you, Lena, to be willing to help them.'

With a little shrug of her shoulders, the pretty girl laughed. 'We appreciate your support too. It's brave of you too to come here and sing for the troops. It has lifted their morale and the memory of these concerts will fill their minds for days.'

Cecily smiled. 'Thank you. Having lost the man I loved, I felt the need to honour his memory by doing my bit for these Tommies. Grief never goes away completely but I wish to face reality and move forward in life.'

'I'm so sorry to hear that, but greatly admire your success with our patients.' She then hurried to help a young man who was in complete agony. Cecily followed to hold his hand and began to sing quietly to him. Confined in bed, he'd missed the show. He blinked at her in surprise and when the song was over, she asked him his name.

'Wilhelm Ackermann,' he murmured.

She instantly realised that he must be a German prisoner of war. Remembering what Lieutenant Trevain expected of her, in return for granting the necessary permission she'd asked for, a quiver of anxiety erupted in her chest. This man's handsome face with its full round cheeks and a square chin was racked with pain and covered with bruises. Clumps of his fair hair fell over his blue-grey, staring eyes and she smoothed them back.

'*Danke*,' he murmured.

'You're welcome,' she said with a smile. 'I feel sorry for the suffering of all prisoners in this war, no matter what their nationality.' He was wearing Blücher boots with no socks, his feet bound in rags, his leg having been injured as his trousers were ripped and soaked in blood. The smell of it was gruesome. Did that mean it would have to be amputated? 'Would you like me to help you take these boots off? Is it all right if I do that?' she asked Lena.

'So long as you take them off most carefully.' Turning to the prisoner, she said something to him in German. '*Hab' keine Angst, hier bleibst du sicher.*'

Cecily was surprised, not understanding a word of the language. 'That's clever of you,' she whispered.

Lena smiled. 'I know only a few obvious words such as – don't worry, you'll be safe – which is what I've just said to him. I do what is expected of me, no matter what nationality they are.' At that point, she dashed away to see to someone else.

Should she be asking this man questions? Because of the panic within her, Cecily couldn't remember what she should speak of. Having so far failed to send any information to Lieutenant Trevain, she still had no confidence in fulfilling her role as a spy or agent, as they were supposedly called. But remembering her love for Ewan, she really must attempt to do what she had promised. Would this Wilhelm Ackermann be willing to reveal anything?

'Have you been in France long?' Cecily brightly asked, wondering how much English he really knew when he stared at her without answering. He must understand a little, having responded to her original question. Receiving no response, she tried again. 'What about your comrades? Are they safe?'

Noticing a slight darkening of his eyes as he stared at her, Cecily ploughed on as best she could, assuming he had little English. 'No doubt you have an important role in this war. And I dare say you feel resentful at being arrested or captured. How did that come about?'

His silence now was echoed with a glimmer of amusement and disapproval in his eyes, causing her to flush with embarrassment. Recalling how Lieutenant Trevain had made it clear that it was the gentleness and attractiveness of women that caused them to be the best at this job, she realised she must not sound as if she was interrogating him, but simply being caring and sympathetic. Giving him a charming smile, she said, 'Oh, your family must be most concerned about you being missing. I'm sure you feel isolated and are anxious to see an end to this war, escape and return home, as are we,' she said with a soft smile.

Lena appeared at that moment, to tell this man that he would soon be taken into the operating theatre.

'Oh dear, what will he have to go through?' Cecily asked, feeling a degree of pity for the possibility of him losing a limb.

'We'll check and see,' Lena blandly stated.

He lifted up his head to cast a smile at Cecily and grasping her hand gave it a small squeeze. 'Hope to see you again,' he said in perfect English, which greatly staggered her. His choice of words sent a chill echoing through her, so similar to what Boyd, a more pleasant man, had said to her when last she saw him, but a far worse proposition. Giving this fellow a brisk nod, Cecily scurried away, quickly moving on to another group of injured patients. Had she made the right decision to agree to act as a spy? Probably not. She was certainly no good at this task and felt a complete idiot.

'Hello, have you come to join us?' another young man asked, again in excellent English with a slightly foreign accent. Cecily merely smiled, feeling confused and inadequate, struggling to think of any relevant questions.

This man's handsome face was badly bruised, grubby and weather-beaten, one of his white teeth chipped behind swollen lips, his bleeding arm tucked in a sling. Feeling anxious not to make a complete fool of herself, she resolved to do better this time and made an attempt to be cheerful rather than ignorant. 'Hopefully, you'll feel well enough to come and watch our next performance. It will take place early this evening.'

He met her gaze with a lopsided smile. 'I wish that I could. However, I have to be seen by the doctor to have this damaged shoulder dealt with.'

His ash-brown hair was a scraggy mess, while his matching eyes were lit with a resolute strength. Cecily felt herself unexpectedly captivated by this man's good looks. 'Sorry to hear that. How did you come by this injury?'

'I was hit by a shell – a bit like being kicked by a horse, only worse,' he grimly remarked.

'Your English is so good I forgot you were – oh dear – you *are* a German prisoner of war on your way to an internment camp.'

He burst out laughing. 'I'm French Canadian and certainly not a prisoner, so will be occupied elsewhere once I'm taken to be treated.'

Blushing with embarrassment, she was about to apologise when there came the sound of a barrage of shellfire. This happened fairly frequently and was always terrifying. Numerous hostile aeroplanes appeared overhead, being attacked by heavy anti-aircraft fire while bombs fell just a few feet away. The roaring sound was horrendous.

'Come on, we need to go hide in a trench,' he yelled.

'Is it far?'

'No, it's over there,' the French Canadian said, pointing to the right. 'Come on, we must hurry,' he urged, grabbing her hand.

As the pair of them ran across the field, she heard a cry. 'I need help too!' Turning, she saw Wilhelm Ackermann, the German PoW with whom she'd spoken earlier. Cecily felt startled to see him seated close by in his wheelchair, his expression a complete picture of agony. Would the sentries manage to protect all these prisoners, let alone the ones trapped in beds or wheelchairs? This camp was turning into a nightmare. It was then that more Hun planes came whirling overhead. Seconds later, a much greater explosion filled the air. Rushing over to him, Cecily grabbed the handles of the wheelchair and began to push it down the muddy path towards the trench. As she reached it, sturdily attempting to safely deposit his wheelchair, she must have pushed it too hard as her feet slipped and she fell. Her head bashing against the wooden framed arm rest, she knocked herself out.

FOURTEEN

CECILY CAME round slowly, the pain in her head so bad it caused her to vomit, her mind a blur of semi-conscious thoughts. The silence after the deafening noise of battle was almost too awful to bear. Staring up into the mist of dust and smoke that filled the air all around her, she could see nothing, not a soul around in the grim darkness of the trench. She feared the hospital might have been destroyed. Dear God, make sure my sister is safe, let alone my mother and Johnny. She prayed the nurses, doctors and Tommies were alive too. Oh, and where was that young French-Canadian chap who'd bravely saved her life? Cecily shuddered, as she could see no sign of him either. And where was the German prisoner who she'd attempted to rescue?

'*Danke*,' she heard a voice quietly say.

Looking up, she felt startled and oddly relieved that he was beside her, alive and well, if jammed in his wheelchair. She tried to move and cried out as pain pounded within her. She too was trapped, her foot caught in the sodden trench beneath it. Why she'd risked her own life for this enemy was not something she cared to contemplate. As a prisoner, he could have called for help from the sentries and soldiers all around. And maybe he'd been aware that those Hun planes would come flying over. Something inside her froze at the thought. She would need to take care not to ask him any of those questions.

'*Ich verdanke Dir mein Leben.* I owe you my life,' he murmured, then seeing the tremor of anxiety in her face gave a wry smile. 'I'd no wish to be left lined up with my comrades in danger of attack. Those of us who were captured and suffered injuries were brought to this hospital by train. Others came by road in most uncomfortable armoured vehicles. In answer to your earlier question, it was not my choice to come to France and fight. We were ordered to do so.'

Cecily guessed he was revealing nothing of any relevance, only the obvious. She felt a certain appreciation for his attempt to console her. 'That is the reality in today's world. Not just for you Germans but British and French soldiers too. I've no wish to be stuck in a trench either.'

'Let me help you,' he said, and tried to shift away his wheelchair.

'Keep still!' she yelled as pain escalated within her, the weight of it far too heavy.

'*Tut mir leid!* he apologised.

They both fell silent. Cecily felt something scrambling over her leg and saw to her horror it was a rat. Knocking it away with her fist, she thanked God it hadn't actually bitten her. She could also sense lice prowling over her. According to that young nurse Lena, there would be slugs and beetles all around too. The stink of this trench was too much to bear, causing her to gag. The odour of urine and faeces was coming from latrines in these trenches that had not been filled in. There was also the stench of gas, creosol, chloride of lime used in water, rotting sandbags, cigarette smoke and even corpses. Some soldiers frequently complained there was a shortage of ammunition, only being allowed to fire the odd round from their gun. As a consequence, many were shot and left buried in the trenches. It didn't bear thinking about. She could catch trench fever, sink into the muddy depth of it and drown. A horrific prospect.

Time passed. She'd no idea how long she'd lain there, drifting in and out of sleep. A gust of wind woke her. Dusk was falling with night almost upon them. Then with great relief, Cecily saw two sentries arrive and watched in awe as they began to lift Wilhelm Ackermann and his battered wheelchair out of the trench.

He raised a hand to salute her. '*Du bist ein wunderschönes junges Fräulein, charmant und unschuldig. Danke für Deine Hilfe.*'

The sentry laughed. 'He says you're a lovely young woman, charming and innocent, and thanks you for your help.'

'Thank goodness you've been saved,' she told him, wincing with relief as her foot was finally free. 'I was trapped beneath the wheelchair and I can't climb out of here either,' she said wearily, as they successfully dragged him up over the ridge.

'We'll be back soon,' they called. There was something about the way they were carrying this PoW away that troubled her. Were they taking him to some place out of revenge for the bomb attack by his German comrades? Don't believe such a thing, she warned herself. They were evacuating patients as a priority, which was surely the right thing to do.

Realising that her legs had slipped deeper into the mud, the fear of sinking caused her to struggle to pull them out. Pain again shot through her and she cried out in agony. Didn't soldiers sometimes get trapped like this and die as a consequence? The ridge was too high for her to climb out. Surely there must be a place of access somewhere along the line. Desperately attempting to cope with the anguish she was suffering, she pulled herself up with her arms and began to crawl on her belly through the mud, keeping an eye out for the duckboards that marked the way to safety. Cecily felt the urge not only to escape this bloody trench but also to find her sister, mother and friends. She could hear cries of injured men, and small whimpering sounds as she strove to keep calm in a blackness so profound it pressed upon her like a suffocating mask. Presumably the sentries were busy helping people in a worse situation or else could no longer find her.

'Help!' she cried, hoping this might alert them. It was then that she heard a strong voice call to her.

'Is that you, girl? Where are you?'

Looking up, to her delight, she saw the French Canadian rise out of the mist like a ghost, one arm outstretched as he searched the empty blackness.

'I'm here, still trapped in this bloody trench.'

As he stumbled towards her, once again Cecily struggled to drag herself out of the stinking mud. The pair of them were suddenly lit by the light from another exploding shell. It felt almost as if she was on stage in some macabre dance as he wrapped his one good arm around her, locked in the horror of a battery of explosions.

Eventually the sentries did return and pulled her up out of the six-foot deep trench. Scrambling up to join her, he wiped a layer of mud from her cheeks, grinned and shook her hand. 'I'm Louis Casey. Pleased to meet you, ma'am.'

'Cecily Hanson,' she said, meeting his glittering gaze with relief and warm appreciation. 'Thank you so much for helping to save me again.'

'My pleasure, honey.'

'I do hope you haven't damaged your shoulder even more.'

'I'm pretty fit, alive and well, so I'm sure it'll be fixed soon.'

They did seem to be caught up in an entanglement of barbed wire, but the stretcher-bearers rushed over to place him on a stretcher. Louis gave her hand a quick squeeze before they carried him away. 'If I don't see you again, thanks for accepting I'm not the enemy.'

'You certainly aren't. Sorry I assumed you were. I'll call in to see you soon. Chin up,' she said, aware of how he'd endured considerable trauma yet still looked kind and friendly.

Cecily too was lifted free of the wire and carried away on a stretcher to the medical hut where she was put in a queue, waiting to have her leg and foot checked. She heard that a number of French and English soldiers, as well as German prisoners, had been killed or badly injured. She kept anxiously asking where her sister and mother were, the nurse attending to her promising to send this enquiry out. How she wished she was fit enough to go searching for them herself. The fear of losing her beloved family, as she'd lost Ewan, was far too dreadful to contemplate.

Later, to her huge relief they came rushing in, each of them enveloping her in a warm hug of love and happiness. 'Oh, thank God you're alive and well,' Cecily said, tears of relief filling her eyes. 'How fortunate we are to have survived this bombing.'

'I'm still around thanks to Johnny,' Queenie said. 'He came rushing to grab me and dragged me away from the falling bombs.' She went on to say how two of the men whose tent he shared were not so lucky. 'They both got hit and killed as they ran for it.'

'So did Corporal Lewis,' Merryn said.

'Oh no, he was such a lovely, friendly man.' Cecily felt rife with dismay at this news. 'What happened to him?'

'He was in the hut that was being used as a ward when the bomb hit,' Lena said, coming to join them. 'Like me, he saved quite a lot of patients and tragically didn't get out in time, poor fellow. I managed to help some escape but for those who were strapped to their bed in some way, it was far too difficult. Such is reality.'

'I feel utterly heartbroken at his loss,' Cecily groaned. 'Lewis will be sorely missed. He was a most brave young man. He was always happy to drive us everywhere, as well as help prepare the stage and props and sort out all the many military rules. He was so kind and accommodating.'

'Indeed he was,' Lena said. 'He had two brothers, the three of them having gone through many campaigns together, including the nightmare here at Ypres at the start of the war. One was lost at Gallipoli in December 1915. Then his younger brother was killed in the Battle of the Somme the following year. Sadly, now his beloved parents have lost him too.'

'Oh no, to lose all three of your sons is dreadful. My heart goes out to them,' Cecily quietly said, intensely aware of the grief they would suffer.

'Mine too,' Merryn murmured, her face pale with fear and agony.

'Enough of this sad conversation, girls. We are in sore need of rest and a good sleep,' Queenie said, with a yawn.

Lena smiled. 'I'm sure you are. I just took this short break from the ward to check that you were all safe. See you tomorrow, ladies.'

'We certainly will,' Merryn agreed and saying goodnight, gave her sister a loving kiss and went off with her mother back to their tent. Cecily settled in the hospital bed and made a quiet prayer of thanks.

∽

It took over a week before Cecily felt able to walk. Her foot was not broken but simply sprained, as Queenie had once suffered on stage. Once she was well enough, she went to the hospital in search of Louis Casey, the French Canadian. Unable to find him anywhere, she spotted Lena who told her that he'd been released, his dislocated shoulder having been fixed.

'Thank goodness for that. He's a most resilient man who did help to save me, for which I thanked him.'

'It's so good to see you're looking better, Cecily.'

'I'm largely recovered, thank you. I have washed myself down, so I don't stink any more,' Cecily remarked firmly, meeting her anxious gaze with a grin.

Lena laughed. 'I wouldn't notice as I'm far too used to the dreadful stench of patients. If you feel in need of a longer break, don't feel compelled to put on a show any time soon.'

'We intend to start rehearsing today. And having acquired a new permit, we'll keep on working until this war is over, assuming we continue to be granted the necessary local passes. Unless that bully of a Major General succeeds in tossing us out.'

'He's sadly no longer with us, having been killed in that recent attack.'

'Oh no, that's dreadful!' Cecily was instantly filled with guilt over the insulting remark she'd made about him.

'He was a long-serving professional soldier for whom some Tommies showed great respect. Others couldn't stand him as he would shout loudly at them on parade and give them a dressing down, either because he did not approve of their appearance or they hadn't done what he'd ordered them to do. A very strict and domineering man.'

'He was indeed but I'm so sorry to hear of his death. How I hate this war and all the losses and tragedy it has created. It's utterly terrifying.'

She next went to check how Wilhelm Ackermann was. He was lying in bed looking morose, his leg hooked up. 'Are you feeling any better?' she asked, attempting to keep a cool distance from him. He smiled, looking pleased to see her, saying how much better he felt, although he was still in pain.

'Thankfully, I too am on the mend, and not as badly damaged as I expected.'

'Good! I accept that asking you to save me in my wheelchair didn't help. We've both been lucky, Miss Hanson. My leg is not infected or suffering from gangrene, so with luck will not be amputated.'

This comment reminded her of Boyd and how he had lost part of his leg while being spared those nasty infections. 'At least you are alive so will fully recover.'

'Once I get out of here, I'll be transferred to an internment camp. I'm not looking forward to that, being a *Generalleutnant*.'

Goodness, he was presumably a Lieutenant General, a most official man. What a dreadful thought that was. However anxious she was to carry out her promise to act as a so-called spy, Cecily did feel a wave of sympathy for him. He was an attractive man, but she had no wish to allow things to develop to a dangerous level between them. Nevertheless, the urge to take the opportunity to interrogate him pummelled within her as she strove to remember the training requirements she was required to apply. What more could she ask, having gained no information from him so far? She said the first thing that came into her head. 'Do you know where the nearest railway station is and where the trains travel to?'

He blinked at her in surprise. 'Why ask me that? Are you planning to leave?'

This had merely been an effort to gain some useful information from him, as instructed. He must surely know a good deal about the area his fellow Germans were attempting to take over. But she'd obviously asked a completely stupid question. 'Oh no, I simply wished to show an interest in how you came to be here. Our small concert party will be going on tour again soon and we cannot assume to always be provided with free transport.'

'I believe the military is in charge of travelling, so you surely won't go on tour by train,' he said, smiling at her with quizzical curiosity.

Nerves pounded within Cecily, keenly aware that she should have asked him something far more important, like where the nearest airfield was, whereabouts in Germany he lived, how long he'd been in the Army and what he felt he was fighting for. And she should also investigate what the enemy's plan was to be and when they were likely to invade England; whether he'd been engaged in this latest attack and if he knew of any future raids. The ability to find the courage to make such an enquiry without revealing she was a spy would not be easy and could put herself at risk. Deciding what and how to ask him was extremely difficult, her knowledge of the war and the enemy being almost nil.

'No one revels in being a prisoner of war,' she said with a faint smile and a sympathetic bat of her eyelashes, as instructed by Lieutenant Trevain. He'd clearly stated that appearing friendly or a little incompetent could be an effective way for women to grow close to a prisoner.

That hadn't worked for her. She'd had great success supporting the suffragists, but now Cecily felt she was making a complete mess of this alleged role.

He looked up at her with a bland expression in his dark eyes. 'Thank you for rescuing me. Otherwise I could have been blown to smithereens, so will make no complaints,' he wryly remarked, meeting her charming gaze with gratitude in his.

Cecily felt quite touched by this remark and not wishing to be viewed as a spy or remind him of what they'd endured on the day they were bombed, she went on to speak of where they'd performed lately and how they were increasingly busy, lightening her tone of voice even more.

He seemed quite interested in this, asking what she sang and which play they'd performed. 'It is amazing that you agreed to involve yourself in a concert party so close to the Front.'

'I love singing if not the dangers and travelling involved,' she said, having no wish to mention why she was doing her bit in the war. 'I used to work on the trams before coming to France. What did you do before this dratted war?'

'I was a language teacher, so can speak English.'

'That's interesting. I do wish I were good at languages but I'm not at all. I expect you miss your family, as we all do during this war, assuming that you have one and are perhaps married.'

'I've not yet found myself a wife, having spent much of my late twenties stuck in this dratted war, as you call it, but I'm still hoping to find one,' he said, a glimmer of interest in his eyes as they slid over her.

'Oh, I'm sure that you will.' Cecily felt a confusion of appreciation and anxiety, as she blushed at this response from him.

'I mostly miss my mother who is old, sick and now a widow, my father having died. I feel I should be there to protect and care for her.' A harsh bitterness came in his voice that seemed to indicate he was not at all passionate about fighting.

'How sad. I lost my father too.'

'I'm sorry to hear that.' Heaving a sigh, he once more thanked her for rescuing him. 'And as my mother is most anxious for me to remain safe, you could always rescue me again to spare me from being locked up. I could then return home to her.'

Cecily laughed and told him that would not be possible. He did seem to be quite a friendly man, even if he was the enemy. Why would she not trust him? But this had not been an easy conversation, probably because of the rummage of nerves and panic within her over how she should be acting as a so-called spy. She'd asked him entirely the wrong questions. 'Now I must go and attend our morning rehearsal,' she said, and quickly marched away, shivering a little with trepidation over this requirement of her that she felt incapable of achieving.

FIFTEEN

ONE MORNING after a good night's sleep, Cecily rose early and quickly dressed, eager to take breakfast then start preparing for their next rehearsal and performance. Lena came over to join the sisters when she saw them tucking into bread and dripping in the Mess, which had thankfully not been bombed. 'Morning, I have some good news. You might be interested to learn that the Lieutenant Colonel now in charge has agreed to hold a dance in order to cheer everyone up. The military does like to hold one every now and then for the sake of morale, particularly following such an attack.'

'Oh, what fun,' Cecily said with a grin.

'I could play some music for it,' Merryn offered.

'That would be most generous of you. They do have a phonograph to provide most of the music. I'm sure they'd appreciate some tunes played on your accordion too. Don't offer to do too many though. They are desperately short of women to dance with, apart from a few nurses. Most of the Tommies haven't danced with a woman in years and accept they have no choice but to dance with each other,' she said, giving a little chuckle. 'So you need to happily accommodate them there too.'

Merryn laughed. 'At least we're available to do our bit.' Excited by this news, she offered to go through the costumes she'd made and choose some that were suitably glamorous.

'You do that, lovey,' Cecily agreed. 'Please can I wear that pink silk gown? It always makes me feel sensational.'

'We all need to look dressy, as we do when we're on stage. I'll find one for you too, Lena.'

'Ooh, that would be wonderful. Now I must return to the hospital, having dealt with the patients stuck here in tents.'

As Merryn trotted off happily, Cecily offered to accompany Lena. 'I feel in need of some exercise, having been clogged up in our tent for so long and still a bit slow on my aching feet.'

They walked together across the bustling camp towards the line of tents where more wounded were now accommodated, those who would eventually be sent to a hospital when someone was able to take them, or else to a detention centre.

'It was brave of you to save that German prisoner. I did see you talking to him earlier and I suspect he took a shine to you, appreciating how pretty you are. He was evidently willing to trust you.'

Cecily wrinkled her nose, still wondering if she should trust him. She had attempted to say how sorry she was for all prisoners in the war and what they were suffering, no matter what their nationality. 'He called for my help, so I did what I could for him.'

'Good for you. Not just soldiers but civilians too have been captured, all trapped in this hellish world. Many of our boys have been despatched to Germany and gone missing for years. Women who work as prostitutes are often locked away for a different reason,' she scathingly remarked.

'Goodness, is there an internment camp near here?' Cecily quietly asked.

Lena nodded. 'Many of our soldiers are being held prisoner in parts of the country, having been taken over by the Germans. Prisoners who are considered a problem or keep attempting to escape are often moved around. The worst camps are those across the border in Germany, particularly those known as a *Strafenlager*, where prisoners are sent in an attempt to discourage the Allies from whatever their next plan is. Wherever our men are imprisoned, they suffer from unsanitary conditions, are frequently beaten and very poorly fed, which results in an increasingly high death rate.'

'Surely that's entirely wrong?'

'It is indeed. Many are forced to work for the German army at or near the Front, despite the danger of shellfire, and long hours spent on railways, roads, agriculture and other tasks such as acting as a stretcher-bearer. Now the French treat German prisoners with equal contempt. They view it as a way of taking reprisals, each blaming the other for treating PoWs in an incorrect manner. Thankfully, the Red Cross is allowed to visit these camps to take in charity parcels of food, as well as check on the injured.'

'That's interesting, and are you a member, Lena?'

'I am. We nurses are allowed to occasionally call in to help care for prisoners' injuries and give whatever support they need,' she firmly stated.

'Are you saying you help them to escape?'

Lena glanced around, as if making sure there was no one to hear, then met Cecily's curious gaze with a calm rigidity in her own. 'We offer the odd tip or advice. Telling them where they could safely go were they ever to manage that. The effect of such treatment in these camps can destroy their lives or give them dreadful mental problems, which naturally tempts them to escape. If they manage to do that, they can receive assistance from a quite well-to-do nurse in Brussels, this country being largely under German control. I'm not allowed to state her name but being a brave English woman and a suffragette, she has saved hundreds of PoWs' lives already by helping to smuggle them out to a neutral country like the Netherlands or else back to England. She has a good team of supporters and I help too, whenever possible.'

Cecily felt a flicker of interest and concern, recalling how Lieutenant Trevain, back in Plymouth, had told her of a dancer with the stage name Mata Hari, caught spying for the Germans. Being Dutch, she'd freely crossed borders and in 1916 when arrested and interrogated in London had claimed she worked for French intelligence. Aware of how she'd transmitted radio messages to the Germans in Madrid, she was accused of being one of their spies. In October 1917, she'd been executed by firing squad. The danger of that happening to her or Lena brought a black pit of fear into her stomach. 'What a valiant woman she must be, and you too. That work can't be easy.'

'It certainly isn't. The team I'm involved with are determined to do their best to rescue men badly in need of assistance, often having been imprisoned for two years or more. If a wounded or mentally distressed PoW is left wandering in a foreign land alone, it can result in him being recaptured or else the Army might assume he's a deserter, which could have equally disastrous consequences. They each need to be taken to a hideaway then dispatched somewhere safe. Even when we find them they can't stay here, as Army Headquarters interrogate these men about what they've been through at the internment camp, what information they can offer about the enemy and other PoWs, before sending them back to the Front.'

Cecily turned this information over in her head, silent for some minutes, saying nothing of what Lieutenant Trevain had required of her, then quietly said, 'I'm a member of the suffragettes, as is that Brussels lady you spoke of. I wonder if I could help?'

'What are you suggesting?' Lena's face lit with a mixture of hope and disbelief.

'I've been trying for some time to decide if there's anything more I can do for these men, so far without success. This could be the answer. As you know, we visit various bases so were there to be someone seeking escape, they could come with us to act as a prompt or help with the props, particularly now that we've lost Corporal Lewis. They would need to be suitably attired and not look like a prisoner. Then at some point, whenever appropriate, I could drop the escapee off wherever he needed to go. I assume there are safe houses or bases available when you rescue someone?'

'There are indeed, but they do need help to get there.' Lena was silent for some moments as she thought this through, then gave a small smile. 'Actually, that's quite a good idea. It might work. The question is, are you willing to take the risk?'

Meeting her friend's wide-eyed gaze, Cecily nodded. 'I am. How can politicians call this a war to end all wars? It's a nightmare and our prisoners must be badly in need of assistance, something I'm more than willing to give.'

'Excellent! Thank you so much for your offer, which I happily accept,' Lena said, shaking her hand.

∾

The dance was held at a Nissen hut that had thankfully not been damaged. It was packed with men, most of them happily dancing with each other. Cecily, Lena and Queenie never once found themselves short of an invitation to dance, while Merryn stood on a small platform happily playing her accordion. Cecily was hoping to take a little rest when a voice whispered in her ear.

'May I have the pleasure of this dance?'

Turning, she found Louis Casey, the French Canadian, facing her. He was smartly dressed in a khaki uniform with two breast pockets, a leather belt, peaked cap and knee-high boots. His ragged ash-brown hair was now neatly washed and clipped, his velvet brown eyes twinkling at her from beneath thick eyelashes. He looked so much healthier and more handsome than the last time she'd seen him when those shells had struck. 'Delighted to see that you've fully recovered and are no longer in the hospital ward,' she said, a flare of attraction lighting within her.

'The doc fixed my shoulder so here I am, fit and well.'

Taking her hand, he led her on to the dance floor. The feeling of his arm coming around her and his cheek close to hers filled her with an unexpected surge of happiness, almost as though she belonged in this man's embrace. The pressure of his strong fit body and the warmth of his legs excited her, a sensation she had not experienced for some time. She remembered how Ewan had loved to dance with her, claiming he welcomed any opportunity to hold her close. Now it was time for her to move forward and not dwell too much upon his death, only the happy experience of their life together.

'Are you married?' Louis asked.

She smiled and shook her head. 'When I was young, I did once dream of being courted by an Italian Count or a Prince of the Realm, as Mama assured me could well happen. It was a dream that quickly vanished once I met Ewan, the love of my life. We became engaged, then I tragically lost him in this blasted war, which is the reason I decided to come and do my bit for the other Tommies.'

'Ah, I'm so sorry to hear that. I've lost many dear friends too. You're sweet and lovely and I like you a lot. In fact, I'm totally captivated by you and hugely impressed at your talent. Would you care to marry me?'

Cecily laughed out loud. 'You hardly know me. I'm not at all obsessed with marriage, unlike Mama and my sister, both of whom believe a woman should find herself a husband and be a good wife and mother. It is no longer on my list, although I'm very aware that some men are in desperate search of a wife, and can be rather demanding.'

Holding her close, he pressed his cheek against hers, whispering in her ear, 'I assure you I am not a controlling vampire. My intentions are entirely honourable. I'd love to kiss you. Having you in my arms makes my heart pound and my head spin. Do I by any chance have that effect upon you too?'

It was some moments before Cecily felt able to respond, equally captivated by dancing with this man. She tactfully chose not to answer this question. 'How long have you been in this war?' she blithely asked, pulling back her head to create a little more distance between them.

He gave a heavy sigh. 'From the start. I joined with my best pals and we went through many campaigns together, including the nightmare of the Somme. I lost several of them, yet I survived against all the odds. Touch wood, fingers crossed, I'll continue to do so.'

'It can't be easy fighting and constantly being involved in battles,' she said, filled with sympathy.

'I'd just turned twenty-one when it started and eagerly joined up as my father had been in the Boer War. I wished to become a hero just like him. That's not easy to achieve but I do my best. Most of the time we've no idea what's happening in the next town, let alone in the rest of the country. When we first arrived, we were marched up a hill to the camp, which was a scrubby mess. The next morning, we were given a medical and a short haircut. Then over the following days, we went through endless instructions, doing simulated attacks over barbed wire and trenches, learning how to throw hand grenades, use bayonets and other ammunition. After that, we were moved on to do our bit in the trenches and faced a barrage of shellfire.' He fell silent, tears welling in his eyes as he obviously recalled the loss of his pals.

'We won't go into the grim reality. You're a brave man.' The dance ended at this point and she gave him a twinkling little smile. 'I'll forgive you all the nonsense questions you've asked of me and wish you well. I hope you get safely through this dratted war, as I call it.'

'*Merci.*' To her surprise, he continued to hold her close in his arms and when the music started playing again, continued to dance with her. 'The entertainment you are providing us here is also brave and the reason you're treated with great respect. We chaps feel in desperate need of your concerts to lighten our gloom and raise our morale.'

'We greatly appreciate our audience who are always wonderfully welcoming. I must admit that when I am singing or playing a part on stage, I feel totally different, not at all myself, just a make-believe person having fun. Such a treat. In reality, I'm a bit of a tomboy and, yes, extremely independent.'

'I am too. One has to look after oneself with great diligence in this war.'

Not wishing to relate the horrors they'd suffered, Cecily went on to tell a funny story about the difficulty of finding fruit to eat in France and how once she'd found an orchard and managed to strike a deal with the farmer by swapping a tin of bully beef for a couple of apples. 'Scrumptious,' she said with a chuckle.

It was then that their second dance ended, and she next found herself dancing with Johnny. He was nowhere near as exciting or as interesting as Louis Casey.

❧

At the far end of the room, Merryn stood watching as she played her accordion, feeling a wave of envy over how her sister was never short of invitations, not only from these lonely soldiers, that French-Canadian fellow, but now Johnny. He appeared totally engrossed in her. Did Cecily find him appealing too? Merryn had often seen them huddled in corners together, supposedly discussing the next production. She'd found it distressing not to be included in such conversations. Was Johnny's main task in life simply to make himself important to her family since he apparently had suffered a poor upbringing himself? Or did he just like to flirt? He seemed perfectly content to amble on in this live-for-the-moment fashion. In one respect, Merryn adored that trait in him, as it made him so delightfully hedonistic.

One evening after a performance, he'd surprisingly begged for her assistance to improve his use of the cymbals, then later to help him learn his lines for the play extract in order to halt Cecily's criticism of him. Merryn had happily given him her full support whenever he needed it, as they were growing quite close. Now she'd begun to dream of a more intense relationship between them, wondering how she might achieve that seemingly impossible goal. Was it her that Johnny liked most or Cecily?

To her delight, once she stepped down from playing her accordion, with the man playing the phonograph taking over, Johnny came to ask her to dance. She felt utterly contrite, quickly banishing her jealousy. 'I thought you'd lost interest in me by dancing with my sister.'

'Why would I when you look so beautiful in that gorgeous gown?'

'I promise to be more trusting,' Merryn said, beguiling him with a smile. 'At least, I hope I will. I've grown up and don't throw tantrums or go off into sulks any more.'

'I'm glad to hear that. So, if I were ever to apologise for letting you down, you'd forgive me, would you?'

Quickly glancing around to make sure no one was watching, she reached up to touch his lips, his brow and cheeks with her fingers. 'Of course I would. Oh, do stop your teasing, I can't bear to wait another moment for you to kiss me.'

'Let's step outside,' he whispered in her ear.

Collapsing into a fit of giggles, they escaped the Nissen hut to walk quickly away over the duckboards, carefully avoiding the mud and shell holes. Johnny led her to the pillbox, one that had been built of concrete by the Germans when they were in control of this district. 'Some chaps hid here to protect themselves from that dreadful shelling. It proved to be quite safe, although one shell did hit the roof. They sensibly chose not to venture out until silence descended and the bombing eventually stopped, thanks to the change in weather. It's empty now that all the Tommies are at the dance.'

Grinning, he took her in his arms and kissed her with passion. His earlier kisses had always delighted Merryn, but were nowhere near as enticing as the positive storm of the ones he was giving her now.

'I can sense how much you want me,' he murmured. 'Come to my bed tonight and I will kiss you some more. Yes?'

'*No*! Absolutely not.' Merryn giggled, wishing to show that she wasn't cross with him as she melted in his arms.

'Then let me make love to you here,' he murmured, sliding the straps from her low-necked gown. Brushing the bare skin of her breasts, he pulled her down and settled himself quickly upon her. Merryn warned herself to put a stop to this outrageous act as her heart flamed and her body refused to obey. Longing to be a part of him, she arched herself instinctively, revelling in ecstasy as he located a rosy nipple, rubbing it gently between his finger and thumb. She was consumed by desire for more kisses, willing to do whatever he demanded, a sensation she really had no wish to relinquish.

The weight and scent of him was so overpowering, Merryn felt all her senses slip out of control. She could see the glint of his teeth as he smiled, then he traced the outline of her mouth with his tongue. It was already flushed a rosy pink from all the kisses she'd previously received. Wanting more, she responded with a whimper of desire. It felt glorious to feel loved, free and safe. Johnny was a wonderful young man, one Merryn was convinced would never let her down. It was then that she felt his hand pull up her skirt to stroke her legs. She gasped as he touched her private parts. Seconds later, he was inside her, the rhythmic pounding of his movement completely enveloped her and she gladly gave herself to him.

Afterwards, she lay panting for breath in his arms, filled with a confusion of ecstasy and a strange sense of shame. It occurred to her that she might come to regret what she'd allowed him to do. Yet why should she when she loved him so much? And he must surely love her too. He'd disposed of her virginity but his lovemaking had been so wonderfully ecstatic, she had no wish to give him up. Possibly she should curb further attempts by him, in case there were unwelcome consequences. This was a vow Merryn fervently made while doubting her strength to succeed in resisting him. Why could they not be true and ardent lovers? And could she explain to him why she needed to avoid temptation and protect herself? Probably not. 'Are you going to apologise for taking me?' she murmured.

He gave a little snigger of laughter. 'Why would I, when you're so delicious I could eat you all up?'

'Mama expects me to be respectable and proper. She can be very dictatorial about what sort of young man I'm allowed to go out with, sending them packing if they're not high-class and rich.'

'I confess I'm just a poor northern lad. She's the one who's rich, so why would it matter? Just keep quiet and don't tell her about us,' he instructed her as he kissed her again.

'Oh, I do so agree. How close we are. Queenie believes it's my sister that you're obsessed with,' she said, with a giggle. 'We know that is not the case. When did you realise you cared so much for me?' she asked, seeking confirmation of his feelings so that she could swathe herself in reassurance for this glorious event.

'Is that an essential question?' he parried, seeming to imply it was entirely inappropriate of her to ask. 'Didn't you eagerly fall for me?'

'Oh yes, when I first met you at the Palace Theatre. Why would I not? And now we are one.'

'You could say that. I always welcome a lovely woman to do what I demand.'

His arms tightened about her and Merryn sighed with contentment. His kisses were increasingly demanding – oh, but why would she not agree to do whatever he wanted of her? Gently pushing him away to study his face more seriously, her cheeks glowed with excitement. 'You do appreciate, Johnny, that you've robbed me of my virginity.'

'I assume that to be the case.'

'Was it your first time too?'

He gave a snort of laughter. 'I'm thirty years old – how could that be possible?'

A man obviously needed to be expert at lovemaking, she told herself and supposed it was naïve of her to believe otherwise. In view of what they had to endure in this war, why would they not relish whatever happiness they could find together? Locked in his embrace, the possibility of enduring what her sister had suffered came to Merryn in a startling panic. Johnny would surely survive any future attacks or barrages of explosion, as had she in the canteen. That had proved to be the most terrifying moment in her life, a fear still jerking within her every time she heard the roar of a gun or a blast of shrapnel fire. Were the worst to happen and she lost Johnny, at least she could live with the memory of their love.

SIXTEEN

CECILY SAT under the tarpaulin watching as Queenie sang to the audience, looking much calmer than on occasions in the past when she was drunk. She seemed to be on the road to recovery, which was something of a relief and it seemed right to allow her to sing again, which might well recover their relationship. Johnny and Merryn were accompanying her, which was also a good thing, bearing in mind this new plan Cecily was about to become involved in. When the performance ended and Queenie came over, beaming with satisfaction, she gave her a warm hug. 'Well done, Mama. You look as if you're back in your star days.'

'You still refuse to call me by my real name, silly girl. I do at least thank you for believing in me at last. But I have no wish to work too hard, preferring only the odd performance.'

'That makes sense.' Waving the latest pass she'd been granted, Cecily happily made an announcement. 'We are to be allowed to do a performance for a local base hospital. Johnny, you'll not be required to drive us there, as you have enough to do. We've been offered the support of a young soldier who is due for some leave, having suffered from various wounds. He's slowly recovering and before he goes home, he's willing to help backstage with props since we've lost Corporal Lewis. He claims to know a good deal about the theatre and actually seems to be upper class like you, Mama, so that could be the reason.'

'Some of us are born with class and cleverness running through our veins,' Queenie stoutly remarked.

'An interesting thought,' Cecily said with a smile. She'd done her best to give a reason for this soldier joining them, without revealing he was an escapee, currently hidden away in a secret bolthole by Lena. They would be sure to object to the risk she was prepared to take by helping these men.

When Cecily met up with him the following morning, she was relieved to see that he was no longer dressed as a prisoner but as a soldier on duty. He appeared scrawny and pale with a bandage round his forehead covering one eye, the other narrow and twitching with a troubled gaze. Many soldiers had such wounds and were fairly gaunt, having suffered badly from the effects of war. He introduced himself as Sergeant Allenby, clicking his heels and giving a smart salute.

Cecily gratefully shook his hand. 'Good to meet you, sir, and thank you for your support.'

His expression changed to one of confusion. 'I thought you were the one offering *me* support.'

'She certainly is, only it must appear to be the other way round,' Lena whispered. 'You'll be working for this concert party today as dear Corporal Lewis used to. Then you'll quietly depart.'

'Rightio,' he said with a smile, his dark eye lightening a little. 'At your service, ma'am. No need for you to call me sir.'

'What a fine young man you are,' Queenie said, coming over to reward him with one of her enchanting smiles. 'If a little weary-looking and injured. I assume that is the reason you'll soon be going off on leave?'

'For a much-needed few days to recover,' he said, with a polite nod.

'Oh my, you sound like a Londoner?' she cried, clapping her hands in delight. 'Do tell me where you come from and more about yourself. What did you do for a living before the war, and are you married?'

Cecily stepped hastily forward, all too aware of how her mother adored young men. 'Mama, please stop your chatter. This sergeant is allowed some privacy, as are you. Now, it's time for us to leave.'

Sergeant Allenby drove them in the battered old wagon, their equipment safely stowed in the back. It was expected to be an easy journey as this base hospital was quite close to the centre of Ypres. However, they were halted to be checked by a French sentry who took some time examining their passports, passes and permits, appearing entirely unconvinced over their identity. Cecily began to sing 'It's a Long Way to Tipperary', anxious to prove they really were here to entertain the troops.

'They've given any number of wonderful concerts,' Sergeant Allenby told him in perfect French.

With a smirk of amusement and a little clap when she'd finished her song, the sentry finally allowed them through the barrier into town.

'Thank heaven for your help,' Cecily murmured.

The matinee and evening show went according to plan, beginning as usual with Cecily singing the Tommies' favourite songs, followed by *Mother Of Pearl*, a one-act play by Gertrude Jennings. Queenie's expressions and gestures were always a delight to the audience, this one including French and British soldiers who had self-inflicted wounds, which they'd hoped would send them home, plus a few German prisoners of war.

'You're still a star in many ways. Now you can sing to them.' Considering she was stone-cold sober, constantly smiling and much less bad-tempered, Queenie looked even more lovely than usual. Her eyebrows were clipped to pencil thinness, delicately arched over her soft blue eyes. The sight of her always made Cecily feel plain and practical. She'd spent hours the previous day closeted with Merryn trying on and altering some of the costumes her sister had made. But right now, she was simply delighted to see her mother doing well.

'Thanks to Johnny Boy's help,' Queenie said, giving the young man a light kiss on each cheek. 'He's spent hours making sure I sing in tune.'

Cecily frowned at this exchange. Glancing across at her sister, she noticed how Merryn was carefully avoiding his gaze. Could that be because she'd fallen out with him or was it an attempt to protect a relationship developing between them? Cecily could well understand if that was the case. Turning to Queenie, she remarked firmly, 'It's Sergeant Allenby we should thank for acting as prompt, minding our props, as well as helping with the sentry checks.'

'He too is a kind young man. We were most fortunate to have you help us, dear boy, though we didn't require too much work from you,' Queenie said, and treated him to a gentle kiss on his bruised cheek. He chuckled with pleasure.

'The show is over, and we can all go off to bed,' Cecily said. 'I'll do any necessary tidying tomorrow.'

She smiled as Queenie and Merryn lay down on their camp beds. Badly in need of rest herself, Cecily fervently washed the stage make-up off her face with cold water to liven herself up, then avoiding her own bed desperately waited for them to fall asleep. It took some time, which left her somewhat stressed, but once she heard their breathing turn slow and regular, she quickly went to find Sergeant Allenby who was waiting for her by the wagon.

Not for a moment did she believe this to be his real name. Nor would she ever ask him what it truly was. Her only wish was to get him to safety. 'It's my turn to drive,' she told him with a smile, 'and having carefully examined the sketch map Lena gave me, I can but hope we don't get lost.'

'Right. We need to stay well clear of the main road to avoid meeting up with that sentry again,' he warned.

'The route this time will take us through this forest, not the town.'

'Excellent. Were we to get stopped by anyone, I do have a weapon,' he firmly stated.

They drove along a straight path through the woodland, making sure there were no lights showing on the wagon, which made the journey more difficult. Cecily could feel her heart thumping, a consequence of fear and excitement.

Possibly sensing her tension, he quietly remarked, 'By the way, my name's Billy, and I greatly appreciate your help to save my life, Miss Hanson. I was frequently tortured and starved at that German internment camp, then managed to escape when we were working on the railway line. You're very brave to be helping me. Do take care you never end up in such a place.'

She turned her head to meet his gaze with a glimmer of apprehension, not wishing to consider such a possibility. 'I'm Cecily. Pleased to help you, Billy. Now we need to keep our eyes wide open. We'll be meeting up with a man who will take you on the escape route to the Netherlands.'

Continuing to drive slowly and quietly through the woodland, it was thirty minutes later when a man wearing the expected navy woollen hat stepped out from behind a tree and flashed his torch three times, as Lena had said he would.

'Ah, is this the chap?' Billy whispered.

'It is.' Seconds later, Cecily pulled down the window to hear him say 'Dover', the agreed password to which she responded, with a brief nod. He then instructed her not to hang around but head straight back. 'Don't worry, I will,' she assured him.

Billy gave her hand a grateful squeeze, then, jumping out of the wagon, disappeared into the woods. Cecily quickly turned the wagon around and drove much faster back to the base hospital, anxious to arrive before her mother and sister woke and found her missing. It might have been quicker to go by road but remembering this young soldier's warning about the French sentry, who might still be at the entrance to the town, she took care to go nowhere near it. This journey had proved to be fairly easy so she stuck to the rough trail through the forest, a sense of success and foreboding within her, delighted that she'd helped put Billy on the route to freedom. She constantly glanced around her in fear of the appearance of the enemy, but did hope to help other young men who had escaped as prisoners of war.

꩜

The following morning Merryn confronted Cecily, sorely feeling the urge to learn the truth of where she'd gone the previous evening, a suspicion shaking within her. 'Where did you disappear to last night till well after midnight? Were you having a fling with that fellow?' Not exactly what she assumed, but it was worth a try.

Her sister looked somewhat alarmed by this question. 'Of course not! What a dreadful thing to suggest.'

'You were happy to chat to that German fellow and then saved his life. You danced and chatted with a French-Canadian chap too. You always claim to be fighting for women's rights with no desire to live a traditional domestic life, any more than our mother had. Yet like her, you seem to be cavorting with various men.'

'Oh, for goodness sake, I accept that Mama has always been attracted by young men and enjoys chatting them up, as she did with this sergeant, let alone having flings with some of the Tommies. You should appreciate that I have no desire to do that. Are you accusing me of being a woman of loose morals?'

Merryn felt a lump of panic clog her throat. Had she said entirely the wrong thing by insulting her beloved sister? Was that because she'd personally taken a mad risk with Johnny at the dance and thought Cecily might be guilty of the same mistake with that sergeant? Why would she when she was surely still grieving for the loss of Ewan?

Merryn felt an urge to apologise and pull herself out of this mess. Then a totally unexpected response came forth.

'The point is that Mama had a bad marriage, as we know, which has created problems in her life and mine too in a way. When Queenie was performing, she'd leave us stuck in some dosshouse with our father nowhere around to care for us. Thankfully we did have Nan. Then she'd make a great fuss of you whenever she returned home. Unlike me, you were often looked upon as Mama's favourite child,' Cecily said with a rueful smile.

'So you're jealous of the favours she gave me? Queenie could be very neglectful and demanding of me too, although I'll admit her attitude to you was far worse. Being three years younger, why would she neglect me as much? I adore her and it's sad that we lost our father. I've no idea when he died. Had he already left us when I was still young? I can't remember but surely you can.'

Cecily sighed. 'I too was quite young at the time and it must have been fairly traumatic losing him, so I've probably blocked the pain out of my mind. I would still like to know if he accidentally drowned or killed himself because of problems they were going through. We surely have the right to know? And no, I am not jealous of you being Mama's favourite child. You are my beloved sister. Nor did she ever tell us much about our father, which was entirely wrong of her.'

'If you object to Mama not speaking of what we wished to know, then why are *you* keeping equally quiet about where you went yesterday?'

Her sister gave a sigh. 'If you must know, the fact is I was simply helping Lena deal with the wounded.'

Merryn blinked with surprise and confusion. 'How odd. What exactly were you asked to do for that man?'

'Sergeant Allenby was injured as a result of those explosions and bomb attack and had failed to get permission to go on leave. Eventually, I helped by taking him to the station.'

'So he's deserted?'

'No, no! Lena had finally achieved the necessary permission,' Cecily hastily said.

Filled with a sense of total disbelief, Merryn gazed into Cecily's eyes, which looked as if she was telling a fib. And there was something in her sister's sharp tone of voice that sounded an entire sham. 'How strange that one minute you say that man failed to get permission, then next said he did,' Merryn retorted, now feeling the urge to express what she'd suspected from the start of this conversation. 'I'm convinced that this tale you've told me is a complete lie. So tell me the truth, Cecily. Were you with Johnny in some secret place? That's certainly likely since he appears captivated by your beauty.'

'Oh, for goodness sake, stop being so rude and stupid!' Cecily retorted, her tone of voice jangling. 'You're talking absolute nonsense.'

'You're the one doing that.'

'As I have explained a thousand times, I've no interest at all in love or marriage. I confess that Johnny has attempted to flirt with me, but I paid him no attention. I steadfastly ignore him. I would advise you to be wary of him too.'

A cloud of anger permeated Merryn's head as she glared at her sister. 'How dare you say such a thing! You've always been a bit of a fusspot, constantly fretting about me and giving me orders about what I should or shouldn't do. But who I decide to love is none of your business.'

'You're my sister, why would I not be concerned about you? I just wish to protect you.'

'I can look after myself, thank you. I have a much better opinion of men than you do.'

Looking around, Cecily said, 'Oh dear, Mama is coming over. We'll talk about this later. I've no wish for her to hear us quarrelling.'

Merryn's heart sank as she saw Queenie walking across the field towards them, Johnny at her side.

'Here we are,' Queenie announced, sauntering over, her arm linked with Johnny's. 'Ready to start rehearsing.'

Glowering at her sister, Merryn made no further comment.

❧

A day or two later, Lena asked Cecily to escort another escapee to freedom, which she happily agreed to do. Once their evening performance was over, she walked over to the wagon, and seeing Merryn approach, listened wearily to her sister's insistence that she wished to accompany her, wherever she was supposedly going. 'Being a team, why am I not invited to help?'

'Because I'm happy to take the risk on my own. This is not a subject I can discuss with you any more, lovey.'

'I'm fully aware that these lies are because you refuse to admit who it is you're again going to have sex with, whether it's Johnny or some other fellow.'

Cecily gave a sigh. 'Stop accusing me of such nonsense. I'm doing nothing of the sort.'

'Then where are you going and why?'

'As I said, we can maybe talk about this some other time and I'll do my best to explain, if it's possible to do so.' Cecily felt a bleak pain spark within her, rapidly coming to the conclusion that she should not have told Merryn a vague form of what she was involved in, her sister's head far too wrapped up in some other suspicion.

'You mean you'll come up with another lie?' Merryn tartly asked, and spinning around marched away.

Nevertheless, Cecily could hardly admit that having agreed to act as a spy, she found it easy to help escapees. Climbing into the wagon, she found Lena had deposited the next one onto the back seat, tucked under a blanket.

'Is it just me you're rescuing?' he asked.

'It is indeed. I'll hand you over to a valiantly kind man who'll see you safely along the escape route to the Netherlands.'

She drove through the woodland at moderate speed and let him out the moment she met the man responsible for leading these PoWs. Giving a friendly wave to his rescuer, Cecily turned the wagon around and began to drive back. After just a short distance she heard the sound of someone moving behind her. Fear escalated through her as she drew swiftly to a halt, realising she had no gun or anything at all to protect herself with. Snatching up a spanner that was lying on the floor, she pointed it at the bulky shadowed figure rising up behind her, hoping it might appear to be a gun since it was quite dark. 'Don't come any nearer or I'll shoot you,' she cried.

SEVENTEEN

T O HER astonishment, Cecily realised it was Wilhelm Ackermann. 'What are you doing here?' she cried, staring at him in shock. 'When you came to see me the other week I did make a request for you to rescue me. Now able to walk again, I've been informed that they are planning to deliver me to a detention centre tomorrow. Seeing you come over to this wagon, I managed to slip out of the ward and hide in the back. You were so engaged in an argument with your sister, you didn't notice me and thankfully drove off before the guards realised I'd escaped. I wish you to take me close to a German base, which I know well and is not too far away.'

'Why would I risk doing that?' Cecily asked, desperately striving to calm her jittering nerves. 'If you are suggesting that I have to cross No Man's Land in order to reach German-occupied territory, it could result in my being attacked by soldiers and their machine guns.'

'I'm asking you to take me a little way through this forest and drop me off a safe distance away, for which I'd be most grateful. I appreciate the fact you saved my life and seeing you rescue that other young PoW just now was most interesting. Why would you not do the same for me?'

'I really don't think I can do that. You are not French or British.'

'That is true, but you helped rescue me once, why not again?'

'I made it clear I can definitely not do that!'

Giving a chuckle, he said, 'Start driving. I have no wish for us to quarrel or to hurt you. You must simply do as I say.'

Appalled at the grimness that had now entered his tone of voice, she viewed this remark as a threat. A dark and growing fear pounded in her chest. Pushing forward the gear lever, Cecily pressed down the accelerator and began to slowly drive, feeling she had no alternative but to do as he ordered. He could have a knife in his hand and slit her throat or else strangle her, were she to refuse. Had she been wrong to save this man's life? He was, after all, the enemy and she was clearly of no importance to him, not at all the impression he'd given when she'd visited him in the ward.

'You're driving too slowly, speed up.'

'I'm unsure whether I'm driving in the right direction.'

'You are. We turn left shortly. I'll let you know when.'

To her dismay, they drove much further than she'd expected, turning left and right whenever he instructed her to do so, a route she confusedly attempted to remember. Panic mounting within her, he finally ordered her to stop, saying that once he'd departed, she could head back to camp by continuing along this rough road until she reached the main one a mile or two ahead. 'Then if you turn left, it will lead you directly back to camp.'

Bringing the wagon to a halt, he jumped out of the back. Relieved to see him leave and having made a mental note of the many turns she'd made, with no wish to drive along the main road, she reversed the wagon and began to go back the way she'd come. She drove slowly and quietly, using no lights for some distance. Turning right, it was then that a German guard stepped out in front of her, gun in hand. A second one yanked open her door and with a flash of his gun, ordered her to get out. Horrified, Cecily realised she'd been captured.

∽

Fully expecting to find herself locked in a prison cell, fear escalated through her. Would she be treated as a spy, having asked that German PoW a number of questions, as demanded of her by Lieutenant Trevain? She'd been no good at the task, being far too polite and nervous. Now she could be the one interrogated and moved to an internment camp. Panic and a dark misery settled inside her at such a prospect, making her stomach heave. How did these Tommies, who saw themselves as sitting ducks, cope when they too were captured?

She was placed in the back of the guard's vehicle and taken off in a totally different direction, her wagon being driven by one of them. Eventually, she saw a hut or pillbox ahead and was ordered out of their armoured car. A barrier was opened and she found herself marched over to a much larger building close by. It was there that she saw Wilhelm Ackermann standing in the entrance.

He glanced at her and at the two officers gripping her arms as they marched her into the building, saying not a word to her. Why on earth had she ever come to trust this man? Moments later, she found herself ushered into a room that looked very like an office, where she was directed to a chair facing the desk. The man seated behind it was clearly an officer, dressed in a smart grey uniform with stripes around the collar and cuffs. Smiling, he rose to offer her a cigarette.

'No, thank you, I don't smoke.'

'Would you care for a glass of wine?' He spoke to her in English with a slight German accent, his tone quite mild.

Cecily shook her head, confused by these offers. She'd expected to be treated with contempt, not such generosity.

'Coffee or a cup of tea, being British? I visited England when I was a student and am aware of your preferences.' When she did not respond to this, he told the guard who had brought her in to go and fetch one for her. With a nod, the fellow disappeared. 'I'm the *Oberstleutnant*, Lieutenant Colonel, in charge of this regiment. What is your name and in what part of England do you live?' he asked, again with a smile.

Seeing no reason not to, Cecily calmly responded without actually revealing her full address.

'Ah, I believe Cornwall is a most beautiful land. I, however, was at the university in Oxford where I learned how tolerant the British are. They have suffered many losses, yet seem to be remarkably confident of winning this war. Why is that, do you think?'

Having no wish to answer this question, she lifted her chin, determined to remain strong and gave him a bland little smile. 'How would I know? As you must be aware, I'm not a soldier, merely an entertainer.'

'Is that how you met Wilhelm, an old friend of mine who was captured and imprisoned some weeks ago by the British?'

'Yes, he was injured and received medical care in the hospital before being moved to a Nissen hut to recover. He watched the performances we held in the wards following our concert.'

'And were you so attracted to him that you were happy to entertain him personally, I assume, with your charm?'

Cecily felt her cheeks growing hot, whether with embarrassment or temper was hard to decide. There was an amused glimmer in this man's dark eyes and before she had time to consider a suitable response, he placed himself onto the corner of the desk and beamed down at her. 'You're a very attractive woman so he is obviously captivated by you. Is that the reason you went out for a drive together this evening? Where were you going and why?'

This was certainly not a question she was prepared to answer. 'The reason I am here in France is because I brought a concert party to support our soldiers. I'm a singer. That is how I entertain men, not in any other way. We also do a little acting and recite poetry.'

He startled her by clapping slowly. 'Ah, wonderful. Well then, you can entertain us this evening.'

This was something Lieutenant Trevain had warned her could happen. A tremor of fear skittered within her, not at all finding the courage to claim exhaustion after spending the afternoon and evening performing. She could but hope to be released soon and not imprisoned.

He led her to a small room packed with officers seated in armchairs and settees, the place full of smoke and the smell of alcohol, as they all sat chatting and laughing. They leapt to their feet when the Lieutenant Colonel entered.

'Relax,' he informed them. 'This beautiful entertainer has agreed to sing to us. Dinner is over, but we can offer you some food later. Please do feel free to entertain us.'

Cecily noticed Wilhelm Ackermann seat himself next to this officer and leaning close, whisper something in his ear. She desperately wondered what he might be saying, hopefully not accusing her of being a spy. What a horrific prospect. Not something she wished to contemplate. And what on earth could she sing to these Germans? She was tempted to sing 'When I Send You a Picture of Berlin,' but decided that would not be at all appropriate, the next line being: '*You'll know it's over, "Over There", I'm coming home.*' Could a good performance result in her freedom? A part of her fluttered with doubt.

She chose to sing 'Hello! Hello! Who's Your Lady Friend' and 'Champagne Charlie'. Music hall songs seeming to be much safer and more fun than any of the war songs she'd sung for her fellow British. When they roared with delight and demanded another, she sang 'If I Were the Only Girl in the World'. Some of them joined in and sang along with her. She continued with one or two more safe songs, noticing how Wilhelm Ackermann kept smiling at her throughout her performance, as well as chatting with this officer.

Eventually, leaping to his feet, the *Oberstleutnant* clapped his hands and loudly announced, 'You may all go now. Leave this instant.'

A sigh of relief echoed through her as she quickly turned to the door, anxious to return to the camp. His voice called out, 'Not you, Miss Hanson, just these men.' To her dismay, they all departed, including Ackermann, and Cecily found herself left alone with this officer who was clearly in charge. 'Are you sure you have no wish for a meal?' he asked.

'No, thank you. I'm not hungry.' That was the last thing she wanted, feeling desperate to escape.

'I'll pour you a glass of our exceedingly good German beer.'

She graciously declined. 'May I now leave?'

His gaze slid over her from head to toe, dwelling mainly on her eyes, lips and breasts, which made Cecily shudder with dread. 'You're an extremely entertaining woman and far too attractive for me to allow you to disappear so quickly when we could enjoy a most pleasant evening together.'

Putting his arm firmly around her waist, he led her to the settee and pushing her down upon it, placed a glass of beer in her hand. 'Now drink this, it will help you to relax and do you so much good. It's far too late for you to drive back to wherever you are situated. I can, however, offer you accommodation. Not in a prison cell. You are welcome to share my comfortable bedroom.'

Tremors of alarm and terror flickered through her, as she realised she was in serious danger of being raped. How on earth could she get out of this mess? She remembered her mother's reaction that time she was due on stage and Cecily had offered her a glass of water in order to stop her drinking. Feeling a strong desire to protect herself, she now repeated Queenie's tantrum by tossing the glass of beer over his head. He furiously pushed her down and flinging his weight upon her, pulled up her skirt to rub his hand between her legs. She screamed out loud. The door flew open and Wilhelm stormed in.

'*Was zum Teufel machst du mit meiner guten Freundin?*' he shouted.

The officer laughed. '*Ich mache mit ihr genau das, was ich möchte.* I am doing exactly as I please with her. Are you a spy, girl? If so, you are not fit to be a friend of his.'

'I'm certainly not either of those.'

'She is a noble and generous woman who saved my life and now rescued me. Not someone you should be assaulting.'

Their conversation swiftly reverted to a furious row in German. Cecily could not understand a word, nor felt any desire to argue in English. Jumping up, she straightened her skirt, struggling to calm the pounding in her chest, deeply aware that Wilhelm Ackermann must have been hovering by the door either to support her or because he fancied her for himself. Taking hold of her arm, he left the Lieutenant Colonel glowering with fury and led her away down the back passage. Would he now demand his own wicked way with her? An equally terrifying prospect. To her relief, he did not take her to his bedroom but led her out into the yard. Saluting the guards, he issued instructions and they quickly opened the barrier to allow them out into the forest. It felt quite cool, leaves blowing down from the trees in the night wind, and relief flooded through her.

'Your wagon is only a short distance away. I made it clear to these guards that you were helping me to escape, not capturing me, so you are free to go. Do you think you can find it all right?'

'I will. Thank you so much for saving me.' Feeling greatly appreciative, the urge to give him a hug was quite strong in her. Thankfully, she managed to control this foolish notion.

He gave her a warm smile. 'Considering how you saved my life, it seemed right for me to save yours. Were it not for this war, our different nationalities would not be an issue. May God preserve you, Cecily. I did, however, give the *Oberstleutnant* the impression that I was taking you to share my bed instead, so I would recommend you hurry back to camp before he notices you have gone. Otherwise, he could well dispatch you off to a concentration camp.' Then giving her a wave, he slipped back through the barrier into the base.

Battling with a spasm of cold fear, Cecily ran as fast as her legs could carry her, jumped into the wagon and quickly started it. She drove the first few yards quite slowly so that no one would hear her departure, then when she felt far enough away, speeded up to head back as fast as she possibly could.

❧

Following the fright of her capture, Cecily at last revealed the truth to Merryn of what she'd done. She explained how she'd felt the need to help British and French prisoners escape, in spite of the risks involved. And how Lena took more risks by visiting them in their internment camps in the German-occupied zone to hint at what she could do for them, working with a network whose names Cecily didn't know. She described her drive into the forest where a rescuer would then smuggle the young escapee along a secret track to the Netherlands, and what a shock it had been to find that German PoW hiding in the back of the wagon. She went on to tell how she was captured and what the officer had done to her.

'Oh, how terrifying,' Merryn said, holding her close when she saw tears flood down her sister's cheeks.

'I was indeed scared stiff when that appalling Lieutenant Colonel almost raped me.' She went on to explain how she'd tossed the beer over him, which brought forth a smile of surprise and approval from Merryn. 'I had become confused over whether or not I could trust Wilhelm Ackermann, but when I screamed out loud, he bravely came to rescue me. He apparently did this in gratitude for my having saved his life. I have to admit I hadn't agreed to rescue him a second time, and chatting with enemies is not something I would ever wish to do again. I will, however, continue to help Lena save our own escapees.'

Merryn gazed at her, utterly astounded, with pride and admiration in her eyes. 'What a darling, brave woman you are.'

Smiling at her beloved sister, Cecily gave her a hug. 'So good that we are friends again. Do believe that I am not at all interested in Johnny. If you and he are becoming quite close, that's your choice. Just be sure it's the right decision. Mama tried to chat him up on one occasion and gave him a little kiss. I didn't mention it at the time and we know how she loves to do that with various young men. Is she aware of this growing relationship between you?'

Merryn shook her head, looking slightly bemused by this information. 'We've carefully kept it a secret because you're fully aware how she demands we choose a man who is rich and high-class. Queenie has been entirely disapproving of every sweetheart you and I have ever had.'

Cecily found herself chuckling. 'She has indeed. Then you're probably right to keep quiet about this relationship, at least until this war is over. I won't say anything either, lovey. I just want you to be certain that you're making the right decision to feel this affection for him.'

'Oh, I most definitely am,' she said, her lips widening into a glorious smile. 'I love him, and I believe that he feels the same about me.'

Gently putting her arms about her sister and having expressed her concern, Cecily ensured that Merryn did not see the flicker of doubt in her eyes. She disliked the way Johnny had attempted to flirt with her, but it might have been a joke. She could but hope that Merryn's belief in him was justified. Her darling sister was young but deserved to find the love she longed for. Facing the possibility of living a lonely life, at times Cecily yearned to find such pleasure for herself while sensing she stoutly resisted the possibility of that ever happening.

EIGHTEEN
SUMMER 1918

OVER THE coming weeks, Cecily helped several more prisoners escape. As a result of sharing her secret information with Merryn, whenever a wounded soldier came to join them for their performance her sister no longer asked his name or why he was here, merely offered him easy jobs to do. Cecily would simply inform her mother and Johnny that these young men liked to help, as it gave them a little respite from whatever trench or battle they were caught up in, or wounds they were suffering from. Not exactly the truth, but they accepted it as reality in this difficult world. If she disappeared for a short while after the show, Cecily would claim to have taken a walk around the camp for the purpose of exercise or to talk to the Tommies in the base hospital.

She always strove never to be late back, being familiar now with the rough track through the woodlands and took great care as it was not as safe a forest as the one near Saint-Omer. One night she accidentally hit a stone and the front tyre of the wagon suffered a puncture.

'Blast!' she cried. It took her some time and effort to replace the tyre, constantly glancing around through the darkness of the trees, fearing the approach of enemy guards or that terrifying *Oberstleutnant*. In view of what she'd suffered, she sensibly kept well away from that area, although the enemy front line was never far away. Once the job was done, she flung the battered tyre into the wagon and drove rapidly back to camp. Parking, she felt surprised and irritated when she saw Johnny come marching over. Damnation, why was he wandering around at this time of night? She then noticed a nurse hurrying away. Had he been chatting or flirting with her?

'Hello,' he said, yanking open the door and teasingly remarking, 'Have you been off somewhere, secretly engaged in an affair with those Tommies who work with us?'

She laughed. 'Don't be ridiculous. I'm just being helpful to them, as they are with us.' Then narrowing her eyes, she said tartly, 'You did once stupidly flirt with me, which was a bad mistake or a stupid joke. Considering you and my sister are apparently growing quite close, I do hope you aren't having an affair with any of these nurses. I did see you with one just now.'

'Indeed I am not. Merryn and I are close and have fun together, although she is a bit exhausted, as we all are right now. If we were properly granted a sum of money for the work we do, I'd take her away for a short break and a rest.'

'We're volunteers, if you remember, so aren't paid anything.'

'Your family has plenty of money. Being rich and selfish, your mother could provide us with some, but I can see that doesn't matter to you. However, I'm not at all well-off,' he coldly remarked.

'At least you are generally smartly dressed, aren't limping these days, and rarely wear those spectacles. I accept you may have used those as a ploy to avoid being recruited, so why would I believe your denial over your possible association with that nurse. Please do be honest and faithful with my sister. That's all I ask. And I'll make sure Merryn has time for a rest.'

As she walked smartly away, Cecily heard him give a grunt of fury. She still couldn't persuade herself to trust this self-obsessed man, let alone his attitude towards women. Her sister clearly adored him, so she could be entirely wrong over her poor opinion of him. And yet he seemed to be making a demand for money from them. What a worry that was. Creeping into her tent, she quickly tucked herself into bed, shivering a little in the cold, then comforted herself with a spark of pleasure at her success at saving so many escapees.

The next one turned out to be a brazen fellow who insisted she deliver him to the right place before the performance, as dusk was already upon them. Cecily attempted to persuade him to wait until later, but he insisted they leave right now. As he firmly walked off along the rough road towards the wagon, he furiously kicked piles of spent cartridge cases along the way in search of bullets, then lit himself a cigarette.

Cecily hurried to catch up with him. 'Please don't kick those cases as some could be live with an explosive. And put out your cigarette. The light from it might be spotted by the enemy who are situated dangerously close by.'

'Nonsense,' he impatiently stated. 'Start driving, girl. I do what I feel the need for and certainly don't have the patience to wait any longer.'

Heaving a sigh, she turned and rushed back to the tent to fetch the key, wishing he'd agreed to attend their performance and leave when it was over. It wouldn't take too long for her to deliver him to his rescuer, and her mother would readily start the singing if Cecily failed to arrive back in time. Snatching up her bag and setting off back up the road to the wagon, she saw a sniper's bullet zip across in front of him. He instantly flung himself into a hole that had previously been cut into the ground by shellfire. Then something exploded and black smoke sheeted over the entire road. Cecily found herself coughing and choking, fear escalating through her as it had done on previous terrifying occasions. Eventually, once the smoke had diminished and the sound of gunfire had stopped, she staggered to her feet and ran over to rescue him. Lena was beside her in seconds, dismay echoing in both their eyes as they found his dead body in the hole, his legs missing and the cigarette still in his mouth.

'Oh my God, I did try to stop him smoking and warned him not to kick those cartridge cases in case one was live. He didn't listen to a word I said,' Cecily cried, tears running down her cheeks.

'Not your fault, love. He wasn't an easy man, never accepting anything I said either. He's maybe a deserter who secretly injured himself so that he could escape. I'm afraid he's paid a dreadful price for his arrogant stubbornness.'

Cecily struggled to accept this, aware she was still engaged in a horrifying routine.

❦

In July, the battalion moved back to Saint-Omer and their concert party happily went with them, filled with relief at leaving this camp in Ypres, so close to German territory and the front line of numerous battles: Lys, Bailleul, Kemmel, Passchendaele and many others. They had seen many soldiers killed or blinded by tear gas, poor men, their own hearts constantly pumping with fear. Lena joined them, feeling a similar need for a change of region. It felt good to be back in a place they were more familiar with. How long they would stay there was not clear, Cecily having received a note from Lieutenant Trevain that he was keen for them to move on to Malta at some point soon, a hospital region desperate for entertainers. She had contacted him with letters of her news about Wilhelm Ackermann, how he'd bullied her into helping him escape then had saved her from rape and internment. She also described the work she was now involved in, which apparently met with his approval.

Today, Cecily was seated beneath a tree planning the next concert when Louis appeared, a smile lighting his cleanly shaven face. 'May we have a word? There's something I'd like to ask you.'

Her senses skittered with excitement at the sight of this handsome Canadian and considering the work she was engaged in, she also felt a flicker of alarm. Did he too wish to escape, as so many soldiers longed to do? 'I hope you don't have a problem.'

Seating himself on the grass at her feet, he gave her a wry smile. 'The fact is, Cecily, I've just been informed that I'm about to be moved on.'

'Oh, I'm so sorry to hear that. We'll be moving too in due course. Are you allowed to say where you're being sent?'

'A number of us have been ordered to join the battalion at Bapaume. It's a small town close to the Somme, apparently caught up in another battle.'

A sense of foreboding jerked within her. 'I do hope you remain safe. I shall miss you.'

Meeting the sadness in her violet-blue eyes, he gave her hand a small squeeze. 'I shall miss you too, but I'm sure I'll be fine. Let's not assume that this war will get any worse. I reckon it will end fairly soon,' he firmly declared, the resilience in his soft brown eyes sparking more admiration within her.

'Let's hope so.'

'The thing is, we'll be despatched at the end of this week. Before then we've been granted a few days' leave, as is often the case. I thought I'd visit Salperwick, a village just a few kilometres from here, which has a magnificent river. I always enjoy fishing, sailing and swimming, and there's a lovely forest for walks. I wondered if you'd find that fun too and would be interested in joining me for a short break. Your presence would give me great pleasure as I confess I've become quite fond of you.'

Cecily listened spellbound, the thrill of this offer running through her like fire. Following that dance, they'd become quite friendly. She couldn't imagine falling in love with him, her heart still wrapped up in Ewan. Nor was he declaring any love for her, which was a good thing. But if this lovely man was to be involved in another horrendous battle, why would she not assist him in having some fun before he left? And should desire arise between them, he deserved a little romantic pleasure. Didn't she too, being a single woman facing a lonely life? 'I too like fishing, sailing and swimming, having lived in Plymouth for some time. However, I don't see myself as being very skilled at those leisure pursuits. I'm more into dancing and singing, and swimming,' she said with a chuckle. 'I'd be delighted to accept your invitation and come with you.'

His expression lit up with delight. 'Thank you, Cecily. That would be wonderful.' Reaching up to put his arms around her, she found herself locked in his embrace and felt a tremor of excitement when he gently kissed her.

❧

'We have one double bedroom and two single rooms available,' the concierge of the small hotel or *pension*, as the French called it, informed them.

Louis softly asked Cecily which one she'd be happy with, lifting his brows with quizzical interest. She looked up at this tall, fit man with strongly muscled shoulders and a delicious twinkle in his brown eyes, to give him a broad smile. 'Oh, the double room, obviously, being now a married couple.' It seemed appropriate to claim that.

With a smile and a nod, he turned to the woman behind the reception desk and said, 'That would be splendid, thank you.'

Picking up both their small cases, the concierge led the way up to the second floor. Unlocking the door at the end of the passage, she placed the cases on a rack then quietly left. Whether she believed in what Cecily had stated about their relationship was perhaps open to question, but they had not been dismissed. Looking around the room, not least at the large double bed in the centre, to her surprise Cecily felt her limbs start to tremble. Foolish as it might seem, the sight of it filled her with a sudden panic. Had frustration made her agree to join him on this trip, and tell that lie? No, she'd simply longed for a little fun in her life. What was wrong with that?

'This is splendid,' Louis commented, also glancing around.

He was so close to her that she could smell not a whiff of smoke or alcohol, only soap and a lingering odour of his uniform. Their eyes met, an electrifying, sensual and certain wild courage in his, while she felt warmth start to glow in hers, her sense of panic quickly subsiding.

It was late morning, and having unpacked their few items of clothes to hang them in the wardrobe, Louis suggested they should go and find themselves some lunch then explore the river. 'I did promise you some sailing, today being sunny and warm, so this could be the best chance we'll get.'

And probably the last they'd have for some time since he'd be leaving in just a few days to Bapaume, and then the troupe could be moved on to Malta. They enjoyed a delicious lunch of pâté, toast and black coffee. The concierge then brought them each a slice of homemade sponge cake, the meal a real treat after the poor food available in camp.

Louis told her how much he had enjoyed their concerts. 'Your singing is superb, and you're quite a talented actor too.'

'I love singing best of all. We might go on to perform an extract from one or two of Shakespeare's comedies: *Much Ado About Nothing* or *A Midsummer Night's Dream*. That would be such fun and make a change from the other plays we've done. I will continue to sing before and after each play extract.'

'You devote so much time and energy to this project, much appreciated by all. This war can leave us pretty shattered, riddled with fear and grief, or completely crackers as a result of shellfire. What you offer us Tommies nurtures and lightens our minds and spirits. You are very brave.'

'So are you, having opted to fight in this war. I do hope you remain safe.'

A small frown creased his brow. 'I believe this battle already taking place in Bapaume is being supported by troops from New Zealand and maybe Australia. I'll find out for sure when I get there. I believe it will finally bring this war to an end. That is the plan it's involved in, part of a series of Allied victories that began with the Battle of Amiens and could well expand again to the Somme, Ypres and many other places. We have to drive the Germans out.'

Seeing the grip of determination in his face, Cecily grasped his hand with both of hers to give it a gentle squeeze. 'Enough of this war talk. Let's put all of that worry out of our minds and enjoy this break. We need to have some fun.'

He laughed. 'We do indeed. An excellent idea.'

Walking through the woodlands down to the river, he hired a small boat and sat opposite her as he began to row. With the sun shining, the sky and river appeared to be melding together like molten gold. A fickle breeze came along to disturb the blue-grey ruffle of waves. It felt a little startling as the boat bobbed up and down, the water slapping against its sides.

Louis laughed. 'Are you all right?'

'I am. You are excellent at rowing,' she said, taking pleasure in watching his skill. And this man had never looked more inviting.

They continued for some distance, Cecily covertly studying him till finally he asked if she'd like to have a try.

'Why not?'

'We could row together,' he said, and passing over one of the oars, he locked it in place then told her to make sure it was held properly in the water. 'Now bend forward, roll your wrists and pull it through the water as you lean back. Don't jerk, just apply strength.'

She made an attempt to do as he instructed, which didn't prove to be easy, and she ended up laughing. 'You are so much stronger than me. I think we're just moving round in circles.'

'I'll use less pressure,' Louis said, joining in her laughter. He rowed much more slowly and it worked perfectly. After a while, he brought the boat safely back to shore with his considerable skill. Helping her to climb out he gave her a hug, which lit her with anticipation. 'Thank you and well done.'

Following dinner, they returned to walk along the riverbank, hand in hand. The soft lapping of water slipping over stones echoed magically in her ears. Ruffled by the breeze and bathed in a pool of pale moonlight, the river glimmered a beautiful shiny grey. They talked quietly, sharing dreams for their future, Louis saying how he ached to return to his hometown of Quebec where he hoped one day to run a restaurant.

'Heaven knows what I will do. I assume I'll continue singing as I can't think what else I'd be any good at,' Cecily said with a smile. 'Assuming I can manage to get taken on by a theatre.'

'You'd be more than welcome to come and sing to us in Quebec. Unless you have a fiancé whom you plan to marry,' he quietly remarked, his brows lifting in query.

She briefly reminded him of how losing Ewan was the reason she had no wish to do that. 'He too loved to sing, although in a much deeper tone of voice, as well as fish and swim,' she said with a chuckle. 'I like to remember the enjoyable time we had together when we were young, not dwell upon his death.'

'Quite right,' he agreed, holding her close to give her a comforting hug. 'You look beautiful,' he murmured, smoothing her cheek with the palm of his hand then admiring the pink silk dress she'd chosen to wear that evening. 'Most enchanting.'

Finding the gleam of admiration in his eyes alluring, it caused a bubble of exhilaration to flow within her. 'You look pretty handsome too.'

When he kissed her, she felt utterly intoxicated. Linking her arm with his, they strolled happily back to the hotel and upstairs to the bedroom. She eagerly helped him to remove her dress, making no protest as he lay her down upon the bed. As he caressed and kissed her with increasing passion, desire flared within her, a sensation far more intense than she'd ever known before. Instinctively, she slid her hands around his neck, drawing him closer, barely able to suppress her need for him. Assuming all hope of intimacy had died, this was an event she'd never believed possible. Not that she and Ewan had ever made love, being far too young and perfectly content to wait until they were married. Now that she had lost him, Cecily felt she had no reason to believe she'd ever fall in love again. And holding fast to her independence would save the risk of choosing to marry simply because of a sense of despondency or loneliness, which could prove to be a disastrous mistake. The prospect of spending her entire life as a virgin no longer appealed. Why should she confine herself to celibacy when she surely had a right to a little fun and satisfaction? And this lovely man was not that dreadful *Oberstleutnant* who'd attempted to rape her.

'Are you sure you're happy about this?' he murmured.

She gave him a sweet smile as he tenderly kissed her lips, cheeks and breasts, promising to take appropriate action to protect her. When finally he entered her, she found herself instinctively moving with the rhythm of his body, the bliss between them escalating to a glorious pinnacle of happiness.

NINETEEN

FOLLOWING A rehearsal and taking into account the amount of work she'd done for months, let alone the last few days without Cecily around to help, Queenie demanded Johnny take her to the nearest *estaminet*, a local café bar close to the railway station. He'd bought her Malaga wine and a pint of stout for himself, together with a Dutch cigar, each costing only a few coppers. They sat at a table for some time just outside the café, Queenie deliciously relishing her third glass. 'Thank goodness you didn't invite Merryn to join us or tell her where we were going. She's my darling daughter but being very anti-alcohol, never allows me a sip. We should take a walk together later, to help me sober up. Will there be any possibility of doing that here in town before we return to the camp?' she asked, flicking her eyelashes at him.

Glancing around at the messy state of the road packed with shell-holes, Johnny shrugged. 'Couldn't say for sure. Depends whether there are any more likely attacks. Doesn't feel safe enough to risk a walk, not here in Saint-Omer, let alone out in the woods.' Hearing a train approach, he looked across at the railway buildings on the opposite side of the street and saw Cecily walking up the road towards the station. 'Good Lord, your other daughter is back. Nor is she alone.'

Queenie jerked, startled and annoyed that Cecily should appear just when she was enjoying this day out. 'You'll have to hop it, Johnny Boy!'

Leaping up, he edged around the corner of the *estaminet*. Keeping his glass of stout and cigar in hand, he crouched down on the pavement, remaining close enough to hear what Queenie was saying.

'Thankfully, she hasn't noticed me sitting here. She's walking to the station accompanied by a man. Could he be that German PoW she saved?'

Johnny shook his head. 'I doubt it. He apparently escaped some time ago back in Ypres. Hadn't you better move away too, Queenie?'

'I will, just as soon as I've finished this glass of wine,' she hissed, hugely irritated to be under pressure to leave, her love of booze far too strong for her to abandon it. 'What a nuisance! I was so enjoying this treat, but she'll be furious if she finds me drinking. Her attitude is even worse than Merryn's.'

Johnny frowned. 'That chap looks vaguely familiar. He could be one of those soldiers who help us perform, or else that French-Canadian bloke she danced with.'

'Ah, yes, you may well be right.' Closely watching as Cecily entered the station, Queenie guessed she'd probably spent these last few days with him. So she liked sex too. Now feeling the urge to escape, she said, 'Oh dear, when she comes back out of the station, she'll be walking towards us.'

'We could go and find another *estaminet*,' Johnny whispered, sounding slightly desperate. 'So long as Cecily hasn't seen us, we're free to go elsewhere.'

'Let's go now,' she said, and quickly gulped down the last few drops of wine. Moments later, her glass emptied, the pair of them quickly crossed the bridge over the Canal de Neuffossé and scurried away.

∽

Cecily gazed up at Louis with sadness in her heart as she walked with him along the railway platform packed with Tommies. How she'd enjoyed their short relaxation together. They'd spent those few days exploring the area and enjoyed rowing, swimming and fishing, let alone making love numerous times throughout the night and first thing each morning when she would wake to find his arm around her. It almost felt as if the war was over and she was allowed to be happy and peaceful at last.

The time came when they had to return to Saint-Omer for Louis to move on to join the next battle near the Somme, not something either of them wished to discuss. In silence, they packed their few belongings and returned to the camp. He changed into his uniform, collected his kit and Cecily accompanied him to the railway station. She would feel so alone once he had left. How she would miss him.

'I suspect it will be a slow journey. I'll spend it remembering the thrill of the time we've spent together, not least the long nights,' he said, holding her close as they approached the train.

'I will remember it with great affection too,' she murmured, giving him a shy smile. 'And I do appreciate being taught more about rowing and fishing, as well as lovemaking.'

He grinned. 'That's good to hear.'

At that moment, the crowds of soldiers began to climb on board. The pair of them stood staring at each other for some seconds, then holding her tight against his chest, he kissed her with renewed passion. 'I loved every minute I spent with you. What a treasure you are. Take care of yourself, Cecily. I'll write to you whenever I get the chance.'

'I'll write to you too,' she said, feeling a prickle of tears flood her eyes. As he turned to board the train, she ran after him to wrap her arms around his neck and give him another kiss. His gaze flickered with a mixture of sadness and desire.

Once all the Tommies had climbed on board, the train shunted out of the station and, moments later, it had vanished and Louis was gone. Filled with a sense of despondency, Cecily made her way slowly back to camp. What a horrific life these brave men were caught up in. She could but hope that Louis was right when he said this dratted war would end soon.

∽

Over the next few weeks, Cecily received several letters from Louis telling of his experiences. He described their endless marching in fierce wind and rain, how they slept in the woods or hid in ditches, dugouts and trenches to avoid the heavy shelling. He spoke of watching the artillery come by, their galloping horses very often panic-stricken and with nostrils flaring.

> There are shells striking all around and many casual-
> ties. We find ourselves picking up abandoned rifles,
> guns and hand grenades since we always feel in need
> of more ammunition. The bombardment goes on and
> we listen painstakingly to the sound of an oncoming
> shell to ascertain whether it might fall within yards
> of us. We pray the enemy will finally withdraw, then
> we could too. I so look forward to seeing you again
> but rumour has it that we're about to be moved on to
> a new front line, so you may not hear from me for a
> week or two. Once we've settled some place else, I'll
> write again. Take care and keep strong.
> Best wishes,
> Louis

Cecily found it heartrending to read his latest letter, pleased as she was to receive it. Following this, his silence brought a sense of despair within her. How painful it was that having developed a fondness for this man, his life was once again rife with danger. Going to speak to Lena, she asked if she'd heard any news of the men who'd joined the battalion at Bapaume, close to the Somme.

Giving a sad shake of her head, Lena said, 'Sorry, I believe many have been injured and killed, but who and where they now are is not easy to discover. Is there anyone in particular you wish to know of?'

'I care about all of these Tommies and I have become quite friendly with Louis Casey, a French Canadian.' Cecily went on to explain how he claimed there would be a slight delay before he wrote again since they were to be moved on to a different front line.

'Let's hope he writes once he settles wherever they send him,' Lena said with a sympathetic smile. 'I'll make a few enquiries and if I hear anything about him, I'll let you know.'

'Oh, thank you, it's much appreciated.'

'I appreciate your help too. More prisoners are being herded along roads by the German enemy. God knows where they are being taken or how we'll manage to save them. I found one unconscious and tied to a tree, very close to death but managed to save him.'

'Thank God for that.'

Valiantly putting her personal worries out of her mind, Cecily continued to work hard with their concerts and thankfully no more PoWs needed rescuing. She then received the expected order from Lieutenant Trevain saying that their concert party was to be taken to Malta, where they felt in sore need of entertainment. Being a small island in the Mediterranean a reasonably safe distance from battles on the front line, it was packed with hospitals for thousands of men, and was viewed as a sanctuary. Cecily was looking forward to entertaining them if feeling sad at leaving Lena. They gave each other a fond farewell, promising to keep in touch.

Their concert party was transported by the Navy free of charge, stopping off briefly at Marseille as they waited for a ship to be found, then once on board spending a lively evening singing and dancing on the lower deck to entertain the crew. When they finally reached Malta, Cecily felt a spur of excitement. She could see clusters of white houses, the church where the Knights of Malta were buried, and a street flocked with a herd of goats. It was an island famous for its megalithic temples, towers and historic sites, if looking somewhat disrupted right now, the harbours packed with warehouses, armaments and military equipment, soldiers and ships. The island was not fully involved in the fighting but was considered to be slightly more dangerous than in the early years of the war, several hospital ships having been sunk by German submarines. Some patients were now taken to Greece but the medical care available in the many hospitals still on the island held a high reputation. Cecily was happy to do her bit for the injured men recuperating here, with thousands of lives being saved.

They were taken to a small hotel, where they gave a concert in a garden filled with lemon and orange trees, and mimosa cactus, the audience overflowing with admiration for them. Such a joyful experience, her heart alive with great respect for these injured men.

Throughout September and October, they went on to give many more concerts at hospitals and various camps as well as on board a troopship filled with a thousand men, plus a battleship. On one occasion, they travelled over narrow roads and up steep hills to St Paul's Bay. It took some time but was quite delightful. They called in to perform at a convalescent camp, also attended by thousands of young men, some of whom were suffering from fever, limb injuries and mental breakdown. There was little food available, mainly bread, fruit, beans, peas and other vegetables. She could see women working in the fields, tending to small patches that were walled in to protect the plants against the winds that roared in over the sea. They then thankfully settled in a different camp for the night, feeling exhausted.

There were many restrictions to protect public safety and defend the island. No one was allowed to involve themselves in conversation with the enemy, particularly with regard to the movement of ships and other naval matters. Cecily became aware that it would be dangerous to speak with any injured PoWs here. Thankfully, she'd stopped doing that ever since Wilhelm Ackermann had kidnapped her. One evening, realising she hadn't contacted Lieutenant Trevain for some weeks and needing to assure him she'd helped more escapees, she took a walk along the harbour in search of a naval ship that would possess the necessary radio-telegraph, only to find herself halted by a stern-looking guard.

'Who goes there?' he roared. With a glower of rage, he informed her that no one was allowed to walk along the coast anywhere near a military post or ship, as there was a danger she could be fired upon.

'I'm so sorry, I didn't think of that. I was wondering if I could use your ship's radiotelegraph?' She readily went on to state her name and that she was a performer. All too aware he might demand to know who she would be contacting and why, she smilingly told him she simply wished to speak to a good friend back in England. 'Is that not allowed either?' she asked, wondering if she should risk using the code Trevain had given her, although some instinct warned her not to mention this unless requested to do so.

To her astonishment, he stepped forward to firmly fasten her wrists in handcuffs. Cecily then found herself escorted by two guards to the naval ship, not at all in the manner she'd expected. Locked in a small cabin that felt very like a prison cell, she was left sitting there for some hours, her sense of panic gradually degenerating into fury. How dare they lock her up just for asking a perfectly reasonable question? Had she been wrong not to use the code word granted her?

The guard finally returned and took her to the officer's cabin on the upper deck. Seated at his desk, he was a sour-faced man who did not offer her a chair, leaving her standing before him. He blandly informed her that he'd investigated her name and history, saying how he'd learned a good deal about her from various sources, making no mention of what these might be. 'You will be required to answer all questions I ask. If you refuse or fail to explain what you are about, then you could be found guilty of a serious offence.'

Cecily could feel herself start to shake with alarm. Was she about to be interrogated yet again, this time by a British naval officer who sounded even more condescending than the *Oberstleutnant*, that German Lieutenant Colonel back in Ypres? How terrifying that had been – now she seemed to be facing the same issue here in Malta. 'I doubt there's much more to tell you, having made it clear who I am and that I'm merely a singer running a concert party to entertain the Tommies. We've performed at the Opera House here and in many other theatres, as well as various parties and festivities.'

'Indeed? I have been informed that you assisted a German PoW to escape.'

She stared at him in utter dismay. Who on earth had told him that? It came into her head that it might have been the escapee who was in the wagon when Wilhelm Ackermann was hidden in the back. He'd possibly spotted him but had said nothing except: '*Is it just me you're rescuing?*' The poor man was probably too afraid and desperate to escape himself to mention who he suspected he'd seen, but had possibly given the information to the Navy. Not for a moment dare she confess to this fact. 'That is a complete lie. I only assisted a German PoW patient who was stuck in a wheelchair when our camp was bombed and dumped him in a trench. Not something that went well.' She really had no wish to describe all that had occurred between them after that. Far too dangerous.

'His name, please, and what did he demand of you as a consequence of your generous assistance?'

Discreetly remaining silent, Cecily worried how to respond to this question.

Pounding his fist on the desk, he threatened to lock her back in the prison cell if she did not reply. 'Answer the damn question! *I* am in charge and even if your colleagues discover where you are, they will be denied all rights to see or rescue you, so silence will do your self-interest no good at all. I require proof of what you're claiming.'

Taking a deep breath in an attempt to soften the tension building within her, it came to Cecily that she could give this officer a small version of the truth. Firmly lifting her chin, she calmly announced, 'Sir, I am under instruction from a certain Lieutenant in England not to speak of prisoners of war I've spoken to, and never to rescue them. I speak to him in England at regular intervals about "Dover".'

Staring at her in dazed disbelief, he fell silent. Then spinning on his heel, he marched away. Some moments later, the guard returned and led her down to the operating room where the radiotelegraph was situated. Assisted by the young man in charge on how to use it, she was then left alone to deliver her latest information: '*More chickens saved and sent home to roost.*' A message she wrote in the strictly disguised way she'd been taught.

Having steadfastly gone through the process with a strong sense of relief, Cecily was relieved when the guard drove her back to their camp in his army vehicle. She did insist he let her out some distance from the entrance so that no one was aware of where she'd been. He readily agreed to do that and wished her well.

'And the end of the war is coming,' he said. He then went on to tell her how the German forces were at last retreating, having lost all support from their allies who had vanished, as well as control of many areas that were apparently in total chaos. 'Even their troops are deserting.'

'That's so good to hear,' Cecily said with a grin.

TWENTY

CECILY WAS organising their final concert in Malta and for the first time ever, Merryn declined to join them, claiming she had a cough and a cold and wasn't feeling at all well.

'I know you may still be a bit exhausted, lovey, and in need of a rest, but this is a most important event as the war is coming to an end. The Tommies do not feel inclined to laugh or cheer, being far too weary after all the fighting, battles and terror that has occupied them for years. So many have been injured, and they dread more possible attacks. It will take them some time to accept that the war may at last be over. We must do our bit to cheer them up.'

'Sorry, I too feel worn out and sick,' she cried, and ran off back to their tent.

One of the Tommies who could play the violin offered to stand in for her, Johnny still playing his drum. It was not too cold a day, the wind known as the sirocco blowing in from Africa, and they were kept busy dealing with horses, guns and ammunition.

Dressed in a gorgeous white silk gown, Cecily sang with joy and vigour, beginning with 'Take Me Back to Dear Old Blighty'. She then went on to sing all the old songs they loved, plus a few new ones: 'Au Revoir, But Not Goodbye, Soldier Boy'; 'Home Sweet Home' and one of her favourites: 'Oh! How I Hate to Get Up in the Morning'. All of these were well received, the Tommies at last cheering, laughing, whistling and whooping.

Queenie too sang some of her music hall favourites starting with 'Another Little Drink Wouldn't Do Us Any Harm'. This caused Cecily to shake her head in despair as she chuckled with good humour. Her mother did appear to be quite sober and as usual, extremely glamorous. She began with her much loved 'Any Old Iron? Any Old Iron? Any, Any, Any Old Iron?', then went on to sing 'Bird in a Gilded Cage' and many more. The pair of them took it in turns and sang more songs, working well together and gladly encouraging the soldiers to join in. It felt most gratifying to see the audience filled with admiration for their performance. Cecily could see relief in their worn-out faces, then as they remembered their lost friends, tears would slide over their ashen-pale cheeks. Life would improve for them once this war came to an end.

∾

When she woke around dawn, Merryn leapt out of bed, ran out of the tent to a ditch and threw up. She'd been feeling sick for the last few weeks, frequently vomiting, not something she wished to dwell upon. Life recently had been a bit of a juggling act. She'd committed the unforgivable sin of allowing Johnny to make love to her whenever he wished, because of her dread of losing him. Merryn had no wish to experience what her beloved sister had suffered. It was true that he wasn't a soldier, but they'd lived in dangerous places for some time and their relationship had become far more intense than she'd anticipated. She loved him and believed he loved her, so didn't that make it right? Oh, and how she adored feeling him inside her, the rhythm and intensity making it seem as if she were a part of him.

Merryn suspected she was now beset with a profound problem and revealing it to Johnny would not prove to be easy, let alone resolving it in this tricky situation. And how would she dare to face her mother's wrath? Certainly not yet. Queenie was occupying a small tent of her own some distance away, having made a fuss and demanding privacy because of her age. As a consequence, she was unaware of the frequent trips Merryn had made each morning recently to throw up. Returning to her own tent, Merryn curled up in bed, keeping her back turned. She'd really no wish to discuss this issue with her sister either, considering Cecily's low opinion of Johnny and how she'd ordered her not to become too involved or trust him. Irritatingly, Cecily was awake and started chatting to her.

'Ah, morning, lovey, there you are. Have you been out seeking breakfast? What time is it? Sorry if I was late coming to bed. Our performance yesterday evening went so well. It's such a pity you didn't feel well enough to join us.' Sitting up, she rubbed her eyes.

Merryn said nothing, locked in silence.

'What's wrong, are you still suffering from exhaustion, lovey? I know you became overtired and I accept that here in Malta we're still pretty busy, so no wonder you look pale and tired.'

Merryn burst into tears. Leaping out of bed, Cecily dashed over to give her a cuddle. 'What is it, darling?' she whispered, thankfully keeping her voice low so that no one lingering outside the tent would hear her. 'I do hope you aren't cross with me again.'

'I've no wish to speak of that quarrel we had,' Merryn said, giving a little whimper of despair. 'Yes, I am still exhausted and don't feel well enough to do much at all right now.' Then her next words came out without a moment's thought. 'That's because I'm expecting . . .'

'. . . something dreadful to happen?' Cecily whispered soothingly. 'Oh, I too keep expecting to receive another dreadful telegram.'

Angrily brushing the tears from her eyes, Merryn met her sister's troubled gaze with fury in her own. 'How naïve you are. It's not a bloody telegram I'm expecting, but something much more serious. A *baby*!'

Cecily gazed at her in stunned disbelief for some long seconds. 'Oh my God, how far gone do you reckon you are?'

'Only a few weeks, I think.'

'I assume Johnny is the man responsible. Have you told him?'

Merryn shook her head, not wishing to go into any great detail of how she'd believed he would protect her by wearing a rubber sheath. He'd obviously failed to do that on at least one occasion. She supposed she should feel some regret about losing her virginity. How could she avoid this sense of guilt, being unmarried? Oh, but how she loved him. Her feelings for Johnny must be perfectly evident in her eyes whenever they met his, and in the way her fingers strayed to touch him at every opportunity. 'I haven't plucked up the courage and surely there's no rush. I might not actually be pregnant or might lose it.'

Cecily jerked. 'Don't do anything stupid to hurt yourself or risk losing either the baby or Johnny. He could well be delighted to learn he's about to become a father, so do tell him.'

Merryn chewed on her lip, feeling confused. It was true that she really had no wish to give him up. They were surely one person now. Was he aware that she did have a problem, as the torment of her situation had begun to mar their love a little? He'd seemed at times to be deliberately avoiding her. Would he promise to stand by her? She could but hope so. 'I'll tell him when I feel it's appropriate. As we'll be travelling back to Blighty with the Tommies soon, let's not worry about this problem right now. I'll sort it out once we get back home. Oh, and for heaven's sake, please don't tell Queenie,' Merryn said, with a little moan. 'If I admit to her that I wish to marry Johnny, let alone the condition I'm in, she'll be furious and most disapproving. She could refuse the necessary permission I need since I'm not twenty-one.'

'I'm perfectly aware of her dismissive attitude to every sweetheart you've ever had, lovey, so I won't say a word to her on the subject, I promise. Not until you receive a proposal. Then I'll do everything I can to support you and convince our snobby mother that you are a devoted couple.'

'Thank you,' Merryn said, and once more bursting into tears, fell gratefully into her sister's arms as Cecily hugged and gently patted her.

❧

When packing in preparation for their departure, Cecily received a couple of letters, one from Cornwall addressed only to her. To her surprise, it was not from Nan, who frequently wrote to express her hope that they were keeping well and still enjoying presenting their concerts. This was from her nephew Boyd. Cecily remembered him with a degree of fondness and sat down eagerly to read whatever he had to say. He began by telling her about Armistice Day on Monday 11 November, the end of the war having been announced by the King, and how Plymouth was soon crammed with people eager to celebrate, including WAACs, WRENs and soldiers, bands playing, nurses dancing and everyone cheering or crying, followed by a two-minute silence in memory of all the lost men.

Cecily smiled, wishing they'd been there to savour that wonderful event. No cheers had been raised here, not until they gave their last performance. The Tommies had been too worn out to celebrate, despite realising they would soon be heading back to Blighty with a new future to look forward to. That was to happen in just a few days when they would all be taken home by the Navy. Cecily would be happy to sing to them again on-board ship, to celebrate their good fortune at having survived this war.

Now going on to read more of this letter, she found herself intrigued by the change of topic.

> The reason I'm writing to you, Cecily, is to tell you
> that I wrote to Lady Stanford to ask if you might speak
> with her, explaining how you wished to know more

about the man who might be your father. Her secretary finally responded saying she could possibly have some useful information and would agree to see you, once you arrived back. She didn't give me a clue as to what that might be. I hope it will be of value to you and not just with regard to the suffrage movement with which she is involved and obviously how you met. I look forward to seeing you soon.

Best wishes,

Boyd

Cecily ran to Merryn to share this news with her. 'I don't believe for a moment it's about suffragists or suffragettes. It looks like she's found out some information about our lost father. Wouldn't that be wonderful? I so look forward to meeting her again and hearing what she has to say. And we can celebrate this victory too, once we get back to Blighty.'

'I can hardly wait to return home to Plymouth either,' Merryn said. Strangely, her tone of voice and the tight expression on her face didn't seem to match this remark. 'But I need to rest, so please leave me in peace.'

Cecily knelt down to give her a comforting hug. 'The war is over, lovey, so all could now be well for you and Johnny, and Mama, once we are settled back home. You'll feel much better in a week or two. Take a little sleep to prepare yourself for the journey while I get on with the packing.'

It was after she'd collected their last pieces of equipment that she opened the second letter she'd received, this one from Lena.

Dear Cecily,

I'm so sorry to have to send you this tragic news. I've been informed that the infantry suffered a bombardment with very little support around, the artillery having withdrawn. A barrage of shells was falling everywhere, killing and injuring more men and horses. And I'm afraid there's no sign of Louis anywhere. He's sadly gone. I should think you're heartbroken to hear this as you were such good friends and he's not your only loss. As you know, millions of men have been destroyed in this dreadful war meant to end all wars. Not easy to accept, but many will live forever in our hearts.

Much love,

Lena

Pain and a flood of grief plummeted through Cecily. This was the bad news she'd dreaded. She was lying on her camp bed sobbing when her mother came in to see her, and confessed why she was in this dreadful state.

'Oh, my dear girl, so you've lost that lovely young French Canadian whom you clearly adored. I'm so sorry.' Sitting down beside Cecily she gave her a comforting hug. 'How sad for you to lose another man you were coming to love. My heart goes out to you, darling, all too aware of how dreadful that feels.'

Cecily was deeply moved by her sympathy as she sank her head against her mother's cheek. Queenie could be an exceedingly conceited and self-obsessed lady, but at times could prove to be most caring, particularly over this issue. Savouring the comfort she offered was very soothing. Louis had been a lovely man, so adoring towards her. Why did she always lose a man she loved or was growing fond of? She would definitely have nothing more to do with any men in future. She felt quite unable to bear this sense of loss ever again. And would her darling sister find happiness, considering the mess she was in? She could but hope so.

PART TWO — POST WAR

TWENTY-ONE

I T FELT so good to be home. Nan gave them all loving hugs, helped them to unpack and handed Queenie her diamond ring, which brought a glow of delight to her face. They were then provided with good food, hot baths and fresh clean clothes. What a relief that was. Somewhere at the back of Cecily's mind was a desire to ask Nan about her nephew Boyd, and how he'd made contact with Lady Stanford, but she couldn't bring herself to do that right now. She would certainly go and speak to her about it as soon as she felt it appropriate to do so.

Cecily felt wrapped in depression, darkly sunk in grief over the loss of Louis, almost as devastating as losing Ewan. He was a lovely man, so kind and considerate. She'd greatly enjoyed the break they'd enjoyed in Salperwick, rowing, fishing and swimming, not least spending those exciting nights together. Would their friendship have developed into a deeper relationship had he still been alive? He'd certainly claimed to be very fond of her, had even teasingly proposed at that dance. There was no chance of that happening now. Any hope she'd originally had of marrying a man she loved was completely gone. She'd known that for some time. How sad it was. All she could do now was to savour the peace and embark upon a plan to build a new life for herself. How she would do that she had no idea, as it was proving to be a more difficult time than she'd expected.

Deep within her pit of grief lay a sense of resentment and anger at the mess this war had made of all their lives. Reading the latest news in *The Daily Telegraph*, Cecily was convinced that the country was in total disarray. Many of the Tommies were angry because they had still not been demobilised. The rule was for them to be released from the Army once they'd found a job. This infuriated them, believing those who were first in should be first out. Even fit men were having difficulties finding employment, and strikes over pay and industrial unrest were taking place in many towns. Wounded soldiers were being treated for a short time in overcrowded hospitals, sometimes for little more than a month. Those suffering from shell shock and constantly reliving the traumas they'd been through were given little help at all. Some could only find work as match-sellers in a market, while others blew their heads off, being unable to find the necessary medical assistance.

Christmas had been taken over by the election, Lloyd George once more winning the role of prime minister. Would he succeed in resolving these problems? Amazingly, some women had put themselves forward as possible members of parliament, including Christabel Pankhurst, much to Cecily's delight. Unfortunately, she was not elected. Only Constance Markievicz, a Countess and Irish woman, had been granted a seat, which she did not accept for political or personal reasons.

Women were being sacked or requested to leave their place of work in order to make way for returning soldiers, including those who had lost their beloved husband and were now the breadwinner, being head of their household. They found themselves ordered back to the kitchen. This turned any hope of them earning a living into complete turmoil. Could they trust any politician to treat women with proper respect?

'You would expect us to have decent rights and hopes of a job after all the work we've done for the country and the soldiers,' Cecily said to Merryn, slamming down the paper in disgust. 'I asked for my job back to work on the trams but was given a dismissive refusal. Did you manage to get yours back, lovey?'

Merryn shook her head. 'Why would I bother asking when we know I'd be sacked the moment I married?'

Seeing her sister flop down upon her bed, Cecily read a worrying message of despair on her face. 'Have you spoken to Johnny?'

She shook her head. 'I will as soon as he too finds a job, which could take a while.'

'What a mess we're in,' Cecily said, tucking the quilt over her.

She felt a deep need to protect her beloved sister. How to succeed in doing that would not be easy. Leaving Merryn in peace for an afternoon rest, she quietly left the room, a small bubble of irritation flickering within her. She would like to speak to Johnny and warn him he should offer support to Merryn since he was the one who'd messed up her life. The reality was that this would not be appropriate. Nor must she speak to Mama on the subject, because that too could create havoc and make her beloved young sister's problem worse.

It was, however, a relevant point that finding work could prove to be a nightmare for all women, not least themselves. She'd visited and written to the Palace Theatre, the Theatre Royal and all others she knew of, including the Pavilion on the Pier. So far, she had received no response from any of them. Their lack of interest was most worrying. Dancers, singers, jugglers and comedians were now in competition with the cinema. Having spent many sleepless nights going over possible solutions, Cecily came to a decision, making an announcement the following morning at breakfast.

'I intend to go in search of local clubs and smaller theatres that may have started up during the war, plus schools, churches and cinemas, any place that might be interested in us giving a performance. I shall do my utmost to acquire us an offer somewhere by making it known how skilled we were at entertaining the troops.'

'I doubt you'll succeed. This community seems to have changed, in keeping with the world, and all local directors who knew me are now gone,' Queenie sharply retorted, seething with fury as she too had so far received no offers.

Cecily marched off to trail around street after street in Plymouth. Finding no small theatres, she called at every club, pub and picture palace she could find. None were interested in making her an offer until she came across one small nightclub in the north of the city. Cecily was at least granted permission to speak to the manager and she briefly explained what their concert party had done for the Tommies over the last eighteen months. 'We'd be happy to put on a performance here for a reasonable sum.'

His expression was oddly scathing. 'The war is over and we have to compete with cinemas nowadays, so mebbe not.' He looked an extremely fussy man, unimpressed by the story she'd told him. Cecily was all too aware that the war had resulted in a new type of management taking over, not people who had been brought up in the theatre, but those who wished to take advantage of the boom years. There'd always been packed houses, soldiers on leave flocking to the theatre with their wives or girlfriends, desperate to see anything amusing or spectacular. Theatre managers' reputations were now no longer good, being looked upon as less caring towards artists they employed than the old-style actor-managers had been.

'It would be our way of celebrating the end of the war,' Cecily remarked brightly, eager to win him round.

'We certainly don't want plays about grim disasters or anything too serious like Shakespeare.'

'We won't trouble you with a play. We will perform merry songs and music. We could put on the first performance for free if you like,' she offered, feeling desperate to make a deal. 'If we do well, you might be interested in offering us the opportunity for paid appearances after that.'

'Hmm, all right then, I'll give it a go. No promises.'

'Thank you so much.' A date was agreed and with relief bubbling through her, Cecily hurried home to give this good news. 'I believe we should sing songs about the war, and dress in uniform, as Vesta Tilley does, to make it a great show of patriotism.'

'I'm not sure that's a good idea,' Queenie commented starkly. 'You are not a star, unlike that great lady. And the war is over, so why would we continue performing for and about soldiers?'

'This concert is for everyone, Mama, not just the Tommies. I feel we should do this as our way of celebrating the end of the war, also in order to get our talent known.'

'Why are we not getting paid?' Johnny grumbled. 'I see no point in working for nothing.'

'It's only a small nightclub and having received no offer from the manager to put on a show for a modest sum, I suggested we'd do the first one for free. I did point out we should then be paid for any further concerts we do following that. If we don't, we might have to consider performing during the interval at a local cinema, which is what some artists are now doing. Not that the pay for that is very good either.'

'Assuming we don't find better offers on our own,' Johnny remarked caustically.

Merryn made no comment at all, still locked in stunned dismay. Being very conversant with her sister's state of health, Cecily kept a careful watch over her during the next few days, which they spent fully engaged in rehearsals. Queenie repeated all her usual instructions on how to breathe, stand and sing, working them harder than ever, resolute to ensure their performance was up to scratch. They all agreed that Cecily could be the first to sing, then she would introduce Queenie as the star of the show, something she had to steadfastly accept, now they were back in Plymouth, where her mother had been a star for some years.

◦◦

When the day arrived, they were delighted to find a queue lined up along the street outside the nightclub, being entertained by a man playing a banjo and a woman walking round with her dog to collect money for soldiers and sailors wounded in the war who were in need of help. Cecily gladly added a contribution and with a grin, quickly ushered her concert party to the dressing rooms. 'Chin up, folks. Time for us to do our bit again.'

Cecily peeped through a crack in the wing curtains to peek across the open stage. To her delight and relief, she saw that small though it was, the club was packed with people sitting around at tables enjoying drinks and jolly laughter. Not only was every seat taken, but many were actually standing at the back by the bar. 'Standing room only. Lord, they've just rung the two-minute bell. Quick, Johnny and Merryn, get yourselves on stage and settled with your instruments. Then off we go. Break a leg.' Settling themselves in the far corner, they started to play.

Just as Cecily was smoothing her uniform and preparing to follow them on stage, a man hovering in the wings behind her approached to hiss in her ear. 'My daughter should be the one doing a show here tonight, not you lot. Hers was cancelled, no attention paid to the fact she'd performed here for years. Because you're doing this for free, you've ruined her career.'

'Oh, my goodness, how dreadful! I wasn't aware of that.'

Unable to discuss this problem with the audience starting to cheer and clap, Cecily hastily apologised and dressed in her smart uniform marched on stage. She gave them a salute and a cheerful grin, then lifting her knees high, stamped her feet and came to a halt. She valiantly began to sing 'Pack Up Your Troubles in Your Old Kit Bag', one of her favourite war songs. Noticing how Merryn's bright expression changed to one of concern, Cecily gave her sister a wink and a wide smile. It was not, after all, her fault that this cancellation had taken place. Surely the poor girl would be offered another date? She'd speak to the manager to make sure of that.

It was halfway through the song that she heard a growing mumble of heckling among the group of people standing by the bar. The sound alarmed her, and the rest of the audience looked slightly irritated by the fact they could no longer properly hear her sing as a result.

A voice rang out. 'We don't want any songs about that damn war.'

'Nor do we want to look at women in uniform,' yelled another man.

Within minutes mayhem erupted and pushing forward, they began to fling rotten fruit and beer bottles on stage. Panic ricocheted through her. It seemed she'd made the wrong decision by wearing her uniform. It looked almost as if some of these cantankerous members of this club might charge up on stage too. A terrifying prospect.

'Get off the stage and leave us with our favourite singers and dancers,' someone shouted.

Cecily recognised this voice as that of the man in the wings who'd accused her of damaging his daughter's career. Could he be the one who had organised this attack? A sense of foreboding flooded through her, reminding her of the traumas she'd suffered during the war when bombs and shells blew down. Feeling powerless and unable to decide how to cope with this, a line of women suddenly came tripping on stage. Attractively dressed in flimsy gowns with their arms linked around each other's bare shoulders, they started to kick their legs high, looking like the Moulin Rouge dancers. The audience burst into fresh cheers and whistles, clearly excited by their image.

Dashing over to her, Johnny grabbed Cecily and dragged her and Merryn off stage. 'Come on, chucks, let's go. There's nothing we can do to save this disaster.'

Their show was thus taken over by other performers, including that bad-tempered man's daughter. There was a smirk of satisfaction on her pretty face as she prepared to go on stage to sing, sparingly dressed in skimpy clothing. Cecily attempted to apologise. Merryn remained locked in silence while Johnny looked utterly captivated by these beautiful dancing women, awe and admiration in his glittering eyes.

The manager then appeared, announcing that they were far too boring, and they were tossed out with no further offers made. Cecily hurried to the dressing room to find Queenie engaged in making up her face and clipping her earrings in place in preparation for her own star performance. She listened in dismay as Cecily explained why they'd been fired. It took some time to calm her down, gather all her belongings and persuade her to leave.

The moment they arrived home, Queenie turned upon Cecily in cold fury. 'I did say this was entirely the wrong thing to do. I will never work for you again, girl. You should have checked the date properly, made sure nothing had been cancelled and never agreed to do it for free.'

'I was doing what I felt appropriate, not at all expecting it to go badly,' Cecily said. 'I desperately wish that man hadn't arranged to attack us, and surely his daughter could have performed on another evening.'

'Don't blame them,' Queenie snarled. 'The responsibility was entirely yours and you made a bad mistake from the start.'

Merryn came to tuck her arm through her sister's. 'It's not fair to say the cancellation was Cecily's fault. Why would you assume that to be the case, Queenie? There are too many people needing work with little in the way of possible jobs, so they'll do battle to keep hold of the one they have. That's the way things are now we're at peace and the country is short of money. So don't blame Cecily when she was doing her best to help us. She's organised things marvellously for us throughout the war.'

'Thank heaven that is now over. From now on I'll do as I please, not what Cecily orders me to do. It's early days for us, having only recently returned from France but I'm utterly convinced I will find employment back at the Palace Theatre because *I* am a star and *she* is not.'

Johnny stepped forward. 'I reckon it's time for me too to build my own future and find work, using no connection either with the war.

You're very talented, Cecily, but made a bad mistake here. Your plan didn't work.'

'I'm sorry about that,' she said, holding up her hands in despair. 'Theatres are struggling postwar but do whatever you think is right for yourself, Johnny. You too, Mama.' Cecily felt a cringe of despair at Queenie's dismissive attitude towards her, as had forever been the case.

'*I* believe you did the right thing to help us, but feel in need of a rest, not more work,' Merryn said, giving a little sigh.

Her sister's support felt most touching, although the bleak expression in her eyes convinced Cecily that, still feeling unwell, she clearly had no wish to confess the reason why she felt in need of a rest. Certainly not while their mother was around. Nor did Cecily have any desire to argue with them all. She no doubt was the one who had made the mistake and as a consequence of the messy response from the audience, it meant their concert party was now defunct, leaving her to face a bleak future.

TWENTY-TWO

1919

MERRYN HURRIED to meet Johnny in a quiet corner of Tinside beach and melted into his arms. It was a cold and windy January day so she'd dressed herself in a pretty long skirt, woollen jersey and smart coat, desperate to look attractive as well as keep herself warm. How delightful it was for them to have some time alone at last. Whether she'd actually find the courage to tell him about her condition was still not clear in her head. He slid his hand beneath her jumper to brush her breasts, causing her to forget all about her morning sickness, which was beginning to ease. Her tummy was starting to feel plump so this issue had to be dealt with soon.

'I'm so glad you still want me,' she murmured. 'The thing is, I have got a bit of a problem.'

He groaned. 'Haven't we all in this dreadful world, not helped by what we went through the other day, thanks to your daft sister.'

Merryn felt in despair as she saw the grouchy expression etched on Johnny's face. 'Please don't blame Cecily. Queenie tends to do that all the time when she's moaning about anything that is troubling her. My dear sister was simply trying to find us employment. Do you think you'll manage to find a job?'

'Like you I feel the need for a bit of a rest, having worked bloody hard over this last year or so, and a chap deserves some time off for hobbies. I've been happy to do my bit, so will do anything within my grasp once I've enjoyed a much-needed break. Why wouldn't I move heaven and earth to help you resolve whatever problem you have?'

'Oh, would you really?' A part of Merryn lurched with fresh hope at this comment.

He gave a little half-smile and then fell into a fit of coughing. When it was over, he drew out a cigarette from his silver case and lit it. 'The war being over, we'll soon recover from exhaustion.'

'I'm not sure I will. But then my issue is not about the war. I'm pregnant,' she said, the words at last leaping out because of her sense of desperation.

'What?' Dropping his cigarette, Johnny stared at her in shocked disbelief. 'Blimey, my ears are popping out like hat pegs. I thought you'd just had a cold or an infection.'

She shook her head. 'I suspected what the problem was before we left France but wished to be sure before I told you, and we did have to face that long journey home. I've worried about it all over Christmas. Now that we are free to create a new life for ourselves, we could marry,' she said, a shy smile lighting her face. What had possessed her to make such a suggestion: wasn't that up to him? Panic rattled through her. 'That's assuming you're ready to be a father and still want me,' she added in a fluster.

He blinked as he released her, gazing at her in startled confusion for what felt like several long moments. 'Good grief, chuck, this problem is putting me in a bit of a flap. I'm not sure I can afford to marry and maintain a wife, let alone be a dad. As you must appreciate, finding a job now this war's over is not proving to be easy. How could I cope, unless you don't need me to provide you with wages, having a rich mother? Has Queenie agreed to help you?'

Merryn was instantly filled with anxiety that Johnny might not feel able to marry her if he became even more poor and unemployed. What a dreadful thought that she could end up a spinster and an unmarried mother. Fighting back tears, she struggled not to show her concern over this remark. 'I still haven't plucked up the courage to admit my condition to her.'

'You must. She's your mam so should offer to help you resolve the problem by providing you with sufficient money for this child.'

'It's not about money, it's whether or not she'll give me permission to marry you, were you to ask me,' she said, blushing with embarrassment. 'I won't turn twenty-one until September 1920. And she's always had silly notions that Cecily and I should marry well-to-do men.'

'Which I am not.'

'That doesn't matter to me. I love you. And don't you love me?'

He blinked, looking confused. 'Haven't we had a good time together? Something special has grown between us, so I reckon it must be love that we feel for each other, right? I trust I'm not wrong in saying that.'

Merryn felt as if she'd stopped breathing and her heart had ceased to beat. What could he possibly mean by describing their relationship in this way? She became aware of his fingers sliding possessively beneath her skirt to caress her thighs and softer flesh, then he started to kiss and make love to her, almost as if that was of importance to prove this statement. Panting with intensity, he pummelled within her, making Merryn gasp and feel a mixture of excitement and panic. However much she might ache for his touch and long to be a part of his life, was he willing to be a part of hers? He sounded no nearer to effectively declaring himself.

When eventually he withdrew, he grinned wolfishly at her. 'You really are quite delicious and belong to a well-off family, not like mine, so mebbe I will come round to the idea of marrying you. Would you like me to speak to your mam?'

Merryn fervently shook her head. 'Absolutely not! I'll tell her myself, just as soon as I can find her in an appropriately good mood, which might not be any time soon.'

'I'll stay close by in case you need help to achieve that.'

'Meanwhile, you'll try to find yourself a job?'

He snorted with laughter. 'It will not be easy to do that, let alone find us a house. We could always live with Queenie.'

'Oh no, I would never wish that to happen.'

The fact he claimed the need for Queenie's assistance was not a good thing, in her opinion. It came to Merryn that like it or not she would have to speak to her mother sooner than she'd planned, in order to resolve this problem.

∽

'Are you certain that marrying him is a good idea, lovey?' Cecily said when Merryn announced that she'd finally told Johnny he was about to be a father and bravely made that suggestion. 'I fear great harm may be brought about if you allow that man to take over your life. He has at times flirted with other girls, including me, which is surely a form of betrayal.'

Flushing, Merryn tightened her lips, looking cross. 'That could be your fault, not his. Why would I blame him for that?'

Realising she'd said entirely the wrong thing, Cecily hastened to defend herself. 'I firmly discouraged him, so please don't accuse me of wanting that to happen. I also tried to explain to you how Mama once attempted to kiss him. I believe he's flirted with the nurses too. You should listen to what I say and not be too trusting of him.'

Merryn's face paled with fury. 'I do not believe he would carry on flirting with anyone now we're a couple.'

'He may also have lied about why he did not join the Army. This eyesight problem he allegedly has doesn't seem to gel. There have been many occasions when I've seen him out and about or even reading, without spectacles on.'

'He does forget to put them on sometimes.'

'That wouldn't happen if he couldn't see well enough without them, and that coughing and limping he apparently suffered from seems to have vanished altogether. He also once demanded a sum of money off me, accusing our family of being rich and selfish. How can you trust him?'

'You're the one who doesn't trust men, not me,' Merryn said. 'Why would I not believe in him? I'd give my heart and soul for marriage with my darling Johnny, and I'm utterly convinced he loves me too.'

'Do take care. You are my dear sister and I'll do anything to protect you, even if you have to remain unmarried.'

'I assure you Johnny will take good care of me, and I do trust him. Now I shall go and speak with Queenie.' She marched off in a huff, her chin held high, leaving Cecily sinking into despair and deeply concerned for her beloved sister.

❦

'May I speak with you, Mama?' Merryn courteously asked, having knocked on her bedroom door. She'd said nothing to her sister about Johnny's grim reaction to her news, not wishing to give the impression that he might never actually make a proposal. Any reluctance he'd felt about agreeing to marry her was simply because he needed a job, Merryn firmly reminded herself. And he had felt the need to make love to her. She could but hope that he would come round to accepting the reality of her situation. Now she must attempt to receive the necessary permission from Queenie. When the door opened, Merryn was, as always, impressed by how lovely her mother looked, elegantly attired in a sky-blue crêpe de chine nightgown that so matched her eyes.

'What is it, darling? Have you at last found me a new role in a show at the Palace?' she asked.

Taking a seat by the fire, Merryn clasped her hands firmly on her lap, striving to hold on to her nerves. 'Sorry, I haven't had time to enquire about that. The thing is, I've not been feeling too well and . . .'

'You're now much better, so please do go and speak to the new manager. You used to be very good at that task, so why would you not assist me? Just make it clear that I can sing and am still a star. Oh, and do please attend to my hair,' she said, handing Merryn a brush.

Ignoring this request, Merryn rubbed her hand over her stomach. 'The fact is, I'm expecting . . .'

Queenie gazed at her with a blank expression in her blue eyes for several long seconds, then screamed out loud. '*What*? You can't *possibly* be!'

'I'm afraid I am.' Merryn could feel her nerves tremble at the sight of the fury in her mother's face. It did not surprise her when Queenie lashed out to smack her, treating her like a naughty young child.

'You slut! Who the hell is the damn father? Was it one of those stupid Tommies?'

Feeling sore and slightly breathless, Merryn rubbed her cheek. 'Actually, it's Johnny, and as I'm anxious that our child should be born within the bounds of matrimony, I wish you to grant permission for me to marry him.'

'Oh my God! You mean you've had an affair with him?' Shock was evident in her mother's gaze. 'You surely aren't claiming that stupid man loves you?'

'I believe he does,' Merryn said, praying that the doubt that niggled within her was not evident in her eyes. 'He is exciting, very loving and we've had a good relationship for over a year.'

Silence followed this remark, and glowering with fierce disapproval, Queenie sneered. 'Don't be ridiculous. You are far too young to marry.

You have all your life and possibly a dazzling career before you, so why put yourself at risk?'

Merryn scoffed at this notion. 'I do not have the talent that you and Cecily have, let alone your good looks, and would never impress or persuade anyone into employing me as a musician.'

'How can you say that? Once you have gained more experience the world is your oyster, dearest, and you can forever work for me. Johnny may attempt to make out that he's a gentleman but has little to offer. His mother is as poor as a church mouse, very northern and working class, and he has no father.'

'Neither have I,' Merryn stoutly remarked. 'As you are fairly well off and my beloved mother, he believes you will help to support me financially. I'm not convinced that would be the right thing for you to do.'

'Quite right, never in a million years,' Queenie screamed. 'Not unless you remain with me. You've put yourself into this mess, so if you walk away and marry him, the pair of you will have to deal with the cost of having a child. Do bear in mind that marriage does not always turn out to be as wonderful as we women hope for. It certainly didn't for me.'

'I'm fully aware that you constantly make this complaint about your personal experience, never having explained why it went wrong. I'm hoping that whatever your disaster was, it won't happen to me. Don't you care about me any more, Mama?'

Distress now resonated in Queenie's beautiful blue eyes. 'Of course I do, my darling. You are my most precious daughter and I have every wish for your happiness.'

'Good, then as I've explained, I *wish* to marry the man I love,' Merryn valiantly remarked. 'If you are not convinced of his feelings for me, I will ask Johnny to come and request your permission. He has offered to do that.'

Queenie's mouth curled into an ironic twist of a smile. 'What a good idea. You can send him to me with all speed.'

'Actually, he's waiting out in the courtyard. I'll go and fetch him and do be kind towards him, Mama.' Giving Queenie a kiss on her cheek, Merryn scampered off and happily brought him to join her.

Johnny stood before Queenie, flattering her by saying what a beautiful and talented lady she was. 'I daresay you will be anxious to prove your love for Merryn, as well as your loyalty to me in justification for all the work I've done for you over the years.'

Queenie glared wrathfully at him. 'Damnation, you never told me you were dilly-dallying with my darling daughter.'

Giving a little shrug, he smiled. 'Since we were involved in the war, we believed our relationship had to be kept private. Merryn was also aware that you'd prefer her to marry a man with riches and high status. I would not allow that to happen. She is young, pretty, madly in love with me and it is my son she is carrying. I strongly hope you have no objection to my marrying your favourite daughter, whom you must surely wish to protect, as do I. I adore her.' Wrapping his arm around Merryn, he pulled her close, his comments filling her with joy. He then went on to make a suggestion. 'Were you to provide me with the necessary funds to support her since I don't hold great hope of easily finding myself a suitable job or a good income, that would be most appropriate.'

'Absolutely not! You're far too demanding.'

Johnny chuckled. 'Ambition for a good life for myself is embedded in me, as well as caring for your daughter. I'm afraid you will have to accept reality to protect her and your future grandson.'

Following this request, to Merryn's amazement, Queenie granted the necessary permission for their marriage, expressing hope for their happiness and also agreed to provide them with a modest sum of money. Days later, Johnny achieved the necessary special licence, banns were called at the local church over the next three Sundays and the wedding took place a few days after that. Merryn radiated with happiness.

TWENTY-THREE

CECILY RECEIVED a note from Boyd to say that Lady Stanford was to be a speaker at the next suffrage meeting in London. The urge to go and see her erupted in her head. What information did that lady have about their father? She could hardly wait to find out, and would be delighted to see Boyd again, such a helpful man. She asked Nan if her sister could offer her accommodation.

'Her husband having died, my dear sister has moved to Bournemouth to run a small bed and breakfast, feeling the need to earn a decent income. It's quite some distance from London, so you'd have to stay at a hostel.'

'Oh, that's a shame. I was so looking forward to seeing your nephew again,' she said, feeling a blow of disappointment.

'He's renting a flat in Shoreditch as he's still searching for a job, as well as grieving for the loss of his father. We've lost so many men during this war and Eric, his dad, died recently of that Spanish flu. Are you sure you wish to go all the way to London for a meeting?'

'I'm so sorry to hear that, Nan, but yes, I do. This is too good an opportunity to miss.' When her sister called in to see her, now living on Mutley Plain with her husband, Cecily told Merryn she hoped she'd come with her.

'Ooh, I'd love to. You know I always find such meetings fascinating.'

Johnny walked into the parlour at that moment, his face appearing even more arrogant than usual. 'Which meeting is this you're talking about, and where?'

'It's a suffrage meeting in London with an important guest speaker,' Cecily quietly informed him.

His tone turned unexpectedly testy and irritable. 'Why would you go so far when you can attend such meetings here? Besides, Merryn is now a wife and soon to become an even busier mother, so how could she find the time and energy, let alone the money for the train fare?'

'I can help her with the cost and it will be a worthwhile visit. They'll be discussing the problems women are facing in finding jobs and how many are suffering a drop in pay, back to the poor sums they received before the war.'

'Why should women be paid the same as men who have wives and children to keep?'

'I do understand that men deserve decent pay, Johnny, but bachelor men too earn more than women who have children to provide for, many having lost their husband during the war. That's not right. A committee was formed to discuss unequal pay, but male members of Parliament were very nervous of being defeated by women at the election because of the shortage of men, which is why the right to vote has not been granted to all of us.'

'You women have to accept the reality that we men are now back in charge.'

Cecily rolled her eyes and laughed out loud. 'Never! Women should be allowed equal rights, the same pay, working hours and pensions as men. We cannot allow MPs or the middle- and upper-class brigade to make decisions without taking into account the requirement of working-class folk.'

'Unlike me, you're upper class, so why would you care?'

'Because I believe everyone deserves the right to vote so that people can build their own future when necessary, no matter what class or gender they are. We should aim for equality for all.'

'Poof, that's nonsense!' he scorned, curling his lip in disgust. 'Men can't do domestic work: cooking, washing and cleaning. They'd look like a stupid music-hall act if they dressed in an apron to do that. Why would we assume women have the right to do men's jobs, now they are freed from the Army or Navy?'

Cecily stabbed her blunt-tipped fingers on the table as she met his dismissive gaze, a light of battle in her own violet-blue eyes 'I reckon your head is stuck in some misty cloud and you haven't noticed that over a million women are now unemployed. They should still have the right to work, particularly those having lost their husband, as well as needing to earn a decent wage. And you should bear in mind there is a terrible shortage of men, thousands if not millions having been lost, so there's a surplus of women.' Remembering that stupid conversation they'd had on board the ship heading to France when he'd revealed his contemptuous attitude towards women, and how demanding he was of them, she never had trusted him. However, her sister did.

'I am not a lost husband so my wife has no reason to go. I require her to stay with me,' he stated, smoothing his hand over Merryn's neck.

There followed a small, awkward silence in which Cecily saw how Merryn glanced up at him, nervously aware of the anger in Johnny's eyes, which filled her with a sense of distress and panic. Clearing her throat, she gave Cecily a little smile. 'I think my husband makes a valid point that I really don't have the time or necessity to travel to London. This discussion seems to be moving away from women's suffrage so I'll give the meeting a miss, if you don't mind, Cecily.'

Cecily struggled not to argue and upset her sister, even if she was allowing herself to be ruled by Johnny. 'As you wish. It's your choice, lovey. I find it useful to visit a meeting where there's a celebrity prepared to give new information. This lady is most interesting.' She made no mention of the fact that Boyd had written to tell her that Lady Stanford might have some news about their father, which she was so looking forward to speaking to her about. This was not a subject she wished to discuss in front of Johnny. He didn't seem to be in a good mood and was behaving far too domineering, his opinion of women seeming worse than ever. Presumably because he too was having difficulty finding employment, for which Cecily did have some sympathy. With a sigh, she gave Merryn a warm hug. 'Sorry I've pestered Johnny to allow you to come with me. It will only be a short trip, but I can perfectly understand your need for rest. I'll tell you all about it when I return.'

'We've finally achieved a vote for some women, if not all. Many members of the suffrage movement are disappointed that Christabel Pankhurst has not been elected. We women must remain strong even if some men view us as being weak as babes,' Lady Stanford announced firmly at the start of her speech. 'We should acquire the strength to make our own decisions. Not simply because we are daughters doing our fathers' bidding or wives obeying our husbands. We are not children, animals or crazy idiots. We are intelligent adults who should be granted our own rights. When children have problems, we expect their father to help resolve them. As wives, we like our husbands to be entirely supportive and not overly controlling. Men should not view us merely as domestic servants and sexual objects,' she thundered, waving her fist in the air and making everyone in the hall jump and cheer. Cecily too felt riveted by these remarks, filled with admiration for this determined lady.

'We cannot go through life as if we are still children. We must learn to resolve our own problems and view our husbands as equals, not as father substitutes. We need to gain their respect in addition to offering them our own.'

Cheers filled the room in response to these comments, Cecily drinking in every word with great appreciation. Lady Stanford's talk had proved to be most fascinating. She went on to speak of how girls who had once worked as domestic servants were no longer interested in returning to those dull tasks. 'They are more concerned with the new jobs they've undertaken during the war and less keen on spending their time washing, ironing and cooking, nor being confined in a fine house. I can understand that, some being obliged to work all hours from morning till night. Thankfully, I've never been so demanding and we do have more equipment and machines to deal with our needs these days. These girls also wish to have the freedom to attend the picture-palace or the *palais-de-danse* of an evening,' she said with a smile.

Why would they not? Cecily thought. She longed for that freedom herself if she could but decide what she was going to do with her life. All too aware that Merryn would be in need of her support over the coming months, particularly after the birth of her baby, she did not see how this could be an easy decision to make.

When the meeting was over, she hurried to stand in the queue of women wishing to speak to Lady Stanford, patiently hoping for that opportunity too. 'Are you here to request employment?' she asked, offering a polite smile when Cecily finally came face to face with her. 'If so, I'm afraid I've already granted two posts to suitable ladies and have no more to offer.'

Cecily blinked. She was obviously a most well-to-do lady who must have felt in need of more servants, not at all what she'd expected to hear. 'No, m'lady, I'm not here to seek work, merely to understand the political problems women are facing and to see you again. If you recall, we did first meet in Plymouth on the day of that celebratory procession for votes for women and I asked if you were related to my father, but you were understandably too busy to respond.'

Her smile fading, Lady Stanford narrowed her eyes to gaze at Cecily with an odd and almost cold expression. 'I believe I pointed out that was not at all the case, whoever your father might be.'

Slightly unnerved at her poor reaction, she struggled to explain. 'You have the same name and I'm aware my father did live in London, which is where I was born. Mama has told us little of what went wrong with their marriage, or when and why my father Dean disappeared, so I'd love to know if you were related. Boyd, my nanny's nephew, said he wrote to you and received a reply saying that you would speak to me.'

'I do not recall agreeing to that. Presumably my secretary responded to his request without consulting me,' she said, giving her a firm glare. 'Who is your mother?'

'Queenie Hanson. I'm assuming that was her maiden name. She did once tell my sister that she reverted to it following the separation from her husband, abandoning her married name of Stanford.'

'You have a sister?'

'I do, yes. She's called Merryn. Could you by any chance be our father's sister?'

'Good gracious, what a ridiculous question! When were you both born?'

Seeing how Lady Stanford's face seemed to have paled to an odd shade of white, looking infuriated for some obscure reason, it sparked curiosity within her over this question she'd asked, plus a sense of dismay. Cecily frowned. 'Why do you wish to know that?'

'No reason, I'm merely attempting to be courteous. I'm sorry to say that I can be of no help. If you'll excuse me, there are other people with more important questions and comments to make. Good evening.' Spinning round on her heel, she began to speak to the next woman in the queue. Rife with disappointment, Cecily felt she had no choice but to leave.

⁓

The meeting being over and a complete disaster so far as achieving the information she'd been seeking was concerned, Cecily was pleased to find Boyd waiting for her outside the hall. She'd written to tell him she was coming and it was a delight to meet him again. He looked much healthier than when they'd first met in Plymouth; he had put on a little weight and was no longer using a crutch. Nor were there any bruises on his head, and his eyes looked bright, wide and lively. 'So pleased to see you looking well, Boyd,' she said, giving his hand a firm shake.

The glow in his velvet brown eyes looked very like a flicker of affection. He lifted his arms almost as if he was about to give her a hug of welcome, then settled for a grin instead and led her into a nearby café. 'Did you enjoy the suffrage meeting and how did it go with Lady Stanford?' he asked, as they settled at a table.

Cecily pulled a face, feeling a resonance of frustration and disappointment. 'What a puzzling woman she was. Quite unwilling to offer any information and far too engrossed in asking *me* questions. Nor was she at all polite.'

'I wonder why that was.'

'I've no idea. Such a puzzle. She certainly had no wish to discuss it, and claimed to have no knowledge of your letter, Boyd.'

He frowned, seeming to match Cecily's despondency with some of his own. The waitress arrived and he quickly ordered afternoon tea. 'As I explained, I did write to her and received a short note in response from her secretary stating that she would look into this issue. She felt certain Lady Stanford would be willing to speak with you. Did she tell you anything about her husband and where he was?'

'She told me nothing, insisting she'd already made it clear my father was not related to her, whoever he might be. It would seem that this effort to see her has proved to be a complete waste of time,' Cecily wearily admitted.

'That's a pity. I did, however, discover some interesting information about her husband. He was called James Stanford, apparently the kind of man who engaged himself in affairs with actresses, singers and dancers. A philanderer.'

'Really? I remember Mama stating that many men treated them as—' Cecily tactfully paused as the waitress appeared bringing a pot of tea and sandwiches, cakes, scones and jam served on a high-tiered cake stand, such a treat in today's postwar world. Once she had gone, she finished her sentence with a little giggle. '—rather like prostitutes.'

Boyd laughed and encouraged her to help herself to a ham or cheese sandwich, which she happily did, feeling hungry. 'This is purely a supposition but it's possible Queenie was her husband's mistress. Unless you have proof they were actually married?'

'Oh, my goodness, that would be astonishing. Mama does claim to have been engaged in a disastrous marriage but has frequently involved herself in affairs. Still does to a degree,' she said, giving a small sigh. 'I guess that as a young woman she must have been pretty stunning. She still is quite beautiful with curly blonde hair, radiant blue eyes and deep red lips. It seems pretty obvious that her husband was not this James Stanford fellow.'

'That's a pity. He was the son of a lord.'

Cecily blinked in surprise as she tucked into another sandwich. 'Goodness, that's extraordinary. Mama does approve of high society and views herself as a most important person, as if she too is high-class, which I'm not convinced she was. Did you find out anything more about this lord?'

He nodded as he sipped his tea. 'I visited the British Library to investigate numerous old newspapers and finally found one or two short articles about him. He was brought up on a large estate in Yorkshire. The family also owned a house in London, where his father Lord Stanford frequently attended the House of Lords. They gave an overview of his life. Let me show you a copy I made of it.'

James Arthur Stanford claimed he'd endured a comfortless childhood with scant interest shown in him by his parents, finding himself confined within the hands of servants. They lived on a large estate in Yorkshire where he was expected to shoot pheasants and grouse, which he had no wish to do. He was taught to ride, ordered to be vigilant with money and diligently learn how to manage the estate. In the main, he spent most of his life from the age of eight in various public schools he considered to be quite grim. He would constantly find himself expelled and moved on to a different boarding school, making few friends as a consequence. When he grew older, he preferred to stay in London where he attended the theatre most nights and indulged in wine, women and song, not being at all interested in politics. Now, for some unknown reason, he has disappeared and has not been seen for some time. If anyone knows where he might be or what has happened to him, please contact your local police or us here at the newspaper.

Having read this through twice, Cecily looked up at Boyd with a puzzled glimmer in her eyes. 'Mama did tell us that our father's name was Stanford, so if this man was indeed her husband he could have drowned, which would be why this article claims him to be missing. Except that if he was a lord and did marry Mama, why is she not called Lady Stanford? Doesn't make sense.'

'James Stanford disappeared and possibly died before his father did, so would not have survived long enough to be classed as a lord.'

'Oh, I see. Did he perhaps have a brother?'

Boyd shook his head as he gave a shrug. 'I've no idea. The information I found about this man is interesting, although I admit there's no proof that he was your father. And there's little point in trying to talk to Lady Stanford as it's not an uncommon name so she and her husband James may not be related to your family. I could continue to search for more details of Dean Stanford.'

'Please don't feel that is essential. I'm sure you have far more important things to do with your time now that you are fit and well, and as you say there's absolutely no proof they are in any way related.' A little disturbed by Lady Stanford's dismissive attitude, Cecily felt touched by Boyd's offer, a part of her wondering why he would bother to waste his time when it seemed utterly pointless. They both remained silent for some moments as they went on to eat the scones with jam and cream, then determined to liven up the conversation Cecily gave a grin. 'I do love this food. What a treat it is after all the boring meals we've had during this dratted war. I really should learn to cook.'

'I keep thinking I should too,' he laughed. 'I'm not very domestically inclined and declined to help Mum with her new B & B. I'm searching instead for a job at a local newspaper, being quite interested in journalism. I am also developing a passion for jazz. It's very African and American. Like you, I love music and greatly admire and envy your work. I wondered if you'd like to go with me to a jazz club. There's one just a short distance away.'

The prospect of spending the evening with him gave Cecily a burst of excitement. And having dressed herself in a pleated silk dress, long beads and an embroidered wide-brimmed hat, in order to look smart for the suffrage meeting, she happily accepted his offer. 'That would be a real treat, never having been to one before.'

'Then let's go and have a jolly evening.'

TWENTY-FOUR

I T PROVED to be an amazing entertainment, the floor packed with happy couples dancing. There was much thumping, stamping and cheering as the Dixieland Jazz Band played 'Mournin' Blues' and many ragtime numbers, pleasure and appreciation very evident among the audience. Cecily didn't find herself very good at this new dancing and because of his peg-leg, Boyd wasn't able to do more than a languorous, rather than an energetic and strenuous, routine. Nevertheless, she loved dancing with him. He would twirl her around, sometimes holding her closely, his velvet brown eyes glittering with admiration and happiness. They managed a slow tango, then tried the *paso doble*, which was Spanish and a little too fast for them both. Cecily tripped up and fell into his arms in a fit of giggles.

'Golly, I think I'm in need of a rest,' she said, noticing that he too looked in need of one, starting to limp a little. They found a table and chairs along the far side of the room and flopped down. He ordered them a glass of wine each and they relaxed, cheerfully sharing details of their favourite music and plays, saying little about the war, memories no one liked to talk of any more. As they danced the last waltz, Cecily experienced a glow of happiness at being held close in his arms, his chin gently brushing against her forehead. When the dance was over, he walked her back to the hostel, saying nothing until they reached the door.

'I'm sorry Mum couldn't accommodate you, having moved to Bournemouth. Hopefully, this hostel will suffice. Could we meet up for breakfast at the café where we had that afternoon tea?'

'That would be lovely,' she said with a smile. He hovered for a moment then tenderly kissed her, the soft warmth of his mouth such a thrill, not at all what she'd expected. Cecily watched him walk away with a stir of excitement in her heart.

The hostel was not exactly comfortable but at least friendly and inexpensive. She occupied a small dormitory along with several other young women, and drifted off to sleep calling to mind how she'd savoured that evening with Boyd. She kept waking up, hearing some of the women snore while others wept having lost their job or loved one, often given comfort and advice by those facing similar difficulties. Cecily wished she too could find a job. She did still receive a small income from her mother, but the cost of her generosity was that Cecily was expected to obey Queenie's demands to carry out various tasks to assist her, particularly since Merryn was no longer around. How she ached to earn her own living and rule her own life.

The next morning, she joined Boyd for breakfast at the café and to her delight, he offered to take her on a bus tour of London. She enjoyed seeing the Houses of Parliament, Big Ben, the Tower of London and various other wonderful places. After that, they took a long walk from Trafalgar Square along the Mall, through St James's Park to Buckingham Palace. When they finally arrived at Paddington Station for Cecily to catch a train back to Cornwall, she thanked him, feeling enormous gratitude for his attention and company, and a slight melancholy as she said goodbye.

'This trip would have been so boring and lonely without you.'

'I've enjoyed our time together too,' he said, his smile warm and alluring.

Was she beginning to feel seriously attracted to him? Of course not! Hadn't she made a decision to pay no further attention to any man? He was merely turning into a good friend. She stood beside him on the platform watching the train puff into the station, almost wishing she didn't have to leave. Opening a carriage door, he helped her to climb on board, putting her small suitcase up on the rack. 'I hope to see you again soon, particularly if I start looking for a job in Cornwall. Not that my aunt is keen for me to do that, insisting I should stay in London, which she claims will be much better for me.'

Cecily grinned. 'Nan can be a bit picky. I hope you find whatever you are seeking. We'd be happy to have you visit us at any time in Plymouth.' A flush of relief flickered through her at the prospect of seeing him again.

Waving goodbye, he met her friendly gaze with a smile of admiration that stirred a deep emotion within her. Considering the losses she'd already suffered, Cecily firmly attempted to block this out. She definitely didn't have the strength to risk falling in love ever again. Oh, but what a kind and considerate man he was. She'd loved every minute of the time they'd spent together, her mind in a whirl of confusion over her feelings towards him. As she settled down for the long journey home, she turned her mind to Lady Stanford's dismissive attitude towards her, greatly appreciating Boyd's generous offer to seek more information about their father. Why he was prepared to spend time doing that was astonishing. Being unemployed, he was perhaps seeking something to occupy him, which made her wonder why Nan was not in favour of him seeking work in Cornwall. Then closing her eyes, she gave herself a much-needed rest having spent a disturbed night with very little sleep.

∽

Arriving back in Plymouth, Cecily took a tram from the station and called in at Merryn's small terraced house behind the Co-op on Mutley

Plain. She was eager to see her sister and tell her what a fascinating time she'd enjoyed in London with Boyd. 'Nan's nephew is a most polite and lively young man. He took me out to tea then to a local jazz club. We had great fun dancing.'

'Oh, lucky you.'

'Wasn't I just? You would have loved it too. It seems that popular tastes have started to change. Ballads and old-style songs have given way to the Charleston, jazz and a different beat of music, which they call syncopation. I tried to learn how to do these new dances with some difficulty,' she said, giving a gurgle of laughter. 'Considering Boyd has a peg-leg as he calls it, he did brilliantly. We had a lovely evening and the next day enjoyed a wonderful bus tour around London. It was a delightful trip.'

'I envy you, Cecily. Apart from the odd bit of shopping, I've spent my days pretty well stuck here in the house, resting or sewing. Johnny is not in favour of my going anywhere, claiming we're very short of money. Besides which, he is not pleased with this house.'

Cecily glanced around the small living room where they were seated together on the sofa. It was not particularly well furnished, possessing only one armchair in addition to this sofa and a small coffee table. It felt quite cold and the fact there was no fire on in the grate was not surprising if they were a bit hard up. But it was small, practical and conveniently close to the centre of town. There was a neat handmade rug and bright blue curtains at the window that Merryn had made, being excellent at sewing, and the walls were a brilliant white, that she'd probably painted. 'You've obviously worked hard cleaning and updating this house, lovey, making it look smart and pretty, so why would he disapprove of it?'

Merryn pulled a face. 'He finds it too far from the sea and has to walk some distance when visiting local theatres in search of work. He also considers it confining and a grubby mess. I've done it up in the hope he'll come to approve of it. Johnny says he'd prefer to live in our home on Grand Parade with Queenie, being much smarter and more convenient. I've no wish for that ever to happen, needing control of my own life now, not one ruled by our mother.'

'I do agree with that. I have exactly the same wish.'

'While you were in London she received an offer to perform again at the Palace Theatre.'

'Oh, that's good to know. So she is still considered to be a star?'

Merryn grinned. 'She is indeed, and so are you. I helped by making her a new gown and dealing with her hair, but declined to do everything she demanded of me, such as wash her clothes or spend hours tidying and cleaning her dressing room. I've recommended that she employ a maid to do those tasks for her.'

'Oh, so have I, being equally pestered to wait upon her hand, foot and finger,' Cecily said, with a sigh and a chuckle. 'It's good to hear she's back on stage, which should calm her temper down. I too am attempting to build a new life for myself if with less success than Mama, having failed to find myself a job, let alone a man to marry as she has insisted upon. Although that shouldn't trouble me.'

'It would me,' Merryn said, giving a faltering little smile. 'Not that I'm riveted with energy or satisfaction just yet. Feeling a little morose.'

Noting a disturbed frown in her sister's expression, Cecily experienced a jolt of concern. Could it be her health or fear of delivering this baby that was troubling her? 'I'm sorry to hear that. I'm sure you'll feel better once this birth has taken place,' she tenderly remarked.

'Except I won't be allowed to find employment once I give birth, not something I'd planned at my young age. I'm sure I'll love him or her, once this baby is born, so will then relish taking care of my family. I just hope my husband does too,' she added, a tiny flicker of anxiety in her lovely hazel eyes.

'You could at some point find work, darling, as Johnny will too.' Cecily then tactfully changed the subject, not wishing to say the wrong thing about this husband of hers of whom she didn't at all approve.

'You wouldn't believe what little I learned from Lady Stanford. I do wish she'd been prepared to answer my questions instead of asking too many of her own.'

'Oh dear, so your trip was a complete waste of time, as I feared it might be,' Merryn murmured.

'Not at all.' And she went on to tell all that Boyd had discovered about James Stanford, showing her the copy of the article he'd given her. 'Not that he found any proof this man was related to our father even if he too went missing. Boyd is a good man and has offered to try and find out more for us. How he'll manage to do that, I've no idea.'

'If Lady Stanford refused to reveal the truth, why don't we ask Queenie? Surely it's time for her to accept we have a right to know more about the death of our father and whether it was this man.'

'That won't be easy,' Cecily said, looking grim.

'Let's give it a go together since we're a good team.' And giving each other a hug, an agreement was made.

❧

Seated in the parlour at Queenie's fine house on Grand Parade, Cecily poured her a cup of coffee. Handing it to her mother she calmly remarked, 'Mama, there is a matter we wish to discuss with you.'

Glancing from one to the other, Queenie blinked. 'You are surely not going to attempt to persuade me to rejoin your concert party? I've made it clear that I wish to maintain my independence, still being a star.'

'You are a most famous person and free to make your own choice on such matters, Mama. This question is not about that. We are wondering if you now feel ready to tell us more about our father? When and why he left you. What sort of man he was. Did he love and miss us when we parted? Is that why he died? Considering you've told us barely anything about him, there's so much we feel the need to know.'

'Do please tell us all you can,' Merryn quietly said.

Queenie glanced from one to the other of them, looking utterly startled by this request. 'You have no right to demand such information. Not hearing the story of my past life may seem irritating, but you must accept that I have no wish to recall the disasters that occurred. It would be far too distressing for me to recall it.'

Cecily gave her a sorrowful smile. 'I do acknowledge that fact, Mama, having lost the love of my life too. But being your darling daughters and now adults, we are keen to offer our sympathy and support over the sorry tale of your marriage, and to understand why it went wrong. We're trying to guess whether that was because he betrayed and hurt you, or else disapproved of the job you were engaged in. Sharing this with us could surely help to make you feel much better and put a stop to those dreadful nightmares you still suffer from.'

Merryn reached over to give her mother's hand a gentle pat. 'Do listen to Cecily; she is making a valid point. We are a close family and feel the need to know what happened to Papa, or at least grow a picture of him in our minds.'

The glare that Queenie gave them brought a shiver into Cecily's soul. 'I have no wish to speak of that man ever again.'

'Why not? You lost but loved him. This issue is important to us, Mama. If you decline to tell us anything about our father, then we'll have to search elsewhere for the necessary information.'

'Utter nonsense! How could you possibly achieve that?' Queenie scornfully remarked.

'By chance, I met a Lady Stanford at a suffrage meeting in Plymouth last year and now in London. I am aware that Stanford was your married name, so I thought it was worth asking if she was related to Dean Stanford. She declared there was no one of that name in her family.'

'Good God, how dare you speak about *me* to someone just because of *their* name?' The ferocity in Queenie's face was quite staggering.

'It seemed a reasonable thing to do. When I tried again at the suffrage meeting in London last week where she was giving a speech, she again ignored my questions, seeming quite irritated.'

Queenie's expression could only be described as an odd mixture of cool derision and panic. 'I'm not at all surprised. I forbid you *ever* to speak to that lady again.'

'Are you saying that she does know you?'

'Absolutely not! I'm speaking of *my* life and *my* privacy, of catastrophes which are best kept out of my mind as they are far too distressing,' she gasped, bursting into tears. 'Never ask me about my husband either.'

Alarmed at having upset her and remembering how Queenie had been most sympathetic over the loss of Ewan, which had created heartache in her soul, Cecily felt filled with guilt. She rushed over to the sofa to hold her close in her arms. 'I'm so sorry, Mama. Obviously, I did not take into account the bad effect the memory of his loss might have upon you, in spite of your disastrous marriage and the nightmares you still sometimes endure.' Exchanging a glance of distress with Merryn, she tactfully pledged that she would not raise the subject of their father's death ever again. Crossing her fingers, she hoped that would be possible.

Slamming down the coffee cup she'd been clutching in her lap, Queenie flicked the tears from her eyes and leapt briskly to her feet. 'You must not speak to anyone on this matter. Is that clear? Were you to do so, I would never forgive you for such dreadful intrusion upon my personal life. It could bring about the demise of my heart and our family.' Firmly lifting her chin, she strode off, the tears having vanished, anxiety and rage now storming in her blue eyes. The subject, it seemed, was forever closed.

TWENTY-FIVE

AT THE end of May, Merryn delightedly gave birth to a tiny baby daughter in a surprisingly easy delivery assisted by Nan and her sister with no doctor or midwife needing to be called. She felt swamped with love and totally captivated by this little one, gazing in wonder at her beautiful blue eyes, golden hair and small neat fingernails. What an adorable baby she was. She cradled her child in her arms and kissed her soft cheeks, loving the sweet scent of her.

Queenie was there too, expressing her delight at being granted a granddaughter. 'What a clever girl you are, darling, to have had such a simple birth. I was never so fortunate.'

'Thanks to Nan,' Merryn said, giving her a warm hug.

'Do you wish me to do anything more?' Nan asked, having bathed the baby and settled her in the cot.

'Nothing I can think of. Cecily has agreed to stay here and help.'

'Then I shall take a little rest and you should too, dear girl. Please leave her in peace,' Nan instructed Queenie, then turning to Cecily with a firm expression on her face, ordered her to take good care of her sister.

'I will, Nan,' Cecily said, a promise that brought a sense of security and relief into Merryn's heart. How supportive and caring her sister was.

Queenie smilingly gave her a kiss and once her family departed and Cecily went to rest in the spare bedroom, she fell asleep. Merryn kept jerking awake as she could hardly wait for Johnny to come home and meet his beautiful daughter. It was a few hours later that he arrived, bursting with satisfaction, to gleefully announce that he'd been granted employment once again at the Palace Theatre, thanks to Queenie's recommendation. He gave her a huge kiss and a grin. 'Life is improving at last.'

'That's good to know, and I've successfully given birth.'

'Ah, so you've finally delivered my son. That's good to know too.'

'Actually, a daughter,' she said, giving him a beaming smile.

'Good Lord, so you've failed to do as I expected. I'd no wish for one of those. Living with a woman as a wife is enough for any man to deal with,' he remarked tartly, scowling at the tiny baby tucked in the cot beside the bed. 'I have five younger sisters and wasn't terribly interested in any of them as baby girls. They were so fussy and demanding, it quite put me off wanting a daughter of my own, much preferring a jolly little boy with whom I could play cricket and football. You should have produced what I wished for!'

A shudder of dismay coursed through Merryn, seeing how he didn't look at all pleased or interested. 'I can't be blamed for this. Besides, your daughter is adorable. Don't you wish to give her a cuddle?'

Firmly shaking his head, Johnny gave a snort of disapproval. 'I have better things to do, like practising on my drum.' Turning on his heel, he marched away.

Tears streamed down Merryn's cheeks, appalled that he'd shown no desire to hold the baby. When Cecily hurried in to give her a hug of comfort, no doubt having been hovering outside and hearing his caustic remarks, Merryn found herself sobbing, 'Why is my husband against our baby girl?'

'Don't fret about that, darling. He's probably too wrapped up in having at last gained employment. I'm sure he'll come round to accepting her eventually. Why would he not find her adorable?' When her tiny niece started to cry, Cecily picked the baby up to give her a cuddle. 'Whoops, I think she's hungry. What are you going to call her?' she asked, as she handed the infant over to her mother to be fed.

'I thought of Josette. It's such a charming name,' Merryn said, wiping her eyes as she attempted to settle her darling child to her breast.

'Oh, what a lovely idea. Hello, little one, pleased to meet you Josette,' Cecily whispered, giving the baby's head a stroke and a kiss, then she quietly sat on a stool close by the bed to watch the feeding take place. Noticing anxiety crease her sister's face as she struggled to persuade the baby to start sucking properly, Cecily helped to settle her in the right position. 'Relax, lovey, she's now found out how to suckle.'

'I'm so lucky to have you here, Cecily. I don't know what I'd do without you,' Merryn said with a sigh.

Once the baby was well fed and had fallen back to sleep, Cecily helped change her nappy and smiled as Merryn tucked her back into the cot. 'You are most fortunate to have this baby. Don't fret about Johnny; he'll come round to accepting her once he grows used to the idea of a daughter instead of a son. Men do have that odd attitude now and then. Now, enjoy a good night's sleep. That is what you badly need after this hectic day. And if you want any help at some point, ring this bell,' she said, indicating one she'd placed on the bedside table. 'I'll just be in the next room and am happy to stay to help for as long as you wish.'

'That would be wonderful, thank you so much.' Merryn met her sister's cheerful face with a smile of gratitude.

Once Cecily had gone, quietly closing the door behind her, Merryn lay down and let the tears roll out of her eyes. She lay swamped in misery but strove to console herself, remembering how excited she'd been when Johnny had agreed to marry her. They'd had no honeymoon, having spent so much time away in France. Instead, they'd simply enjoyed making love, no longer with any reason to worry about the consequences. That had to stop eventually in view of Merryn's condition. She remembered attempting to explain to him she was no longer capable of it, being close to the birth. He'd laughingly ignored her protest, but she'd finally made her point and banned him from her bed. It was now some time since they'd last made love. Her baby having been born, she would soon be free to resume their intimacy, which would surely restore their happy relationship. And as Cecily assured her, Johnny would surely then come to accept and adore their daughter.

Dreaming of these benefits, she drifted off to sleep to be woken three hours later by the sound of the baby crying. Happily sitting up in bed and thankful that Johnny was sleeping upon the sofa in the living room since Cecily was in the spare room, she settled Josette at her breast several times during the night. Merryn felt concerned and weary at the length of time it always took to feed her. Oh, but she loved the feel of her baby daughter. Once Josette seemed contentedly full, she tucked her back into her cot and fell asleep herself, not waking until dawn broke and the baby was again eager to be fed.

The door opened and Cecily crept in. 'Morning, lovey. Here's a cup of tea and a pile of new nappies. I'll bring you a tray of breakfast once Josette has enjoyed hers.'

'Oh, thank you. I do appreciate you being around to help.'

'I'm happy to do what I can, at least until I manage to find myself some form of employment. Then my life will change.'

'Mine already has,' Merryn murmured, and gazing at her beloved daughter, a smile of contentment came into her face. How could she not be happy with her life?

❦

Cecily lay in bed in the spare room at her sister's small terraced house feeling utterly shattered and in desperate need of a good night's sleep. She'd spent the last week running up and downstairs, fetching and carrying food, nappies and endless cups of tea for Merryn as she coped with caring for her baby. Josette would gaze at her with her baby blue eyes and was so adorable Cecily felt an ache of longing arising within her. The hope of ever having children of her own had died, along with darling Ewan.

Giving birth must be physically taxing. Nan had wisely called the local doctor to check all was well with Merryn as a consequence of this quick birth. He'd carefully examined her and agreed she was fine but insisted she must stay in bed for a little while to fully recover. Cecily had happily agreed to stay and care for her sister, aware how much Merryn needed her and what little support she got from Johnny.

Yet again she could hear the baby crying, not sounding as if she would ever stop. Cecily dragged herself out of bed, pulled on her dressing gown and went to help. Merryn was again in a panic, holding her in the wrong position as the baby screamed. It couldn't be easy to cope when one was so young. Eventually, Josette settled in the right position and began to suckle much-needed milk from her mother's breast. Leaving mother and child in peace, Cecily gave her a kiss and crept out. On reaching her room, she was surprised to see Johnny hovering at the door. Thankful that she'd remembered to put on her dressing gown, she tightened the belt and pulled her collar up closer.

'Is that damn baby ever going to stop yelling?' he snarled.

'Your lovely daughter is now happily being fed. It can take time for some babies to get the hang of how to do this. Why don't you go in to give your wife some support, and see how Josette is getting much better?'

He gave a snort. 'Not my job.'

Giving him a disdainful glance, Cecily walked past him to open the bedroom door. It was then that he stepped in front of her and she felt his hand slide over her breasts. 'Men are more interested in these for personal reasons, not supplying milk to babies.'

Cecily slapped his face in fury. 'Damn you! How dare you touch me like that?'

He laughed. 'It was just a joke.'

'As you allegedly said that time you attempted to flirt with me. Don't you dare ever do that again, and be more caring of my sister. Your wife!'

Marching into the bedroom, she slammed the door shut behind her, then hooked a chair beneath the handle to hold it fast. Not for a moment would she ever trust this stupid man. She worried so much for her darling sister who naturally had some despondency in her head because of his dismissive attitude towards that lovely little girl. What a problem Johnny was, almost as irritating as that German PoW and how those dreadful officers had behaved towards her. Heaven knows why Merryn had fallen in love with him. Cecily could but hope he truly loved her and would come round to being a good husband.

~

Each afternoon while Merryn took a little rest, Cecily spent hours minding her niece. How she loved to cuddle, kiss and chat with her, feed her from a bottle if needed, and change her nappy. Johnny kept announcing it was time for his wife to get back to caring for him as well as her child. What a selfish man he was, still not showing any interest in his precious daughter, let alone offering any support to his wife. It was as if his reason for marrying her had been so that he could have someone to look after him, as well as provide him with regular sex. And she feared he still had an obsession with flirting. Cecily kept her bedroom door firmly blocked and herself well out of his way. Could her opinion of him have become too negative? These venomous thoughts melted a little as she reminded herself how much Merryn loved Johnny and at times looked a little woebegone.

Being responsible for doing all the cooking, Cecily rose early each morning to prepare breakfast, having risen on the odd occasion during the night to assist Merryn. Right now, she could hear baby Josette crying for her next feed. Quickly dressing and splashing her face with cold water from the jug on the chest of drawers, she hurried downstairs to put the kettle on the stove. She felt exhausted and was irritated to see Johnny fast asleep on the sofa in the parlour, having come home late last night, as usual. An hour later, after baby Josette had been fed and Cecily had taken up a tray of breakfast for Merryn, he burst into the kitchen, his face scarlet with rage, to find her busily engaged in washing nappies.

'Where's my breakfast? Why didn't you call me?'

Cecily paused to give him a scathing look, then nodded her head in the direction of the oven. 'There's a plate of bacon and egg in there. Help yourself. I assumed you were perfectly well aware of when I deal with breakfast and must hear me going up and downstairs. It's not my fault you are dozy and late.'

'Why would I not be, when I work late each night?' he snarled, and pulling the plate from the oven gave her a glare. 'This is barely lukewarm.'

'Well, if ye aren't satisfied with me cooking, *m'lord*, I'll hand in me notice this minute,' she mockingly remarked as if she was a servant.

'Oh, shut up,' he growled, and plonking himself down at the kitchen table began to quickly consume the food. Minutes later, he pushed aside the empty plate. 'It wasn't good but I had to eat it as I was hungry. Make sure you provide me with a better dinner.'

Standing before him with her hands on her hips, Cecily gave a sarcastic laugh, even though fury lit within her. 'Will do me best, *sir*. It's quite surprising how well I'm learning to cook, being new to this job, *sir*. And not well paid, *sir*.'

'Stop talking nonsense! Why would you be paid a penny when you're here to look after your sister? Don't stand there chortling. Get back to the washing or you'll still be elbow-deep in suds for hours. My shirts too require washing and ironing, then there are other jobs needing attention: cleaning the carpets and windows, mopping the kitchen floor, sweeping and dusting and many more.'

'Heavens, no wonder Merryn is in dire need of a rest. What will you do to help her, once she feels able to cope with all these domestic duties?'

With a blank expression in his grey eyes, he gave a sniff. 'She'll manage perfectly well, once she gets the hang of caring for that baby. I shall do my bit by working hard every evening, which is what we men do. You are provided with an income from Queenie so don't have to work or sing ever again. Lucky you!'

'Actually, I am seeking the occasional performance, if not on the Pier or any large theatre, and hope to find something. Meanwhile, having time on my hands, I love to assist my sister.'

'Merryn doesn't have to perform either and should be engaged doing her own domestic work, now she's fully recovered. She no longer needs your assistance, being perfectly capable of caring for her own child and me, her precious husband. So you can leave, once you've finished these jobs. I've no wish for you to be in charge of her or interfere in our relationship.'

Cecily turned away with a frisson of anger in her stomach, aware of how fragile Merryn was, but knew the fruitlessness of arguing with him over this matter. He was a stubborn and condescending man. She suspected he'd agreed to marry her sister simply because of their well-off mother. On many occasions during the war, he'd insisted men should be in charge of women, instructing them what to do. He seemed to be getting worse in that respect, which surely meant that Merryn was in greater need of protection. Pushing up her sleeves, she went back to battling with the washtub and nappies and furiously scrubbed the kitchen floor.

'Would you believe your husband has ordered me to leave?' she told Merryn as she assisted her to bathe Josette. Receiving no response, she glanced up at her sister to see a tight expression on her face as she remained silent for some long moments.

Lifting up the baby to dry her, she finally said, 'Actually, Johnny is probably right. I am better now so can surely look after myself.'

'But he's such a bully, expecting me and now you to do all the domestic work while he has done nothing to help,' Cecily said, struggling not to mention how she'd felt the need to keep her spare bedroom door fast shut.

'I'm his wife, so why would I not since I've recovered from Josette's birth? Thank you for your assistance but I now feel it is more appropriate to spend time with my beloved husband, instead of with you, my sister. Your attempt in the past to put me off marrying Johnny, probably because you rather resented he'd given up flirting with you, and your poor opinion of him now, is not helping one bit.'

Hearing this, Cecily felt utterly desolate. It came to her that she'd said entirely the wrong thing. Johnny's sarcasm had revealed why she should not be spending her time waiting hand, foot and fingers on him, or listening to his whims and peccadilloes. He'd accused her of interference, with which her sister was surprisingly agreeing. Cecily strove to convince herself that she could indeed be interfering in their relationship. As she was now married, Merryn had the right to make her own decisions. Flushing with dismay, it came to her that an awkward distance and coolness was developing between them. 'I'm so sorry, lovey. You're probably right. I could go off and find myself new employment, and you should feel free to organise your own life.'

'Quite! You may call in to see me on those occasions when Johnny is involved in rehearsals.'

'I will, and you can call to see me whenever you wish. Just take a tram, as they aren't expensive. I shall see you in a day or two, lovey.'

Saying goodbye, she packed her bag and receiving no hug, quietly left, steadfastly keeping a smile on her face and making no further comment about her sister's so-called precious husband. She'd been delighted to care for her sister and little niece. Now a part of Cecily was filled with relief that she no longer had to remain in this house with that dreadful man. But she felt deeply anxious over leaving her sister.

TWENTY-SIX

IN THE weeks following her departure, Cecily would go swimming each morning, feeling the need for exercise, then occasionally cycle over to visit her sister. Sometimes she'd mind the baby while Merryn was engaged in her domestic routine. Other days they would go shopping together and Cecily loved taking a turn at wheeling the pram. Much as she enjoyed spending time with her beloved sister, there was still a slightly detached feeling between them, and she no longer dared ask anything about her marriage or husband. She certainly appeared far more grown up, quiet and independent. Cecily could but hope things were improving for Merryn.

As for her own life, a part of her was growing increasingly frustrated and bored. She'd failed to find any decent employment here and had lost so many friends. Most of the boys she'd known were gone, leaving many of her female friends widowed and tied up with their children too. She too had lost the men she'd loved or grown fond of. Cecily saw herself as a spinster who would never be fortunate enough to have a child herself, let alone find any hope of marriage since there were few men around. Being the only male friend she had left, would she ever see Boyd again? She secretly hoped that one day he'd come to visit her.

Cecily firmly believed it was much safer to remain single. The dream of wedded bliss was long gone from her head, replaced by a desire to explore the possibility of creating her own future and economic security, safely away from domineering men. More single women were becoming self-sufficient, so she must make every effort to do the same. There was definitely a limit to how long she could rely upon the funds her mother provided. Desperately feeling the need to manage her own independence and purpose in life, she resolved to make enquiries on how to develop a new career for herself, the concert party having folded. Whether she could continue singing or find some other form of employment seemed to be an issue that would not be easy to resolve.

At least she was free to make her own decisions, as all women should be allowed to do. Those who'd worked on the local trams throughout the war and had retained their jobs were now going on strike, demanding the same increase in pay as men. There'd been women workers on strike in London, so why wouldn't local women here in Plymouth do the same? They surely deserved equal rights. It came to Cecily that having been involved with the suffrage movement for so long, she could possibly attempt to assist them in this battle.

'Are you managing to resolve this problem?' she asked Sally Fielding, one of her former fellow tram workers. A group of them were standing on the Old Town Street holding posters high, one stating: *Is a Woman's Place in the Home*? Another said: *We Believe in Equality*. 'I can understand why I was not granted my job back on the trams, having been away entertaining the troops in France. Those of you who've worked for them throughout the war should have that right.'

'Indeed we should,' Sally agreed. 'They accuse us of having less strength and more health problems than men. Absolute tosh! The bloody government treats us like servants. We were doing our bit for the duration of the war but are now being dismissed and replaced by men they consider to be more skilled. We women have worked damned hard and done well. They see us as less productive, which we're most definitely not and we surely have the right to the same pay.'

'Did you join a trade union?' Cecily asked.

'We did indeed. Once we'd registered to work in the war, why would we not protect ourselves? It was recommended we do that when we were sent a leaflet issued by the War Emergency Workers' National Committee.'

'Are you managing to provide some funds for unpaid women on strike?'

'Not very well,' Sally said, pulling a face.

'Right, I'll help with that.' Cecily remained with them for the remainder of the day. Taking off one of her boots, she held it out to passers-by, begging a donation as a token of their support. When dusk fell, she handed over a fair sum of money to Sally. 'I'll try to collect more tomorrow. How long will this strike last?'

'Maybe just a couple of days this week. Then if we don't get anywhere, even longer next.'

'I'll be there to join you,' she promised.

Cecily continued to spend time each day assisting more women by raising money to provide them with an income, as they received none while on strike. It felt such a satisfaction, giving her a fresh purpose in life. Despite the troubles they were enduring, she too sorely missed the work she'd been involved with during the war, and the opportunity to display her talent. She wrote a brief letter to Boyd, to tell him of her satisfaction in helping these women on strike, being a suffragist. She sorely missed him too.

'Can I do anything more to help?' she asked her friend Sally.

'Aye, you could write a newspaper report depicting our success and why we deserve to receive the same rate of bonus that is being given to men workers, as a result of the war.'

'I'll be happy to give that a go,' Cecily agreed. She wrote at length about how many women during the war had worked in munitions, coal, gas and power supplies, factories, transport and various offices.

As a result, this war feels like a revolution. Now they are being compelled to return to domestic service and even those still in work are having their wages cut to the low rate they received before the war, not raised as is the case for men. If women are doing the same work with equal skills, they should be paid the same rate. No woman should be paid less than a living wage and the return of men to their jobs should not destroy women's lives. Many have lost their husbands and must now raise their children alone. In order to provide their loved ones with a good future, they should be allowed to keep their occupation or be granted alternative work. Please help support these hard-working deprived women.

She delivered copies of this article to all the local newspapers in Plymouth, Devonport and beyond. As the strike continued over the following week, she happily continued to collect donations to support those women in need of income. She visited church congregations, the Hoe, where she found there were always caring folk quite close to the war memorial, the Pier, theatres and football grounds. The following week, Cecily was delighted to find her article featured in local posters, several newspapers and magazines. It was weeks later that the tram bosses agreed to an equal minimum wage rate for women.

'Success!' they all shouted.

'And thanks for providing these funds to stop us from starving while we were on strike,' Sally said, giving her a hug.

Cecily smiled. 'Happy to help and so glad of your success.'

Once again finding herself at a loose end, having done her bit for the women on strike, the Tommies and her beloved sister, Cecily greatly felt a desire to build a better life for herself. She still loved singing and had visited many theatres here in Plymouth, Devonport and other towns within easy distance but had received no good offers so far. She had been granted the opportunity to give an occasional performance in the interval at a cinema and the odd evening at a small hotel. Not that she'd made much money from either of those, so she must seek some improvement.

Cecily changed into a smart lavender dress and decided to go out for a much-needed walk along the Hoe and head for the Pier. She could hear music playing and went along to the Pavilion. It was a lovely July day, the sun shining and people swimming, laughing and having fun. She almost felt the urge to jump in and take a swim herself, having always enjoyed taking the plunge. She looked up at Smeaton's Tower and the war memorial, now packed with names of lost men, her mind slipping back to the anguish of the war and how glad she felt that it was over at last.

Would the manager at the Pavilion be interested in her? Shortly after they'd returned from the war, she'd sent him a note requesting an audition but to no avail. According to Mama, there was now a new manager, so that might help. Queenie was unlikely to object to her going back on stage, as she had sternly done in the past. Deliberately shutting out that possibility, Cecily asked the lady at the office if she might speak to the manager. She dutifully hurried to fetch him, and he respectfully listened as Cecily explained where she'd been performing during the last eighteen months of the war.

'I wondered if you'd be prepared to give me the opportunity to sing here? I dare say you know that my mother is something of a star. She is once again performing at the Palace Theatre so I'm sure she'd have no objection to my working here.'

He gave her a puzzled glance in response to this. 'Can't see why that matters.'

'It did use to bother her once upon a time,' Cecily smiled. 'As a consequence of war, I now have lots of good songs to offer.'

'Indeed? Well, I'm afraid the kind of concert and songs you performed for the troops would no longer go down well. Do you have any new songs to offer?'

Taking a breath, Cecily realised that she'd again made a mistake. Hadn't the same thing been said when their concert party had performed some months ago at that small nightclub? That could be the reason she'd received few offers since. The interest now was in lively trivia, jazz and silent pictures at the cinemas, which were becoming increasingly popular with many people attending. A piano would be played in the interval and sometimes a singer would be permitted to accompany it, as Cecily occasionally was. Old-style concerts were most definitely out of favour, performances that were a bit naughty and jolly being much more the in thing. Why hadn't she remembered that and devised a new routine? Probably because she'd been too caught up in caring for Merryn and Josette, and then those striking women.

'I'm sure I can provide whatever you wish,' she hastily assured him. Seeing him return his attention to a folder he was carrying and starting to jot notes in it, it was clear that he was not interested. 'Will you be holding an audition at some point?' she asked.

'We've plenty of performers available, thank you. I'm not currently seeking any more.' And with a nod of his head, he turned to walk away.

Hurrying after him, she said, 'I'm so sorry to hear that, being desperate for work. Do you know of any company that is seeking new artists?'

Pausing to glance at her and noting the anxiety in her face, he gave a sympathetic smile. 'You could always apply to perform on board a cruise liner. They are definitely seeking new entertainers.'

'Really? Good gracious, I never thought of that. I'll give that some consideration.' Thanking him, she quietly left.

Bearing in mind what that new manager had said, would it be appropriate for her to go travelling again? She would miss Merryn, but her sister was now well recovered and determined to live her own life with a man Cecily had failed to approve of, and at least she had a darling child. So why not go and do something more exciting with her own life? She did love Plymouth. It was a lively town with regiments garrisoned at the Citadel, many of them sailors and marines, and there were plenty of pubs and bawdy houses available to entertain them. Having spent her youth living in digs and enduring dozens of shambolic places for years, which had never been easy, coming to live in this town had felt utterly blissful. Cecily believed that her mother had only been prepared to move here once her parents were both dead – a puzzling and depressing attitude. Putting all of that out of her mind, she began to spend time writing songs for herself, feeling in need of making a dramatic change in her life.

Once she had a collection that satisfied her, she popped in again to ask the manager if he could recommend a company worth trying. He readily handed over the address of Carabick Cruises. 'The cruise industry is back in action now the war is over. There are quite a few companies to choose from, but start with this one. It's classy, smart and efficient, and their small liner sails from Portsmouth to Corsica, Sardinia, Malta, parts of Spain, Italy, Greece, and numerous other places around the Mediterranean. They could contact me for a reference if that was required. And if you don't get taken on as an entertainer with them, Cecily, come and see me again and we'll talk about what you could perhaps perform for us here on the Pier.'

'Thank you so much,' Cecily said, surprised by this implication of a possible offer.

She spent the following days correcting and testing the new songs she'd written, as well as teaching herself some classic ballads that were not at all war-oriented. Having finally convinced herself she was still good at entertaining, Cecily then wrote a carefully worded letter to Carabick Cruises, giving the envelope a kiss of hope when she posted it. Oh, how she hoped she'd succeed in getting an offer.

TWENTY-SEVEN

MERRYN WAS thrilled to have her adorable daughter but badly missed the support of her sister, since Cecily only called in for a few moments most days. Johnny's interest in their baby was still poor and he gave her no help. His attitude towards her too was not at all considerate, and he was constantly pestering her for sex. Merryn had attempted to explain why she wasn't able to give in to that just yet, still feeling sore and tired, let alone bleeding. 'I'm sorry, love, I will come round to it soon,' she promised him.

Now that Cecily had gone, he had returned to their bed and demanded she succumb to his needs. Pulling the blankets off her, he snarled, 'Get up and strip off. You can at least give me the pleasure of seeing you naked, even if you claim not to be available. You're an artist, so it's time you entertained me.'

'I – I don't think the sight of me would appeal to you right now. I'm still a little plump following the birth and have stretch marks and other issues,' she said, giving him a shy smile and not wishing to describe the fact she felt clogged with infection and her breasts were swollen and sore.

'Don't be ridiculous, that baby is nearly a month old, so what's the problem?' Pulling her out of bed, he stripped off her nightgown, then taking off his own clothes lay down on the bed to gaze at her, his hands stroking his member. 'Walk around and do a little dance.'

Merryn struggled to do as he instructed, embarrassment fluttering through her, this being something she'd never done before.

'Put your arms up, open your legs wide and push yourself towards me.'

'Oh please, no, Johnny.'

'Do what I say!' he roared, giving her a push.

She fell, shuddering with humiliation and a vivid sense of guilt that she'd refused to allow him to make love to her. Then being dragged up to her feet, she did as he ordered. It was then that she heard Josette start to cry, obviously having been disturbed by the loud shouts he'd made. She quickly dashed over to the cot only to find herself grabbed by Johnny as he leapt out of bed. He slid his hands over her, fingering and caressing every part of her body, not only her swollen breasts but also those private parts still sore after the birth. Josette was screaming louder than ever and Merryn desperately strove to push him away. Why would he not appreciate the responsibility involved in caring for a first baby, and the pain involved in the birth? He seemed to have an insatiable sexual appetite and not a shimmer of respect or understanding for what she'd been through. 'Please let go of me, Johnny, Josette needs attention.'

'So do I, and I'm much more important than that child,' he said, grasping her breasts so firmly she cried out in agony. Then with a rumble of excitement, he pushed her back on to the bed and entered her without bothering to give her a hug or a single kiss.

Scenting the stink of alcohol on his breath and hearing his panting and grunting without him showing the slightest glimmer of affection for her, Merryn felt utterly traumatised and abused. Once he flopped away from her and fell almost instantly asleep, she pulled on her nightgown, picked up Josette and fled downstairs to feed and change her as well as wash herself, aware of a trickle of blood running down her legs and tears rolling down her cheeks. Why had he been so demanding? Did he find possession of her totally enthralling, wishing to treat her as an obedient and submissive slave? Or had he simply required proof that she still loved him? If the latter notion was the reason, then she could have been entirely wrong to attempt to put off his sexual needs just because of her condition. Hadn't she always enjoyed him making love to her, and felt a desire for him to be a little more compassionate? That being the case, she must try to be a better wife, and encourage him to become a loving father.

❧

Delighted to have received a friendly reply from Boyd in admiration of her efforts for the women on strike, on a spur of the moment Cecily took it into her head to visit him. Aware that he too was keen on music, she would greatly appreciate his opinion on what she'd achieved with these songs she'd written. She wrote a short note to say she felt the need to visit London again, not wishing to state her reason until the appropriate moment came. She was thrilled to receive a reply the next day saying he would meet her at Paddington Station.

She chose to wear a long pale blue checked skirt, white blouse, matching jacket, and a wide-brimmed hat upon her chestnut-brown hair, anxious to look appealing. Carrying her bag and a summer umbrella to protect herself from the sun, she found herself equally delighted to see him. He looked so smart and handsome in a light grey suit with a striped waistcoat and boater hat. And most welcoming with a warm smile on his face.

As they walked through the city, a silence fell between them, although their attraction was very apparent in the way he kept glancing at her and holding her hand whenever they crossed a road. A whirl of emotion flared through her at his touch.

'Where would you like to go? We could visit Spitalfields Market, Princes Theatre or the Gaiety. Or simply take a walk in St James's Park. I assume you're staying at the hostel and will escort you there whenever you wish. Although if you don't care for that uncomfortable place, you could always stay at my flat.'

There was something in his velvet brown eyes that excited her. Nevertheless, instinct warned her not to agree to this offer. It was far too tempting and dangerous. Hadn't she messed up her life before by allowing Louis to make love to her, even if they weren't falling in love? And could she be certain how Boyd felt about her, let alone any emotion she had for him? Cecily met his smile with a gentle shake of her head. 'I'll be quite happy staying at the hostel, thank you. I've no wish to go to it just yet, so a walk in the park would be lovely.'

They took a wonderful stroll, the sun shining in a bright blue sky, then enjoyed a delicious lunch, the pleasure of his closeness running through her like fire as they chatted happily. Wondering if she should now mention her reason for being here, instead Cecily blandly stated how she'd been hoping he'd visit Cornwall.

He looked sideways at her, his lips lifting into an enticing smile. 'I certainly was considering coming to look for a job in Plymouth, feeling the desire to see more of you, and hoping to stay with my aunt, your Nan, until I found a place of my own. She then wrote to say that your mother does not welcome visitors so I didn't feel I could come.'

Cecily chuckled, thrilled by his interest in her and understanding Nan's reason for that latter comment. 'That's not entirely true. Queenie does tend to be a bit fanatical about young men. Nan would simply be attempting to protect you from being seduced.'

He roared with laughter at such a prospect. 'So if I did, I'd better stay at a local youth hostel to remain safe, just as you do here.'

'You'd always be most welcome. Have you found yourself a job in journalism?'

'No, I've failed to find employment at any local newspaper here in London. I used to work with my dad at Spitalfields Market, fetching and carrying stuff before joining the army at a young age, so maybe I don't have the necessary skill. My aunt is urging me to go to Bournemouth, Mum being desperate for me to work with her at the B & B. As you know, I've no wish to do that and as she is planning to soon retire, what is the point as she'll no doubt go to live with her sister.'

'Really? Oh, we'll sorely miss her.'

'I'm sure you will. Have you yet managed to find yourself a job?'

Cecily felt strangely relieved at his lack of employment, filling her with the hope he might indeed come to Cornwall, even if Nan did retire and leave. 'I've done the odd small performance at a local cinema and hotel but nothing long term has been offered.' She went on to explain the suggestion made by the new director on the Pier that she could apply to work on a cruise ship. 'I'm quite passionate about travel as well as singing, but as our concert party is now defunct and Merryn cannot come with me, it's not an easy decision to go off travelling alone. I'll have to decide soon though. Being a changed world, I feel the need for more importance in my life.'

'So you reckon you may choose to work on a cruise liner?'

'Actually, I've written to Carabick Cruises and am hoping for an offer,' she softly admitted.

He grinned. 'That's good to know. Were you to succeed in achieving employment on a cruise, would you entertain them with the songs you sang during the war?'

'Indeed not. They are now considered to be out of date.' Finding the courage to pull her sheets of songs from her handbag, she said, 'Actually, I've written a few for myself but I'm not sure if they're any good. I rather hoped you might give me your opinion.'

He looked fascinated as he studied them. 'I'd love to hear you sing these. The flat I rent is quite small in an overcrowded part of the city, not at all as glamorous as your house in Plymouth, but made available to me thanks to the local council. I'm grateful for that as there's a shortage of houses and I'm stuck on my war pension. I do, however, have a piano there. Would you care to come and sing to me before disappearing off to the hostel?'

Sorely tempted, Cecily blinked in delight. 'You have a piano? That's wonderful. Are you saying that you're a pianist?'

'I'm not claiming to be expert at the task, since my parents were only able to afford a few years of lessons for me when I passionately begged them to buy me a piano. I would be happy to do my bit, or maybe you have a grand piano and can play too?'

Cecily laughed. 'I do, although I never play a piano in public, not feeling good enough. But I do play for myself whenever I practise singing and would be happy to sing some for you if you were interested.'

'I am indeed.'

She happily seated herself at the piano in his small kitchen-living room. The flat didn't have much furniture, merely a couple of chairs and a table, yet looked very clean and tidy. Boyd quietly took a seat to listen while she concentrated on performing one of her favourites, rather than one of her own compositions: 'How Ya Gonna Keep 'Em Down on the Farm After They've Seen Paree'.

When she'd finished, he gave loud applause. 'I love that song. It's very popular and such fun. You're an excellent singer and I'm most impressed that you can play the piano for yourself, which you do well. Can I play for you now?'

'Please do.' Cecily quickly rose to make way for him on the piano stool, presenting him with a fresh sheet of music. As he played, she was instantly convinced by his skill and began to hum, then sing:

After you've gone and left me cryin',

After you've gone, there's no denyin',

243

You'll feel blue, you'll feel sad,

You'll miss the dearest pal you've ever had.

When the song was over, Cecily applauded him. 'You played really well. I'm highly impressed.'

'I like this song too,' he said with a grin. 'May I now play those you've written for yourself?'

He spent the next hour playing these and as Cecily sang, to her delight he sometimes joined in and sang with her, whenever it seemed appropriate. How she loved that. 'My goodness, you can sing as well as play.'

'I only do that occasionally but I'm so glad you approve of my playing,' he said, then something in the way he rubbed his chin and fell silent made her worry that he was about to criticise what she'd written – not a reaction she would relish. 'Your songs have a good pace and interesting lyrics. Were you to receive an offer from that cruise company, I wonder if I could join you?'

She gazed at him in astonishment. 'Goodness, are you saying you wish to work with me?'

He nodded, giving her an enchanting smile. 'Why would I not, assuming you consider my playing to be good enough? I would find such an adventure absolutely irresistible, and you know how I love all music, not just jazz.'

'Oh, that would be wonderful! That's a deal if and when I ever get offered such a job.' She held out her hand to shake his, but slipping his hands around her face he gave her a tender kiss. Cecily's heart raced, loving the taste and pressure of his mouth against hers. She felt the stroke of his fingers on her cheeks and a wave of desire flared within her. Flushing with excitement, she gently stepped back. 'Now I must go as I have to be at the hostel before nine, and tomorrow I take the train home. I'll be in touch with you, Boyd, as soon as I receive a reply to my application.'

❦

A few days later, to her surprise and delight, Cecily received a response, offering her the opportunity to attend an interview and audition the following week. Quickly sending Boyd a postcard with this news, she then told Merryn, mentioning the possibility that Nan's nephew might accompany her. Her sister listened in awe then gave Cecily's hand a squeeze. 'Singing on a cruise ship sounds great fun. I do hope that works for you, although I will sorely miss you.'

'I'll miss you too. I hope we're still close, lovey.'

'Of course we are.'

'And as I'm prepared to give this cruise a go, I trust that you're contentedly settled in a happy marriage?'

'I am,' Merryn said, and turning away to tickle Josette's face as she lay in her pram, avoided meeting Cecily's warm smile with one of her own.

'That's good to know,' Cecily said, giving her a hug and Josette a sweet kiss. 'You are most fortunate with this lovely baby. Right now, I desperately need to search through my wardrobe for an appropriate costume for the audition. Please do help me find one.'

Merryn chose her an elegant ankle-length gown of pale green silk, adding a wide lemon sash and matching new shoulder straps lined with a tiny row of floral buds. Meeting Boyd in Portsmouth for the audition, Cecily was hugely impressed by Boyd wearing an evening suit with a tailcoat, together with a white waistcoat, shirt and smart bow tie, which he'd apparently hired. How classically well dressed they both looked.

'I'm trying to squash a stir of nerves,' he admitted as they sat waiting to be called.

'You look most handsome.'

'And you look beautiful, as always,' he said, bringing a blush of excitement to her face.

There were so many other people taking part in the audition that Cecily almost lost hope, feeling an unusually strong degree of stage fright. Once Boyd began to play and she started singing one of her own songs, 'My Life is Bliss', this quickly vanished. It received a good applause and appreciative comments, being new and well performed by them both. To her delight, they were later called to the director's office and instantly offered a job. Seconds later, they were signing a contract and given instructions of when and where they were to leave, and what would be required of them. They were then taken along to the dressing room to be measured for costumes and suits.

'Oh, if only Merryn could come with us too, wouldn't that be fun?' she said as they excitedly sat chatting over a coffee in the café.

'We'll have fun too,' he promised. 'I did make it clear to the director that we require separate cabins, as we aren't a married couple.'

Cecily met his gaze with a certain sense of reality and longing. Why did she want him? She shivered with desire and gave him an enchanting smile. 'I'm delighted you're willing to join me, Boyd. It will be so much better than travelling alone.'

TWENTY-EIGHT

MERRYN SAT having coffee with Cecily in the café on the Pier, as she so loved to do, her baby snuggled close in her arms. She listened to her sister's wonderful news that she and Nan's nephew had been granted the role of cruise entertainers. Tears flooded Merryn's eyes as she nodded and smiled. 'I'm so pleased for you, darling. Oh, how I wish I could come too. I can't possibly do that now that I'm a married woman with a baby, not unless Johnny was agreeable to joining you too, which he isn't.'

'Not since he's no longer interested in the concert party.'

'I thought it was wrong of Queenie, and even Johnny, to put an end to our concert party, considering all we went through together during the war in France. Not that there was anything we could do about that and they both thankfully started working again for the Palace Theatre, which is a good thing.'

'I can perfectly understand that. Why would they not?'

'Johnny is so busy he spends less time at home than he used to.'

'Oh dear, is that a problem?'

'No, no, I'm happy that he's doing so well, and being an equally busy mother I'm willing to accept that.' Merryn frowned, not wishing to explain how a distance seemed to be developing between them, maybe because of the work he was engaged in rather than simply losing interest in her.

Cecily gave her a sympathetic smile. 'With regard to Nan's nephew joining me in this project, neither his aunt nor Queenie must be told. Nan has tried to persuade Boyd to work with his mother in her B & B, which he has no wish to do. So we can't tell them about this cruise until we have proof our professional partnership works.'

'I won't say a word,' Merryn promised. Judging by the excitement in her sister's eyes and all too aware of her talent, she suspected Cecily could be absent for weeks or even months, a situation she dreaded. 'I'm so glad you have this young man's support. Could you become a serious couple?' she teasingly asked.

Cecily gave a shy smile. 'Who knows. I do find him most caring and attentive, and really quite attractive. I'm also impressed by his skill as a pianist. We leave in ten days so I must now go and check what I should take with me. They do provide us with a few costumes but we're allowed to take some of our own. Would you help me sort that out and do some shopping, lovey?'

'I'd be happy to help you get yourself sorted.'

The next few days passed in a whirl of activity, Merryn rigorously engaged herself in helping Cecily go through her wardrobe to choose appropriate stage costumes, day dresses, hats, stockings and suitable shoes to take with her, as well as spending several hours shopping together for items she required. She also spent much of her time watching Cecily rehearse, listening and applauding while she sat mending and improving garments in need of attention. Baby Josette would lie on the hearthrug waving her legs about, also seeming to enjoy the music. At times Merryn would give her baby a cuddle and let her sit contentedly on her lap. She was over three months old and growing increasingly lively.

Queenie too would sometimes come to listen and offer advice. She generously loaned Cecily a few garments, demonstrating how they should be folded and properly packed. Cecily always thanked her mother for this support, making it clear she would be working alone, carefully avoiding details of this new partnership. On the day she was due to leave, Merryn happily smiled as she saw her mother give Cecily a warm hug.

'Do enjoy this trip and don't misbehave with any men you don't know well.'

Cecily burst out laughing. 'As you've never done, Mama?'

Queenie gave a wicked little grin at this remark. 'I'm suggesting you do not make the same mistakes I made. My own mother was somewhat foolish over men and I have been too, so make sure you find one who is rich, high-class and most caring, as I have advised you to do on numerous occasions. And do take care of yourself, dear girl.'

Seeing a glow of happiness in her sister's eyes as Queenie gave her another hug and a kiss, Merryn could see Cecily was savouring this rare moment of closeness between them, their relationship having never been easy. Or could their mother simply be relieved that Cecily was leaving? Not a pleasant thought. And it was interesting to hear Queenie speak of her own mother.

Merryn accompanied Cecily on the train to Portsmouth and walked with her down to the dock, pushing little Josette along in her pram, fascinated to see Nan's nephew waiting for her sister on the dock. When the time came for the ship to depart, she enfolded her with warm affection, fighting back tears in an effort to remain calm. 'Johnny sends his best wishes and apologises that he wasn't able to come and see you off.'

'I expect he's busily engaged in rehearsals,' Cecily said.

Aware that her husband and sister had barely spoken a word to each other since he'd ordered Cecily out of the house, Merryn said, 'Actually, he claimed to be in need of rest today, probably because he's been working too hard recently. Thankfully he's slowly coming round to accepting our daughter as a small treasure. He spends time watching her being fed and I've sometimes persuaded him to sit her on his knee.' It happened once following an argument, but she tactfully made no mention of that.

'Excellent! I do hope he becomes a good father to my adorable niece,' Cecily drily said, giving Josette a sweet kiss.

'Do enjoy your performances, as well as exploring all the fascinating places you'll be visiting. It was nice to meet you, Boyd, and good luck,' she said, shaking his hand, then giving Cecily another big hug, as tears rolled down her cheeks.

'I'm sure we'll have an exciting time. You take care of yourself too, darling, as well as your lovely baby,' Cecily said as she too began to weep, locking Merryn close in her arms. Finally releasing her, she walked hand in hand with Boyd up the gangway to board the ship.

Once they were up on deck, Merryn saw how this young man pulled her sister close to put his arms around her. When she heard the blast of the ship's horn and it slowly began to sail away, she bleakly watched them depart, doing her best to smile and wave. Merryn then took the train home and fell into Johnny's arms in a flood of tears. She was in a sorry state of emotion, which he instantly attempted to resolve by having sex with her. Merryn made no protest even as she again found herself unimpressed by his harsh lovemaking.

❧

In the weeks following, Merryn became increasingly lonely, not having seen much of Cecily. Thankfully, she did come home for Christmas and as always, the two sisters had been delighted to see each other. They'd spent a happy Christmas Day with Queenie, Cecily thrilled to see her lovely niece, a fun and lively child who was rapidly growing. Merryn saw herself as a devoted and caring mother if at times a little subdued, perhaps because it troubled her that Cecily would be leaving again soon on more cruises. Following the Christmas dinner, Johnny had ordered her to provide him with a glass of port, even though she'd been fully occupied with feeding her baby daughter.

As he was just lying on the sofa, Cecily had told him off. 'I believe you're capable of pouring yourself a glass, whereas Josette cannot feed herself. Mama does now have a new maid to do the cooking, appointed by Nan when she retired, but there's no butler around.'

Queenie hooted with laughter. 'I've never been able to afford one of those nor wished to. Do pour me a glass too, Johnny.'

Frowning, he marched off to fetch a bottle of port from the table in the corner, making no further comment. Once Josette was fed, Merryn did a lot of dashing to and fro refilling his glass, fetching his cigarettes, providing him with nuts and a slice of Christmas cake, as well as plumping up the cushions behind his back. Much to her irritation, he did nothing for her, his wife.

When Cecily ordered a carriage to take them home, she gave Merryn a little whisper of advice. 'Make sure you don't allow this husband of yours to boss you around, lovey. You're not his slave.'

Were Cecily still around, Merryn would seek her sister's guidance on how to deal with Johnny. She'd so appreciated the thrill of marrying him and the heady excitement of setting up home together, regardless of his displeasure at renting this small shabby house. He had always seemed to be a polite and amusing man but was now becoming increasingly bad-tempered and domineering, for no reason she could understand. And he was still not at all interested in their lovely daughter. The fact that Johnny had at last found a job was a great relief. He'd made it clear that as his wife, Merryn would have no reason ever to go back on stage or to work. This was something of a disappointment, being young and having loved those performances. However, now she was a mother she had no wish to be as neglectful as Queenie had been. That being the case, Merryn involved herself in tasks far less boring than washing nappies, cooking and cleaning.

Greatly relieved that Queenie insisted she'd no wish for them to live with her, she'd done her best to perk up this old house. Oddly enough Johnny didn't approve of her doing such work. Not the walls she'd painted white, the curtains, cushions and rugs she'd made, or even the pretty pictures she'd drawn and put up on Josette's nursery walls. His attitude seemed almost as though it was wrong for a young wife to be active and have a sense of independence. Not that hers was as strong as it was in Cecily. Nevertheless, having survived the difficulties of war, it now felt a part of her.

Today, when he came home for lunch following his morning rehearsal, he found her busily engaged in painting the kitchen cabinets. 'What the hell are you doing?'

'I've chosen to carry out this task, again using a creamy white paint to make them look more clean and sanitary. Isn't it lovely?'

'It's not your task to do such jobs. You should hire someone or ask the landlord to do it. Concentrate on cooking, which is what women are expected to do. Where is my lunch?'

She smiled consolingly at him. 'There's a cheese and onion pie keeping warm in the cooker for you, dear. I did get permission from our landlord for me to do this painting, which I'm perfectly capable of. I'd no wish to pay someone when we're still a bit short of money.'

'We might be forever, unless my wages rise. Your mother is well off, so why don't you ask her to give you some more?'

Merryn stifled a sigh, finding him far too obsessed with money. Queenie had granted them a small sum when they first married, if not as much as Johnny had hoped for. Merryn had felt deeply grateful for her providing them with a reasonable income until her husband had found employment. Her mother could be a difficult woman and very neglectful, but at times most generous and caring. Why would she ask for more? Merryn had no wish to be subject to the demands Queenie used to place upon her for all manner of tasks, determined to rely upon her own independence. 'Now that you have your job back, Johnny, we thankfully no longer require Queenie's assistance. I surely have the right to engage myself in other household tasks, not simply cooking and sewing, as well as run my own life.'

'No, you damn well don't. *I* make the decisions on how we run our lives. Turning yourself into an odd-job person is definitely not what I want from you. You're my *wife*, so do as you're told. Fetch me my lunch *now!*' he yelled, and snatching the paint can off her, he flung it into the sink.

'Oh no, look what you've done, Johnny! You've splashed paint all over the sink.' Dashing over, she quickly lifted up the can before it dripped out any more and began to scrub the sink with a large brush.

Grabbing her arm, he yanked her round to face him and raising a fist, shook it dangerously close to her face. 'Listen to what I say, girl,' he hissed, spitting in fury. 'Get my lunch out of the oven *now* or you'll live to regret your neglect of me.'

A shiver of trepidation rippled through her. She knew that it was not wise to disagree with the decisions and comments Johnny made. He rarely listened to her opinion or needs, becoming a most meticulous and dictatorial man. Each evening, Merryn was expected to ensure that his bow ties were hung at precisely the right position in the wardrobe, his shirt was folded once he'd taken it off, and his trousers put in the press. His clothes had to be perfectly attended to. 'Please calm down, Johnny. I'm attempting to improve our life, not neglect you. Why would I when we survived the war together? I've certainly no wish to impose further demands upon Mama now that her income is starting to fall.'

Panic and guilt flickered in his grey eyes, clearly visible, as he wasn't even wearing his spectacles. Had Cecily been right that he lied about his poor vision in order to avoid being called up? And he did seem to be obsessed with money. Unclasping his fist, he pulled her into his arms. 'Sorry, sweetheart, you're right in saying the war was damaging, which does affect my mood at times. Performing for the troops was dangerous and we were most fortunate that none of us were injured. I will try to calm down.'

The sound of their infant crying echoed loudly down the stairs and Merryn attempted to pull herself away from him. 'That's good, now help yourself to lunch while I go and see to Josette.'

'Not just now,' he said. Then pushing her down upon the kitchen table, he yanked up her skirt and thrust himself into her.

Later, when he'd returned to the theatre, Merryn finally fed her distressed and hungry child and scrubbed the sink clean. Then she sat at the kitchen table feeling even more confused and depressed. She'd once believed that all was well with their marriage, now she was beginning to think it was going terribly wrong. Certainly, her early sense of excitement had disintegrated. She remembered Cecily warning her to carefully consider whether she should marry Johnny. Had she made a dreadful mistake in doing that? Wiping the tears from her flooded eyes, Merryn told herself she must be content with life and hope that he would improve their marriage, whatever his current problem was. Was he under considerable pressure at the theatre? It was difficult to know since he never allowed her to attend and watch him play. Merryn felt increasingly confined to this house and kitchen. Surely she would eventually convince him, not least her mother, that she was no longer a child since she would turn twenty-one next year. Thereafter, she should be considered old enough to run her own life.

TWENTY-NINE
1920

EACH OCCUPYING a small single cabin on the lower deck of the ship, Cecily and Boyd ate with the other entertainers, crew members, photographers and artists, which gave them very little in the way of privacy. Living in close quarters with strangers definitely required tact. As Cecily was accustomed to working with soldiers and was very independent, she had no problem with that. Boyd was great fun and on their first cruise they visited some marvellous places: Alicante, Gran Canaria, Tenerife and Funchal. She did welcome his presence and was delighted to be singing with him. They worked long hours, seven days a week, there being a great deal involved in these cruises. Each morning, Cecily would wake up around seven o'clock and go to the crew's buffet for breakfast. They would then go on to rehearse and practise for two or more hours.

'Do not allow yourself to fall into stage fright,' she'd warned him when at the start she'd seen his hands trembling. 'Pretend there's no one around listening to you and you're simply playing for yourself.'

'I'll remember that,' he'd said with a grin.

'It also helps if you pay attention to other musicians on occasion. I love to listen to many singers and learn a lot from them. In the meantime, we'll keep on practising.'

Now, with Christmas over and it being the start of the Twenties, they sailed to Venice where they enjoyed a gondola trip along the Grand Canal to the island of Murano, then on to Corsica, Barcelona and Malaga. Occasionally they were granted a little time off, and Cecily always loved spending it with Boyd. Here in Tangier, they visited an ancient mosque, walked through streets packed with donkeys and watched men making pottery or painting candlesticks. One group were working in a tannery, looking soaked to the skin as they trod in the stinking pools that processed the leather. When Cecily expressed sympathy for them, then admiration of a beautiful bag they had on sale, Boyd purchased it for her.

'There's really no reason for you to be so generous,' she said, flushing.

'Why would I not? Let's revel in this trip since we enjoy each other's company.'

Experiencing a coil of pleasure at this remark, she gave him a dazzling smile. 'I love it too. I'll find something to buy for you.'

When they were approached by a salesman urging them to come and view rugs he was selling, she gave Boyd a quizzical glance and he laughingly declined the offer. 'Where on earth would I put such a thing in my small cabin? Nor do I own a house. But maybe one day . . .' There was something in the glint of his gaze that seemed to be saying she could be part of it. But would she ever agree to that, having resolved never to fall in love again? Oh dear, Cecily was finding it extremely difficult not to care for this man. Noting the confused emotion in her eyes, he smiled and gave her a kiss, making her mouth fall dry with desire. 'You can buy me a glass of mint tea instead,' he said, which she happily did. She also ordered tajine, a lamb stew, for their lunch, both of them savouring its delicious flavour, as well as the fun they enjoyed together.

What a wonderful man he was.

Merryn was carefully making no complaints to Johnny, concentrating on being a good wife and mother, even if her husband was becoming increasingly controlling. Caring for little Josette, who was growing into a lively toddler, having recently celebrated her first birthday, took up hours of her day, although she now slept well all night. Merryn made sure that she only carried out difficult jobs on the house once her daughter was fast asleep and Johnny had left for the theatre, knowing he would not be home for hours. So long as his meals were provided on time and his clothes dealt with exactly as he required, he never noticed any further improvements she made upon the kitchen as he rarely visited it. He was spending even more time at the theatre, no doubt fully wrapped up in his performances. When he returned home late at night, Merryn always had to make certain she was tucked up in bed, for he would rapidly make love to her. That was surely a good thing, although much less of a pleasure than it used to be. He rarely bothered to caress or kiss her, which made her feel used rather than loved.

One morning in the summer, Merryn was alarmed when she received a message from Queenie saying she was not well. She hastily put Josette in her pram and took a tram over to Grand Parade, fearing her mother had been drinking too much again.

'I am in a dreadful state,' Queenie moaned, dabbing her face with her lace handkerchief as she lay on the sofa in her parlour. 'I'm desperately in need of your care.'

'But Nan hired you a new maid when she left before last Christmas.'

Her mother gave a sniff of displeasure. 'I had to dismiss that girl as she was absolutely useless. Finding decent servants these days is quite impossible, therefore you and Johnny will have to come and live here with me.'

Merryn stared at her in astonishment. 'You always said you'd no wish for us to do that.'

'Well, things have changed.'

'I'm not sure that would work for me. I have a baby and husband to look after, and Johnny spends hours involved in rehearsals and his performances at the theatre. Besides, I've done a great deal of work to improve the house we're renting, so have no wish to abandon it. I could try to find you a new housekeeper and I'll be happy to call in to help whenever I can.'

'I'm afraid that will not be good enough. You must move here permanently, darling, since I am not at all well. The doctor has checked my pulse, heart and other organs, and informed me that I have a problem with high blood pressure and possibly with my kidneys.'

Dismay ricocheted within Merryn, realising her beloved mother could be seriously ill. 'Oh no, I'm so sorry to hear that, Queenie. I assume this has come about because of your obsession with gin. Does the doctor intend to send you to the hospital?'

'I refused to allow him to do that.'

'Goodness, that was entirely the wrong decision.'

'Please do not scold me – he admitted I needed to be examined but there's no guarantee of an available cure.' Queenie began to weep.

'I'm sure there could be, Mama.' Holding her mother close in her arms to offer her a comforting hug, Merryn felt desperate over how to deal with this issue. Why on earth had she refused to go? Because she'd no longer be able to drink there. Merryn had always feared Queenie's health could worsen because of her addiction to alcohol. However distressing this was, she really did not feel capable of acting as a housekeeper and a nurse. Surely she could find someone far better skilled at such jobs than herself. She made a mental note to speak to the doctor about that, and what exactly Queenie required. 'Let's hope it's simply an infection or a mild bladder disease such as cystitis, from which you will soon recover. Has the doctor offered you any medicine?'

'He has given me some pills, ordered me to rest and eat mild food, no fat or meat and plenty of fruit and vegetables. As you will appreciate that doesn't appeal to me in the slightest.'

'You should do as he recommends and agree to be examined. Meanwhile, I'll find someone to cook for you, dearest Mama, and see that you're well looked after. I'll also arrange for the doctor to send a nurse to call in regularly.'

'No need for that, darling. Caring for me will be entirely your task.'

Over supper that evening when Merryn told Johnny about her mother's problem and her demand they go to live with her, he looked and sounded surprisingly pleased. 'I agree we should do our utmost to help. In fact, realising Queenie was unwell I made this suggestion to her. I'm delighted she has agreed. And I assume you must love her.'

Merryn stared at him in a confusion of astonishment and concern. 'She's my mother, so of course I do. But you had no right to make this suggestion without discussing it with me first. I've offered to find her a far more skilled housekeeper and a nurse to care for her day and night, not feeling up to the task myself and having no wish to move.'

'Damnation, why would you not agree to do that? Your mother's home on Grand Parade is far more beautiful than this messy cottage, however much time and effort you've wasted on trying to improve it.'

Merryn firmly shook her head, worrying whether it was right for her to feel this reluctance to sacrifice her own life and give in to her mother's demands. Working for Queenie had never proved to be easy despite often being treated as her favourite daughter. Maybe she was not truly ill, but Johnny had convinced her that she was in order to accommodate his desire to live in a better house. 'As you spend most of your time at the Palace Theatre, were we to move, caring for Queenie would be left entirely in my hands. I have enough to do looking after Josette, as well as you, my dear, so I'm not in favour of that unless it's absolutely essential. I will call in regularly to check she's all right, but she has always been far too demanding.'

'She may be a very dominant lady yet has been most helpful to us. If Queenie needs assistance you should offer to care for her,' he coldly informed her. 'And we do still require her financial support.'

Merryn blinked in surprise. Was this another reason he'd made such a suggestion to Queenie, not simply his desire to live in that lovely house, and she'd come up with this tale of her being ill in order to comply with his request? If this was another of her lies, that would explain why she hadn't agreed to go to a hospital for an examination. 'I certainly have no wish to live with Mama simply for financial reasons. If you don't feel you are earning sufficient money, Johnny, then I could try to earn a little by doing some sewing for people.'

'No, you damn well won't. You've never appreciated how important money is and that it is *my* responsibility, not *yours*,' he snarled. 'Get back to the washing up or you'll still be elbows deep in suds when that child needs feeding. You're far too obsessed with this damn cottage, let alone your own self-sufficiency.'

Merryn was instantly filled with guilt at this remark. Aware of how caring her dear sister was, she could find no appropriate response to this comment. Noting the glimmer of anger in her husband's eyes and remembering the time he'd raised his fist to her, almost as if he might hit her, she felt a prickle of warning that it would be dangerous to disagree with him. Besides, if Queenie truly did have kidney failure and was in need of full care and attention, special diet and treatment, it would be wrong of her to refuse to move in and care for her if only for a little while. How could she neglect the mother she loved? Taking a breath, she gave a nod of acceptance. 'Perhaps you're right and this is what we must do, however difficult it may be.'

'Excellent! You've seen reality at last. I'll have a word with Queenie to arrange our move.'

Oh, how Merryn missed her sister, feeling dreadfully lonely and far too controlled by her husband and mother. But, as Johnny said, she must face reality, overcome this sense of depression that had been with her for some months and take into account that she at least had a darling daughter of her own to love and care for. Pouring a kettle of boiling water into the sink, Merryn valiantly returned to her domestic duties, hoping Johnny wouldn't see the tears dripping into the washing-up bowl.

෨

Several more cruises took place over the following months. They called at Florence, Genoa, Cadiz, Marseille, Gibraltar, where they went on many exciting trips, as well as revisits to some of their favourite spots. Sometimes they were unable to go on shore, having a list of tasks they were obliged to do on board ship. These might involve cleaning and tidying, washing and ironing, or taking part in lifeboat safety drills. They became quite expert at that as every crew member, including entertainers, were required to guide and support the guests as they too were trained on how to wear their lifejacket and where they must assemble if they ever had to evacuate the ship. Not a prospect Cecily wished to consider possible in this peaceful world.

'Perhaps working on these cruise ships will help us to gain a job back in Cornwall or some other place in England if and when we wish to do that,' she said one morning over breakfast.

Boyd snorted with laughter. 'I doubt it. Confined within this ship feels like being locked in another world and most of the passengers will be unlikely to remember our names, even if they do enjoy our show.'

'What a sad thought.'

'The benefit is the money we're earning, plus the fact we do not have to pay rent for our accommodation or this good food we're provided with, even though it may not be quite as classy as that cooked for the passengers,' he said with a chuckle. 'Performing is always hard work, but on these cruises it's great fun, don't you think?'

Cecily smiled. 'I do agree. Some shows are a little stressful, but never as much as they were in the war. Those concert parties were far more demanding and traumatic, a part of my life I now wish to block forever out of my mind.'

'I do too,' he said with a sigh.

'And we're a good team. You've become master of the grand piano, performing well for the audience and have brought excitement into my life.'

'As you have for me,' he said, and she felt her heart squeeze with happiness.

Most days they performed in the lounge, bar or dining area each lunchtime. In the evenings, they entertained the guests before or after dinner so Cecily was required to be more glamorously dressed, with no sign of the uniform she'd first worn in front of the Tommies in France. Boyd would always be suitably attired in his evening suit, looking most handsome. Once a week, they would give a much longer show in the dance hall where Boyd would play ballroom music and jazz tunes appropriate for dancing. This went on till after midnight and he was very popular, receiving a great deal of applause and appreciation from the audience.

Cecily felt determined to revel in this new decade and enjoy the madness of the early Twenties. She would sing new songs such as 'After They've Seen Paree'. Her favourite one was 'I Want to Hold You in My Arms'. She would cast teasing little smiles and a flicker of her hands across at Boyd as she sang it, making the audience chuckle. She also sang some of the ones she'd written, which were also well received.

Occasionally she would be obliged to dance with a man if requested to do so, passengers needing to be treated with respect. Cecily never involved herself closely with any of these well-to-do-men who could afford to go cruising, simply remaining studiously cautious and polite. Not that there were many around, the ship being largely occupied by women and retired gentlemen, as was England right now. Dancing with a stranger raised not the slightest twinge of emotion within her.

As she moved across the dance floor singing, one quite good-looking fellow, if rather old, constantly pestered her, asking her to dance. The scent of him was very like Queenie whenever she'd been drunk. Finally feeling obliged to accept, he surprised her by offering a proposal.

Giving him a wry smile she laughingly declined, treating it as a joke, as she had with Louis when they'd danced together that lovely evening. A relationship had grown between them over time. Had she actually loved him? She couldn't be certain but felt privileged to have given him those delightful few days and nights before he was lost. Now revelling in this new job, her growing affection for Boyd was becoming very apparent.

'Did you fancy that rich, drunken man and accept his proposal?' he asked, pulling her close into his arms as they walked down to the stairs to their rooms on the lower deck.

Glancing up into his gentle gaze, she grinned. 'Definitely not. Too many men consider actresses and singers as terribly naughty ladies who spend most of their time drinking champagne, flirting and mis-behaving with admirers, or lazing about, doing nothing too strenuous. Mama's life to a T, not mine. I'm more interested in my career, although Queenie is obsessed with hers too,' she added with a chuckle.

'That's a ridiculous attitude for a man to take. Entirely wrong.'

'It is indeed. Our critics should appreciate that hundreds of artists, mainly women, have provided entertainment for the Tommies, not sex and booze. We helped to boost their morale. I'm told that Vesta Tilley did the same and raised money for the troops by selling signed photos of herself, as well as sending them postcards and gifts. A lovely and most talented lady.'

'So are you, Cecily. I love our increasing closeness.' Drawing her into his arms, he whispered in her ear, 'I adore you. In fact, I think I'm falling in love with you.' He kissed her most passionately and her entire resolve to stay clear of men slipped away. He was so intoxicating, drugging her with sweetness. Curling her hands into the tousled locks of his hair, Cecily felt a soar of happiness. Then lifting her hips, he pressed her up against the hardness of him, his desire for her very evident, and in herself too.

'Oh, I love you too,' she said, eagerly kissing him again.

Slipping into his cabin they made love, an intoxicating excitement flooding through her.

THIRTY

LIFE WITH her mother became even worse than it had been in the past. Merryn was constantly scolded for not combing her blonde hair correctly or tucking up the ends neatly enough. Let alone pinning it in the right place. That had happened so many times at the Palace Theatre that Merryn had found herself dismissed on countless occasions. If only Queenie would do that now, but her mother's demands had grown beyond endurance.

Each morning when Merryn took in her tray of breakfast, as was expected of her, Queenie would recite a number of jobs she was required to do. 'Carry out all the necessary washing and ironing, as well as changing my bed sheets each day. Keep the floors of this beautiful large house well scrubbed. Make sure all doors and windows are closed tight each evening and that all fires, which you must light each morning, are safely put out before you retire at night. Trim the lamps, keep the dining table, dresser and all other items of furniture well polished. Brush and clean my shoes, hats and clothes, and deal with the pile of underwear and gowns in my dressing room that require mending. Do bear in mind that should I require your attention, I shall ring this bell.'

'Good gracious, I'm your daughter, not a servant. As Cecily would say, you are very Victorian in your attitude. I'll do what I have time for,

Queenie. I've put a request for a cleaner or housekeeper in the local paper. The doctor has agreed that a nurse will call in most days to attend to you. Once you recover, we will return to our own home.'

'Don't you dare do such a thing. I require you to live here to look after me for as long as I need you. Oh, and please go and purchase a bottle of rum. I'm in need of it to deal with my troubled nerves.'

'No, Mama, don't talk nonsense. You are sick with possible kidney failure so I would never agree to your addicting yourself to alcohol ever again,' Merryn calmly informed her.

'Do as I order you!' Queenie screamed in fury. The fierce look in her eyes seemed to indicate that was indeed how she viewed Merryn, as a Victorian servant. Her intention being for her daughter to spend her life waiting hand, foot and finger on her whims and peccadilloes. 'Roast some meat for my dinner, leaving just a touch of fat with it.'

'I thought the doctor instructed you not to have meat, let alone fat? I could make you some vegetable soup.'

'Listen to what I'm telling you, stupid girl.'

Venomous thoughts echoed in her head as Merryn marched downstairs and burst through the kitchen door, her cheeks scarlet with anger. If only Nan were still here. She'd always dealt with Queenie so much better. Being now quite old, she was entitled to retire and Merryn did not feel she had the right to call her back.

After lunch, having provided Queenie with a meal of lukewarm kippers, being unable to get the oven to heat up properly, she went to examine her dressing room. Merryn was appalled to find it littered with gowns, underwear, shoes and hats, as if when Queenie returned from the theatre each evening she'd simply tossed them around in a haphazard manner, many scattered on the floor. Clicking her tongue with fresh annoyance, Merryn gathered them all up, smoothed and ironed the crumpled gowns and began to hang them carefully in the wardrobe or folded them into a drawer.

It proved to be a time-consuming task, a little enlivened by watching Josette playing with hats and shoes she fancied. By the time Merryn got around to making her daughter's supper, bathing and putting her to bed, Queenie's bell had been loudly ringing for some time. No doubt this was because she deemed it was time for her dinner, for which Merryn had dutifully roasted her some beef, as instructed. What a nightmare she was.

◠◡

Merryn became utterly exhausted, finding all the domestic work in this large house far too taxing. She would constantly run up and down stairs to provide Queenie with food, cups of tea and pills, all applicable to the orders issued by the doctor. She did eventually manage to engage a nurse, and a woman as housekeeper to cook and clean. With a sigh of relief, Merryn began to relax. To her dismay, within days Queenie had dismissed them and when she found replacements, they too were sacked. 'Why would you do that, Mama? I cannot possibly cope with all this work or the demands you are placing on me.'

'Yes, you can. Pay proper attention to what I tell you, not least because those women were useless and that nurse far too interfering. As a result, I feel even worse.' Falling back on to her pillow, she cried out in pain and began to weep.

Hastily rushing to comfort Queenie in her arms, Merryn was filled with a wave of pity and confusion. How on earth could she manage to cope?

Queenie became oddly silent and increasingly distant, treating her like a stranger with whom she had no wish to discuss her health issues. She barely even glanced at her, looking extremely blank as she sat eating her breakfast in bed. Was that because of a resentment she felt over the amount of time Merryn spent with her own child and husband, instead of carrying out every single duty she was ordered to do? Or was Queenie again suffering from nightmares, filtering into her mind from her past? That might explain why she would often be asleep during the day for hours at a time. Whatever the reason, she seemed to be wrapped up in herself and sinking into depression. How Merryn wished she could cheer her spirits and help her to recover.

Seated beside her and bouncing her child up and down on her lap, Merryn sang to Josette: '*Sing a song of sixpence, a pocket full of rye, four and twenty blackbirds, baked in a pie.*'

Giggling with delight, Josette clapped her hands, looking thrilled by this. Merryn sang it again, then turned to Queenie. 'Would you like to cuddle and sing to Josette too?'

'No, she's your child, not mine.'

'If you are in pain, Queenie, it might help if you enjoyed the presence of your grandchild.'

'Why would I? She cannot cure me.'

'No, but she could cheer you up.'

'Take her away, leave me in peace and get on with your jobs.'

'Keeping you company is surely better than spending all my time cleaning and washing,' Merryn remarked drily.

'No, it damn well isn't.' And picking up the tray of breakfast she'd only half eaten, Queenie flung it across the bed on to the floor. The crashing sound as cups and plates smashed and tea flooded everywhere made Josette jerk with alarm and burst into tears.

'There, there, darling, don't cry. Mummy will see to this,' Merryn said, and quickly settling her child in the armchair, ran to gather up the mess. 'I know you're in pain, Mama, but that was a stupid thing to do and greatly upset my daughter. You really should try to remain calm and not be so self-obsessed. Did you neglect and irritate Papa just as you are doing with Josette and me? That must have driven him away, and could have that effect upon us too. How would you cope if we left?' Merryn struggled to mop up the tea with her handkerchief and pick everything up, feeling a spurt of anger as she cut her fingers on a broken plate.

'I'm bored! Don't you *dare* leave me. And I've no wish to speak of that man or discuss the problems I had with him. Concentrate upon reality, girl. *I am sick!*'

Josette cried all the more as a result of her grandmother's temper.

Merryn furiously struggled to calm her down, having countless times over the years asked for the identity of their father. Despite the fact her mother would not be long in this world, she still refused to reveal any details of her past. It was entirely against her nature to tell the truth and being a most neglectful, self-opinionated woman, she was now treating her grandchild with equal disdain. Piling all the broken crockery on to the tray and picking up her weeping child, Merryn walked out in a huff.

Later that day when Johnny came home, she explained the problems Queenie was suffering, and how she claimed to be bored. 'She's constantly aloof, unsociable or sleeps for hours on end. I suspect she is again drinking too much alcohol. I can smell it on her.'

'Don't talk ridiculous. I doubt she drinks gin any more. How would she find any?'

'Maybe she persuaded those various maids I employed to buy her some gin or rum, and then sacked them if they refused to get her any more. Now, she obviously doesn't consider the state of her health or the dreadful number of jobs she insists I do, making me wait upon her every hour of the day in order to save the expense of a nurse and housekeeper. I'm sorry but I don't have the necessary time, ability or energy to do all the work necessary in this huge house, let alone fully care for Mama, being more involved with my darling daughter. Not only is she ruining my life but putting her own in mortal danger, which is so worrying.'

'Don't talk nonsense. You have plenty of time and if her health is growing worse, just provide her with another pill,' he said, and giving a snort of laughter, marched away.

∽

How Cecily missed her sister, receiving few letters from her, care of the cruise office. Merryn never spoke of her marriage or whether Johnny had come round to adoring his daughter. She did write to say that Josette was growing fast and had celebrated her first birthday. That was some months ago when Cecily had sent her niece a birthday card and written regularly to her sister, but she had received no response since. When she was away at sea on the ship, Merryn could only contact her via radiotelegraphy if she had an urgent message. Cecily hoped she'd never feel the need to send one of those. Oh, but she regretted not being able to call and see her. Whenever they arrived at Portsmouth or sometimes Southampton, they had no free time to take a train and visit Plymouth. Once the current passengers had disembarked, they were required to assist in the preparation for the next ones, who came on board later the same day. Then the ship would sail away again. She worried about that, wishing all the more that she could see her beloved sister and ask how she was.

She said as much to Boyd as they were busily working on stage, practising for their next performance that evening, then asked him, 'Have you written to your mother recently?'

'I've written to both her and my aunt, telling them that I'm enjoying a good job on a ship, but giving no specific details, and only received one letter in response, care of the office. As you know, Aunty had instructed me not to tell Mum that I was planning to move to Cornwall. When she replied to this latest news, she ordered me to explain exactly what I'm doing and when I'll give it up and come home to work at her guest house, as requested, having no wish for me to upset Mum. I wrote to say I'd no plan to do that, which probably hasn't gone down well.'

'Oh dear, I wonder why your mother would be upset? Is she something of a worrier?'

He frowned. 'I was never aware that she was. I think she may be concerned for me to join her in Bournemouth because Dad died.'

'I'm sure Nan is most caring of your mum, as she was of us, and will ultimately help her to accept reality. Do tell her that you are a successful pianist,' she said with a smile.

He gave a puff of disbelief. 'I'm not convinced I am. If there were more men around, you could have chosen one much more talented than me.'

'Nonsense! You're doing fine.'

Hearing the blast of the ship's hooter, he said, 'We're off again. So these issues will have to be put on hold.'

It was proving to be a busy life, and stimulating to be working with Boyd.

Their next port of call was Malta, an island of which she had mixed emotions. When they landed, Cecily felt utterly speechless, her heart pounding as she recalled the dilemmas she'd gone through here, largely remembering Merryn's state of health and the dreadful interrogation she'd experienced. Not subjects she wished to discuss. The island looked far more beautiful than it had back then, lit with glimmering golden sand and with no sign of munitions or jeeps anywhere around.

'It did feel appropriate to visit this island towards the end of the war. It was a place filled with hospitals for injured men, but not as horrendous a battle area as Saint-Omer, Ypres or the Somme, places we were happy to leave. That war was so terrible that I find it far too difficult to speak of the horrors we faced.'

'So do I.'

They both fell silent as they took a walk along the coast, much lovelier despite the odd sign of bomb damage. Cecily had no wish to recall being grilled over allegedly rescuing the German PoW, nor how she'd been trapped in the trench with him, or the threat of rape she'd faced when caught by that German officer. At least Wilhelm had saved her in response to her saving him. Neither had she any wish to speak of the loss of hundreds of soldiers and close colleagues like Corporal Lewis as a result of the bombing they suffered. Boyd was equally silent, making no mention of what he had endured. Cecily felt it would not be appropriate to ask him. Those men who had returned to Blighty, injured or not, never spoke of what they'd had to live through either. It was much better for her heart and soul to merely speak of the plea-sure they'd enjoyed as entertainers and the benefits they'd given those brave men.

'We performed great concerts here at various hospitals for the Red Cross, convalescent camps, troopships and many other places. Our audiences were always huge – laughing, crying and cheering, giving us a thunderous applause as they did even in battle zones. And we had a standing ovation when we gave our final performance. We enjoyed coming to this beautiful island, delighted to hear that the end of the war was in sight but then received dreadful news about Louis Casey, a French-Canadian friend. He saved my life when our camp was bombed, so it was shattering to hear that he died in a battle close to the Somme right at the end of the war. What a tragedy.'

'It sounds like he was a brave man.'

'He was indeed.'

'Was he a man you fell in love with?'

'Certainly not,' she said, wondering if that was true as she recalled their close relationship. Smilingly shaking her head, she gave Boyd a quick kiss, he being the one she adored now. 'We were just good friends who enjoyed some time together rowing, swimming and fishing.' She carefully made no mention of their other activities. 'He was definitely not the love of my life.'

He gazed at her with devotion in his velvet brown eyes. 'Can you guess who is the love of my life? Someone I hope I'll never lose. One day you may receive an offer you cannot resist.'

Was he implying that could be from him? This was a prospect that filled her with nervous excitement, despite having resolved she would remain single because of the losses she'd suffered. Oh, how she adored Boyd. Working on this ship with him was utterly delicious, and they spent much of their spare time together making love. 'Do you think we'll ever take part in a cruise to Canada?' she asked, as they walked back up the gangplank to the ship. 'If we do, I'd like to pay my respects for how Louis saved my life by placing flowers beside a war memorial in his name.'

'We'll look into that,' he said, giving her an affectionate smile. 'I too would be interested in visiting America and Canada and would happily support you with this wish.'

THIRTY-ONE

I T WAS late summer when they were involved in a cruise across the Atlantic, this time in a much larger ship, to New York. The streets were crowded and a little rough-looking, but packed with cars as well as wonderful buildings. Much work was apparently being done to provide electricity, running hot water and new industries for the citizens.

'It feels a most modern city, quite impressive,' Cecily remarked, relishing Boyd's decision to walk across Brooklyn Bridge and visit Central Park, where she loved watching squirrels playing in the trees. She so much enjoyed sharing these trips on shore with him, as well as their performances. They did their bit for the company by assisting passengers and then savoured time off to explore whatever town or city they were in, which was so exciting.

They next moved on to sail to Canada, far more important so far as Cecily was concerned. First they called at Newport on Rhode Island, a pretty town that was rich in history, where they were welcomed at a Quaker meeting house for afternoon tea. It reminded her of the one they'd enjoyed together in London. Would she ever see Lady Stanford again and receive from her the information about her father she'd once felt desperate for? Another lost man. The next port of call was Sydney in Nova Scotia, where apparently many immigrants from Scotland had arrived in the nineteenth century.

'It feels quite Celtic,' she said. 'Quebec, however, is very much French and I'm so looking forward to our visit, hoping there'll be a memorial where I can place a wreath of flowers in memory of Louis.'

'We'll look out for somewhere appropriate,' Boyd remarked softly.

When the ship moored at the dock in Quebec, Cecily felt nostalgia over the memory of her time with Louis and sadness for his loss. She was greatly impressed by this lovely walled city, remembering Louis's description of his hometown that he'd loved. They walked along the curved cobbled streets up the hill, quite a long climb but most pleasant, and visited Cathedral-Basilica of Notre-Dame de Québec. They then went on to admire the magnificence of the Chateau Frontenac, a hotel so tall and magnificent it seemed to dominate the town.

'The guidebook says this hotel has been very popular with rail travellers since it was built back in 1893. Thankfully, although we too are travellers, we don't need to pay to stay here,' Boyd said with a laugh, as they walked past it to the wall set around the square to look out at their splendid cruise ship moored in the harbour below. The view across the St Lawrence River was utterly breathtaking, making Cecily feel so privileged to be here. 'Can we now move on to the Citadel, occupied by the soldiers?' she suggested.

'Good idea.'

As they approached it, situated in a flat wooded area of land high above the city, she paused at the entrance to lay down the small wreath of flowers she'd bought. 'Since we're staying in Quebec for a couple of nights, I'd love to give them a performance in memory of Louis and other Canadian soldiers?' she said.

'That's a good idea, why not? Let's go and make them an offer.'

Cecily and Boyd performed the following evening in the courtyard in the centre of the Citadel, surrounded by walls, cannons and beautiful green land. It was packed with a large audience of soldiers, many of them disabled or injured, reminding her of their audiences back in the war. As she stepped forward to sing, she was stunned to see Louis seated on the front row. He was not looking at her or grinning like he used to do. The state of his face was a shrunken mess, his nose twisted, and his eyes hidden behind a pair of dark spectacles. He sat holding a white cane in his hands and it came to her in that startling moment that the poor man must be blind and badly injured. At least he was *alive*, thank God! Beside him sat a young woman who fondly had her arm looped through his. Cecily felt so transfixed at the sight of him, she momentarily lapsed into silence. Then keenly aware Boyd had noticed her reaction to seeing him, she pulled herself together and began to sing: 'Goodbye, France'. After that, she sang 'Till We Meet Again', which somehow seemed appropriate.

At the end of the show, she turned to Boyd and whispered, 'It's so astounding to discover that he's still alive.'

'Maybe you knew that he was, and that's why you wanted to come here.'

She blinked in surprise. 'I'd no idea! I must go and speak to him, if you don't mind.'

'I'll come with you,' he said, an expression of curiosity and concern in his gaze as he watched her hurry over to him.

Cecily was delighted to find Louis standing waiting for her. 'I can't see you, Cecily, having lost my sight but when I was told you were going to perform for us, I couldn't resist coming. I recognised your voice instantly. I'm so delighted to hear you sing again and amazed to find you here in Quebec.'

He sounded so pleased if looking in something of a pitiful state, Cecily felt the urge to give him a warm hug. Thankfully, she managed to control that emotion. 'Oh, and it's even more remarkable to find you, Louis. I thought you were a goner. You must be so pleased he isn't,' she said with a smile to the woman standing beside him.

'I am indeed,' she murmured, squeezing his hand.

'This is Caroline, my wife, who bravely agreed to marry me in spite of the mess I'm in.'

'You're doing fine, Louis, don't fret. I confess to having been his girlfriend on and off for some years, so was only too delighted to marry him, even if he can't see that I'm older and less attractive than I used to be,' she said, giving a little laugh. 'He did tell me what a good singer and friend you were, Cecily, and thank you so much for supporting him back in that terrifying war. He often speaks of how much he enjoyed the concerts you put on. Very noble of you.'

'I was just doing my bit, as we women did back then. I'm now working on a cruise ship: much more pleasant than life in a camp or hospital during the war.'

'And is this your husband?' she asked, reaching out her hand to shake Boyd's.

'Actually, Cecily is a very special friend of mine and she did tell me about the loss of Louis. Good to meet you both,' he said, happily shaking her hand, but not moving over to shake that of Louis's.

'I'm so thrilled and relieved to see that you are alive and well, but so sorry about your blindness.'

'I'm pleased to meet you again too, Cecily,' Louis said, reaching over to give her a hug while his wife smiled cheerfully at his kindness. 'I want you to know how much I appreciated our friendship and the dancing we enjoyed together. I hope you were later informed that I'd survived, although I couldn't write to anyone as it took a while for me to recover since I had lost my eyesight and had a smashed face as well as other parts of me. Caroline had no objection to my blindness.' He then put his arm around his darling wife and spoke to her in French, making her flush with happiness as he clearly said *Je t'aime*, saying he loved her.

Watching him with his wife, it came to Cecily that she had never been in love with this man. She had simply enjoyed the friendship they'd shared and the fun they'd had together at a difficult time during the war, which he'd most cautiously described. Kissing them both on each cheek in the French way, she said goodbye and wished the pair of them every happiness.

'How extraordinary that was to find him, even though he does have a sorrowful problem,' she said as they strolled back down the hill. 'And our performance went well, I think.'

'It did indeed. You looked excited to see that man. I assume you were less pleased to meet his wife and jealous to discover that he'd married someone else.'

She gave her head a firm shake. 'I was totally uninterested in involving myself with a man ever again, having lost Ewan, my fiancé, determined not to consider marrying anyone.'

'I'm aware there are few of us men around, but I can't believe you would make the decision to remain single. I'm sure he was once a most handsome man. Did he make you a proposal that you accepted in order to improve your future?'

'Of course not.' Cecily felt her cheeks go a little pink as she recalled the offer Louis had made to her while they danced, which she'd treated as a joke. Not something she wished to mention, seeing the frown on Boyd's face. She felt a prickle of panic, realising he'd seen her blushing and didn't believe she'd received no offer from Louis.

They fell into silence as they continued walking down to the dock. Maybe she'd said and done entirely the wrong thing by insisting they come to Canada in memory of him. It could well have damaged their intense relationship, Boyd convinced she was still pining for Louis. She doubted she'd ever receive an offer from him now.

As they boarded the cruise ship, she struggled to find something appropriate to say. 'He did once tease me when . . .' Then found herself interrupted by a young man who came dashing over to hand her an urgent message. Cecily was shocked to discover it was from Merryn stating that Queenie was seriously ill and could be dying of kidney failure. Horrified at this news, tears filled her eyes as she passed the note to

Boyd. 'I must go home.' She definitely felt the need to see Mama one last time, and to be with her sister.

'It will take a week or more for this cruise to end. Once we reach Portsmouth, you can quickly take a train home. We'll have to make it clear that we won't be joining the next cruise.'

Seeing the darkness in his eyes and recalling all he'd said about her meeting Louis, it came to her that he would still have had no wish for them to continue as a team, even if she'd never received this bad news. He no longer believed he was the love of her life.

∽

One morning, Merryn was startled when Queenie demanded her assistance to help her dress. 'I may be suffering from some illness or other but am bored stiff with being stuck in this bed. I intend to return to the theatre.'

Utterly alarmed by this decision, Merryn protested. 'Are you certain about that? How would you cope with attending a rehearsal, let alone performing each evening?'

Sounding breathless as she dressed, which took a considerable amount of time because of the pain she was experiencing, Queenie acidly remarked, 'You know damn well it's what I love to do. I'm sure I could perfectly well stand on stage to sing and protect my stardom, which could make me feel so much better. You will have to attend the theatre with me.'

'No, Mama, I cannot do that, having a daughter of my own to care for, and you are not at all well enough to work. You need to rest and take better care of your health.' She thought she sounded a little delirious and hoped that her refusal to attend would persuade Queenie to stay home.

Turning away, she paid no attention to this advice and insisted Merryn call a taxicab. How obstinate and difficult her mother was.

Surely she would return within a few hours? Oddly enough, she did not, coming back quite late and claiming she would attend rehearsals much earlier the following morning.

In desperation, Merryn wrote to tell Cecily how ill their mother was, possibly in danger of dying if it truly was kidney failure she was suffering from. As Queenie refused to visit the hospital she couldn't be certain of that, but feared it was the case, as the doctor had suggested. She carefully made no mention of the bad effect this problem was having upon her life, feeling that would not be at all appropriate. She was attempting to return to work, which would take far too long to explain. The next morning, she took the short note to the cruise company, begging them to send this urgent information to her sister, which they thankfully agreed to do. Then Merryn once again sought Johnny's help as she fed him breakfast.

'Despite Queenie's claim that she's unwell, she's foolishly gone back to performing at the theatre. That is entirely the wrong thing for her to do. You must have seen her performing last night, no doubt badly. Do please help me persuade her not to do that again.'

Looking rather surprised at this remark, he shook his head. 'If, being a star, Queenie valiantly keeps performing, that is most brave of her. But if you don't wish her to go, give her another pill and lock her bedroom door.'

Dare she do that? Merryn rather thought not. When she woke her mother, not as early as demanded, Queenie looked bleary-eyed and didn't seem able to speak, simply grunted and whinged as she again went through the tiresome process of dressing and then departed. But she still refused to listen to Merryn's urge for her to stay in bed.

Later that day, deeply concerned for her mother, Merryn made the decision to call at the theatre and view her rehearsal, feeling anxious to find out whether she truly had recovered and was performing well. It was a pleasant walk over from the seaside, Josette happily enjoying the ride in her pram on this lovely sunny day. Merryn was looking forward to visiting the Palace Theatre after all these years. It was a fine-looking Art Nouveau building with glazed tiled floors, a dome-shaped roof and arched bays and windows where people could look out over the town.

Entering the theatre, she could see no sign of Queenie, nor was Johnny anywhere around. When she asked where her mother was, the manager informed her that she had again fallen ill, having done so the day before when he'd allowed her to sleep in her old dressing room. 'I then called a taxicab to take her home, firmly ordering her not to come again until she'd fully recovered from whatever she's suffering from. She foolishly came again today, insisting she was well but recently collapsed in her rehearsal and I again dispatched her by taxi. I recommend you do not allow her to come again.'

'Quite right. I'll make sure she retires as she is not at all well,' Merryn tactfully agreed. Anxious to seek Johnny's help, she asked where he was.

'He no longer works for us,' the manager stated, blinking in surprise at this question. 'When he left to entertain in France we employed a new drummer.'

Merryn stared at him in disbelief. 'I – I thought he told me that he'd got his job back.'

Giving her a sad smile, he shook his head. 'I'm sorry to have to say this, believing you were aware of the fact that we could no longer employ him, Johnny is now working for a restaurant nearby. He mainly helps them to wash and tidy up. It was the only work he could find.' Giving her a gentle pat on her shoulder, he went on to say, 'As for your mother, she was a great star and I would love to believe she'll make a full recovery but, like you, I have serious doubts that will happen. Good day and God bless, dear girl.'

Merryn stood frozen in silent disbelief as he walked away. Was this dreadful job the reason Johnny was constantly in such a bad-tempered frame of mind? Aware that he'd lied to her, probably from a sense of shame, she felt a spark of pity for him. Not wishing him to know she'd called at the theatre, she did not linger in Union Street but quickly hurried home. That evening as she gave him his dinner, she said nothing about what she had discovered, merely wishing him well when he left, allegedly for his evening performance at the theatre.

Later, after feeding, bathing and putting Josette to bed, and singing to her till she happily fell asleep, Merryn sat in the parlour wondering how to resolve Johnny's dilemma. Maybe she could find an appropriate moment to discuss his lack of suitable employment and help him to find a way back to playing his drum. Merryn wondered where this instrument was, not having seen it around for ages, always assuming it was stored at the theatre. Could Johnny by any chance have sold it when he claimed he was in need of more money? What a dreadful thought.

When she decided it was time for bed, Merryn realised she'd forgotten to collect Queenie's supper tray but felt it would be inappropriate to retrieve it. Her mother always insisted upon having supper in her room and opted for an early night, not wishing to be disturbed, a decision Merryn fully sympathised with, considering her poor state of health. Queenie had at least agreed to make no further attempt to visit the theatre, which was a great relief. Feeling in need of an early night herself, as Merryn went upstairs she was surprised to hear the sound of grunting coming from her bedroom. Was she not sleeping well and suffering another nightmare? She quietly opened her bedroom door to check how she was and was shocked to see Johnny lying in bed, making love to her.

THIRTY-TWO

MERRYN SPENT a sleepless night in her daughter's room, feeling far too furious and distressed by what she'd seen to speak to her husband, leaving Johnny a note to say Josette was teething and needed her attention. When he allegedly returned from the theatre, she certainly had no desire for him to make love to her. Instead, he'd had sex with her mother. She felt sick at the thought, her heart sinking into a dark pit. Why would he do that when he supposedly loved her, his wife? And how dare Queenie allow her darling daughter's husband to make love to her? Being far too wrapped up in each other, they hadn't heard the door open nor Merryn's gasp of devastation. She'd quickly smothered that by putting a hand over her mouth. Feeling anxious to escape, she'd fled to Josette's room to sleep in the single bed.

Throughout the night she'd quietly wept, careful not to upset Josette or alert her mother and husband. Hadn't Cecily once told her that Queenie had attempted to kiss Johnny? Merryn had paid no attention to that, flirting with young men always having been one of her mother's favourite hobbies and not something she'd ever taken seriously. What an atrocious woman she was, with no respect for anyone but herself.

Heartbroken, Merryn rose early and calmed herself down over a most welcome cup of tea. She cooked bacon and eggs for Johnny, leaving the plate in the oven at a low temperature to keep warm, then put a note on the dining room table saying she had to stay with Josette who wasn't feeling well. The last thing she wanted right now was to speak to him, so she hurried back to her daughter's nursery on the top floor. It was after she heard Johnny depart, slamming the front door behind him, that she slipped back down to the kitchen to make Queenie's breakfast. Steeling herself and taking a deep breath, she carried the tray upstairs, leaving Josette safely playing with her dolls in her new playpen in the parlour.

Merryn sat in silence as she watched her mother eat her favourite breakfast of scrambled egg and toast, the memory of what she'd witnessed bringing a sour skim of distaste within her. Queenie looked composed and content, elegantly attired in a creamy nightgown, her lovely blue eyes shining brightly. The sight of her gave Merryn the distinct impression that having Johnny make love to her last night had quite cheered her up. When Queenie had finished eating and taken the first of the pills prescribed by the doctor, Merryn placed the tray on the table by the door to avoid it being flung aside yet again. Queenie then began to issue her usual list of instructions, her voice slurring as it generally did these days.

'Today, I wish you to clean all these dusty windows and wash the curtains. After that, you can cook me a lunch of lamb cutlets and . . .'

'Enough. Say no more. How you find the strength to nag me and eat so well when you are allegedly so ill is beyond belief.'

'I beg your pardon? I definitely feel the desire to remain steadfast and brave. You are obliged to listen to what I require for the good of my health. Food and cleanliness are important to me. First of all, I will need to take a bath. Please run and prepare one for me.'

Ignoring this request, Merryn folded her arms and stared coolly at her mother. 'I called in last evening and guess what? I saw Johnny engaged in sex with you, instead of me, his wife.'

Queenie jerked with shock, then covered her cheeks with shaking hands. 'Oh my God, when did you come to my room, and why?'

Seating herself back in the armchair and feeling a strange calmness in her soul, Merryn coolly informed her that she'd come to collect her supper tray. 'Why did you allow my husband to do that with you? Were you again drunk?'

She saw a shocked glimmer of guilt in Queenie's eyes as she turned her face away to avoid meeting her glare. Then with a sigh, she said, 'Because of my nerves and ill health, Johnny does provide me with rum and I pay little attention to what he does with me after I've drunk the several glasses I long for. I confess we did have an affair in France. I was completely unaware that he was also involved in a relationship with you at that time. Once I realised that you were to be married, I did attempt to call an end to it, darling. Sadly, he paid no attention and still took me to bed, as he has done many times since.'

Merryn felt sick at such a thought. 'For goodness sake, Queenie, couldn't you find another lover to provide you with sex?'

'I admit I found Johnny hard to resist, there being such a shortage of healthy men. And it was a price I had to pay in order to keep myself supplied with the necessary alcohol,' she wearily remarked, flopping back onto her pillow. 'I guessed I had little time left in this world, so badly felt the need for love. I remember when I was a young girl, a boy I truly cared for became a dear friend and a good sport, then left the country so I lost him. Johnny is kind and considerate, ready to help me cope with the difficulties in my life and sympathises with the glums I suffer from by helping me to relax and find amusement. So long as I provide him with the money he badly needs, since he's still unable to find a decent job for himself, poor man. Once I found employment again at the Palace Theatre, I've kept working far too hard for that reason.'

Merryn frowned. 'I called at the theatre yesterday to check if you were all right and the manager informed me you were far too sick to work. But what has that got to do with his lovemaking? You've destroyed my marriage, Queenie, just as you ruined your own. Why would I ever forgive you for that?'

As Merryn turned to walk away, she heard her mother start to cry. 'I'm so sorry, darling. I've no memory of what happened last night but do recall that he came in to give me a couple of pills, as he tends to do each evening to help me cope with the pain I suffer, as well as rum. I'd probably fallen asleep after that, unaware of what he was doing, and certainly no longer in the mood for sex these days.'

'Oh, Mama! Two extra pills on top of the normal amount you take are far too many. No wonder you keep falling asleep.' Halting her angry steps, Merryn rushed to gather Queenie in her arms, tears of despair sliding down her cheeks. How could she put the blame entirely on her mother when Johnny ruled them both in a dreadful way?

∽

Merryn spent the rest of the morning fiddling with only a few basic jobs as she found herself quite unable to concentrate, a confusion of fury and pity for her mother echoing within her. She spent most of the time playing with Josette and cuddling her, which gave her so much comfort she strove to come to terms with how best to cope with this catastrophe. Queenie must have suffered considerable distress in her life to cause her to make such a stupid mistake, as well as being addicted to alcohol. What could that be? Merryn had no idea, since she still refused to speak of her past. It was most likely the issue of her failed marriage with that unknown husband.

Realising that her own marriage with Johnny was most definitely over, Merryn was coming to the conclusion that she should return to their small house back in Mutley. She could call here each day to care for her mother, as was only right and proper. But bearing in mind she'd not found another housekeeper and the nurse only called in briefly at some point each day, would that be sufficient? Furious as she might feel towards her mother's betrayal, how could Merryn desert her when she was ill? And, feeling determined not to ruin her own life either, she came to an entirely different decision. Johnny should be the one to leave, not her. Going to their bedroom, she began to pack his belongings.

It was late afternoon when he returned home, claiming his rehearsals had gone well and he would require an early dinner before returning for the evening's performance.

Merryn gave a dismissive shake of her head. 'I discovered yesterday when I went to the Palace Theatre to check how Queenie was, the reality of the work you are engaged in. I have some sympathy with you, Johnny, even though you've lied to me for months about your alleged job with the Palace Theatre.'

His face flushed red with fury. 'Damnation, why would I admit the reality of the only rubbish work I've managed to find?'

'As your beloved wife, I would have been most supportive if you'd discussed it with me. I'm sure there are other places you could have found employment and I'd have willingly done my best to help. If you are no longer playing your drum, Johnny, where is it?'

'I had to bloody sell it to the pawn shop, being short of money,' he scowled.

'Goodness, what a foolish thing to do. Before we even married you harassed Queenie for money, and have demanded an increasing amount of finance from my star of a mother. Possibly this was the reason you chose to move in here, convincing her she was in desperate need of care and attention. That wasn't right either. And despite my being here to care for her health, last night I saw what you were doing with her, which is no doubt another reason. You love having sex with her.'

Now he turned ashen, sinking into silence for some seconds before he answered in a smarmy tone of voice. 'Don't blame me for that. Queenie seduced me back in France. I swore not to allow it to ever happen again, but it did.'

Merryn gave a snort of derision. 'I don't believe a word you say. Queenie claims she attempted to call an end to your affair, once she discovered our relationship, yet you did not comply with that decision. In fact, neither of you succumbed to it, so you are both equally guilty of what has gone on between you for some time. And you still clearly relish having sex with Queenie although she's unwell. Nor have you any right to give her extra pills each night. That is absolutely wrong and dangerous as it could damage her health even more.'

He snorted with derision. 'Why would I risk her being in pain when she loves to have sex with me? Much better to make her calm and drowsy.'

'My sick mother claims that she is no longer interested in continuing this affair with you, saying that she falls asleep when taking those extra pills, unaware of what you are up to. Because of your betrayal, I have no wish to live with you any longer and intend to put an end to our marriage, which has proved to be a total disaster. She is still my darling mama, and sorely sick, so you are the one who must leave, not me.'

'Damnation, where the hell could I live? You're fully aware that I've let out our old house. Why should I live on my own when you're my wife and it's your duty to look after me?'

Merryn gave a smirk of derision. 'Not any more. In future, you'll have to cook your own breakfast, tea and dinner, clean, fold and hang up your own clothes. You must acquire the ability to look after yourself.'

'You know damn well I can't bloody cook and I do enough washing up and tidying in that bloody job at the café. If you force me to leave this house, refuse to remain my wife and provide me with the fortune your family clearly has, I won't allow you to keep that child.'

A coldness flooded through her. 'Our marriage is over, so what I do and how I care for Josette, the daughter you never wanted, is my decision, not yours. I believe Queenie has only a small amount of savings left. Not that I care about money, only my own life and that of my daughter. I'll happily find myself a job, as many women do these days, once I have the time and opportunity. I've packed your bags, so please go and collect them from your room and leave now. Goodbye, Johnny.'

'I'm not damned well going anywhere.'

'I'm afraid you must,' Merryn frostily remarked and turned to open the kitchen door for him. Stepping forward, he slammed her across the head and sent her flying. As she crashed down upon the tiled floor, fear escalated through her, and seconds later he was kicking her in the back over and over again, pounding her with fury. Cramping small to desperately save herself, she let out a scream, finding blood streaming from her bruised head and face. Her mind then went blank, a haze of blackness filling her head as she fell unconscious.

THIRTY-THREE

DOCKING IN Portsmouth at dawn the next morning, Cecily reluctantly said goodbye to Boyd. He was on his way to Bournemouth to see his mother and explain where he'd been working these last several months, which he admitted he had not properly done in any of the letters he'd sent her. She wasn't convinced they would meet up for another cruise, a strange awkwardness having developed between them, possibly because of a sense of jealousy he had and the belief she'd fooled him by saying she loved him when it was actually Louis she'd felt desperate for. Entirely wrong, but she'd been so wrapped up in concern for her mother and sister, Cecily had been unable to find the strength to convince him otherwise.

'Let me know if I can do anything to help,' he gently offered, much to her delight as he placed her luggage on the passenger rack. 'And if and when you would be available for another cruise, assuming I'm free too.'

'Thank you, that depends upon how ill Mama is and how much help Merryn needs to care for her,' Cecily dejectedly remarked, feeling most anxious to see her own family and seriously afraid Boyd was not planning to be free to join her again. She waved goodbye when the train left for Plymouth, giving him a sweet smile, thinking she saw a flicker of sympathy in his gaze.

The journey took several hours, much longer than the one Boyd was taking. It felt good to see her beloved land, but she couldn't bear to imagine what dreadful state Queenie could be in, tormented by the fear she might not recover. And she was so eager to see her sister and niece, hoping all was well with them. Fully aware that Merryn had been obliged to move in to care for their mother, it would be wonderful for them to be living together again if only for a little while. She would tell her all about the places they'd visited on these wonderful cruises, including the hard work involved, the love she'd found with Boyd and was now in danger of losing. She could but hope he'd come round to believing in her love for him.

When she arrived in Plymouth approaching twelve noon, Cecily took a tram to her home on Grand Parade. She dropped her suitcase in the hall and called out, 'Surprise, surprise, I'm here, lovey!' and went on to sing a little of 'Dreaming of Home, Sweet Home'.

The silence following this was something of a disappointment. Was Merryn out shopping or upstairs giving lunch to Queenie and hadn't heard her singing? Running up to her mother's bedroom, Cecily gently pushed open the door, a grin lighting her face as she planned to sing again. Then she fell into silence, appalled at what she saw. There was no sign of Merryn, the room empty save for Queenie who was lying in bed fast asleep, her face pale and withered, looking seriously ill. Creeping over, Cecily stroked her blonde curly hair. 'Wakey, wakey, Mama, I'm home.' Queenie didn't move or open her eyes, clearly locked in sleep for some reason and entirely unaware of her presence. Looking around, Cecily frowned. Where was her sister?

Slipping out quietly, she quickly glanced in Merryn's bedroom, also empty, then hurried back downstairs to look in the kitchen, parlour and drawing room, not finding her anywhere. She again called out on her way back upstairs. 'Where are you, Merryn lovey?' and was astounded when she heard her niece cry out from her nursery on the top floor, possibly in response.

Dashing up the next flight of stairs, she was alarmed at the sight of Josette standing in her cot, clinging tightly to the rail. She looked very grubby, the sheet beneath her bare feet soaking wet as if she'd peed on it. Stuck in her cot, she was sobbing her heart out.

'Oh, my little love, why are you stuck up here in the middle of the day?'

Wrapping her in a cloth, Cecily gathered her in her arms and gave her a warm cuddle, relieved when the little toddler stopped crying to slip her arms tight around her neck. Not that her darling niece would remember her, it being months since she'd last seen this lovely little girl, but she was obviously feeling in need of comfort. Now being around seventeen months, she turned her little head to look around and cried, 'Mummy!'

'My poor darling. I wonder where she is?'

When the little one began to cry again, Cecily gave her a kiss, noticing how she stank. 'Don't worry, we'll go and look for her. First we'll change your nappy, love.'

Her precious niece looked in a dreadful mess, her face flushed as though she'd been sobbing for some time, her entire body wet with tears and urine, and she sounded badly in need of food. Stripping her off, Cecily gave her a quick wash in the bathroom sink, not wishing to spend too much time fussing over bathing her right now when she felt the urge to search again for her sister. Once she'd found and dressed her in some clean clothes, Cecily gave her a warm hug. 'Now we'll go looking for your mummy, shall we, darling? After that, we'll have some lunch.'

Looking equally eager to find her, Josette took hold of Cecily's hand and trotted with her as she searched. Cecily investigated each room much more carefully, looking in every nook and cranny in case Merryn had suffered a fall. Being a large house with three floors, she lifted and carried the little one as they went up and down stairs, not wishing her to come to any harm. Also feeling the necessity to care for her mother, she kept popping back to Queenie's bedroom to see if she was awake, only to find her still fast asleep, not having stirred an inch. Cecily could only assume that her mother had fallen unconscious, due to her ill state of health. It came to her as she walked endlessly around, that the house appeared to have been ransacked, many pictures, vases and other items missing, which was a puzzle. More importantly, where was her beloved sister? Finding no trace of Merryn filled her with deep concern. Had she gone to fetch a nurse or doctor? If not, where else might she be? And wherever she was, why leave her daughter behind?

Striving not to reveal the sense of fear growing within her, she gave Josette a smile. 'Are you hungry, darling? While we wait for your mummy to come home, let's have a bite of lunch.' Carrying her down to the kitchen, Cecily poured her a cup of milk. Then finding some dry bread and cheese, she quickly toasted her a slice of Welsh rarebit, which she happily nibbled. Cecily couldn't bring herself to eat anything, feeling far too distressed by her sister's unexpected absence.

It was then that Johnny walked in, jerking with incredulity when he saw Cecily seated at the kitchen table with Josette. 'Good heavens, what the hell are you doing here?'

'Er, I live here and felt the need to come to see Mama. I've also been looking for Merryn. Where is she?'

'Isn't she here?' he remarked coolly. 'That's odd, she's usually with Queenie. I expect she's gone shopping or is busy doing one of the many tasks her mother demands. Does Queenie not know where she is?'

Cecily stared at him in startled disbelief. 'Why on earth would Merryn go out and leave her child and sick mother here all alone? She would never do such a stupid thing. Even this house is looking in something of a mess. It hasn't by any chance been burgled?'

'Not that I am aware of,' he tartly commented. 'The truth is that Merryn isn't coping too well with all the cleaning and work involved in caring for this house, as well as her mother, so she may well have made a mess of it.'

'I thought Mama had employed a housekeeper or cleaner, once Nan retired to her sister's in Bournemouth. I can't find any of them either.'

'Queenie has disapproved of every single one Merryn employed, always giving them the sack.'

'That's ridiculous. So are you saying that Merryn has to do everything herself with no assistance, and as a result is in a sorry state because of the pressure?'

He gave a sigh, turning away to boil a kettle and help himself to a cup of tea. 'I am concerned about her state of mind. She could have gone for a walk to escape Queenie who, as you know, is not an easy woman and they do tend to disagree about what needs to be done.'

Pulling his spectacles out of his pocket, he put them on. There was something in the way he was avoiding her gaze that greatly troubled Cecily, none of this conversation quite making sense. Glancing at Josette who seemed to be watching and listening to both her father and her aunt, she gave the child a gentle smile then, picking her up, said to Johnny, 'You may well be right. Queenie has never been easy to work for, and if Merryn is in a desperate state of mind, she may have gone for a walk. I shall take little Josette down to the beach and see if she's there or on the Pier, both being her favourite spots. If I can't find her, then we'll have to call for help from the police.'

Swivelling briskly round, his expression now was one of complete desolation. 'Actually, I doubt she will be in either of those places or easy to find. I should confess that she left last night in a fury, having stated she no longer had any wish to care for her mother. I haven't seen her since.'

The thought of her beloved sister abandoning her child because of issues over her sick mother was too dreadful to contemplate. 'Good Lord, why would she do such a thing? Had she quarrelled with Queenie?'

'I'm afraid it was me she fell out with when I objected to the fact she was refusing to properly care for her mother and had given her far too many pills, which was surely a dangerous thing to do.'

She wasn't convinced Merryn would do such a thing – it was more likely to be him who'd issued too many pills. Cecily reacted as calmly as she could. 'Is that why Mama has been asleep all day?'

'Obviously. It may spare her the pain she badly suffers from but was quite the wrong thing for Merryn to do. I too was upset that she no longer cared about her mother, daughter or me and declared her determination to leave, claiming to be exhausted and in need of a break, just as she once did back in France.'

'That was for an entirely different reason. And why would she abandon her child? Are you suggesting that she has some mental issue?'

'I am.'

'That's a terrifying thought,' she murmured, and seeing a shifty expression in his eyes, felt filled with dread. 'I must go and look for her.'

'As you wish. God knows where she'll have gone, certainly not to our old house as she's fully aware our landlord plans to let it out to someone else.'

Grasping at straws in order to get away from him, Cecily said the first thing that popped into her head. 'She could have gone to stay with one of our suffrage friends. I'll take Josette with me, in the hope we'll find her.' She certainly had no wish to abandon her darling niece. There could be much more to this tale than Johnny was prepared to tell her. Leaving Queenie alone was not an easy decision, but she must go and search for her sister. 'I'll also call at a company I know and find someone to help care for Queenie and this house.'

'As well as for me,' he said, giving a dry smile.

Cecily was putting on Josette's coat when she heard the doorbell ring. She rushed to open the front door, hoping it might be Merryn and was astonished to find Nan standing there, a suitcase in her hand. 'Hello, my dear. The moment Boyd arrived, he told me you'd come home because Queenie is now in a worse state of ill health, so I thought I'd help to look after her.'

'Oh, thank heaven for that. I'm so pleased to see you, Nan,' she cried, giving her a hug.

Nan picked up Josette to give her a hug too.

Carrying her suitcase, Cecily led her into the parlour, quietly closing the door in order to guard their privacy. 'Queenie has been asleep all day, either because she's drunk or in a state of unconsciousness having been given too many pills. I've no idea what is the case. I believe the nurse will be calling in at some point this afternoon, so could carefully examine her.'

'I'll see that she does,' Nan calmly remarked, as she sat on the sofa with Josette happily settling on her lap. 'Why on earth didn't Merryn let me know how ill Queenie was?'

'I'm not sure, but there's another problem too,' Cecily whispered. 'Possibly due to the stress Merryn has been through, she's gone missing.'

'Oh no, why would that happen? Where can she have gone?'

Cecily gravely shook her head. 'I've no idea, but will you please look after little Josette and Queenie, while I go out and search for her?'

'I will, dear. I'll take great care of them both while you look for Merryn. I do so hope nothing dreadful has happened to her.'

'So do I. Thank you so much for being here, Nan. Do go and settle in your old room on the top floor and I'll just tell Johnny that you've arrived. I recommend that you do not discuss this matter with him. I'm not convinced of a word he says about Merryn running off last night in need of a break. I do not believe for one moment she would leave her darling daughter behind.'

'Neither do I. She is a most adoring mother.' Opening her bag, Nan pulled out a small card. 'If you need any help from Boyd, he told me to give you this. His mother has had a telephone installed in order to get bookings from her guests. It's quite an amazing contraption, but works wonderfully for her, so you could ring him if you need his assistance.'

'Oh, that would be wonderful. I'm afraid I've no idea how long I'll be out or how far I'll need to search for her. Wish me luck.'

When Cecily popped into the kitchen, she was surprised to find it empty. Johnny must have returned to work, not caring about the loss of his wife, the stupid man. She wrote a note telling him of the arrival of Queenie's dear friend, left it on the table and quickly departed to search the beach, the Pier, the Hoe, then the Barbican, where Merryn loved to visit the market and watch the fishing boats sailing in and out. Alas, she failed to find any sign of her.

After several agonising hours of searching, with dusk starting to fall, Cecily felt so alarmed and frightened that she took Nan's advice, found a telephone box and rang Boyd. How heartening it was to hear his voice when she felt in sore need of him. She quickly explained that something mysterious had happened to Merryn. 'She's disappeared, heaven knows why or where. I think there's more to it than Johnny is prepared to admit. Nan has thankfully arrived to help care for Queenie. I greatly appreciate your sending her and feel badly in need of your help too since you're such an important part of my life. I cannot for a moment believe Merryn would willingly abandon her mother and daughter.'

'I agree, that doesn't make sense. You're an important part of my life too, darling. I'll catch the first train I can find and come to help you look for her. It might be around midnight by the time I arrive. Otherwise, early tomorrow if there's no train available. I'll get there as soon as I can.'

THIRTY-FOUR

ONCE SHE had spoken to Boyd, Cecily rang all the local hospitals, asking if her sister Merryn had been injured, perhaps while swimming, and was being treated there. Each receptionist or nurse she spoke to checked their files and told her they had no one of that name, suggesting she call the police if she didn't find her soon. Agreeing that she would, Cecily hurried back home, hoping Merryn might have returned by now. Finding she was still absent as little Josette came running into her arms, she struggled to smile and quell the pit of fear she felt. After all they'd survived during that dratted war, it felt dreadful to be facing yet another possible loss of her sister, whom she loved most in the entire world. As though this agony wasn't enough to deal with, she was then confronted with the problem of her mother.

Nan told her that the nurse agreed Queenie had taken too many pills and alcohol. 'I found a half bottle of rum under her bed and poured it away. I have also hidden the pills well out of her reach. She has now finally come round, thanks to the nurse's assistance. I did manage to persuade her to eat a small sandwich and have a cup of tea. As I showed the nurse out, she didn't offer any good news about the state of Queenie's health. She sorrowfully explained that she now has a limited amount of time left.'

'I rather thought that might be the case,' Cecily murmured, feeling a spurt of sadness. Queenie looked quite pleased to see her and as Nan went off to take a little supper, she spent the next hour sitting with her. Having no wish to upset her by saying that Merryn was missing, she spoke about the success of the cruise tours she was involved in, Queenie happily listening to her tale. 'I found a lovely young man who can play the piano to accompany me, and would you believe he now claims he loves me.'

Having spoken to him on the phone and heard his devoted attention to her, Cecily's faith in their relationship had soared back up.

'I'm so pleased to hear that, dear. I'd love to meet him. Is he good-looking and rich?'

Cecily gave a chuckle. 'He is the former but not the latter. Does that matter, Mama?'

Giving a smile, she gently shook her head. 'Probably not. I have always been obsessed with that, because of the fact my mother abandoned me for no good reason. I would seek love too, although I failed to properly find any. I did build my own life, which was not easy. I do hope you have a much happier one, darling.' She then started to drift back to sleep. Filled with emotion at the tenderness she'd shown towards her, Cecily gave her a hug and a kiss, murmuring, 'God bless you, Mama, and thank you for all the wonderful training you gave me, which has helped enormously, as well as your sympathy for my own losses. I'm sorry I failed to protect you, since I do love you so greatly.'

Opening her eyes and blinking back tears, Queenie whispered, 'I always loved you too, darling.'

Cecily felt choked with emotion and deeply moved by this, words she'd never heard her mother say before. Then with a little chuckle, she said, 'Even though Merryn was your favourite child and you never allowed me to do anything I wished, whether it was performing on stage or marrying Ewan?'

'You are a lovely, talented girl and I always feared I might lose you because of the difficulties in my life.'

A glint of adoration was amazingly evident in her faded blue eyes and Cecily was struggling to decide how to respond to this astonishing remark when Nan came bustling in. She was carrying a tray bearing a small dish of soup, a bread roll and a cup of milk and gave Queenie a beaming smile. 'Now, dear lady, here is a little supper I'll be happy to help you eat and drink.'

Cecily leapt up to allow Nan to take the armchair close to the bed. 'Can you manage to cope on your own while I see to Josette?'

'Don't you worry,' she whispered softly. 'I'll feed Queenie and make sure she doesn't reach for any more rum or too many pills. Once you've seen to the little one, who's in her playpen, do go and take a rest. It's late and you must be tired.'

Leaving Nan to sit beside Queenie and feed her, Cecily went off to bathe Josette, put her to bed and sing her a little song. She then lay upon her own bed, feeling exhausted but comforted and touched by the discussion she'd had with her mother. Why on earth had Queenie's own mother treated her so badly? Not having bothered to undress, Cecily's mind slipped back to her concern for Merryn, which she'd carefully made no mention of. What a long traumatic day it had been, not at all what she'd expected or hoped for. Her heart was hammering over the feared loss of her beloved sister as she drifted off to sleep. Where on earth could she be?

❧

Much to her relief, Boyd arrived around dawn. Having him here to help search for Merryn made her feel so much better, particularly as he wrapped his arms around her, keen to offer her comfort, support and proof of his love for her. Gently stroking his cheeks, she whispered her love for him too. They then sat down to discuss where they should look for Merryn, which was not easy to decide. When he'd consumed a quick breakfast of toast and jam and a mug of tea, he said, 'Right, where do we start? I assume you've already searched this house?'

'I have, twice.'

'Then let's give it a third investigation, just in case, before heading out across the seafront.'

She moved diligently around the large house close by his side, searching every room, cupboard, wardrobe and closet, even looking under beds. They then went across to the seafront, along the harbour, round the Pier, up to the Hoe and various other possible places in town, looking beneath shrubs and trees, in pools and dressing rooms by the sea in case she'd collapsed there. Hours later they were back in the parlour, slumped in silence.

'Where will we look next?' Nan asked, handing them each a cup of coffee and looking deeply concerned. 'I wish I could assist you in this search but feel the need to stay close to Queenie. She's looking worse.'

Cecily gave a weary sigh, a dark flow of unease sinking into her stomach. 'I can't think what we should do. I've looked everywhere, so many times. Yesterday, I even rang all the hospitals to check she hadn't been taken in as a result of an injury. I dread to imagine that Merryn may have gone for a swim and drowned. Do you think I should call the police?'

'We may have reached that stage,' Boyd forlornly remarked.

Silence fell as they all considered this possibility, then a few moments later Nan said, 'I assume you've also checked the cellar.'

'Good Lord, I'd forgotten all about that part of the house, never having been involved in working in it,' Cecily said, jumping up.

Boyd too leapt to his feet. 'Where is it and how do we find the way down?'

'It's in the basement. The door to it is out in the scullery,' Nan told him, before heading back upstairs with a tray of coffee and biscuits for Queenie.

The two of them ran through the kitchen out to the scullery but when they found the door leading to the cellar, it was locked. 'Where's the key?' Boyd asked.

'It should be hooked up on this board but it isn't,' Cecily said, with a groan of irritation.

'Why would this door be locked? Had I two legs I'd kick it open. Can we find a hammer or an axe?'

'Those are kept down in the basement.' Cecily ran back into the kitchen and returned with the poker. 'Will this do the trick?'

Grabbing it, Boyd bashed at the lock in the door several times until finally it broke. He pushed it open and carrying the lamp she'd also brought, Cecily followed him down the stone steps. Lifting it high in order to flash a light and look around the dark and gloomy cellar they saw nothing, save for a pile of logs and coal. 'I'm not sure how big this cellar is, as it's years since I've been down here. I remember it has more than one area, running quite a length beneath the house. Should I go and fetch another lamp so that we can see a little better?' Cecily asked.

'That might be a good idea. I'll look into this next room.'

As she turned to hurry back upstairs to fetch one, some instinct within her made her pause and call out in her loud singing voice: 'Merryn darling, are you by any chance here? I've been searching our "Home Sweet Home" for you since early yesterday.'

It was then that she heard a muffled cry.

❧

They found her in the far corner of the next part of the cellar, her wrists tied to a water pipe and a scarf fastened around her mouth. Traumatised at finding her locked in this dark freezing cellar and at the sight of bruises marking her face, her eyes quite black with trails of blood upon her neck, Cecily tenderly removed the scarf while Boyd released her wrists from the rope.

'How long have you been down here, and who tied you up? Could it have been the burglars who have stolen many of our pictures, vases and other items?'

Shaking her head, Merryn winced at the pain this caused her. 'I've no memory of when or how I was brought down here. More likely it was not burglars who have stolen our goods, but the same dreadful man who beat me to a pulp.'

'Oh no, who was that, lovey?' Cecily quietly asked, fearing she knew the answer to this question, but was nervously wary of declaring she suspected her sister's husband to be the man responsible.

Seeing the tears in Merryn's eyes and how she was shaking with cold, Boyd halted the conversation. 'Let me carry you upstairs, dear girl. Then when you've warmed up and recovered a little, you can tell us what happened in your own time.'

It was an hour later after she'd bathed and been fed by Nan that Merryn sat on the sofa in the parlour clad in her dressing gown. They all gathered round to listen to her story and she told them what she'd seen the night she'd gone to collect Queenie's supper tray. This shocked them all, save for Cecily.

'I always feared that might happen, but not after you married him, darling.'

'I wish I'd listened to your suspicions, Cecily, when you saw them kissing. We were always fully aware of Queenie's passion for young men, so I assumed she was simply flirting with him. When I accused her of this betrayal, she did admit to their having an affair, so cannot claim to be innocent. Neither can Johnny. He persisted in having sex with her, paying no attention to the fact we were married, and she succumbed to that, believing she hadn't much time left in her life. In recent weeks because of her ill health, he apparently fed Queenie too many pills and could actually have raped her most nights, as she claimed to be unconscious and no longer interested in sex. But she is still fond of him.'

Merryn went on to describe the threats her husband had made upon her, as a consequence of what she'd witnessed. 'Johnny has controlled my life far more greatly than I ever expected, turning out to be a most domineering man. He finally threatened that he would not allow me to keep my child if I did not agree to remain his wife and provide him with the fortune he believes our family possesses. He has always been obsessed with robbing Queenie of her money. I explained that she has little left and told him our marriage was over. That's when he struck and beat me.'

'Oh, lovey, what a dreadful man he's turned out to be. He no doubt resented the lack of cash available and also stole those precious items from the house,' Cecily said, engulfed in fury over his controlling attitude and greed.

'I expect he did. How fortunate I was that you all arrived to help Queenie, and me too,' Merryn whispered.

Feeling compassion for her beloved sister, Cecily sat holding her hand while Boyd went off to call the police. Two policemen arrived fairly shortly to also listen to Merryn's tale, stating that tying her up in the cellar could well have resulted in her dying of injury or starvation had her family not arrived and found her in time. They took her to the local hospital for a doctor to examine her, and then went in search of her offending husband. Cecily seriously hoped they'd find that bastard and lock him up.

She accompanied her sister and although Merryn did have a badly bruised spine, which was alarming, there was no serious damage to her heart or lungs. The doctor placed an ice pack on her back, explaining this would help to reduce the swelling. Her legs were thankfully still moving so she was in no danger of paralysis in spite of the beating she'd received.

'Thank God you will not end up confined to a wheelchair as many soldiers have, lovey,' Cecily said, giving her a warm hug.

The doctor informed them that it might take some time for her to slowly recover, and recommended that she must take some rest, then engage in gentle exercise to help her muscles improve. Something Cecily would be happy to help her achieve.

∽

When they returned home later that evening and Cecily settled Merryn in bed, they learned from Boyd that the police had found Johnny selling goods on a market here in Plymouth. He had then been arrested for theft, plus the assault and attempted murder of his wife. Thank goodness for that, Cecily thought, exactly what he deserved. Feeling exhausted they all retired, Boyd to a spare room on the top floor and Cecily tactfully not joining him. First thing the next morning she checked Queenie, who was still deeply asleep, then going down to join everyone for breakfast, carefully explained to Boyd that she couldn't contemplate going off to work on another cruise with him just yet, and how she hoped her mother might recover.

'Maybe we could later,' she remarked shyly.

'I'm quite happy to wait and hope for that too,' he said, giving her a gentle smile.

Nan frowned, looking displeased by the news they'd been working together on board a cruise ship. 'I confess that although I happily came to assist Queenie when you told me she was ill, I was startled to learn that you'd chosen to work with Cecily instead of your mother, Boyd. You'd make a good assistant at running her guest house, and it would be a much better project for you.'

'It would not,' he laughed. 'I love my darling mum and I'm sure you're brilliant at helping her, Aunty, but that job would not work for me. And because of this issue over Merryn, I haven't had time to tell her much about this cruise entertainment Cecily and I are involved in.'

'It's just as well you haven't. My sister would strongly disapprove of what you are doing. Please hand in your resignation and move to Bournemouth.'

Greatly puzzled by Nan's disapproving attitude and noticing how Boyd was looking equally frustrated, his face tight with distress, Cecily said, 'Why would she disapprove? I told Queenie about the success of our entertaining and how happy we are working together, and she was delighted to hear this. Although I didn't risk upsetting her by speaking of your disaster, Merryn.'

'That's very sensible,' her sister agreed. 'And despite what she's foolishly done, I still love her.'

Cecily smiled. 'I love her too. Do come upstairs to say hello, Boyd. Mama has said she would like to meet my musical partner.'

'That would not be at all appropriate,' Nan remarked sternly. 'Queenie is still in something of a comatose state and will not be with us for much longer.'

Cecily gently patted her shoulder. 'Don't fret. We need to spend whatever time she has left with her. She has been most kind to me recently and if she is awake, I'm happy to do as she asked and introduce her to Boyd. Why would I not wish to make her happy before she departs this world?'

Nan bustled behind them as they all went upstairs, looking oddly disconcerted. Stroking Queenie's hair and giving her a kiss, Cecily noticed how ragged her breathing sounded, sometimes as if it had ceased altogether. Greatly relieved when she saw her tired eyes open, Cecily smiled as Merryn instantly assured her mother not to be concerned about the sorry state she was in, as she quickly described what had happened. 'Do be aware I have forgiven you, although not my husband. He's now gone.'

Stroking her daughter's cheek, Queenie smiled. 'I'm so glad, darling. He is a dreadful man.'

With tears in her eyes, Merryn nodded. 'He is indeed. I love you, Mama.'

As her sister stepped back, Cecily took hold of Queenie's hand to give it a gentle squeeze, pleased to see she was still wearing her diamond ring. 'I've brought my friend to meet you, as requested, Mama.'

Gazing up at Boyd in wonder, she said, 'Oh, I know you, dear boy, having seen a photo of you.' Then lifting her arms, she drew him close with a radiant smile. 'How wonderful to see you at last. What a lovely young man you are, and my darling son.'

THIRTY-FIVE

SHOCK EXPLODED within Cecily and seeing how Boyd jolted, looking equally astounded, she gave a little frown. 'I assume you are suggesting he could become your son-in-law, Mama.' It was then that she heard an odd rasping breath followed by complete silence, Queenie's eyes frozen wide open. Stepping forward, Nan slid them closed and informed her daughters that their mother had sadly passed away.

'Oh no, are you sure she's gone, Nan?'

'I'm afraid so, my dears.'

The loss of her, considering what she'd just said, was too dreadful to contemplate. Cecily heard Merryn start to weep and took hold of her hand, finding a prickle of tears flood her own eyes, both experiencing grief for their loss. 'When I was with her last night, Mama said how she loved me and had feared she might lose me because of the difficulties in her life. I was deeply moved by that if not properly understanding a word of what she said.'

'She has always kept her past a secret. Now we'll never find out anything, let alone who our father was. That's a reality we'll have to live with. Thank goodness we were here with her when she departed,' Merryn said, wiping the tears from her eyes.

'But calling Boyd her son was surely simply a joke, assuming we'd marry. Why would she say such a thing and then slip away?' Glancing up at Boyd, she saw that he was seated on a chair some distance away, rubbing his head, his face a picture of agony. 'You didn't believe what she said, did you, Boyd?'

Looking up at her, he appeared ashen. 'When my father was dying of that dreadful Spanish flu, he whispered a sad goodbye, saying he loved me as though I truly were his son. Naturally, I was astounded by this remark and asked him to explain what he meant by that. He confessed that I was adopted, Mum apparently unable to have a baby of her own. Then realising he should not have revealed this information, as it would upset her, he begged me to say nothing on the subject.'

Stunned by this remark, Cecily stared at him in silence, her heart pounding in panic, feeling desperately traumatised and dreading to think that what her mother had said could be true.

'Did you know this fact, Aunty?' he asked.

When Nan gave no immediate response, he asked a further, more obvious question. 'If I was indeed adopted, do you by any chance know who my natural birth parents were? I do need to know the answer to that, as does Cecily. Is Queenie my mother as well as hers? Or was she simply assuming we are to be married, as Cecily suggested?'

Clearing her throat, Nan said, 'She gave birth to you in 1894 when she'd just turned seventeen.' It was then that Boyd got up and walked out of the door.

❦

The funeral took place a few days later. Boyd attended but was entirely silent, his glorious velvet brown eyes looking deeply distressed and never meeting Cecily's. Cecily felt wracked with pain. Why on earth did something always go wrong whenever she developed affection for a man? She would love Boyd forever. Their life together this last twelve months or more had been wonderful and exciting, a couple who felt they belonged together. Now she'd discovered the worst possible news – that he was her half-brother. They could have a different father but apparently the same mother, and they'd made love countless times, which meant they were guilty of incest. Cecily felt a strong desire to run away and hide.

Queenie had always been entirely focused upon her own stardom and reputation, so it was not at all surprising that she'd blocked her son out of her mind and never mentioned his existence. Heaven knows who his father was or whether Queenie could even remember his name, having had several lovers throughout her entire life. She'd never been an easy mother, in view of problems in her life she'd never disclosed, even though she'd thankfully proved her love for Cecily before she died, and had always been most sympathetic about the losses she'd suffered. Now she'd lost Boyd too.

Once it was over and they sat in the dining room eating a light lunch, Nan made an announcement. 'You are aware that I have known Queenie since she was a young girl. Back then, her name was Martha. There were many facts I was ordered not to reveal throughout her life. Now that she has left this world, I am permitted to tell you everything I know. She did make that clear to me. I can't guarantee it will resolve everything, but I will do my best to explain what I can.'

'Oh, yes please, Nan,' Cecily said.

'We do need to know more,' Merryn agreed.

'May I listen too?' Boyd asked.

'Of course, dear boy,' his aunt said, then settling back in her chair, began to tell her story. 'Queenie was a spoilt only child, an attractive young girl who enjoyed a happy and privileged childhood in Whitstable. As she grew older, she became quite fond of the son of a fisherman. But when that boy developed no wish to be one himself, he left for America. She sorely missed him, having believed he'd adored her as he would give her sweet kisses and had been most caring over her family problems. She'd believed that she was falling in love with him. Discovering her daughter was pregnant, Mrs Gossard was of the opinion that the young lad was the one responsible, assuming he was guilty because he was working class. The truth was that after her father died, her mother had soon found a new lover to come and live with her. That rogue constantly abused young Martha, giving her gin to drink at night in order to make her vulnerable to his assaults.'

Cecily flinched with fury. 'Oh, that's dreadful! No wonder Mama kept having nightmares.'

'And became addicted to alcohol,' Merryn wryly remarked. 'Queenie too had little faith in working-class men, presumably because that boy she loved had deserted her.'

Nan nodded. 'She did attempt to tell her mother the truth, but she refused to believe her. Despite being unmarried I'd helped my own mam to deliver many babies, so assisted at the birth. Mrs Gossard had no wish to risk calling the doctor, thereby revealing the state her daughter was in. She'd kept her locked away for nearly five months in order to protect her own reputation. Nor had she any wish for her to keep an illegitimate child. I was therefore instructed to take the baby to a local orphanage for adoption. I set off to do that. However, aware that my sister, by then thirty-three, was unable to have children, I instead gave her this boy child.'

'So I am her son?' Boyd asked.

'You are indeed, dear boy. During the war when I became distressed over your injury, I finally confessed to Queenie what I'd done. She was truly delighted to learn about your existence and happy life. Thereafter, I kept her informed of how well you were dealing with the loss of your leg, writing to her often while she was away in France. She was so glad to know that you'd recovered and was obviously delighted to at last meet you.'

Cecily met his devastated gaze with equal misery, a slur of depression again erupting within her. 'So what happened to Queenie after her baby son was taken away?'

'She ran away from home with very little money, barely more than the cost of the train to London, being anxious to find somewhere safely distant. She had nowhere to live, slept rough and once her money was gone, she was starving and stole odd bits of food from bakers. One shop owner threatened to arrest her, but she managed to escape and run away. She was sitting weeping one freezing cold night close to the Thames in East London when a woman approached to offer her assistance and employment. Martha gladly accepted, only to find herself turned into a prostitute.'

The two sisters exchanged a horrified gaze of disbelief. 'That cannot have been right. Why would she do such a thing?'

Nan met their expressions of dismay with deep compassion. 'Being in dire need of food, income and somewhere to live, she decided that seamen were much more caring than her family. Obviously, she had grown accustomed to being exploited and out of habit would take a drink in order to allow her body to be used.'

'It really doesn't bear thinking about,' Cecily said. 'Poor Mama.'

'Indeed! However, months later, she grew increasingly resentful of the fact that much of her earnings were taken from her by the pimp who ruled her. She lived in a house of ill repute, packed with prostitutes with barely a penny to her name. Becoming despondent about this, she resolved to earn herself money in some other way. Aware of her ability to sing, as she'd used to do as a child in local schools and churches, one day she valiantly stood in the market place, putting her hat on the ground in order to collect donations. To her delight she did surprisingly well, developing a number of fans. Fearful the pimp might discover what she was about and steal that money from her too, she moved on to perform in various other markets or else under a bridge on a wet day.

'It was when she was singing in the West End of London close to the Gaiety Theatre that she was approached by a distinguished young man. He praised her talent and made a suggestion for her to attend an audition at the local theatre, offering to organise it for her. She felt eager to give that a go, assuming he might want more from her by way of payment. She attended the audition and to her delight did indeed receive the offer of a job.'

Merryn smiled. 'I can see why they would do that. She has always had a wonderful voice, except in her later years.'

Nan nodded in agreement. 'Her career went well and a year or so later she wrote and begged me to come and work for her, saying she was turning into a star. I happily agreed, having been her maid and most fond of her. I was not allowed to make any mention of this fact to her mother.'

'So who was this man who got her into the theatre?' Cecily asked. 'Was he the one we've been investigating, assuming him to be our father?'

'He was James Stanford, son of a lord and a well-to-do man who filled her with hope and excitement for a new life. She happily gave herself to him with gratitude and a relationship developed between them. She loved calling him Dean, choosing it as a jokey name because he was a man of authority and high status.'

Finding herself unable to say another word, the dismay at discovering Boyd was her brother pumping within her, Cecily was relieved when Merryn spoke.

'I'm sorry that we never knew our father or why our mother spent her entire life remaining obstinately silent. Being her so-called favourite child, it's also astonishing that she paid no attention to my attachment to Johnny, using him for her own amusement. She did finally apologise to me for doing that, having become filled with guilt as she suffered from kidney failure. Showing her love for me, I felt relieved at feeling able to forgive her. Hearing what she suffered as a child, it's not surprising that she became addicted to alcohol and sex, despite developing a career of fame. As a consequence, she failed to find the time and energy to give us much attention or love when we were young. Thank goodness we had you to care for us, darling Nan.'

She reached over to hug them both, and her nephew. 'Never having married, you all felt like my darling children.'

'And you were like a mother to us,' Cecily whispered, giving her plump cheek a kiss. 'What a relief and pleasure that was.'

'I agree Queenie was not an easy lady, mainly because of the abuse she'd suffered as a young girl. She never had any desire to return to her family home in Kent, still being riddled with nightmares. When Mrs Gossard died, she left the family home to her lover, still not believing what her daughter had endured. Being successful, Queenie didn't care about that and eventually bought this Victorian terraced house here in Plymouth. I then insisted you girls should spend all your time here and no longer be involved in her constant tours.'

'That was a good thing. We loved living here with you. I'm trying to remember if Stanford, presumably our father, shared this house with her?' Cecily asked.

'I do not recall him coming here,' Nan said. 'He was no longer around by then, although they were a couple for a number of years.'

'Did she ever confess to him that she'd acted as a prostitute?' Merryn quietly asked.

Nan shook her head. 'She didn't, praying he never would find out. She told him both her parents had died when she was young, leaving her homeless and with very little money because of their huge debts. I'm afraid lying became an important part of her life.'

'So nothing she has actually told us has ever been true, is that what you're saying? Was that man truly our father and did he drown in the Thames, as she claimed?'

'She did lose Stanford but lived in hope that one day they would reunite and again become lovers. The years slipped by and he continued to supply her with funds, but she never saw him again. As a consequence, she grew weary of you two girls asking questions about who and where your father was and when he'd be coming home. That was the reason she claimed he drowned. She hoped it would silence you both for good, as well as protect herself from worse problems. She firmly believed that your future husbands should be rich so that you would each have sufficient money to sustain your lives if a marriage went wrong, as had hers. Queenie certainly took advantage of her money and status for that reason and . . .'

Cecily interrupted. 'Sorry, Nan, but if you are saying that she claimed he drowned simply to shut us up, does that mean our father is not dead?'

Taking a moment to respond, Nan astoundingly said, 'Actually, Lord Stanford is still alive and well. He lives in the far north of Scotland. When I heard from Queenie some months ago that she was seriously unwell with suspected kidney failure, I did write to him. He replied to say he'd be delighted to meet you both, as he has wished to do for years, were you ever to be interested in seeing him.'

'Oh, my goodness, that would be wonderful!' Cecily said, feeling utterly astonished by this news.

'This is what we've wanted for so long,' Merryn agreed.

Nan nodded. 'You can meet him too, Boyd, if you wish. Lord Stanford has generously invited you all to visit him, and is willing to tell his part of the story regarding the mistakes both he and Queenie made. I contacted him once I decided to tell you the facts of her life, now that she has passed away. I booked you the train journey,' Nan said, handing over three tickets. 'So you can go whenever you feel it's appropriate, perhaps tomorrow?'

THIRTY-SIX

T HE TRAIN journey was long and interesting, taking them up into the highlands of Scotland via Inverness to Nairn, fifteen miles away on the coast of the Moray Firth. The silence between Cecily and Boyd had been somewhat profound. Merryn at first attempted to chat with them both until even she fell quiet, suffering from a sense of grief. They arrived on a mild autumn day, filled with anxiety at the possibility of meeting their father at last. The town had long narrow streets with a harbour and flat sandy beaches, and looked very Victorian. Finding a horse and carriage, Cecily showed the driver the name of the house they were seeking: MacMarron Hall, and was amazed when he informed them it was not a house but a Georgian castle set a few miles outside of the town.

'So this lord really is quite rich,' Merryn whispered, as they climbed on board.

It did indeed prove to be a magnificent building with a small turret set to the left and right of it, a huge number of tall chimneys on the roof, sash windows and a pillared entrance porch clothed in wisteria. 'What a beautiful place to live,' Cecily said, as the carriage drew up in the courtyard, surrounded by a walled garden and woodland.

As they climbed out, the front door burst open and a man appeared. He looked quite elderly and plump with white hair, a moustache over his wide smiling mouth and most elegantly attired in a grey double-breasted suit. Beside him stood a small sable and white Shetland sheep-dog. He hurried over to quickly shake their hands, grinning happily at the sight of them, the dog trotting close to his heels. 'I was delighted to receive a telegram telling me you were coming. My goodness, how pleased I am to see you. I never dreamed it would ever be possible. Do come in.'

Cecily felt deeply moved by this welcome. He seemed to be a most charming man.

They entered the hall, impressed at its size, glittering chandelier and a grand staircase, surprised to see an ancient suit of armour by the door. 'He's standing guard,' Stanford said, with a laugh. 'This way, dear folk.'

Moments later, they found themselves seated in a large drawing room filled with chairs and sofas, a fire roaring in the grate and huge portraits and tapestries hung upon the walls. The little Sheltie, introduced as Shep, had a soft, sweet temperament, not barking or showing any resistance when each of them gave him a gentle stroke. He merely offered a little sniff, then went off to sit peacefully close to his master.

Coffee was brought in by the housekeeper, together with a large cake stand, scones and biscuits, oatcakes and cheese: an astonishingly appetising afternoon tea. They chatted about the mild weather as they ate. 'This area has an interesting climate with cool summers and mild winters. Not as warm as Cornwall,' he said with a chuckle.

'So you do remember Cornwall?' Cecily asked. 'I assume you have not visited for some years.'

'I remember it well, dear girl, and you too.'

She almost flushed with excitement at this comment. Putting down her cup and catching Merryn's anxious glance, she gave him a smile. 'We are delighted to be here to meet you too, Lord Stanford.'

'You can call me James, or Dean if you wish, as your mother did,' he said with a chuckle, leaning forward to look more closely at them both, and at Boyd.

Cecily quickly explained how they'd had no idea he was still alive until Queenie had passed away and Nan was at last permitted to tell the story of her past. 'We were told how she first met you but only learned a small portion of her life, so would love to hear about the time you spent with her if you're willing to share that. Mama has always refused to tell us anything about our father, so we'd like to know if that is you.'

Giving a dry smile, he settled back in his armchair. Shep gave a sigh and settled his chin upon his master's feet. 'I will not bore you with anything irrelevant but will happily provide you with the honest truth, which has been kept secret for my entire life. I'll explain why later. We did have a most happy relationship, being young. She was a beautiful woman, tightly bound in a corset, her gowns sleeveless with a low cleavage.'

'She was indeed,' Cecily said with a smile.

'Then one day, to Queenie's complete astonishment, I confessed that my previous mistress had given birth to a baby. I told her that she had tragically lost her mother who'd died of scarlet fever. I pointed out that I needed to protect my reputation and not reveal to my father how I'd indulged in many mistresses and now possessed an illegitimate child. Queenie did pay attention to that remark, probably because she'd had an inappropriate early life herself, something she never spoke of. That being the case, I asked if she would look after this child until I could find someone to adopt her. She agreed but only if we were to marry, assuming my dalliance would then stop. I succumbed to her request, quite entranced by her and wishing this infant to be safe, so long as she never revealed the child's true parents.

'I did insist upon a quiet ceremony, expressing doubt of my parents' attitude towards Queenie for being only middle class and not nobility. I promised we could have a grander wedding once I'd won them round.

She happily called upon the local vicar and arranged a small private service in the local church.'

'Who was that child?' Merryn asked.

'I'd like to know too,' Cecily said.

'I will tell you shortly.'

With agony in their faces, the two sisters clasped each other's hands, saying nothing more.

'Queenie hired a nanny to care for the child and after the wedding took place, I moved her into a much better house in London. We were quite happy and I'd bought her a diamond ring, which she loved. But I was not able to live with her quite as much as she'd hoped. She assumed this was because of my disapproving parents, taking into account my words of warning. Then one day when she was performing at the Gaiety Theatre on the Strand, she saw me seated in the audience with another woman by my side. I should have realised she was in that show and not attended. When I visited her a day or two later, she flung herself into my arms in a fury of tears, telling me what she'd seen and accusing me of inappropriate behaviour with another woman. I confirmed I'd had affairs with many and asked if she wished to call an end to our marriage. She steadfastly refused, saying, "You are my husband and I love you. Being a man of high status who provides me with ample funds, why would I wish to leave you?" She then took to drinking more and embarked upon a few affairs of her own in retaliation.'

'Who with?' Both sisters asked this question, speaking as one person in need of names and detail. Boyd still remained silent.

'I've no idea. She was involved with several men and I paid no attention to who they were. When later she became pregnant, she admitted that the child was not mine because I'd neglected her for some time. We had a furious row and I finally spilled out the information I'd kept secret for so long. The lady she'd seen me with was my wife, Seraphina. "*I* am your wife," she screamed. I apologised and coolly explained that before we'd gone through that quiet wedding ceremony, I was already married. I hadn't felt able to admit that fact since she wasn't prepared to care for my illegitimate child unless I agreed to wed her.'

'Are you saying Seraphina is the woman we know as Lady Stanford?' Cecily asked.

'She is indeed and still officially my wife. We have not lived together for years, not at all getting on well as a result of this issue. That was the final straw in our difficult marriage. She did, however, inform me how she'd met you, Cecily, and had resolutely told you nothing about me, not wishing to create problems for me or more importantly, herself.'

'So you were a bigamist?' Boyd quietly remarked, clearly attempting not to sound too condemning.

'I was indeed. Queenie threatened to report me to the police, saying I could be charged and imprisoned for five years. I begged her to remain silent, having no wish for that to happen. I also admitted that if my parents discovered I had an illegitimate child, I would be cut out of my father's will and lose my inheritance. Being a fierce and arrogant lord, he would also ensure that her career was destroyed, along with her reputation. Seeing how furious Queenie was as a result of what I'd told her, and fearful of this threat, I promised to provide her with a new home wherever she wished to move to. I also offered her a good income so long as she did not have me charged. Fearing she too might then lose everything worthwhile in her life, Queenie felt obliged to grit her teeth and accept reality. She insisted upon quite a large income, chose to move to Plymouth and a few months later gave birth in 1899 when she was twenty-two.'

'That must have been me,' Merryn said, her freckled face creased with anxiety. 'So that's the reason she never told me anything about my father, because she'd no idea who he was.'

'That is the case, I'm afraid.'

'And was I your illegitimate child?' Cecily asked, giving a little gasp.

'You were indeed, dear girl.'

Boyd cleared his throat and swiftly asked, 'Are you saying that I am not Cecily's half-brother?'

'Absolutely, dear boy. You are Queenie's son but not mine, as I believe Nan explained to you. She was, however, unaware that Cecily is the daughter of my former mistress who died of scarlet fever, not Queenie's daughter. But, yes, I am her father.'

'Oh, my goodness!' Something lit within Cecily as she met Boyd's glittering gaze. He looked equally thrilled and excited by this news. 'So the fact I am not actually Queenie's daughter is the reason she never showed much interest in me, almost resenting my presence. Merryn was mainly her favourite child, although just before she died she did tell me she loved me and had lived in fear of losing me.'

He looked racked with guilt as he nodded his head. 'I apologise for foolishly being guilty of bigamy in order to save my reputation and inheritance. As a consequence, my so-called true marriage also collapsed and I quickly left London to retreat to our estate here in Scotland, not wishing to risk being charged by either of those ladies. I remained absent from Queenie's life but did fund her care of you, Cecily. I would occasionally ask if I might visit, being very fond of you, dear girl. She always refused to allow me to come, possibly fearing I might take you away, particularly once my father had eventually departed this world and I was free to do as I pleased.'

'Are you saying she had no wish to part with me, or else feared you might thereafter stop supplying her with the income she depended upon?'

'Who knows! She definitely had no wish to lose you. Nor did she ever wish to see me again. And as my very determined wife Seraphina also threatened to charge me with bigamy, I stopped making that request and kept well away from both ladies. As a consequence, I've had no children to care for, simply the companionship of a small dog, this one my latest,' he said, giving Shep a loving tickle.

Then giving Merryn a pitying look, Lord Stanford said, 'We have no idea who your father was, dear girl, but you are indeed Queenie's daughter.'

'I can live with that reality, particularly now that I have a daughter of my own whom I adore, and am about to rid myself of a violent husband.'

'Ah, if that's what he is, good for you! Do take care of yourself and your dear child. Also take note that although you two girls are not, strictly speaking, sisters, you can surely continue to act as such.'

'Oh, that hadn't occurred to me,' Cecily said, looking startled, then wrapping her arms around Merryn, gave a little chuckle. 'I still feel as if I am and always will.'

'We grew up as sisters and will forever be so in our hearts if not by birth,' Merryn agreed, hugging her too.

He gave them both a beaming smile. 'I'm so glad to hear that. Oh, and the house I bought for Queenie in Plymouth belongs to you both forever and a day, my loves.'

He kindly urged them to stay for a couple of nights, taking them for lovely walks along the beach and the woods, Shep trotting everywhere with them. He drove them out in his Humber to visit Nairn, the local golf course, Inverness and many pretty villages in the area, fed them well and happily applauded the songs they sang for him. He was a most caring and accommodating man, the kind of father Cecily had always longed for. What a delight it was to feel that she'd found him at last. And even Merryn looked quite content, even though she was not related to him. They had finally resolved the puzzle in their lives.

On their first evening, Boyd took Cecily out for a walk along the beach, where he pulled her into his arms and kissed her with passion. 'This news is something I've been dreaming of but had little hope would happen. Thank heaven you are not my half-sister. I love you so much, darling.' Then sinking down upon one knee, he asked her to marry him. 'I know you claimed that you had no wish to fall for a man ever again, but you have made it clear that you do love me. I'm so relieved to know that. We're more than a professional team. We belong together, my darling, and ever will.'

'Oh, yes, I do love you,' she happily told him, excitement within her. 'I gladly accept your proposal. Thank heaven we have learned the truth from this man that we are not related. How wonderful he is, behaving like a father to us all. And how wonderful you are too.' Flinging herself into Boyd's arms, she experienced the thrill of his loving embrace. The deep emotion she felt for him pounded in her heart.

When they left, Lord Stanford assured them they could visit him any time they wished, and he promised to visit them too. 'I consider you both to be my daughters if that is all right by you, dear girls.'

'It certainly is,' Cecily declared.

Merryn said, 'If I can be your adopted daughter, that would be lovely too.'

'We are most definitely a family,' he said, giving each of them a kiss on their cheeks. 'What a treat that is for me.'

❧

A month later, following their wedding, Cecily and Boyd gave a performance on the Pier, Merryn and Nan sitting happily in the audience with Josette. Cecily had written to Lena to give her latest news and was delighted when she came to visit and watch their performance. Lieutenant Trevain, the officer who had granted them the necessary permission to go to France, also attended, including several of the ex-soldiers they'd entertained over the years, and many whom Lena and Cecily had helped to escape. The performance went remarkably well. Cecily sang some of her own songs plus the ones they'd performed on the cruises. Towards the end, she invited her sister to join them on stage and Merryn smilingly came to play her piano accordion while Cecily sang a few of her favourite war songs: 'It's a Long Way to Tipperary' and

'Pack Up Your Troubles in Your Old Kit Bag', which also went down well, the audience joining in to sing the chorus with her. When the show was over, they gave a standing ovation, cheering and applauding her with great admiration, many tossing bouquets and roses on to the stage.

Afterwards, Cecily held a party at their home on Grand Parade to celebrate seeing these old friends and their recent wedding. Life suddenly felt perfect, her sister free of the misery she'd been through and happily content with her child. And Cecily had amazingly found a wonderful man to love and marry. What could be better than that?

ACKNOWLEDGMENTS

The inspiration for this book came from the pleasure my husband and I enjoyed with amateur dramatics and musical theatre for many years. It was always great fun and so satisfying. The idea of how girls were keen to entertain troops in the Great War greatly intrigued me. Members of my family in the past were involved in World War One. How brave they must have been. Some sadly did not survive. I love to write historical romance and always enjoy the research, the timing of which I sometimes adapt slightly to suit the story. Here is the interesting list of books I read to get the feel of the era:

British Music Hall: An Illustrated History – Richard Anthony Baker

The Odd Women – George Gissing

Modern Troubadours, a Record of Concerts at the Front – Lena Ashwell

Lady Under Fire on the Western Front: The Great War letters of Lady Dorothie Fielding MM 1914–1917

Kate Parry Frye: The Long Life of an Edwardian Actress and Suffragette – Elizabeth Crawford

Dr. Elsie Inglis – Lady Frances Balfour

Singled Out – Virginia Nicholson

Fighting on the Home Front – Kate Adie

The Great Silence – 1918–1920 – Living in the Shadow of the Great War – Juliet Nicolson

Johnny Get Your Gun – A Personal Narrative of the Somme, Ypres and Arras – John F. Tucker

A Woman's Place – 1910–1975 – Ruth Adam

My thanks to Klaus Doerr, a German friend who provided the necessary sentences in his language. I am most grateful for his support. I also appreciate the excellent Amazon Lake Union team and my editor, Victoria Pepe. My wonderful agent, Amanda Preston of the LBA Agency, for her faith in me. Thanks always to my husband, David, who as well as keeping me well fed and cared for when I'm busy writing, helps with proofing and other administrative tasks. I would also like to thank all my readers for their kind messages and reviews telling me how much they enjoy my books.

Kind regards,

Freda

For further details, or if you wish to sign up for my newsletter, please visit my website:

Facebook: Freda Lightfoot Books

Twitter: @fredalightfoot

Website: www.fredalightfoot.co.uk

ABOUT THE AUTHOR

Photo © 2014 by Roger Moore

Sunday Times bestselling author Freda Lightfoot hails from Oswaldtwistle, a small mill town in Lancashire. Her mother comes from generations of weavers, and her father was a shoe-repairer; she still remembers the first pair of clogs he made for her.

After several years of teaching, Freda opened a bookshop in Kendal, Cumbria. And while living in the rural Lakeland Fells, rearing sheep and hens and making jam, Freda turned to writing. She wrote over fifty articles and short stories for magazines such as *My Weekly* and *Woman's Realm*, before finding her vocation as a novelist. She has since written over forty-eight novels, mostly sagas and historical fiction. She now spends warm winters living in Spain on the hills above the Mediterranean, and the rainy summers in Britain.